Turkish Wedding

Once There Was, Once There Wasn't

JUDITH REYNOLDS BROWN

PublishAmerica
Baltimore

© 2008 by Judith Reynolds Brown.
All rights reserved. No part of this book may be reproduced, stored in a retrieval system or transmitted in any form or by any means without the prior written permission of the publishers, except by a reviewer who may quote brief passages in a review to be printed in a newspaper, magazine or journal.

First printing

All characters in this book are fictitious, and any resemblance to real persons, living or dead, is coincidental.

PublishAmerica has allowed this work to remain exactly as the author intended, verbatim, without editorial input.

Softcover 1-60563-062-4
Pocketbook 978-1-4560-0788-1
PUBLISHED BY PUBLISHAMERICA, LLLP
www.publishamerica.com
Baltimore

Printed in the United States of America

Dedicated to Jack Ross Brown

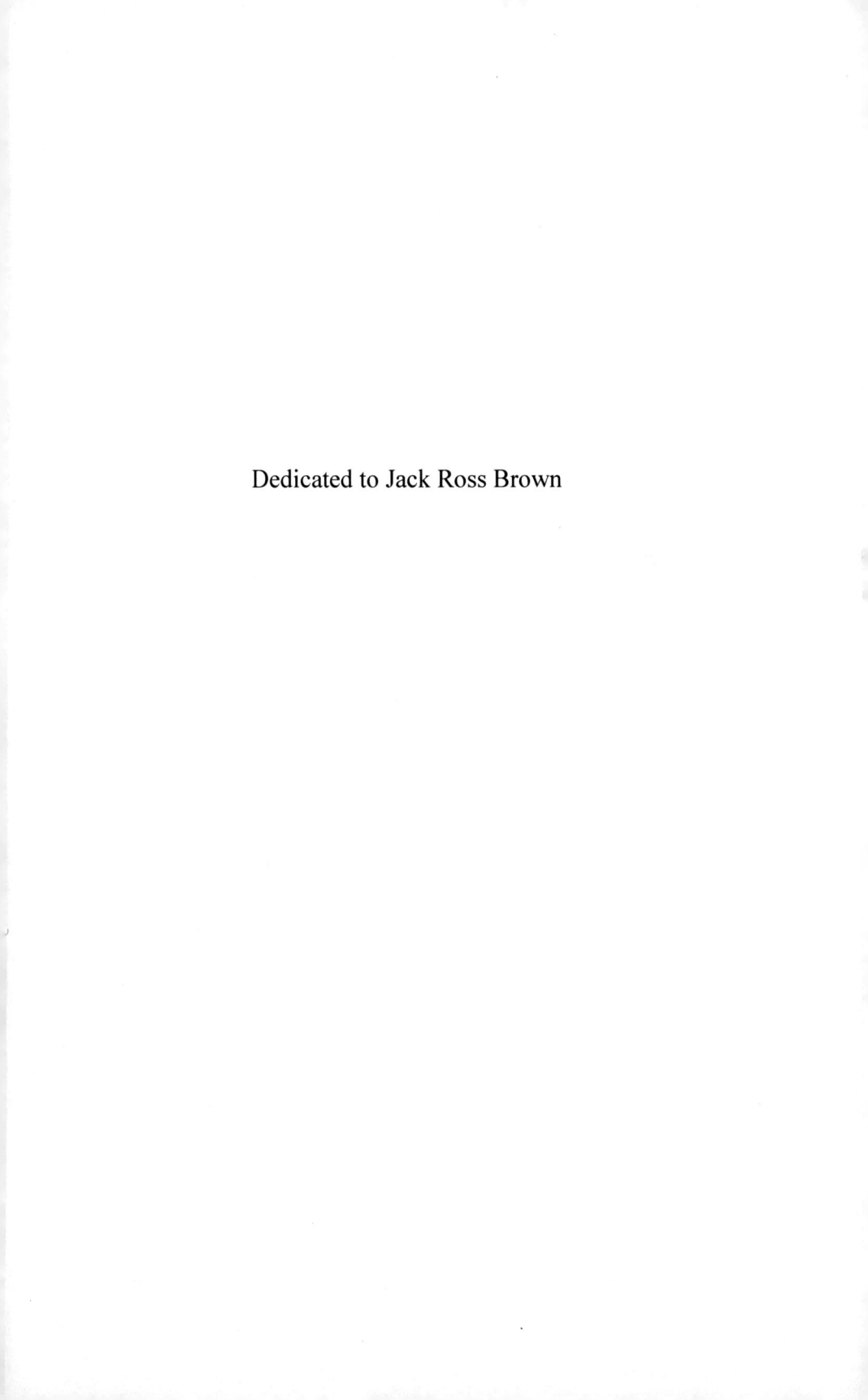

Turkish uses the Western alphabet with some additional marks, called diacritics, attached to certain letter characters, which indicate a different pronunciation. Due to technical limitations in rendering these letters with diacritical marks the author has used the English spellings of Turkish words and names.

CHAPTER ONE
Perhaps There Was, Perhaps There Wasn't

Turkish folktales begin, "Once there was and once there was not, a long time ago, when God had many people but it was a sin to say so, when the camel was a town crier and the cock was a barber, when the sieve was in the straw and I was rocking my mother's cradle, *Tinger, mingir.*" Once there was and once there wasn't a young lady named Anne McClellan who was not Turkish, and a young Turk, Orhan Demir, whom she had decided she loved. Their tale begins in June of 1960 when they found themselves traveling in a 1951 Chevrolet Sedan taxi with a cracked windshield on the road between Adana and Gaziantep in southern Turkey.

Anne stared ahead at the mirage of shimmering heat waves rising from the hot pavement on which their taxi traveled. From what she could see their road shot straight through cultivated fields until it came to treeless mountains and began to wind and climb through scrubby, dry vegetation. It was now the brass gold hour of evening, but heat waves could still be seen dancing above the tarmac.

On a promontory ahead and just off the road loomed a ruined castle whose huge black boulders lit by the setting sun towered above the fields. "That must be a crusader castle," she said thinking back to the guide books she'd read on this area of Turkey.

"I don't know. What I know is it has always been there. For me it is no more than a pile of rocks." Orhan flipped a dismissive hand at the dark ruin.

"You don't care then that it could have been there since the 1200's? Are all the other Turks like you? Would those women working in the field below it care that crusaders built it? Probably not." She indicated three bent women working the cultivated field surrounding the promontory and its scattered stones. They wore full blousy trousers which seemed to sway in an easy rhythm as they worked.

"They are clever. They work when it is more cool in the evening."

"But you are really so lucky! I had to read about castles like this in history books. The ancient world peppers the very ground you've always walked on!"

"You say luck. Is it? I want to unglue Turkey from this past. We need to grow up, be like Europe. The name of that castle is Snake Castle. People around here must know it is dangerous to go there. The snakes come out on the rocks to sun themselves."

"Can I come back here? I could be careful. The idea of exploring a crusader castle is exciting to me. Just think, those misled crusaders built that castle."

"Gaziantep has a castle. I don't know maybe the crusaders built it, maybe some other people a long time ago, but it's a castle. You will not need to come so far."

"Will you take me there, then?"

"My grandfather knows it. He'll take you."

"If I'd grown up in Gaziantep, I can't believe I wouldn't have been curious. I still say you're lucky!"

Glancing again at the dark, high silhouette against the cloudless sky she was struck by the incongruity of this stark, man-made castle planted as it was in the midst of lush grain fields. The new grain was the same green of the spring fields in the U.S. but in this country the crops pushed up in a myriad of smaller plots. By contrast the mountainside their taxi was about to climb was uncultivated, rocky. Parched cracks in the soil mapped the dry earth just off the road. Water had chiseled its course down over the hardened earth in small gullies. The threat of erosion appeared more rampant here on these bare mountains than at home. This land had been deforested longer. Yes, living in Turkey, if she decided to marry and stay here, might expand her world in ways she could not have imagined.

Orhan glanced at this young American woman beside him, grinned and gestured toward the mountain their taxi was beginning to climb. "This is *Gavur Dagh*. Means Infidel Mountain. I bet you never thought you were infidel before you met me."

"What does infidel really mean?"

"Means you match the mountain." Tentatively he put a hand on her knee.

Nearly ten months ago when Orhan had been a newly arrived graduate student in business and engineering at the University of Washington, he had charmed Anne with his impish grin and mock helplessness when she met him at a University reception for international students. Now when they were returning together to his country, he was suggesting she might be a stranger to Turkey in a way that she hadn't thought much about, a religious outsider. The idea was somehow frightening.

Hoping to mask her discomfort, Anne decided to make an irrelevant comment. "We have a saying about mountains: 'They shall not be moved.'" In this Islamic country how uneasy should she be at being labeled a non-believer?

She and Orhan were nearing the end of a twenty-three hour journey which had begun in Seattle on the Western side of the U.S. When the third plane of their journey, the one from Istanbul to Adana in south central Turkey, had landed in the tiny Adana airport, the airline representative at the desk had informed Orhan in apologetic, bleating tones that their flight to Gaziantep had been cancelled. As if plane cancellations happened to him every day Orhan took the news calmly, walked straight out of the small building, eyed the three taxis waiting outside, and engaged the driver of the shiniest and most ancient among the automobiles. "In Turkey," he told her, "you always choose the oldest taxi. It is a sign the driver wants to keep it, so he keeps you safe with extra good care of it. Means he owns it and drives carefully to protect his taxi."

The taxi began the long ascent upward on what she would call a huge hill rather than a mountain—she was from a place where "real" snow-covered mountains dominated the winter horizon. Anne noted that in the muggy heat her rayon blouse had begun to stick to her back. She pushed away from the seat's plastic cover and in an attempt to distract herself she seized on the first odd thing she saw: in one cultivated field, perhaps ten feet off the ground on makeshift wooden poles, stood a small platform enclosed by dry, leaf-covered branches. It appeared to be some kind of make-shift shelter. Were there more such shelters? Glancing about she saw only more scrubby, dry-gray vegetation and hairpin turns as the road wound up and over the barren mountain.

"That platform—what's it for?"

"They guard the field at harvest time. A watchman sleeps there to be high, to see."

Anne settled back wondering about a country where people were poor enough that crops had to be guarded. Don't be overwhelmed, she told herself. Just observe the contrasts, the things I can learn because I grew up in another world. All the history of this older world...it's going to be right at my finger-tips. She thrust a hand up to push a lock of hair off her moist forehead, and took a deep breath. The dry odor of the air seemed good.

She and her friend Orhan—adamantly she had made it clear to everyone they met on their journey that they were just friends, not man and wife—were traveling together to his home in a city of some 125,000 people in southeastern Turkey. Bradley Owen, the foreign student adviser for whom she worked at the University of Washington, when he heard his assistant thought she was in love with one of the international students she'd been working with, assumed a fatherly role to give her his advice. He had suggested to Anne that before she married anyone from another culture, she ought to live in that culture a while first. Anne's own father had echoed the same advice, and she herself had begun to see this trial as vital. Southern Turkey was now welcoming her with a blast of muggy late June heat. Thank God, however, the sun was setting.

"Wait until we're over the mountain," Orhan said protectively.

"Gaziantep is more high, more dry than here on this low plain. You will not be so hot there."

Anne reached into her handbag for a handkerchief and wiped the moisture from her hairline. The taxi continued to climb, switchback by switchback up and out of the Adana plain. They reached the top and when the road began to descend on the other side of the mountain Orhan lit a cigarette.

The next sharp turn threw Anne against him. "I'm afraid I'm going to be sick."

"My cigarette bothers you? I'm sorry."

"It's the curves, not the smoke."

Orhan snuffed out his cigarette in the ashtray set into the back of the seat in front of them. "I don't need to smoke.... I...I need to tell you that to use the word 'sick' is not good in Turkey. Better instead to use the word 'ill.'"

Better if she didn't mention sickness at all. Anne wedged her body back into a corner of the seat. Thank God it was cooling off. Now they were in Turkey, the shift Orhan had made to being more formal with her puzzled her. Was he nervous about how she would react? Or was he worried she would behave in some way that embarrassed him?

It grew dark. The taxi increased its speed when it reached the base of the other side of the mountain and began to hurtle over the potholes of a straighter road. They had descended to another flat plain on the far side of the mountain and Orhan pointed to three dimly lit small windows set back from the road. "See those? The light is from oil-lamps in village houses. It is 1960, but most villages here have no electricity. Behind the mud walls are villagers. They are my countrymen. They eat, they talk, they argue, but business, engineering, the things I studied in the U.S. mean nothing to them. They don't know, they don't care that another Turk spends a year studying in a faraway graduate school. They never heard of graduate school. Means nothing to them that my father's textile factory will be better now I am back. The cloth they buy will not fade so fast, but they will not notice. They will eat. They will talk. They can argue. They may not even read. Oh, maybe a sometimes newspaper—Ayee!"

The unlighted rear end of a horse cart loomed dead in front of the taxi and skillfully, the driver pounded his brakes and swung out at the same time.

Knocked forward, Anne clutched at the seat in front of her while the taxi jerked to a stop. What she could see of the driver of the cart indicated he was scarcely aware of the calamity he had escaped. He continued placidly holding the reins while his horse continued plodding over the potholes.

Orhan opened the window next to him to lean out and shout. "*Esholeshek!*" Afterward pulling his head in, he said, "That's swear word. It means 'son of a donkey' but women don't use it. That man is lucky our driver didn't hit him."

"His cart had no lights, no reflectors!" Anne gasped. The taxi hurtled on and they were silent.

Orhan, having collected his composure, said, "I want to tell you more customs. This time it is about the educated in our town. I want to tell what happens when your parents arrange marriage for you."

"Your parents want to arrange your marriage, don't they," Anne asked. "And I mess all that up, don't I?"

"They had begun to find me a wife, yes, before I told them about you. I mean this story I'm going to tell you is true. It happened three years ago. I have a friend, Mehmet. He's older than I am. He studied engineering in Switzerland four years. That is long time, and he loved a girl. Like you say, fell in love. When he came back to Gaziantep, the Swiss girl came with him. Like you, she came to see if she wants to marry and live in our town."

In the dark, Orhan thrust a hand out to touch her knee and she understood that he was telling her something important to him.

"This Swiss girl only stayed about a half year. While she was living in a hotel—they sent her to hotel because it was not right to have her stay with Mehmet's family—while she was in Gaziantep, my friend's mother, she talks too much. His mother told all her friends at the women's reception days that her son had a Swiss woman who would be his wife, she made it sound like it was settled. She told about how her son found his own wife and didn't wait for his parents to find for him.

But then the girl decides she can't live in Gaziantep. She goes back to Switzerland. So, Mehmet was left and his parents, they have to find another wife for him."

Anne placed her moist hand over Orhan's dry one on her knee. "If I decide to go home again, are you telling me what would happen to you?"

"Yes...well...maybe. My friend's mother talked too much. This is good family. They need a bride from a good family, and the first family in Gaziantep they asked said no. Aintab—that is the short name for our town—Aintab families knew too much. They knew their daughter was only second choice, so refusal. Everyone who is educated knows everyone else in Gaziantep who is educated, and *Eyvah!*" Orhan's voice shook. "The second family refused."

"My friend's family asked, asked again, and always it was the same answer, no! Finally they traveled to Ankara to find a wife. The family they asked in Ankara must have heard what families had said in Gaziantep. They refused. Finally after more tries my friend found a wife in Izmir. She is educated. She is pretty, but she is...well... strange. I think her family was happy anyone wanted her. They did not ask about Mehmet. They knew he was from good family and he studied abroad. Still, my friend—is the word you say 'deserves'?—better."

Anne spoke slowly, choosing her words carefully. "Are you trying to warn me? Are you saying that Turkey's village culture...and also Turkish educated culture is also very different from the one I come from?"

"Yes. That is what I am telling you. We have so far two signs we are back in Turkey. One, they canceled our plane. Two, we slammed to stop just before we drove over the back of a horse cart. There will be more signs. But now I hope you sleep. Before you meet my parents, you must sleep. We will arrive late, but I think someone will wait for us. They know I'm still coming because I have not come."

"What does that mean?"

"In Turkey we don't telephone about when we come because the telephones are not good. It's 1960. They will be good soon, but they are not now. So...sleep now my friend An-ne." He pronounced her name in the way he had told her meant "mother" in Turkish.

She had not yet decided if she liked the implications of that pronunciation, but now because she needed to, she took being called "mother" as a sign of his fondness for her, relaxed somewhat, and let herself doze.

At length Orhan nudged her to wake her and pointed ahead. "Look, We are almost home. Soon, we will see the lights of my city. For a year I have not seen Aintab." He pushed himself forward on the seat and peered ahead "Waaait..." he said softly. The taxi had dropped into a low spot in the road between two higher knolls. "There, the lights!"

Laced out on the hills in front of them, perhaps several kilometers away, were the lights of a city. "I am home. *AllahAllaha*. What a sight!"

"Its bigger than I had pictured it."

"It has been growing. I think now it has many more people than when I left a year ago. It is good we came by car on this road. We see it first all lights, sparkle...like fairy city."

As he spoke, a dip in the road made the city's lights vanish again.

"See, perhaps there was, perhaps there wasn't. My favorite folktale goes...oh, I can't translate it into English. It tells about a camel who is barber and an owl who is judge. Then it goes on. It is good sounding nonsense in Turkish."

"Ah, what I came to Turkey for was charming nonsense. I'll have to learn it in Turkish and English both."

Orhan pulled forward abruptly on his seat, stared ahead, and cleared his throat. "I want to tell you more. What I say now is not nonsense. I have not told you yet. Now I have to tell because you will meet my parents in a few minutes. I have to tell you...I told my parents we are married."

Anne's body went numb...except that her stomach felt as if it had been punched hard. Her throat tightened.

Orhan shifted backward in his seat and gently laid a hand on her knee. "No way...I could not take you home with me if we were not married. My parents must accept you...so..."

Anne brushed his hand from her knee. "Orhan, how could you?" Unwilling now to look at either Orhan or his city, she turned her face away. "You mean...you mean...your parents will treat me...like we're married. They'll expect us to act like we're married? You mean this is like my wedding night!" Her foot pushed forward to the floor awkwardly as if she could press a brake. "I'm not ready…not ready! How could you?"

"I…I just did it. I told you the story about my friend Mehmet. I could not come back with you if I was not married to you. I…did not think." He paused. "I did not think you would be like this. I did not think about how you would be. I did not think. I am sorry."

"Oh…oh Orhan. I was frightened before to meet your parents…but now? Now when they think I'm their new daughter-in-law…? Oh…Orhan…how could you? How could you do it? What will they do? How will they treat me, and it will all be false. They'll be angry with me for a hoard of empty reasons. And you didn't tell me until it was too late to turn around and go back. Oh…Orhan how could you do it?"

"Easy…I told them what I want. I want to marry you, so I made it happen."

CHAPTER TWO
ONCE THERE WAS A STUDENT
SEPTEMBER, 1959

Orhan pulled two ties from his luggage, one of dark blue silk, the other a polka dotted bow tie. He decided for the jauntiness of the bow. In the two days since he'd rented this student room, and begun to play at establishing himself as an "honest to *Allah*" U.S. student, each move he'd taken across his room had necessitated steering around his bags. Gingerly. Since he'd put them there, he had been reluctant to actually open his rough leather luggage and remove his things. Three large bags lay as yet unpacked in the center of the room's tiny open space. He had not yet accepted the idea of staying in this room with its scarred chest of drawers, its iron bedstead with a sagging mattress, its window-sills with chipping paint. Was it the musty smell of the chest's drawers that put him off? Was there a chance he could find a better place for less money? Or more money, it didn't matter!. His landlady had insisted that to find another room this late was unlikely. Still, as long as another place remained a possibility, the three large bags might remain in the middle of the threadbare rug. His mother's insistence that he take care to keep the crease in his pants meant he had removed slack hangers from his luggage and hung two pair of slacks in the narrow closet. Now he chose the navy blue slacks hanging there instead of the jeans.

Maybe he'd unpack when he came back tonight. At the last orientation session, he'd been handed a printed invitation to an international student's reception and had decided to make it the first event he had *chosen* to attend since arriving in the country. All the other places he'd been to on every corner of the campus—the International Student office to find housing, the University of Washington Business school to register—had by contrast been places he'd been required to go. Until now he'd done nothing but take care of essentials! Yes, he'd sleep-walked through a scattering of activities connected with "orienting" international students to their life in these United States. Now, he'd decided to do something he actually wanted to do: try a social event. So far, he'd been too occupied to feel lonely, and he had avoided thinking about the things he missed about home. A reception for international students might be good: to speak English with some handful of people who did not approach him for academic reasons. It might feel good to be talking small talk!

For a reception, he'd need to wear a tie. The dark silk was too formal, the bow tie set the right tone. He moved to the mirror above the chest of drawers and noticed for the first time that the glass had a long crack across its lower part. His reflection came back awry: head and shoulders separated by the crack. His waist wasn't reflected, being below the mirror. His groin was cut off from the rest of his body. Was something trying to tell him that his lower desires would have to be subordinate to the way his head needed to function in this U.S. setting? Carefully, he adjusted his tie.

His mother would be appalled to see him in this seedy room with a worn out oriental rug, a cheap one at that, and a cracked mirror. Her son deserved the best the Turkish lira could buy! But when the Turkish lira in this year of the dominant U.S. dollar, 1959, amounted only to something like two-and-a-half to the dollar, her darling son would have to accept the low-cost lot of a student. Life in penury! Penury might not be one of his favorite English words, but he was proud of the fact that he knew it.

With his tie in place and knotted, he pulled the invitation from his suit-coat pocket. Reading it again, he remembered he had no idea where he would find Eagleson Hall on 15th Avenue, which was where the reception would take place. His landlady would know. He'd ask her.

One more glance in the cracked mirror to make sure his mustache was unruffled, a transfer of his comb and wallet from the top of the chest to his pants pockets, an observation that his shoes needed shining, and he was out of the room. Descending the dark stairway, he wondered where he'd get a shoeshine. The countless shoeshine boys with their shiny brass stools who cluttered the streets of his Turkish hometown were missing in Seattle. Nearing the front hall, he began to hope he'd find his landlady on the davenport in her living room. Yesterday when he'd left the house she'd been lying there on her couch, smoking.

This time, also, she lay, clad in a sagging housecoat, on her sofa. "Pardon, Ma'am" he lowered his chin, "Could you…help me?"

"Is it Orha-an?" She propped herself on one elbow above the flowered slip-cover of the sofa. His name came from her mouth pronounced as if he were a leg of lamb. "First, perhaps you…could… please, say my name right?" He paused, shaken to be so readily correcting her pronunciation. "My name does not rhyme with 'can.' It rhymes with your English name 'John.' It is Or-hahn," he said, coming down hard on the long "a."

"I'm so…oo sorry," Her voice was low, grainy. "Elizabeth's my name, but you can call me Betty. What is it that I can do for you?"

Hesitant, Orhan walked into the living room, pulled the card from his pocket, handed it to this woman lying below him, and, because she wasn't fully dressed, turned his head away. "I have a invitation to a reception, but I don't know where…." He paused to look at the card again. "Eagleson Hall…where will I find 15th Avenue?"

While his hand vacillated, hers darted up, grabbed his and pulled it down toward her breast. "It's a breeze," she mumbled.

He pulled his hand away. American slang must use "breeze" to mean something like easy.

"Fifteenth Avenue runs along one side of the campus," she continued. As she spoke her stubby fingers shot out to stroke his lowered hand. Her moist hand felt soft, soothing to his dry hand holding the card, but her gesture also shocked him. Again, he pulled away.

Disregarding his retreat, she pushed herself up from the couch and moved past him to the hall. "Lemme jus' get a piece paper…draw you a map."

"That would be very kind."

He noticed that her fuzzy slippers were matted and they accentuated her thick ankles as she moved through the open French doors into her dining room. She disappeared through a groaning swinging door, and he thought he smelled the cabbage she had cooked for dinner. Her stroke of his hand, was it just a motherly gesture, or was she starved for affection? He hadn't met a husband yet…but assumed she had one.

She reappeared through the same groaning door, put a small scrap of paper on the table and drew a street map with a pencil. When she leaned close to his face to explain it, her breath smelled of whisky.

"Would'ja like a ride, my son?" Her offer lacked enthusiasm.

"I want fresh air." He straightened his body to make a show of independence.

"You can't miss Eagleson Hall. Walk straight south along Fifteenth. It runs beside the campus."

The oak trees that bordered the campus side of this noisy street charmed him when he reached Fifteenth Avenue. The air at dusk on this autumn evening felt moist. After a rainless summer, Gaziantep's air had been dryer this autumn than most years. No trees were left beside streets in Aintab, and the clatter of the traffic on 15th Avenue contrasted also with his home city. Horse carts and men milling about on foot wearing *shalvar* and bright colored *kushak* crowded central Gaziantep's narrow streets. No smell of horse dung here on 15th Avenue. With no sidewalks, the pedestrians that walked Gaziantep's streets had to be alert for the few cars. Not that the Gaziantep streets were quieter, but the sounds were different: horns warning pedestrians to scatter; street vendors hawking their wares; villagers shouting at their horses; the clatter of donkey hooves. Sidewalks in this American city meant people didn't walk in the streets. No need to honk pedestrians from the path of automobiles. At this hour streets in Aintab would be nearly empty, anyway.

Drivers drove at an alarming speed here. The fast pace and the danger in a U.S. city had made him cautious during these first days. How long would it be before he himself drove through these U.S. streets? He'd been driving in Turkey for some five years. He recalled the crestfallen face of his father's chauffeur who felt cheated whenever Orhan elected to drive himself. But to drive in Seattle? That would be some feat. He wouldn't have a car anyway. One less complication.

The encounter with his landlady disturbed him. His home life here should be uncomplicated. Having to be wary of this woman would...not be good. He'd come to study, to learn business. He wanted no distractions, but neither did he like feeling lonely. He could nearly hear his father's admonitions in stern Turkish about working hard. His parents had money, and could send him abroad to study without sacrifice. That wasn't the point. He had been sent here to learn Western business methods, and they wanted him to bring know-how back as rapidly as he could absorb it. He was expected to allow no breaks in his concentration, to endure being lonely. He and his father had a job to do. Their factory would be deeply involved in bringing Turkey into the modern European industrial world. An exciting goal!

He glanced up again at the trees beside 15th Avenue, wondering if he might get some of their seeds to take back for Gaziantep's streets, or at the least, the yard of his family's apartment house. His return to Turkey was time enough for a normal, less lonely life. A suitable wife would be found for him. His parents had already indicated they'd find him a wife while he was away. The time here was to be spent working hard, observing, and enjoying things like these trees. An early patch of gold in one of the broadleafed trees stirred and shimmered in the brassy light of dusk. He'd never see those leaves in Turkey! Could their turns, their twists be described by the idiom "topsy turvy?"

While still focused on the tree, he stepped off the curb to cross the street. The traffic light glowed red, but a car swept down on him and forced him to jump backward.

"*Ayee! Esholeshek,*" The driver of a dark sedan had run a red light.

No horn, no warning—just expected the world to get out of his way. Or had he even thought about the rest of the walking world? No. That driver wouldn't do well in Turkey.

Eagleson Hall was a finely appointed building—fancy brick work, Gothic arched windows on the outside and dark, wood paneling on the inside. Its builders must have been selected to make it match the Gothic-style architecture of the University of Washington campus. Another amazing thing about the U.S.: people built ordinary buildings with a design and ornamentation meant for something other than functional purposes. In the past the buildings of this University campus had been built in ornate styles. But he could recall no such frills on the building he'd watched being built this afternoon.

He paused just inside Eagleson's two doors to consider when this building might have been built. The elaborate carving on the wainscoting put this building in the class of the older campus buildings. He glanced at the clusters of foreign-looking people milling about in the entrance hall. There was a dark-skinned, aquiline-featured man wearing a turban speaking to a woman in a cobalt blue *saree*. Indian women seemed to him to be beautiful. Their long flowing clothing accentuated that beauty.

But to talk to anyone? Earlier he had thought he wanted to make small talk, but now that desire had vanished, and he felt hesitant. What did you say to anyone at a gathering like this?

A gentleman who appeared to be some kind of host came into the entrance hall and announced in an official voice that the actual reception was downstairs in another room. Would this be the time to turn and go back out the door?

No. He persuaded himself to follow the people moving down the dark wood-paneled stairway to a large low-ceilinged room at street level. The large room's many paned windows looked out on 15th Avenue, and once there and drawn to the movement of traffic he glimpsed outside, he wound around the clumps of people talking to a place beside a window. The same loud-voiced man announced that he hoped everyone would pause to pick up a name tag, but Orhan decided to forego leaving the window. A strange American custom, that, wearing your name on your chest for everyone to be able to read. People in Turkey went mostly by their first names, and that made names easier to remember. What difference did it make if people knew your name? In Gaziantep everyone who was anybody knew the name of everyone else who was anybody. Of course there were a lot of nobodies—villagers and workers—in Gaziantep as well, since it was no small town.

"And can you give me a reason why you're not wearing a name-tag?" a saucy low-pitched woman's voice spoke from behind him. Some Americans didn't enunciate. This woman spoke clearly.

"I...I won't stay long," he said.

"I know. To speak English so constantly makes you tired." He turned to see the woman speaking to him in such a forward way. She was tiny, had a perky behind, and had an air of being iron-strong, not pretty. She did have an intriguing puckish face.

Orhan stiffened. "Not that. English I've used my whole school life. University, too."

"Where was your University?" She used that same certain manner to toss her head.

To be so sure of herself didn't fit a woman. Made him want to challenge her. Why did she want to know where he'd studied? Silly. She was probably only making conversation. He looked at her short-bobbed hair—demure. It was only her manner that made her seem forward.

"I went to Robert College in Istanbul, Turkey. Anyone wants to go anywhere in Turkey these days he must learn English. We study in English."

"And are there women who want to go somewhere, and are they allowed?"

"I met you, just. In Turkey it would not be polite to ask me such a question before you'd asked 'How are you?'"

She lowered her chin and looked down. "I'm sorry. We've heard so much in this country about the position of Muslim women, I was only curious."

He hadn't meant to challenge her but he'd come for small talk, not serious talk about a subject that embarrassed him. He looked at her name-tag. "Did you know your name means Mother in Turkish? We pronounce it Ahn-neh."

"I'm not sure I like that. I'm not even certain I want to be a mother."

"Don't go to Turkey, then." Astonished at himself, Orhan pulled his chin in. Five sentences spoken and he was already giving this woman advice. He'd intended a more helpless stance.

"That seems a bit inhospitable! I've heard Turks are famous for their hospitality."

"They are."

"We've somehow got on a strange footing. Let's start over." She cocked her head and grinned. "As you have observed, I'm Anne McClellan and I came to ask you to get a name-tag because I work in the International Student office that sponsors this reception." She paused after her recitation, and smiled again. She had lovely even teeth. She wore a plain short sleeved pink sweater with a single strand of pearls at her neck. Her figure was rounded. He preferred bodies like hers.

"You looked as if you could use a greeting, looking out the window like that, and I pounced. I needed to greet someone. I'm as new at this as you are. I just landed this job. For a woman just out of college in these United States, believe me, this job is pure luck. I dislike admitting it, but I think my father pulled strings."

"Is it 'in common?' Do you say 'in common?' That's something we have in common. My father pulled strings to get me into the University of Washington Business School. I am not from a big, important city. I am from the backwoods in Turkey. My city, Gaziantep, has a population of some 125 thousand, but it is still backwoods."

"You really do amaze me. How do you know words like 'backwoods?' You have an accent, but I haven't heard a single grammatical mistake."

"Thank you. I speak mistakes, I know."

"And what, besides being backwoods, makes Gaziantep important?" She spoke the name of his town as if she had said it already some fifteen times.

"We're known for our energy. You see, we're away from all the modern distractions of Western Turkey and we work hard. My family owns a cloth factory. We weave cloth. Plain fabric, but plain fabric is what most Turkish villagers buy to wear. I went to high school and college in Western Turkey. Western Turkey is different from Eastern Turkey. I'd prefer to live in Western Turkey; it's closer to Europe. But our factory is in Eastern Turkey, so that is where I will live."

As if she hadn't heard him—her saucy manner had vanished—she was staring off across the room. "Forgive me. I don't mean to be rude. I just got the signal I am to come and help make name-tags, help welcome people. I'd forgotten I'm on the job! That's a compliment to you." Again, she flashed him a smile that showed all her even teeth. Another American phenomenon. Few people had crooked teeth. He'd been told that anyone who was anyone made sure their children's teeth were straight at an age when it could still be easily done.

"Do not go!" His delay in replying made him nearly shout, and his own insistence shocked him. "I…I have something I need from you. Does your office have listings of rooming houses? I am not…I am not sure about mine." He had got the address of his present rooming house from an office he was almost certain was the one from which she worked.

"Yes, of course we do. I can probably help you with that."

"Where will I find you? I will come tomorrow."

"Our office is in the Student Union Building. Did they give you a map of the campus? It's shown on there."

"I will come. I am in a room, but I am not sure I like it…."

"I really have to go. I'll expect to see you. Now go make conversation.

"If you're hesitant, let me suggest a trick. Ask questions. If you get the other guy talking, your exchange is made. What's more he'll think you're ever so clever. At ease, even when you know you're not."

He watched her go off, again noticing her perky behind. He was still feeling out of place. He'd go get something to drink—they were serving punch across the room—and go home.

While Orhan waited for a red-faced middle-aged woman to put a glass of punch in his hand, the man wearing the turban he'd seen upstairs came up beside him. Receiving punch at the same time, the two men moved off together. When it became clear his companion expected him to say something, he asked the obvious. "Where are you from?"

His companion launched an answer about being a Sikh and from India and continued for what Orhan guessed was nearly ten minutes explaining his silver bracelet, and the fact that Sikhs don't cut their hair, and that Sikhs were persecuted. His English was heavily accented. Orhan had difficulty understanding it, but it seemed nonetheless to be nearly flawless. Still, Orhan didn't relish hearing about all the difficulties Sikhs encountered. He didn't know what he did want to hear, but not that.

Walking back home along 15th Avenue, he saw visions of the lovely Indian woman in the blue *saree*. He could have come up with countless questions for her, but it wasn't worth waiting around to maneuver himself into a position where he would be near her. While the Sikh had been talking, Orhan's wandering mind had remembered what he could do once he was home. He would go to work to install the high-fidelity speakers and record player which had been his first purchase upon arriving in Seattle. Music was a necessity in his life. Even his sagging bed could be made acceptable if he were lying on it listening to Mozart. Having acquired a sense of purpose, he knew he could avoid all other distractions on this empty evening. The U.S. was, with Europe, a center for the musical world he cared about. In this country he could buy records and hear as much good music as he could afford. He now had the high-fidelity equipment to begin to make good on that aim, and he had the beginnings of a record collection, two discs. Get his equipment operating. That's what he'd do!

Nearing his house, he began to hope that he could come in the front door without encountering his landlady lying on the davenport. She was an agreeable enough woman; he might not be lonely living in her house, but tonight he didn't want to answer her hoarse-voiced questions. She might ask why he was home so early. He didn't know himself.

CHAPTER THREE
ONCE ONE REFLECTS

On a Sunday morning in late October Anne arrived at a meeting for worship of the Society of Friends. Neither a store front, nor like the buildings where congregations ordinarily conduct their worship, this house looked like a family residence. A small group of Quakers, as they were more commonly called, had built themselves this Meeting House. The simplicity of this house suggested to Anne that the quality of worship, rather than its venue, mattered to the people of this faith, and she liked that. Her father had been born a Quaker, but as an adult he had attended their meetings only rarely. When she was a young girl Anne's mother had dressed her blond, blue-eyed little girl in patent leather baby doll shoes and swept her off to Sunday school at a Congregational Church. By her high school years Anne's interest in any church had lagged. It was only in college, after her mother had died, that she wanted to launch some kind of spiritual exploration. Her father told a joke about the Society of Friends: Quakers were like manure, spread them out and they do a lot of good, pile them up and they generate a lot of heat. His quip hadn't frightened Anne, but it did make her wary about becoming too involved with Quakers as a group. She liked their appearance of being more counter-culture and materially simple than other spiritual seekers. It didn't matter to her that this group had evidently decided that they needed no comfortable chairs and carpet to help worshippers listen for the "Light within."

On this particular morning she had brought her own agenda to the meeting for worship. The silent meeting was anything but silent since the bare wooden floor of the meeting room creaked as latecomers tried to slip in noiselessly, and the folding chairs seemed to groan when anyone on them shifted. Noise, however, didn't appear to jar the beatific expressions of the gathered worshippers. A small boy entered the room, located his mother across the circle, and stomped on his chubby legs over to climb on her lap. Anne glanced at him, and decided that the attention from this assembled group must be essential to his sense of himself.

Anne had entered before the service began and had chosen a chair in the back of the four circular rows. Having placed her feet solidly on the floor, she shut her eyes to avoid the distraction of others taking their places around her. She had come not so much to listen for the voice of the Light within, the stated purpose of the gathering, as to think about her own dilemma. She had landed a new dream job, one that fit well with the philosophy of this faith she was exploring. Didn't Quakers work at making peace in the world? But already her new job had presented her with quandaries. Nothing was simple.

Three weeks ago Orhan Demir had come to the International Student office, and looked at the listings of the available rooms. He had decided to look at a room which was beyond walking distance and persuaded her to drive him there. To let herself be thus cajoled was a mistake. One of her boss, Bradley Owen's, admonitions was that it was unwise to have personal relationships with the students who came for help to the International Student office. She had been on the job only about four weeks and was already ignoring this advice. To be impersonal with other students had been easy, but her dealings with Orhan Demir had thrown that aim awry. He had not rented the room he'd looked at with her—asserting that his present room was within walking distance of the campus and had become more liveable now his high-fidelity was operating. But a spark between them had flared by the end of their room-hunting jaunt. Four times since then they had met each other for coffee. In itself, a coffee date would have been innocent enough. But the excitement she felt after those meetings, and the way he seemed to want to see her socially puzzled her. Each time she thought about this engaging man with the bushy mustache she was uncontrollably driven to want more than just a professional relationship with him. He broke all her stereotypes about Turkish men. He had a childlike urbanity, if such a trait were possible, and he seemed genuinely interested in her as a person. Something to *do* about this man was what she hoped to find during this Meeting for Worship. But was there anything to be done?

The mother whose little boy had entered with so much *eclat* now went out with him and as the child went out he made more stomping sounds, and Anne opened her eyes. The assembled people were a captive audience in this carpetless room. The child's delight in his ability to make noticeable noise in the midst of so many silent people charmed Anne. What did Quakers do about small children who disrupted their meetings? But she hadn't come to explore the issues of the group gathered here. She had come to listen for the voice Quakers believed spoke to them from within. She put her two hands on her knees, palm up, shut her eyes again, and waited. Foiled! What came to her was Orhan's voice speaking about his aim to bring Beethoven to Turkey. Last week at coffee he had waxed poetic—at least for his boyish temperament he had seemed poetic—about how one of his missions was to bring Western classical music to his home town, Gaziantep. Right there in the restaurant where they had met, he had taken a pencil and beat out the time of Beethoven's *Ode to Joy* while he hummed it. To speak about music somehow transformed this complex and somewhat stoical man into an enthusiastic boy. That change fascinated her.

"There's no melody to Turkish classical music. You can't hum. It's boring," he insisted. "It repeats phrases over and over. It's mostly religious—they say it makes the worshipper adore the one God, but that kind of religion is for my Sufi grandfather who lives with us. Impossible, that music!"

Now, through the silence the picture that came to her mind was of this good looking Turkish man sitting across the cafe table from her. She recalled her father's claim when as a small girl she had complained that his mustache scratched her cheek. He had pulled out his sing-song voice to mock her: "A kiss without a mustache is like a potato without salt." Orhan's mustache added to his good looks. Did it add to his kisses? No way of knowing. She squirmed in her noisy chair as some inner voice told her "I want him, I want him." A spiritual voice? Surely not. The voice of the Spirit would say something like "You shouldn't, you shouldn't." But why shouldn't she want him? Why shouldn't she let herself go, have a fling? He was a personable young man in this country for only a year. He'd come determined to concentrate on his work in the graduate school of business. A simple friendship with him would make his stay in the U.S. more pleasant for him, yes, and for her it could mean the expansion of her world. But no. The warnings she'd had from her employer were too serious. She would keep this relationship impersonal. Even as she recalled that admonition she knew she would disregard it. She was as eager for Orhan's kiss as she was for salt on a potato. But what kind of thoughts were these in the middle of a silent Meeting for Worship?

Her thinking was interrupted when the same woman whose child had earlier stomped out stood up. In a shaky voice, she spoke out of the silence. "The Society of Friends believes there is a bit of God in every person. My problem is to believe there is a bit of God in me." The woman sat down and the Meeting continued in silence. The other worshippers and Anne were left to integrate that message, make it fit somehow into their sense of worship. If there was a bit of God in her, Anne McClellan, how might it express itself with Orhan? Was not the Spirit of God always a connecting spirit? It would be contrary to cut Orhan off before they had had any chance to know each other. Or was she only kidding herself when she longed to move ahead…be cautious…but connect?

An image from a Marianne Moore poem came to her: an image of the sea rising and falling in a chasm. Moore had said something like "he sees deep and is glad who accedes to mortality and in his imprisonment rises upon himself as the sea in a chasm struggling to be free and unable to be, in its surrending finds its continuing."

Anne imagined herself to be like a riotous sea foaming and churning in a rock chasm, its turbulence confined to rising on itself and crashing back—water without the freedom to flow where it might go naturally. Rock walls kept it churning inside the one chasm, flowing nowhere, only dashing upward. This relationship with Orhan could be limited, controlled. As such, couldn't she let it happen? Like that sea, it could stay confined, rise only within limits. Let it happen…as it happens. With that thought, Anne relaxed and finished the hour in an emotionally fraught day dream: yes, controlled relationships were possible.

Once the meeting was over, speaking to no one—small talk seemed difficult after the deep feelings of worship—Anne slipped out into the dry autumn noon-time and walked up 15th Avenue toward Eagleson Hall. The October sunlight had paled for the winter, but as it shone on the tulip trees on the campus along 15th, their gold colors shone more brilliantly. Lifting her chin, she drew in air and hummed *Ode to Joy* as she walked to the restaurant where she and her friend Nancy would meet. In Friends' silent meetings she missed music. Music had been one of her favorite parts of the church services she had been to as a child. There'd been a hymn which went something like "Joyful, joyful we adore Thee" to the tune of *Ode to Joy*.

Nancy, a good friend whom she knew from their time together on the University's swim team, was now back in town after traveling in Europe for most of the summer. She would have myriad tales to tell. Ann expected she would again feel cowed by her friend's accomplishments. For Nancy life was an experience collection and she had begun to collect in earnest now her college career was finished. Nancy was also attractive. Her dark eyebrows set off her Mona Lisa face, and she drew men like moths to a light bulb. This friend had always spoken of her own exploits and triumphs with a bravado Anne felt she herself couldn't muster. Still, nothing dimmed Anne's fascination with Nancy's stories. Defensively, she reminded herself that her friend wasn't purposely telling her tales just to make her envious. Her amazement at Nancy's adventures needn't make Anne herself long for similar exploits. She could fashion her own adventures rather than try to keep up with her friend's. Nancy craved the exotic! Anne's aspirations were quieter, less ambitious; they had more to do with a widening of the world she knew about.

Anne was already seated when Nancy walked in, one hip canted as Anne remembered was her habit. Full of her own story, her friend didn't seem to notice Anne cupping her palms around her coffee cup and staring down at it's liquid while Nancy described meeting an American business man in Venice. "Italians were all really oily. When I met this American guy I felt like I'd swung back to sophistication." Nancy went on to tell about the dinner they had shared in a candlelit restaurant, and a night time gondola adventure. When she began to describe avidly the details of what happened in the bed of a shadowy hotel room Anne stopped her. "Do you really want to tell me all this? I'm not sure I want to hear all the curlicues of your illicit love affair?"

"None of this could have happened if I had stuck with that bunch of creeps I went with," Nancy leaned across the table. A lock of her straight bobbed hair fell forward across her arched dark eyebrow, and she lowered her voice. "American tourists—particularly in a group—are a drag to be with in Europe. You just have to pluck up your independence and get away from them."

Anne felt outclassed. "I'm not gorgeous like you are. I'd have to stick with the group to protect me from the creeps."

"And Venice wasn't the end of it. This was no one night stand—I sensed it wasn't at the time. I'm still hearing from this guy. He's married—without kids, thank God—and he claims he doesn't want me to slip through his fingers. I'm not sure what to think except that it's nice to be with him and wallow in the money he has… I'll just play it cagey, see what develops through letters. He's a very important guy in his company, I'm thinking…and…well… he has a nose as beautiful as Nuriyev's. I really like him."

Looking up from her coffee, Anne saw the animation on her friend's lovely face and waited for Nancy to look at her. "You're not the only one with intriguing news. Mine's pretty tame compared with your story—but I now have a 'male interest'." Lowering her voice, she mocked a playful sense of mystery as she said 'male interest'.

"Really, and where'd you find him?"

"At the very first reception our office had for International Students. That's the trouble. He's a Turk!"

"No! Wears baggy pants? Waves a scimitar? What's he like?"

"Nothing like the stereotypical Turk. Must be that's why I like him. He comes from a wealthy family and a medium sized town in Eastern Turkey. His family owns a textile factory. But you'd never know he's wealthy. He's self-effacing…gentle. His nose isn't shaped like Nuriyev's, but he does have a cute bushy mustache."

"Does he have a name?"

"Orhan Demir, pronounced with a long 'a.' He says no one had last names in Turkey until after 1922 when Ataturk declared the Republic and made everyone choose a last name. His family chose Demir because it means 'iron' Say's they're proud of the solidity of that name."

"Sensitivity? Sounds pretty macho to me."

"He loves classical music… He's here to learn good business practices, but his passion I'm finding is to find a way to take music back home. We're just friends…My boss, my father, the whole world's warned me about getting involved with a foreigner. Everyone tells me about some intercultural marriage that ended in disaster. I just want a friend, one who expands my world… that's what he does for me… we both love music."

"Love music, huh? You go to concerts with him?"

"The only night-time date we've had was one where we went to my house, sat around talking to my father and Bonnie, and spent the rest of the evening, after they finally left us, listening to music on my father's hi-fi."

"Who's Bonnie?"

"I told you at the beginning of the summer…But you were so full of your own trip you weren't ready to hear my news. Bonnie's the new wife my father married. She was a secretary in his department until he married her. Now she thinks its like her full time job to take care of him. I know I told you because in June when they got married I was afraid of her. Afraid she'd displace me…in some ways she has. But Daddy's still Daddy. He still finds ways to let me know I'm his daughter—like my mother, I am…I don't know. I like Bonnie but…oh, I don't know."

"You gotta get out of there. Home with a new wife for your father is no place for *you*." Nancy's eyes went wide. "Hey, home's no place for me, either. Let's get an apartment. I'll get a job. We can divide the rent. My mother bugs me. I gotta get out of there!"

"We'd rent an apartment, move in, and whammo, you'd get a letter from your exciting man and fly off to San Francisco—leave me holding the gap for the rent check. Let me think about it. I will."

At forty-fifth and University Way, Anne waited twenty minutes for the bus home to Laurelhurst and then decided to walk. It was Sunday and the bus might not be coming without a long wait. The trees on this side of the campus were deciduous instead of the more common evergreens in the Pacific Northwest, and she savored the brilliance in their golden glow. The next wind would probably bring their leaves down.

As she passed the corner of 17th and 45th, the horse-chestnut trees on the road's median strip reminded her that an apartment up 17th in some basement might not be bad...at least affordable. Come to think of it, Orhan's rooming house was on 18th. He'd said it was seedy; his landlady didn't keep it clean. Maybe coming from his background in Turkey he expected his landlady to clean his room. Anne promised herself she'd talk to him about that. Maybe he'd like to learn a few elementary skills like how to make his bed.

Since some of the leaves were still green on the trees beside the 45th street viaduct, she decided that area must be more sheltered...To her left she could see the new shopping center which she would like to blot out of her awareness. She had celebrated when she heard it had taken a while for shoppers to get used to going there, she wondered now how it was doing, and hoped it was not doing well. It was crassly commercial to have filled the open space in this valley with a huge asphalt parking lot and only a scattering of buildings. She picked up her pace down the viaduct, and at the bottom, crossed the street and walked past the slough. They'd filled that wetland in as well and were proposing to make another parking lot. The city's garbage had been used for that fill. From a slough with cat-tails, to garbage, to asphalt—an ugly progression. Orhan came from an under-developed country.

He'd told her cars were scarce. Parking lots were probably not one of Turkey's problems. He had spoken with approval of all the Turkish villagers moving into the cities to find jobs! Maybe his family's factory needed workers. Did he think about his city and the facilities it needed to receive villagers? Did Turks think about having a social conscience?

Why all these questions about Orhan? Was she mothering him? She didn't like the idea. He didn't need a mother! Anne's impression was that his mother was a very strong person in his life. Silently, she vowed not to mother him.

It had been a while since she'd walked home. It gave her time to think. But by the time she reached home her feet were dragging through the fallen leaves on the sidewalk outside her father's house.

Inside, she found her father and Bonnie on the love seat in the living room, each reading, and the record player was playing Vivaldi's Four Seasons. The tableau they composed irritated her. She flung her coat onto a hanger in the hall closet and stood in the arch, hesitating to enter. On the striped loveseat in her family's living room, her father sat reading with a new woman—not her mother. What's more, her father's manner suggested his companionship with this woman was every bit as satisfying as it had been with her mother! Jealous for her mother, she felt envious for herself. Theirs was a kind of intellectual companionship she knew she wanted, but it didn't seem possible with Orhan.

Instead of entering the living room, Anne sniffed the air. "I smell pot roast."

Bonnie smiled the obsequious smile Anne was coming to dislike. "I thought you'd like that. I cook it in dill pickle juice. Arthur loves it," she said, slipping her arm into the arm of the man beside her. To Anne, the gesture seemed excessively clinging.

"Where you been? You look rosy-cheeked," her father said.

"Since you asked, I'll give you the mundane run-down. I was where you seldom go any more—at Friends' Meeting. Then I had coffee with Nancy and then when the bus didn't come, I walked home. It was a longer walk than I remembered."

"I tell you what," Anne cringed at the way Bonnie cooed, "Wouldn't it be cozy to have four of us for dinner tonight. Why don't you call your

Turk and see if he's ever had pot roast. Wouldn't you like to do that?" This final inquiry was spoken as if Bonnie were speaking to an eight year old.

A pleasant tone could not be mustered. "I'll phone him." Anne growled. "Can I have the car to pick him up?"

CHAPTER FOUR
Once There Was a Turkish Guest in a Home that Wasn't Turkish

The smell of meat cooking—an unfamiliar one to him—boded well to Orhan in the entrance hall of Anne's Laurelhurst home. His parents apartment building was said to be one of the marble palaces of Gaziantep, but this home with its elegant upholstered furniture and thick living room carpeting made the apartment building his parents had built seem plain, bare. The oriental rug on the slate floor of this entrance hall wasn't Turkish, but its rich red coloring made him feel at home.

He had heard Anne's father had a new wife. The moment he and Anne arrived she jumped up and disappeared instead of coming to shake his hand, welcome him. Mr. McClellan helped Orhan remove his coat (an assistance Turkish etiquette would not have allowed him to accept). But this was America. He hung the coat in a tiny room right off the entrance hall which appeared to house nothing but coats. Americans built useful places right into their houses. His parents, in the new apartment building they had built two years ago, had needed to purchase a large wardrobe to stand in their entryway for their guests' wraps. At least the wardrobe had a long mirror in its door as this room had. Mirrors placed as you were poised to leave home were useful.

From where he sat in the living room he could see into the dining room. The table set for only four people looked empty. His family seldom had dinner guests, but when they did, the maid usually set some ten to fifteen places. This table looked luxurious with its blue and white patterned dishes and carved crystal water glasses. His mother's idea of elegance was to set a table with dishes and tablecloth all in white. Her aim was always to have many guests and an abundant table. The more guests they seated, the more honor to the Turkish host family.

Bonnie came from the kitchen smoothing the front of her bright apron with plump hands to invite them into the dining room for dinner. A Turkish hostess would never wear an apron in front of her guests, nor would she call them so immediately to the meal when they had just arrived. "I'm afraid the pot roast's not up to snuff," she whimpered. "It got overdone, waiting."

Another odd thing: when Bonnie had brought the platter of pot roast and potatoes and a dish of bright green broccoli (was this strange vegetable served plain without any sauce?) it was Anne's father who distributed the food to the plates. Orhan's mother always served her guests herself. When the servants had brought the large platters for each course, one of his mother's proudest moments was to spoon food onto the guests' plates.

Although it was strange to refrain from eating with his plate full in front of him, it seemed a pleasant bit of reverence when they paused to thank God for their food. Anne introduced this "moment of silence" claiming calmly that she had persuaded her father and his wife to give thanks for their food at least on special occasions like this. To postpone tasting one of the dark wedges of meat on his plate made its aroma that much more inviting.

Having only picked at her food, Bonnie put down her fork. "Now you have to tell us all about the food you have at home." Her voice had a sing-song sweetness to it he couldn't identify, except that it reminded him of some Turkish friend of his mother's.

"We eat little beef. That is why I have never had pot roast."

"Orhan tells me that in Turkey they have three kinds of meat. Sheep, lamb and mutton," Anne quipped. Her father chuckled.

"Actually," Orhan picked up his blue napkin and dabbed at his mustache, "we eat much less meat in Turkey. We eat any vegetable that's in season—in winter it's cauliflower and cabbage. We cook most vegetables with tomato sauce and small bits of ground lamb."

"Orhan tells me they have 99 ways of cooking eggplant in Turkey." Anne seemed eager to talk. "And guess what its name means? *Patlijan*. It means exploded soul."

"But...we use the word so much we never think about that meaning," Orhan explained to Mr. McClellen. "We have wonderful names for eggplant dishes. There's one called *imambayildi*, or the priest fainted, and then there's one called *hunkar beyundi* which means the sultan approved."

"Do tell me why the priest fainted." Bonnie cocked her head with its bright pink round face and flashed Orhan a smile.

"Well, we make *imambayildi* with small eggplant—not like the ones here, and we stuff it with onions and garlic, and lace it, you say? with tomatoes. It maybe looks bloody. Maybe that's why the priest fainted. But there's one dish that looks bloodier and it's called *karni yarik* or split stomach. Ground meat and tomatoes makes it look like a stomach that someone opened up, spilled out."

"How *can* you eat it?" Bonnie feigned shock.

Anne broke in as if she were in a hurry. "Your mother's a good cook. What do you miss most that she cooks?"

"In Gaziantep we have special foods. My mother says the cuisine is good in Aintab because the women use cooking to show off. She says in Aintab they don't have all the new ways and distractions they have in Istanbul to take women's time away from home, so they cook better. I miss what we call *ichli koefte* most. You cook meat and nuts and onions and put them in a shell made of cracked wheat. *Ichli koefte* looks like little American footballs. They would look very good on this china."

"You like the china? It's the only thing I brought to this marriage," Bonnie said.

"Bonnie means it wasn't easy to marry me and move into this house filled with lovely things my wife had collected." McClellan looked at Anne as he spoke.

"Do you think you could show me how to make these little footballs? I could try." He decided that Bonnie's voice reminded him of his sister's friend, not his mother's. The friend was a young girl. Why was Bonnie so friendly? At least she wasn't bothersome like his land lady. Would he ever understand American women? "The shell is made of fine cracked wheat you can't find here. You maybe keep to your kind of footballs in this country. My mother makes it around her thumb. I can't. Takes practice."

"I could try if we could find the right cracked wheat." Why was she so eager?

McClellan sawed at a slice of pot-roast, left off, and looked at Orhan. "Tell us about your father's factory."

Bonnie, having seen the effort required to cut the meat, spoke before Orhan could begin. "It got a little too done, tough, while we waited for the kids to come..."

"It's quite all right," McClellan soothed. "Let's hear about this Turkish factory."

Anne's father was a diplomat. Orhan liked him. "My father is very energetic man and he has many good ideas. They grow much cotton near our town on the Adana plain across the mountains, and my father studied engineering in Germany. In 1950 he learned German factories had machinery—not modern enough for Germany, but not obsolete?, you say? He bought machinery and shipped it to Turkey, to Gaziantep and started a factory. It was difficult. It took too much work, but my father did it. He started, and now he makes good cloth in his factory. I am an engineer. He wants me to study the way they make cloth here, but what he wants more is that I learn about business in the U.S. I will. I have studied four weeks now and I know I will learn much. You in the States are masters at business!"

"I wish Americans were known for mastery of something more than making money!" Anne spoke playfully. Was she joking? No, she was serious.

"There's a lot we do well here," her father said, "but what Orhan's saying is he needs to learn about our capitalist system."

"That's right," Bonnie echoed.

Anne said nothing. It had shocked Orhan when she told him that in politics she didn't always agree with her father. Now, he wanted a subject that would make her happier. "American democracy is very important to Turkey. We're a new democracy in Turkey. But democracy doesn't go well at the moment. It takes a long time to get uneducated people—our villagers—ready for democracy. We didn't have even a republic until 1922 when Atatürk pushed the Greeks out after the first World War."

"But he was a dictator, an army man!" McClellan's tone grew hard.

Orhan paused to find a way to reassure this man. "In English you could say a *benevolent* dictator! We educated Turks are grateful to Ataturk. He forced us into the Western world."

Anne sat forward and gripped the table's edge with both hands. "Imagine what it must have been like! Orhan tells me Ataturk hired linguists to develop a script, then decreed overnight Turks had to use the Western alphabet." Anne was being helpful and he was thankful.

"Now, my father thinks Ataturk's like Allah! I wasn't born yet, but my father had to wake up one morning and try to read the newspaper in a completely new written language."

"You call that benevolent?" McClellan asked.

"We call it necessary. We have to come into the Western world."

"And he made it illegal for women to wear the veil," Anne added.

"My mother says that was difficult for women. When they had to take off their head covering, it was like they were going in the streets naked."

"How do you like the pot roast?" Bonnie asked. Talk about Turkish politics didn't interest her.

"Delicious. We would say *elinize saghlik* which means health to your hand."

"Aren't you nice!" Bonnie appeared to purr.

"But what's happening now in Turkey is not nice." There was more to be said about Turkish politics and Orhan felt compelled to tell it. "We grew up. We had an election. But villagers don't know how to vote. Bad politicians got in. We thought Menderes was a good man, but he is the one who is dictator. Our newspapers are censored now. Men get into trouble just for using their freedom."

"Have you no recourse?" McClellan asked, and while Orhan was wondering about the exact meaning of *recourse* Anne spoke, "Orhan says he's actually hoping for the army to step in—"

"Some kind of coup?" McClellan was further alarmed.

"Yes. We need revolution. You see, our army is the main force in Turkey supporting democracy. The army is determined to protect what Ataturk started."

"These days when I'm thinking about the Quakers' peace testimony, I find it hard to believe that any army could make a revolution and be good." Anne spoke calmly, but her tone carried a force no Turkish woman would ever use when speaking about politics. Did she feel caught between her father's opinions and his?

"But you Americans believe democracy is good. We're losing ours."

Anne was still frowning. "How can an undemocratic institution like an army protect a democracy?"

"How can it…but…well, I trust the army more than this present government."

McClellan laughed a little grunt of a laugh. "If I've learned anything in my lifetime, it's that we Americans don't know everything, either."

"We are infant democracy…. You are grandfather."

"And we just went through the McCarthy era. Democracy's always fragile."

Anne was still frowning. "McCarthy made some of us think we'd learned nothing from what happened in Germany in World War II."

Orhan had never known a politically alert woman. Surely no Turkish woman would ever speak like this at the dinner table.

Her father rose and reached for a serving fork. "More meat. Who wants more meat?"

"I do." Orhan lifted his empty plate, observing its blue willow design. Patterns on china were another aspect of the west he liked.

"Have more potatoes as well," Bonnie added, and the talk moved to safer topics.

Dinner finished, Anne suggested they have their coffee in the living room. "The Turks, Orhan tells me, always do it this way," she said when they all sat with their coffee cups in front of them.

"Anne tells me you like Mozart and Beethoven," McClellan had moved to his hi-fi equipment. "They're pretty pedestrian fare in this country, but I've got a few recordings."

Orhan wasn't certain what "pedestrian" meant but he sensed he needed to defend his musical tastes. "Western classical music is new for us. Turks are not ready for anything too *avant garde*. Turkish classical music is atonal, monotonous. I don't like atonal music, so you can't expect me to like Schoenberg."

"At least you've heard him." McClellan drew a recording from his record cabinet. Orhan watched his ruddy hands handle it delicately as he placed it on the player. "Here's a Mozart I particularly like—violin and viola together—Sinfonia Concertante."

"I know it. I like it." Music would be calming, and while listening he wouldn't have to talk. He continued to find it difficult to speak English socially for a whole evening, especially when there were more people than just Anne.

"Put it on, Arthur. I'll just go do the dishes and know I'm not missing anything." Bonnie said.

"Except she will miss great music," McClellan chuckled.

"Would you like help?" Anne's tone made it clear she hoped Bonnie would not want help.

"You've been running all afternoon. Rest...I'll just load the dishwasher." Orhan was curious about the dishwasher, but decided this was not the time to ask to see it.

"That's kind of you." Anne's sweet tone sounded false. Why didn't she like this woman?

McClellan put the record on and as the music began, the three listeners fell silent. Orhan leaned back into an easy chair, wondered if it was impolite to shut his eyes, and decided not to. After listening a short while he spoke. "There is such order in this music."

"And the harmony of the viola and violin sooths," McClellan said.

Anne sat motionless in her easy chair, eyes shut, and said nothing. To close the eyes was probably polite.

"Hear the modulation in those strings!" her father crooned.

The music set up a yearning in Orhan, but what he yearned for he didn't know, and in a social situation you didn't talk about yearning. The record ended too soon.

McClellen must have sensed Orhan's pleasure. "How much piano music have you heard? I think you'd like Schubert. Have you heard his piano Impromptus?"

"I'd like to," Orhan said, and McClellan put a new record on. "I have a favorite in one of these. I'll signal when we reach it. In it Schubert takes a bold unorthodox step. He allows the piece to come to a violent close in the minor." Had he heard music before, Orhan wondered, which pressed toward the thing it yearned for with such clarity and power as this music of Schubert's? But McClellan—this research genetics professor—awed him by knowing things about music that he himself couldn't begin to know.

When the pianist moved to still another Impromptu, McClellan spoke again. "Listen to how the coda juxtaposes its two tonalities and attempts to reconcile them." Orhan had no idea what he was talking about, but he wasn't bothered. It was enough just to listen, to absorb the movement of the music.

The record finished and Orhan, not knowing how to say what he wanted to in English anyway, was relieved when McClellan turned to a new subject. "Anne tells me you two went to the football game yesterday. What do you think of American football?"

"I don't understand it. It looks just rough to me."

"He prefers soccer. He says they play some soccer in Turkey." Again, Anne was helping. Orhan decided to speak frankly.

"The players—they act like they are angry at each other—it is like what they want to do is beat each other up. I would never play! Soccer takes skill. American football? It does not seem it does."

"Its the strategy that's interesting, the judgment calls. The plays."

"You need running skill in soccer, but to stop, think about strategy? No. But I should not have an opinion…In Gaziantep we do not have much sport. Except if you count our children's holiday when we all go to a sports field and march around, wave flags." Having fallen out of his element again, Orhan longed to listen to more music.

Bonnie came into the living room, sat in a straight chair, and straightened her back. Then she did something which would have been impolite at home—crossed her legs. But this wasn't Aintab. Orhan enjoyed watching her plump leg bob about as it did. "We need to liven this group up," she said. "We've got four for bridge. Let's play."

"To make an international student learn Bridge!? Not fair," Anne protested. "He should have to learn that only when *he* says he's ready." Again Orhan was grateful for Anne's help. He would have a go at Bridge some time, but tonight the talk had been complicated, and he was weary. In the end, they played a game called Crazy Eights, and after six rounds of it he decided some card games were easy to learn and restful. Bonnie purred like an ancient cat every time she put a card on the pile, and Anne played with a kind of grace, even when she was losing. McClellan tolerated his boredom amiably.

"Nancy and I decided to look for an apartment in the University District this morning," Anne said. "I've had a job, now for three months. It's time I stopped mooching off my father."

Now McClellan frowned. Clearly, the idea of Anne's living anywhere besides her own home displeased him, but Orhan could not begin to guess at this University professor's reasons.

CHAPTER FIVE
ONCE THERE WAS A TURKISH COURTSHIP

The day that Nancy and Anne moved into a one-bedroom furnished apartment in the basement of a two story, stucco house Orhan spent long hours helping them load and unload Anne's father's station wagon. Thereafter it seemed fitting to invite him to dinner frequently. Besides several suitcases, they brought three straight chairs, dishes, kettles and other miscellaneous pieces needed to make the kitchen function in a sparsely "furnished" apartment. Their search having begun only after the opening of fall term, it was difficult to find an inexpensive apartment near enough to the University. It had taken three months. More persistent than Anne—Anne was busy evenings with Orhan going to concerts and introducing him to American phenomena like football games—Nancy had, in the end located this low-ceilinged three room apartment. It was not the place either woman had dreamed about, but it was the one they could afford.

When Anne sniffed at the dull flowered draperies in the living room they smelled of cigarette smoke, and she borrowed her mother's sewing machine—Bonnie never used it anyway—to make replacements. Her next project was to make herself a twin bed size quilt. While her mother was alive, she had observed her mother and other quilters fashioning geometric patterns and putting together fabric in intriguing color-combinations. Now she went to the library, found an

Amish quilting book, pored over it until she found a design and instructions she liked, and launched herself. She could at least try. When she had progressed to actually putting the quilt together, however, she took comfort from the Amish belief that no craftsman could match the perfection of God. This conviction was what made Amish women build a mistake right in to any quilt they made, and although Anne wasn't sure she thought even God was perfect, this Amish tolerance for mistakes reassured her. She made countless mistakes—her points did not always come together, her seam lines were not always straight—in this, her first quilt. When observing the squares she'd put together askew she shrugged and told herself, "Only God is perfect." She was, at least, inordinately fond of the blue, aqua and green she'd chosen as a color scheme. Nancy claimed these colors were "too cold for *me* to sleep under."

"*If* I make you one, friend, I'll make it chartreuse and hot pink," Anne told her. Cooking was the other domestic pleasure Anne began to enjoy. During her mother's long illness her father had hired a housekeeper. "We can't have your mother sensing her domestic order is collapsing," he'd claimed. Betsy was a big-hearted, saggy breasted woman who willingly doubled as a cook when she was hired to do light cleaning. To keep watch over his ailing wife, Anne's father was eager to have another presence in the house. This meant that when Anne was a student, she had been able to leave domestic chores to Betsy. Her mother died when Anne was in her senior year and still more pre-occupied by academics. Her father, by contrast, began to welcome domestic chores and became what Anne dubbed "officious" at planning and cooking. Since on the week-ends when they were at home together he had made a big production of their meals, Anne suspected he might still enjoy cooking and wondered why he had let Bonnie take over that part of the household tasks so completely.

For Nancy, who ate as little as she could and only to keep her energy intact, Anne didn't particularly enjoy cooking. But to read cook books, and glean ideas about what to cook when Orhan joined them, inspired her. Since his was a rooming house and all his meals had to be eaten out, Orhan informed Anne with a boyish coquetry that he would be pleased to join the two women for dinner any time he were invited. This began to happen whenever Anne planned ahead, began preparations the night before, and telephoned him.

For one of the dinners to which she invited Orhan, he requested pot roast. She agreed, but was nonetheless chagrined to think that she considered cooking it in dill pickle juice. Remembering this was Bonnie's recipe, she searched the newspapers until she found a recipe for pot roast cooked in beer. Secretly she was elated when Orhan claimed that this pot roast had an even better flavor than the only other one he had tasted. She knew, and he didn't seem to remember, that Bonnie had introduced him to pot roast.

At the end of the first evening they spent alone together at her father's house listening to music, Orhan told Anne that in Turkey sexual encounters before marriage were taboo. He followed that revelation with a gesture Anne remembered as gallant. He took her wrist, ran a light finger along the veins on the back of her hand, and kissed it. This reminded Anne of a conversation she had had with her mother about sex before marriage. Her mother had been an advocate of "saving yourself for Mr. Right." Since her death Anne's inclinations to respect those admonitions had strengthened. Orhan's delicate kiss reassured her. Another warning of her mother's had been to stay out of the situations that led to "being swept away." With that advice in mind Anne had arranged for Nancy to be present on most of the occasions when Orhan joined them for meals. Not that Anne had no clue of how passion could sweep her out of control. On another evening she longed to throw prudence to the winds when she and Orhan stood together in her father's living room while softly he caressed her lips with his. That evening, she recalled, she nearly melted with desire: to press her body against his, to have his hand explore her breast, anything which would be more than he had done.

The evening after Anne cooked the pot roast Orhan left their apartment late to go home to his boarding house. The late hour was in hopes his landlady would have gone to bed. Anne and Nancy had coached him on how to "handle" his landlady who was still finding small ways to force her attentions on him. Nancy, who faithfully helped with the dishes since she did so little of the cooking, jabbered incessantly all evening and now during the washing up turned thoughtful. While Anne scratched the meat marks from the edge of the cooking pan Nancy said, "You know, I think you may be on to something with this Orhan."

"You make him sound like some kind of commodity—'on to something'?"

"I mean...I mean he's Turkish. He's exotic...different. I remember when you first met him you said he didn't seem like a domineering male, and you thought he was good-looking. Now what do you think?"

"I still think he's good looking. And now I know him and he still doesn't seem like a domineering male. *And* as a person I like him a lot."

"Then what are you worried about?"

"Turkey." Anne tried, without succeeding, to keep her voice calm. "I have no idea if I could live in that culture. His family has a lot of money. Of course that's handy. He says his grandfather lives with them in their family apartment and there is an empty apartment in the building his parents built two years ago just waiting for the married Orhan. There's even an apartment rented out at the moment that he says they have reserved in their minds for his little sister who's still only sixteen and away at school in Istanbul. But could I live happily that close to his family? Could I live in a town so Turkish that I'd be cut off from all the Western customs I know? And... I'd lose my friends."

"But you wouldn't be marrying Turkey. You'd be marrying him."

"All right, I'd be marrying Orhan. A man who in the U.S. is a delightful boy. He's uncertain of all kinds of social graces and manages them. But I can't be sure what he'd be like in Turkey."

"Isn't that putting the cart before the horse? I certainly wouldn't marry him without going to bed with him. That's the first thing!"

"That's you, not me. I'm still bound by what my mother told me. I can't go to bed with any man before I marry him. I want to go to bed with Orhan.... Oh, I want to...bad! But when I get swept away, I hear my mother's voice...stay out of the situations where you'll want to go all the way. It's awful. I'm not a free woman."

"Your mother? You can't be that much of a prude!"

"I can't be, but I am. My hesitation may be wrapped up with my mother's death, but she's dead. I can't do anything about bringing her back to talk her out of the way she felt."

"He'll think you're frigid."

"He'll have to think it then. Still, somehow I think he's a creature of his culture and 'nice' girls in Turkey are married as virgins."

"You can't mean it!"

"He says unmarried men go to prostitutes. He says at holiday time the houses where prostitutes live have long lines outside them. Men aren't ashamed to be lined up like that, and prostitution is legal in Turkey."

"Remind me not to be a prostitute in Turkey. All the things those women must have to teach!"

"Wow, Nancy!"

"I'm up-front. Hal's good in bed. I'm learning a lot."

"But you're not the one who's thinking about marrying and going to Turkey." Anne threw the dish-rag into the dish-water. "Oh, I'm not either. Yes, he's talked about it casually, and… I've told him that no woman should make up her mind about Turkey without going there. I think he respects that. I'd marry him in a minute if he'd settle and live here, but he's committed to his father's factory. He's also determined that he's going to modernize and make it still better. The only Western thing he's committed to is classical music. I gather that's a pretty exotic thing to want to bring to Eastern Turkey."

"Your thrill, not mine, but…"

"But to live in a place where classical music is the only contact with any of my past scares me."

"You've begun to cook, to sew. Those things all translate to another culture. You could learn Turkish cooking." Nancy banged the cooking pot she was putting away with a wooden spoon.

"His mother's already a good cook and she's huge. I don't want to end up like that. Besides, domestic stuff is fun; I'm really beginning to like it, but I'm an intellectual. I like ideas better than anything else, and to be cut off from literature, theater, even if I had classical music on records is…well…it's scary…even if I manage to learn Turkish well."

"A new language would sure scare me! But you should take to that!"

"I can learn enough Turkish to get along, sure, but what I'll really want is to learn it well enough to talk about ideas. I'm not sure I'll be able to do that. Orhan says Turkish is regular but difficult. It turns the way we think all around."

"He does well with English. That's a good sign."

"He does, doesn't he."

"How like you. You have to know how to talk about ideas, don't you? I should marry a Turk. All I need is to know how to act in another culture."

"You're a free spirit! Life's some kind of experience collection for you."

"Right you are! Experience is what it's all about."

"And one of the experiences I don't want to have in my life is a failed marriage!"

"You've rationalized all this beyond reason. I thought you were flirting with Quakerism, and Quakers believe in making peace around the world, don't they? One way to make this world smaller is to increase its connections, isn't it?"

"I'm an idealist, but…but I'm human, too. I have to live with myself and the man I marry!"

"Let yourself go. Get swept off your feet. Take a risk." Nancy threw an arm out with a dish towel hanging on it like a white flag.

"Not yet…The closest I can come to marrying Orhan is to take time next summer, go to Turkey, and get some idea of what I might be marrying into."

"Will that work? Does he accept that kind of uncertainty?"

"I think so. He's pretty surprised himself at how fast things have moved." Anne slid the last cooking pot behind the makeshift curtain onto an open shelf below the sink. "It's late. We both have to work tomorrow."

Heading for bed, the two women brushed their teeth together at the chipped enamel sink in the tiny bathroom. But when they both lay in bed with the gooseneck lamp over Anne's bed switched out, neither woman shut her eyes. Anne lay stiff, the blankets pulled up under her chin. Moonlight shone through a clear window in the clouds, hit the rain-spotted window of their bedroom, and made Anne still more restless.

"The trouble with you," Nancy said, "Is that you still think you can control your fate...I love that about you...but..."

"Yes, and you make me think I'm too cautious, too afraid to take risks."

"Why don't you take spring break and go off on a trip with him—see how he holds up under stress."

"If I go off with him it won't be as some kind of test. Now you're the one who's too rational...too calculating."

"Talk to your Dad about him then."

"I wish I could. With Bonnie at home, I can never get him to myself."

"Go see him in his office, student to professor."

"Novel idea. I'll think about it."

Three days later Anne found herself in her father's University office, his dusty books staring down at her from the shelves behind his head.

"I've come here to talk to you. At home I can't talk because... because I just don't know Bonnie well enough to talk about anything personal when she's there."

"Clever of you to come here, then." Her father put his cupped hands together, so that his spread fingers touched at the ends.

"Oh, don't treat me like a student. I'm your daughter!"

"All right. My daughter...what is it?" He dropped his hands, and accented his question with raised eyebrows, the ones that extended without break across his entire forehead.

Anne began, felt the tears springing, and paused to quell them. "You know Orhan. What do you think? Should I marry him?" Why did she have such a need to blurt it all out?

"Should you marry him? I can't answer that. I'm asking you."

"Oh, don't try that non-directive stuff on me."

"I'm not able to be direct. I don't know Orhan like you do. I like him. I like talking to him, but I have no idea what he'd be like to live with."

"That's just it. I don't either. I met him and thought it was important in my job, in what Quakers tell me, to connect, to make the world smaller. It was all intellectual, rational. But now there's no way I can be rational about him. I think I love him."

"And you still don't know, because you can't, what he would be like to live with."

"And if I married him he'd take me way off to Turkey where I'd be completely isolated and I'd be married! No matter how much I think I love him, that scares me."

"That makes sense."

"So what do I do?"

"I have no idea. I have ideas about things to do to help you think about it, though."

"What?"

"You need to be with him on a day to day basis. You need a feel for what he's like in ordinary living."

"And how can that happen?"

"It's spring break soon. Bonnie doesn't like camping. You and I and Orhan could go to the Olympic peninsula—maybe Quinault—we could camp and hike. That'd separate the sheep from the goats of his temperament."

"You'd go with us, really? Because there's no way we could go without a chaperone according to what I get of Turkish custom."

"We'll take two tents—one for you and me—one for Orhan."

"When?"

McClellan pulled his calendar from under a pile of papers on his desk and they chose the days "See, I'm not a man who stews and thinks. Research begins with working on hunches."

"And for that, I think I like you better." Anne rose from her chair, left his office and began choosing the words with which she would invite Orhan to go with them, partake of an American phenomenon: a camping trip.

****

The hypnotic effect of the lashing windshield wipers made Orhan sleepy as he sat on the vinyl front seat of Mr. McClellan's station wagon.

It was an early Friday morning in April, and Anne's father had just invited him to call him by his first name. His doubts about accepting such an invitation made him even more sleepy. Too familiar. Informality with one's elders took gumption. He hadn't acculturated so far as to be comfortable calling this man Arthur. Alternatively, Anne's father would have to find it acceptable to hear a "Bey" after his first name.

Manifest on the windshield were the rain drops of the song he'd heard sung on the radio about April showers. What was it? April showers brought May flowers. This soggy month in the Pacific Northwest ought to yield some kind of reward. However, in this year, 1959, were they traveling in rural Turkey through heavy rain on an untraveled road like this one they'd be plowing through a solid sea of muck. U.S. roads—their smooth paving, order-producing signs, painted center lines—continually astounded Orhan.

"We won't insist you like camping, but in the Pacific Northwest we would be remiss if we didn't introduce it to you. It's part of our culture!" McClellan's voice broke Orhan's mood-lull.

"As you say, the word is 'introduce' Turks do not camp. We go into rural areas to hunt, maybe, but near Gaziantep there is no forest either to hike in, or camp in."

"What do they hunt?"

"I never went, but my father and a doctor friend of his hunt birds. The word in Turkish is *keklik*. I think in English it might be grouse."

"I don't hunt either. There are men in this country who hunt deer every year in season, but…"

"To speak truth, everyone thinks when I'm Turk I'm fierce, I'm 'real man', but I don't like guns. What I like is my mother's *keklik kebab* when they bring birds home. *Kebab* means meat in chunks on…a skewer, I think you say."

"I don't like guns either!" Relief… this Arthur Bey didn't like guns either.

"We like to *see* animals when we're camping," Anne added from the back seat.

Orhan gripped his thigh. "No animals this time, I hope. Are there bears?"

"There are bears on the Olympic peninsula, but they're rare. The important thing is not to surprise them. If you think one's near, talk in a loud voice. You want them to hear you, not see you, and go away. And they will, usually, unless they're protecting a cub. People scare them."

Orhan took in this advice, hoping he wouldn't need it. The smooth road continued and his reverie settled as it did so often on the differences he found in this culture. Odd that Americans so accustomed to traveling in automobiles should choose to put packs on their backs and walk into the forest... What was this camping all about? How could anyone enjoy pitching a tent and sleeping on the ground! Anne's family had lent him her mother's sleeping bag, but it was so light—down they said—he couldn't see how it was going to keep him warm. If there were bears, did he really want to sleep alone in a tent? Anne had assured him that bears seldom came into tents to maraud. But he'd feel safer being in a tent with other persons instead of by himself. Still, could he rein himself in if he were sleeping in the same tent with Anne? He'd have to have restraint in a way he wasn't sure he could manage. He chuckled under his breath thinking how he himself might turn into some kind of marauding wild animal. But with her father right there! Who wouldn't be frozen out?

Later, when the rain had stopped and he found himself walking on a needle-padded trail Orhan's doubts eased. Small, sharp rocks jutting from the trail bed made it necessary to keep his head down, watch where he stepped. But even with a heavy pack on his back, walking had never felt better. The trail climbed gradually beneath a canopy of huge evergreen trees—hemlock, fir and cedar, Anne named them. From Nancy, (who didn't seem the type to enjoy this kind of hiking) Anne had borrowed a backpack for him and now the pack, holding a small tent, sleeping bag, and packets of dried food, didn't feel as heavy as he had expected. A river bed ran beside the trail some twenty or thirty feet away and the sound of water rushing over rocks invigorated him. One of the first Western symphonic works he had come to know was Wagner's Forest Murmurs from Siegfried, and that music began to ring in his mind over the rush of the river rapids. Wagner could have got his musical ideas from a forest like this.

When they had reached a clearing, pitched their tents, and built a fire to cook their dinner, Anne began to cook. The picture of Anne squatting above a campfire stirring the beans and wieners in a large pot blackened by the flames was a sight he would not soon forget. This was no usual woman and he liked her for her sense of adventure. Village women in Turkey might squat, knees high as she was, while they were rolling out bread, but no educated Turkish woman would ever lower herself to such a position! Anne's flexibility...her versatility...all those good English adverbs that described her, put him in awe. For that matter, what educated Turkish woman would ever go off hiking with a loaded pack on her back like Anne had? Turkish educated women would consider themselves too feminine, maybe even too helpless to put a pack on their back. Our women might be frightened to take a trip like this. He admired Anne's willingness to take risks. Conventional Turkish men might well be threatened by a woman like Anne, but as this year continued, he was more and more intrigued with the daring in this woman.

After dinner, with their hands wrapped about coffee in tin cups—camp coffee didn't seem so thin and insubstantial as American coffee usually did—the three campers sat on large fallen logs around the campfire. It seemed a cozy behavior if nonetheless foreign.

"I told Orhan that the fire would keep the animals away. Am I right?" Anne asked, when the fire had burned to embers, and they continued to sit huddled about the coals.

"That's the legend." Her father seemed flip. "Never tested it, except that it's been daylight when I've seen the only elk and deer I've seen in these parts. And those animals are rare. Never have seen a bear."

"I'm disappointed. I'd hoped we'd see deer," Anne said.

"That's O.K. with me! We don't think the same way about animals. You never compare any human to any animal in Turkey! To call someone a donkey or dog is a insult."

"Geneticist that I am, I see animals as all part of the living family. You know the research on gorillas—they're amazing, intelligent animals!"

"That research hasn't touched Turkey yet. If it had, we'd ignore it. We want to go on thinking of animals as the stupid beings they are."

"Orhan!" Anne's disappointment sounded like an animal bleat.

"Sorry. I can overcome a lot of my culture, but I can't manage on that one!"

"Stick to your guns, then!" Arthur Bey said. "I can forgive a lot of odd things if people only own up to their own idiosyncrasies!"

They fell silent and when their coffee cups were empty—no longer keeping their hands warm—Anne suggested that they crawl into their tents. It had been a long Friday.

Orhan slept readily, but was awakened when outside the tent he heard the sounds of metal pans clunking together. Chaos. The cause? Cautiously, he pushed his head out of the sleeping bag to listen. Ann could be up early to start the fire. But it was still dark. She wouldn't do that, and if she did she wouldn't make so much noise. Some marauder was in their camp—an animal? Not tame? The taste of fright invaded his mouth. *AllahAllaha* It meant harm! If he called out, lying down as he was, whatever it was might attack. Pans continued to clatter, and he was sure he heard the heavy breathing of some animal. *AllahAllaha*, the sound of breathing was closer than the clatter of the pans had been! Leave his sleeping bag? Somehow... Open the tent flap enough to see? Carefully he crawled out of the warm bag. Cold air hit him in a blast. Still more cautiously, kneeling, he turned on all fours to the front of his tent, and peered out through the slit. He saw a dark form emerging from the tent next to his. "Get away!" Arthur Bey bellowed.

This man had the bravado to grab a club and shake it at the creature! At least Orhan sensed some kind of a stick in the rumpus. He couldn't tell for sure. Had he actually struck at the bear? Orhan peered fruitlessly into the black night until the beam of a flashlight fixed outward revealed the black hair of some creature not ten feet from their tents. Would it turn... rush Arthur? The dark form lumbered round and Orhan heard underbrush crackle under the creature's feet. It had moved away!

"A bear? I couldn't see." Anne's voice was shrill.

"A bear." Her father's voice was oddly formal.

"Will it stay away?" Orhan asked.

"Our food's all hanging in that tree. He smelled food, but he couldn't reach it. Found our pots and found nothing."

"Thank God you scared it."

"I hope so. Now let's get some sleep."

Reluctant, Orhan crawled back into his sleeping bag, cold. How could anyone sleep when a huge bear was near? Clearly Arthur Bey knew bears better than he did, but sleep? Impossible. Orhan found himself trembling, his whole body wracked and stiff. But slowly, in perhaps an hour, he was lulled by the warmth of the down bag about him. Still, he remained on guard listening. Only when there was light coming in the flap of the tent did the sound of the wind in the trees and the warmth of his sleeping bag sooth him into sleep.

The sound of rattling pots woke him again but this time a brighter light was making it possible to distinguish objects. And when he peered out the front flap he saw Anne squatting over the fire. The aroma of bacon frying lured him from his sleeping bag. Bacon was rarely available in Turkey, and when it was the only people who ate it usually were the non-Muslims who observed no restrictions on pork. But in the U.S. Orhan had discovered how much he liked bacon. Wafted on the open air its smell was still more appealing, and he only just suppressed a wave of desire to go to Anne, put his hand on the back of her neck, and caress her.

At breakfast, as the three hikers again cupped their hands around their metal coffee cups, the talk was about where to go from here. Their decision was made more crucial in Orhan's mind by last night's bear and the rain which began to fall. The alternatives were either to hike further on the mountain trail and make a new camp for Saturday night or hike back and find rooms somewhere. Anne's father claimed to know a lodge on the shores of a lake. Orhan hesitated to offer an opinion. Because the trip had been planned to show him a rain forest in Washington state, he felt obligated to go on if that is what his host decided. Neither Anne nor Arthur asked him what he wanted to do. If they had, he would have been ashamed to let them know anything about his fear last night. The advantage of bedding down alone in a tent was that no one had seen how badly he had slept.

"There's a good camp ground in another half day's hike—Enchanted Valley. The last time I was there it rained and there was an abandoned ranger station we sheltered in."

Orhan noted his own lack of enthusiasm for this alternative.

Anne looked up at the sky. "But it looks like more rain."

"Let's go on, then," Anne's father said, rising. He hadn't heard her. "You clear up the breakfast stuff. Orhan and I will get the tents."

The decision was made. Slowly, Orhan pulled out the pegs of his tent. He and ArthurBey folded each of their tents.

"They call these pup tents," Arthur Bey said, as he pushed his into his back pack. "Never have been able to figure if it's because the tent itself is so small, or if it's because they're only big enough for a small dog!"

"Both ways fit," Orhan hoped he sounded casual. He knew he wasn't.

Their camp broken, their campfire shoveled under, the three hikers started on the trail which wound upward only gradually.

Orhan surprised himself. He felt peaceful walking until a light rain began to fall. At first he felt only a few drops on his face, then slowly there was more and more rain until finally, when Arthur Bey turned his head to look back Orhan saw that water was dripping from the professor's parka hood into his eyebrows and eyes. Why wasn't he miserable?

Orhan slowed to look back at Anne. Water ran across her chin in spite of the sou'wester style yellow hat she wore. Grey moss hung from almost every tree limb. The trees looked to him like old men with scrawny beards. He had had his view of the rain forest. He was ready to turn around.

Anne looked up. Orhan's expression must have told on him. "We've had it, Daddy. This is dumb."

"It is dumb, isn't it," Arthur Bey said. "Let's go back to the car, drive to Quinault lake, and see if we can locate dry rooms to sleep in."

Without a word, Anne turned and the men followed her. They were nearly a day's hike out, and Orhan settled in for a wet slog. The path had never been a steep upward climb, but it would have seemed easier in its descent had it not been for the rain-water which collected and ran downward over the rocky trail. Orhan had pulled the hood of his parka over his head and a small visor protruding over his eyes further limited his view. In places the sharp rocks jutting from the trail meant he trod carefully looking only downward. To focus on something pleasanter than a rocky trail he looked to its sides strewn with countless varieties of moss. Feathery tendrils holding the rain, spike shaped foliage with yellow and gray green shades carpeting the forest floor on either side of the path, all of this intrigued him. This is what could happen when nature was lavish with water. Where he came from, nature was niggardly with water. Niggardly or lavish, either condition made a region seem awry, but he couldn't choose which was more difficult. This forest had its own kind of beauty, but so did the lichen-flecked rocks and sun-scorched bare hills around Aintab.

They reached the lodge, and although it was off-season, they found there was only one room available. "You men can have the room, and I'll put the seat down in the station-wagon, and spread my sleeping bag," Anne proposed.

Orhan was again astounded by the risks Anne was willing to take. No fears? None about sleeping alone for a night in a car? She didn't appear to think about either her safety or her comfort. No educated Turkish woman would be allowed to sleep alone—much less want to sleep in the cramped quarters of a car. Orhan sensed Anne might be unusual in this willingness among American women as well. His hunch didn't stop him from admiring her.

The lodge living room rose to a high pointed ceiling, and in its center was a broad stone fireplace large enough to hold five-foot long logs burning in it. After dinner in the lodge's restaurant, the three of them sat in front of the fireplace watching the flames. Orhan had never seen indoor, open fires like this. In Turkey there was no wood for them. This one was not only a new experience, but a good one to sit in the comfort of a pillowed wicker chair and watch this fire leap and lower. But the dry heat and the let-down from the trail walk meant that very soon each of the three of them admitted to being weary. When they retreated to the room they had rented Anne used the sink to brush her teeth. Orhan watched her ritual, intrigued with the way she brushed in circles and finished with three knocks of the brush on the side of the sink. To watch her go off with her nightgown and her sleeping bag bunched together and carried in front of her chest, to observe her calm at settling into the back of the ford station-wagon made him uneasy. But he was not ready to offer to take her place.

"Be sure to lock yourself in," her father told her, and again Orhan was surprised at the casualness with which he dismissed his daughter.

When Orhan found himself stretched in a twin bed parallel to Arthur Bey, the dark stimulated him. Had he the courage?

"This is not a conventional Turkish way to do this," he began. "I didn't expect I would do it, but..."

"You haven't got the idea we're conventional Americans, have you?" Arthur Bey's voice sounded into the dark.

"I don't know yet what is a conventional American. Out of my country I find myself doing many things I would never do in Turkey. This is one of them.... I want to ask you for your daughter. Americans talk a lot about love. I think maybe this is love. In Turkey I would get my parents to do what I am doing. They're not here. I do not know how they would feel about me wanting a foreign bride, but..."

Arthur Bey's voice came gently out of the dark. "In the U.S., too, your question is unconventional...I can't answer for my daughter. You'll have to let her answer for herself. I admit, if she talks to me I'll be on her with all kinds of cautions—not about you, but about your culture. Still, that's no reason not to ask her. Go ahead, do it...and now, as we say in English, we'd better sleep on it. See if you really want to marry this woman. She's a great woman. I know because she's my daughter, but you haven't seen her in Turkey...." and with that this man's voice trailed off.

The next morning it was still raining. They took a short walk on trails near the lodge, walked out to stare at the lake with its pock marks of rain, and at check-out time headed in the dry car for home.

Anne borrowed the station wagon to take Orhan home. On the way to his house, still through the rain, Orhan wondered if his hesitation was from the fact that he was not in the driver's seat, or that the windshield wipers were again working their hypnotic effect. He was more hesitant to ask Anne herself if she would marry him than he had been to ask her father. "What do you think? Shall we get married?" He started abruptly and neither his voice, nor the question came out as he might have liked. Anne turned to look at him. It was as if he had asked her to drive on the wrong side of the road. Her father must not have told her he had spoken to him.

If he'd planned it, he could have set it up for a more romantic situation. But he hadn't! Anne continued to drive straight ahead, said nothing for a long, dreadful silence.

"I...I can't say. Orhan. I can't. I think you know I've been thinking about it. I...I'm not outright rejecting the idea...but... you've caught me off my guard. I can't say."

His bones went weak. They had reached the street in front of his rooming house. As he got out of the car he nearly stumbled over the curb. It was as if she had punched him in the stomach. He didn't know what he had expected, but neither did he know what to do or say. He didn't bid her goodnight, or goodbye. Feeling panic, he nearly ran to climb the cement stairs to the porch, unlocked the door, and was relieved his landlady was nowhere about. Stealthily, he climbed to his room, put a record on, and lay down on his bed to listen. The stereo tones of Wagner's Forest Murmurs filled the room. His proposal, which in his imagination had seemed good and right, rang phony now.

The record was too short. It finished and he was nowhere near feeling normal.

CHAPTER SIX
Once There Was What Didn't Work

The headlights of oncoming cars glared at Anne as she drove back to her father's house. Having handled Orhan's proposal badly, she wanted to talk to her father. At home, she found him in the basement cleaning the camping gear making it ready to be stored away.

"Come help me spread the tents out," he said, when she called to him from the top of the basement stairs, and descending downward she felt strangely soothed beneath the huge gray insulated heating ducts running out like tree branches from the monstrous oil-burning furnace back of the stairway. Smelling the basement's musty odor, she remembered how as a child on rainy winter days she used to hide in the cellar's dark crannies alone, in cozy retreat.

She took the edge of the tent canvas he thrust at her with two hands. "Daddy...He's asked me to marry him." Her voice didn't sound normal as she heard it.

"I know. He asked me first."

"What did you tell him?"

"I told him he'd have to ask you."

"Why didn't you tell me? I would have had a better answer ready."

"I wasn't alone with you. Remember?" The sight of her father's large frame kneeling on the basement's cement floor in the jump suit he used for hiking trips wasn't normal either.

"Maybe I couldn't have had a better answer. I don't know. I just don't know. Help me!"

"Do you love him?"

"Yes. I love him," She spoke without hesitation, then considered. "The way I love him isn't a calculated thing. I really care about him."

"What *was* your answer then?"

"I bumbled. Marrying him *has got to be* a calculated thing. He's wedded to his country, and I don't know if I can live there."

"Does he love you?"

"I think he does. He's never said so, but against all the rituals of his culture would he ask me to marry him if he didn't? What's more we respect each other. The more I see of the way Orhan does things the more I admire him."

Arthur got up and began to spread the second tent out on the dry basement floor in front of the furnace. "I saw this week-end. I think he admires your sense of adventure. How does it feel when you're with him?"

"Oh God, I want him, Daddy.... I want him."

"Whoa! That's only part of what I'm asking. I mean do you talk? Do you have a lot to talk about?

"What is this? Some kind of examination? It's too calculated! I love the guy. Why can't I marry him? Did you calculate when you married Bonnie?" She hadn't intended that question.

Her father dodged it. "Here, can you clean the black off this?" He thrust the pot in which she'd cooked the beans and wieners at her.

Anne grabbed an old rag, took the pot to the laundry tub, and began scouring the camp-fire soot from its sides and bottom. The pause seemed good. Where was this conversation going? Where did she want it to go?

Arthur cleaned the tent pegs with another old rag before he spoke again. "I guess what I mean is, do you like being with him? Do you enjoy the things you do together? You're going to have to really like him if you go off to Turkey with him. He'll be all you've got until you learn the language and make friends of your own."

"This is all too rational!" She slammed the pot down into the laundry tub. "I don't want to be so reasoned about someone I love."

"You'd better be. New love's exciting! But its not going to carry you through many years in Turkey. It's good you respect him. I would too. He held up well this week-end. He dealt with a lot of new stuff and a lot of discomfort. Respect for him's going to last a lot longer than this crazy blush of love—it'll feed your love. But it's his culture you have to think about."

"How can I think about his culture when I haven't even been there?" Anne heard herself whining and didn't like it.

"Pretty tough, isn't it."

"It's impossible."

"Well, then maybe you'd better arrange to go there."

Anne retained that idea through the ride while her father drove her to her apartment. Riding beside him, she longed to talk about Bonnie. She wanted to tell her father how good it had been with him this weekend on the hike. Since hiking was not Bonnie's thing, she had had her father and Orhan all to herself. It felt right to leave and go back to her own apartment when Bonnie was there in her father's house. She'd never be able to tell him she didn't like Bonnie, but she didn't. She didn't like the way Bonnie tried so hard. It had to be phony. Made it difficult to be with her. Made her miss her mother all the more. The ride home continued in silence.

"Do…do! Go to Turkey. I'll help you pay for it if you need help," her father said, as she got out of the car. "Arrange to take three months this summer and go to Turkey." The following day she and Orhan met for coffee. Their coffee dates had become a ritual.

"I didn't sleep well last night. Did you?" he asked.

"I'd guess neither of us slept well. You had talked to my father. I talked to him."

"What did he say? We Turks expect to hear what parents say in these things."

"He said I should go to Turkey, see what it's like before I marry you."

"You've said that before. What's so important about going to Turkey? We'll go there when we're married."

"But I have no idea about the country I'm marrying! Turn it around.

How would you have felt coming to the U.S. if you knew you were coming for your whole life."

"Lots of Turks do. I need to be in Turkey for my father's factory, but there are plenty of things that make the U.S. look good to us Turks. Life's easier here, in lots of ways."

"But..."

"Besides... You would not be marrying my country. You are marrying me!"

"But if life's easier here, wouldn't it be more difficult for me in Turkey? And you knew English well already. I'll have to learn Turkish...I won't have any friends...You've said yourself ordinary things like cooking and, and...just living will be harder."

"But you are smart. I know that. You will learn Turkish fast. When you miss your friends, you will make new ones. I have many friends. They will like you."

Anne looked at the rigid sides of the booth she and Orhan sat in and felt boxed in. He didn't understand. She didn't know herself why she wasn't willing to just take the risk, jump into marriage, go to Turkey. "I do want to marry you! I love you. I want to be with you for a lifetime. I'm just not sure I want to leave the country I grew up in for a lifetime."

Orhan looked pained. Was it too forward to have told him she loved him?

"In my country we say love comes after marriage, but...but I love *you*. I love you already, so why can we not marry?"

Across a formica top table from her, here in this most unromantic of settings this handsome man had just told her he loved her. Why couldn't she say yes, just say it, plunge?

"Oh, Orhan...marriage isn't supposed to be something you're so rational about. It just...isn't. But please believe me. I don't know why I just can't say yes and marry you. But what I *think* I say yes to is going back with you to Gaziantep this summer. I want to meet your family. I'll see Aintab. I'll see where we would live. It'll make me sure."

"My little sister, Nermin, speaks good English. She's at school in Istanbul...in English. She will be right in the same family, there will be someone who speaks English."

It wasn't irrelevant, but still, it wasn't entirely relevant to the question at hand to think about having her husband's little sister for her only friend. "Let's take a week, think about it. You decide if you're willing to wait, take me to Turkey while I decide. I'll think about whether it's likely that I can say yes after I've been to Turkey."

Manipulation! She was engineering the making of a major decision. Willy nilly, she was mixed up! American or Turkish, it felt odd. It wasn't a woman's place to be so shrewd.

The following Sunday someone had brought a bunch of dark purple lilacs and placed them on a small table near the door to the Quaker's Meeting room. Anne thought she caught their odor as she settled into her noisy chair. The clattering chairs were still out of place in the meeting's silence.

What were Turkey's spring odors? Orhan had been so proud that he lived in the fertile crescent, near the Tigris-Euphrates rivers, in the very cradle of civilization. That area surely had some harbinger of spring to count on.

Anne closed her eyes to shut out the distraction of the toddler on his mother's lap across from her. He was playing with a lock of his mother's hair. Children. She wanted children. What would it be like to raise a child outside the U.S.? Impossible to answer that question, but it would be vital not to have children until she knew. Maybe she'd decide not to have children. Would Orhan understand that? Oh center down, she told herself. Its not a time for questions…it's a time to still the mind, listen.

When her mind was quiet, the image of the sea in a chasm from the Marianne Moore poem came to her as it had so many times when she tried in these meetings to center herself. She saw the sea rising and falling in a rock chasm and as a contrast she saw the sea washing untrammeled up a sandy beach. The waves washed over the beach and broke without restraints, with one flashed moment of translucence. But when the sea rose and fell within a rock chasm, the water's very rock walls, its limitations, made the water's turbulence more powerful. More beautiful? Perhaps not, but surely more exciting. And what relevance had these sea images to the question of whether to go to

Turkey, whether to marry Orhan? She didn't know...except that marrying Orhan had its turbulent side. It was for her to decide if his limitations were powerful enough to crush her, or only powerful enough to make him more exciting. There she was! Back to her quandary. Through the winter Orhan had often entered her mind as she attended these meetings and sat in silence, but her thoughts had most often centered on exotic things about him that expanded her world. This now seemed more urgent. It involved a huge commitment from her...to be willing to expand her world, to endure whatever came, not for this mere school year, but a lifetime.

Another line came to her from the poem "A Habit of Perfection" by Hopkins, as it often did in these silent Meetings for Worship: "Elected silence sing to me." However, just as she was settling into the silence she had elected, a man of some years rose to speak. Quakers had been taking risks, he said, since the beginning of their history and in today's world they should not be afraid to be "holy fools," as he termed it. The gentleman sat back down and Anne tried to return to a blank mind in the silence. But when her mind would not be still, she wondered what being a holy fool had to do with her. It was foolish but not holy to marry Orhan without having been to his country. And was it perhaps taking a risk to go to Turkey experimentally?...permanently?... The word permanent tripped her. It frightened. There was the possibility that she might determine she could live in Turkey and find she couldn't live with Orhan... Then it came to her. It was essential that when Orhan went home he accept her going with him. That was what she had to do. Oh yes...yes. She was a holy fool...in love...rash.

Then another woman got up to speak who quoted John Woolman, the Quaker who in the early 19th century had so strongly opposed slavery. This time the ministry was about love. Was it relevant? What she said was: "Love is not soft like water, it is hard like rock, on which the waves of hatred beat in vain." What was the paradox? There wasn't time to figure it out before the meeting ended.

Walking back to her apartment she remembered the chat she had had with the International Student Adviser this last week. She had gone to explore with him whether it would be possible to keep her job if she took a leave of absence for three months beginning next month in June. When she took the job he had cautioned her against personal relationships with any of the international students. His advice this week had had a tinge of "I told you so," in it. It was an "essential component" of her decision now, he claimed, to go to Turkey and see what the experience of living there might be like. What was important about their talk was that he'd promised to hold her job for her through the summer. There was assurance in the knowledge that she could come back to her job, begin again, if she decided that Orhan and his country was not for her. "This year is rather like you've been in training," he said. "You'll be more useful next year."

Calculated? Anne thought. Everyone's attitude was calculated.

That evening Nancy and she had invited Orhan to dinner. Nancy, her affair with the exciting business man having petered out, was at home many weekend nights of late and had seemed to welcome Orhan's invitations to join him and Anne at films, and concerts.

"Don't you know, two's a couple, three's a crowd," Nancy had asked him the first time he invited her.

"Not in my country!" he told her. "Turks can't make mischief in a crowd," he added.

Now Orhan stood arms folded, leaning against the kitchen counter watching as Anne wielded the hand electric mixer to mash potatoes to go with the chicken she'd fried. "How do Turks mash potatoes?" Anne asked.

"We don't have mashed potatoes much. A pity. I like them. We have rice or bulgur pilav."

"But could I make them without an electric mixer?" Anne kept her tone light.

"You better not come to Turkey, then," Orhan quipped, and Anne observed that the question about her coming to Turkey did not have to be dead serious. A good thing!

At dinner Anne said: "I think potatoes might be good, even if they weren't perfectly mashed." The question looming over her, she thought, made her say inane things.

"What's all this about going to Turkey?" Nancy asked.

"Anne is thinking about coming back to Turkey with me when I go, but I haven't invited her yet," Orhan spoke playfully. Another good sign.

"Hey, don't leave me behind! I want to go!" Nancy seemed almost serious.

"Three's a crowd," Anne said, "although I guess it isn't in Turkey. But I'll promise to write you about it. I'm afraid you'd be too much like a chaperone."

"That's what you need, a chaperone," Nancy said playfully.

"I'll thank you not to suggest what I don't agree to! Just expect copious letters."

"Actually, if two young women came with me, just to see what Turkey's like, my parents would be less suspicious. They'd think two women were just coming to see what Turkey was like."

"They wouldn't suspect us of coming to see what *you* were like?" Nancy joked.

"Turks don't think like that."

Nancy withdrew to the bedroom after dinner, leaving Orhan and Anne alone. "Let's do the dishes." Anne suggested, opening the dishtowel drawer.

"I hope you know that no other Turkish male would wipe dishes for a woman," he said, as he took a towel from the drawer.

"I know... I do," Anne said. "What I don't know is whether you would wipe dishes for me in Turkey!"

"I wouldn't have to. We'd have servants to do dishes for us."

"And what does that mean? Would I ever get to do my own cooking, cleaning? I like to cook!"

"You can't tell me you like cleaning. I'm glad you wouldn't have to mop floors in my country."

"I think I'm glad of that, too."

"And I've told you. My mother cooks. She just has someone to help her... But she supervises all cooking, everything about the house."

"But she doesn't do anything outside the house."

"No. She doesn't want to."

"And I do. Oh, Orhan that bothers me." Anne heard the pleading in her own voice. "Sure, I'm a nest builder. But I'm an American woman and these days American women want more than to build and line their nests. We're birds! We want to fly. I just have to go and see if I'll be able to fly in Turkey. Please understand. I have to see."

"I see. I think I see. We'll go. We'll see," he said.

As Orhan left that evening Anne stood by the door to see him out, and in a gesture that spoke to her of reverence he took her fingers lightly, lifted her hand to his lips and kissed it. Then still holding her fingers, he touched the back of her hand to his forehead.

His reverence convinced her. She could marry him.

CHAPTER SEVEN
ONCE THERE WAS A BRIDE WHO WASN'T
JUNE, 1960

At the first crossroads in Gaziantep the taxi driver turned to ask Orhan for directions. After indicating in Turkish where the driver should go, Orhan explained to Anne in English that the road going the other way would have taken them past a hollow where peasants live in caves in the rock. "The road going that way is bumpy cobblestone. But on our side where the new apartments are—where educated people live—there is smooth road—asphalt."

It was dark and late. Nothing moved on the tarmac. Orhan peered out at the shadowy looming apartment buildings on either side of the wide, paved road, and instructed the driver to stop outside a three story rough cement-block building. He jumped out, opened the wrought iron gate of the low garden wall, and ran up to the door. By reaching through the door's ornamental iron gate, he could bang on the frosted glass behind it. "Ali," he shouted. "I think that's his name. Our *kapici*—that means doorman—was new when I left. I think his name was Ali." He spoke to Anne who had come up behind him. It was important to keep her a participant in his homecoming. Since he had so upset her with the idea that his parents would think they were married, he was still more eager to involve her in their arrival. He hadn't expected her to react as she had.

"Did you let your parents know our plane was canceled?"

"No need. In Turkey we expect travelers when we see them—*AllahAllaha!* I am at my own house and I cannot wake anyone." He hit the door again, this time with his palm.

Now, a light came on behind the glass of the door, and the heavy iron-trimmed door swung open. Behind, with the light shining on him as he unlocked the base of the door was a young man in striped pajamas. He brushed a dark brown forelock beneath the visor of his baggy cap and extended his calloused hand to Orhan. *"Eyvah! Orhan Bey."* Then he offered the traditional Turkish welcome, *"Hosh geldiniz!"*

"Have they all gone to bed?" Orhan asked in Turkish.

"We expected you earlier" the doorman said. Orhan began to explain how their plane had been canceled, and noticed Ali observing Anne behind him. "She is your new wife?"

Orhan was startled. This doorman was calling Anne his "new wife." According to his station, Ali neither looked at Anne nor took the hand she offered him as he spoke *"Hosh geldiniz, Hanim Efendi."*

"He calls you by the most respected title we give to women: *Hanim Efendi.* Come, we will find my parents." To distract himself—although he rather liked this dangerous idea that he had a new wife—Orhan bound up the first flight of polished marble stairs to the landing outside his parents apartment. Left behind, Ali and Anne plodded upward each carrying bags. Having reached the landing, Ali lifted his chin and pointed upward "Your parents have your apartment ready above on the top floor," he said.

"You think I would go there directly, not wake my family!" Orhan moved to the door and rapped on its frosted glass. *"Annem, babam!"*

Having risen when he heard the noise below, a pajama clad man opened the door, and gripping Orhan's upper arm, he kissed him on both cheeks. "My son. You've come. Let me get your mother!" Wiping his bushy brow, his father departed before he noticed Anne.

"He looks so much like you, I'd know he was your father if I saw him in Iceland. That wavy hair—it must have been dark like yours once."

"Something has made him more gray!" Orhan muttered.

"Do all Turkish men wear—" Anne caught herself before she said "pajamas without bathrobes?" Was she not too new to ask such a question?

"My son, my son!" A large woman, still tying a neat gray dressing gown about her ample middle lumbered into the hallway and embraced Orhan. "I could not believe this day was coming." She reached a puffy hand into her pocket, withdrew a white handkerchief and wiped away the tears washing her cheeks.

"*Annem*, this is my wife." Orhan did not want Anne ignored. He wished, however, that the two women might have met somewhere other than in this small entryway where his mother's perspiration odors were aggravated by excitement. "*An-ne*." He emphasized the break in pronouncing his guest's name. "How do you like that? Her name can mean mother in Turkish." He turned to Anne. "My mother, Selma Hanim, my father Abdullah Bey." His introductions might sound formal, but initially they had to be that way.

Anne appeared frightened, as if she didn't know what to do. He should have told her—showed her—how to kiss his mother on both cheeks. She muttered "How do you do," in English and of course his mother didn't understand.

His mother also seemed uncertain, but she lunged forward and kissed Anne on both cheeks. His father shook Anne's hand with one of his hands and with the other squeezed her arm as if he meant more than a simple welcome.

Selma stepped back to look at Anne and spoke to her son in Turkish. "She's too thin. We'll get her fattened up!"

"She's the way they like them in the U.S.," he said.

"Her blond hair and blue eyes will be choice in Turkey," his father added.

Orhan comforted himself that Anne could not have understood what either of his parents had to say. Still there had been too much talk that Anne did not understand. He had drilled her on what to say when she met other Turks, but he couldn't expect her to remember that in the stress of this new situation? "Where's Nermin? I want Anne to meet someone who speaks English. Then we'll go to bed."

"Go get her, Abdullah," Selma ordered, "We won't wake my father. He needs his sleep." As she spoke she turned her head to Anne, who answered with a strained look before she and Orhan followed Selma as she moved slowly into the sitting room and lowered herself cautiously onto the *sedir*. Orhan leaned against the heavy dining table and Anne perched tentatively on the straight chair Selma indicated she should occupy.

"Sorry to wake you in the middle of the night, but our plane—" Orhan paused as the lights flickered and dimmed. "*Eyvah!* The current! Bad light at a time like this!"

"Ali," Selma called and the doorman appeared from the hallway. "Get a lantern. The current's going off." She turned to her son. "Lately it's off a great deal."

Ali went for the lamp and the other three persons sat awkwardly silent in the dim light. Then a plump teenager wearing a red silk dressing gown and high heeled slippers, her long black hair shining in the dull light, ran into the sitting room and flung herself into Orhan's arms. "*Aghabey,* I thought you'd never get back!" Then she pulled away and looked around. "Where's your wife? This must be Anne!" Rushing across to her, the seventeen year old took Anne's two hands and kissed her eagerly on both cheeks. Then with an affected accent, she spoke in English. "My be…e…eg brother has good taste—long blond hair, blue eyes."

"See," Orhan stepped away from the table. "Nermin's English is good! You'll have someone to speak with."

Then because his father must have unintentionally roused Omer Asim Bey, Orhan's grandfather shuffled into the room followed by Abdullah. Their coming made it unnecessary for Anne to answer. The old man kissed Orhan on both cheeks before he turned to Anne who was observing his mismatched pajamas—the stripes of the pants were wide and green and the shirt was of a different red stripe—when the room went dark. Suddenly each person became no more than felt presences. Abdullah must have moved to the window. "It's a general failure. There's no light anywhere."

"Ali, light the lamp." Selma ordered.

"Fate isn't fair." The old man's Turkish words rang out in the darkness. His deafness had made him miscalculate the tone needed. "I catch a glimpse of a beautiful young lady and the lights go out."

"Yes, Dede," grateful his grandfather had called Anne beautiful, even if she hadn't understood his words, Orhan used the affectionate term for grandfather. "I want you to meet An-ne, but we will wait for the lamp." Ali struck a match. Abdullah reached over to hold the chimney of the lamp for him, and a dull light filled the center of the room again.

"We will arrange a brighter welcome tomorrow." Omer Asim Bey's loud tones made him sound irate. Uncertain that this new wife had understood, the old man fumbled for and shook Anne's hand.

His grandfather was trying hard to make Anne feel welcome, and Orhan was grateful. "She will understand Turkish better later," he explained.

"Would you like tea?" Selma asked, indicating by her tone that her son should decline.

"We want nothing," he obliged.

Selma pushed her heavy frame upward. "Ali will take us to our rooms with the lamp. Afterward he will take you and your wife upstairs to your apartment and leave the lamp with you. We're happy you are home. Your bed's ready, and I'm sure you'll sleep well."

Her words sent a chill into Orhan. Anne had said she wasn't ready to be his bride. He also was not ready. His wedding night!? This! He had not thought so far ahead. Following a long tiring trip. Two tired people! They should not try to consummate anything! Worse still, a marriage that hadn't happened. Dazed, he followed Ali up the final flight of stairs and Anne followed him.

When Ali unlocked the door, the odor of naphthalene enveloped them, suggesting the apartment had been shut up for a long while, but Orhan was glad for the distraction of an odor. He found himself entering an apartment with a woman to whom his family believed he was married. But he wasn't. In the dim light he saw his parents had made a great effort. The sitting room was furnished with furniture he'd never seen before. In fact, too much furniture.

"Look." Orhan struggled for the English words for what he had to do. "I'm sorry…about the odor…I'll show you the bedroom and the bathroom. Then I'll take a blanket and sleep in the living room. In the morning we'll tell my parents we're not married. I didn't think. It won't work to be married…I'm sorry."

"I haven't a clue how you'll get us out of this mess. But I'm grateful you want to try." Anne's muddled words scarcely reached him through the dull lamp-light.

****

Orhan slept badly, rose early, and decided it was best to go down to breakfast and arrive well before Anne. If he was lucky he could maneuver having two breakfasts—one with his family and one with Anne.

Dede was already sitting cross-legged on the floor in the dining room smoking his water pipe when Orhan came into the down stairs sitting room.

"*Eyvah,* Dede!" Don't you know that smoking is bad for your health?" Orhan spoke with what he intended to be affectionate gusto.

"Of course I know. I've lived a long, useful life. Why should I be afraid of dying? When—like last night—I get little sleep, smoking gives me energy."

"You know better than I. Who am I to tell an old man anything! I learned a lot about the U.S. and the textile business while I was away, but maybe I got confused when it came to life."

"Too early in the morning for anything so serious!" Dede took a long draw on his pipe.

"It may be too early, but I'm glad I found you alone…to try my problem out." Orhan sat on the *sedir* and massaged his brow with one hand. In Dede's position, a Sufi mystic removed from every-day affairs, even with all the knocks he'd taken in his life, the chances that

Dede would hear his quandary, take it calmly, were better than…what? His mind stalled. He didn't know what kind of comparison to make. Dive in, deal with whatever comes, he told himself. "You see, Anne and I aren't married!" He paused. Dede continued to sit cross-legged in his miss-matched pajamas. "I want her to marry me, but she won't until she sees what Turkey's like."

"Smart woman! Essential you have her, eh?"

"In the U.S. I was sure I wanted her. But…"

"Makes sense. You long to be drunk with the love of a woman, do you? Me, I'm old. Have to save my energy to be drunk with the love of God."

"What does longing to be drunk have to do with it?"

"Don't know. Just thought about the difference in our ages."

"But…I'm asking you what to do. The family thinks I'm married. But when I told Anne that last night, she would have turned around and gone home if I'd let her. I'm stuck. I didn't sleep with her last night. At least I didn't do that! I wanted to but I didn't. So…what do I do? What?"

"What should you do? I don't know any better than you. What can you do? If Anne wants it, you could go out now secretly and marry her. If she doesn't maybe you have to tell your parents you're not married, see what they do. If they'd known last night you weren't married, they surely would have sent her to a hotel."

"I know. I remembered that and that's why I think I told them I was married. It seems inhospitable to send a woman who has hosted me so many times in her home to a hotel. Especially when she comes home with me. *AllahAllaha*! I want to marry her. I want her to decide she can not only live with me, but live in Turkey! But…"

"Then, you'd better tell your parents. They have to know. You can't live that kind of falsehood. Don't expect them to take it easily, but you'll have to tell them."

Then, as if this wife of the *kapici* somehow knew not to disturb Orhan until he made such a decision, the doorbell rang. Orhan went to the door and found the maid Hatije. She wore flowered baggy pants and a plain gray headscarf, and carried in her hand some six flat unwrapped *pida* breads, which she had just purchased for breakfast. She made a small fuss, taking his hand, kissing it and putting it to her forehead to welcome this son of the house home before she moved past him into the tiny kitchen to begin to lay out the breakfast.

Next, Selma and Abdullah came into the dining room, and Selma, without saying anything, disappeared to supervise the preparation of breakfast.

"You won't want to come to the factory today, no doubt," Abdullah said to Orhan. "But—" he paused, remembering he should let his son set his own schedule. "What do you want?"

"Give me just today to settle Anne in. Then tomorrow I ought to be ready. I've got all kinds of ideas and—"

"Only a day? Only a day it will take you to settle back into Gaziantep life? A new wife and a new apartment?!"

"Well, you see," Orhan paused. "You see…we're not married."

"*AllahAllaha!*… And you traveled alone with her all this way!"

"I was a gentleman you'd be proud of."

"You think our friends in this town will believe that!"

"Turks may not believe it, but I *know* it. Even last night, I slept on the living room rug upstairs."

"*Eyvah!*" Abdullah indicated the kitchen with his head. "You're going to have to tell your mother."

"I am. And what I most hope is that she will not turn on Anne. I want her to blame me."

"How can you hope for that?" Abdullah's voice fell. "Anne's a stranger. You're her son." As if Abdullah had called Selma, she entered the sitting room carrying a tray. Hatije came behind with the *samovar* for tea.

"It's been a long time since you had white cheese and olives for breakfast, eh?" his mother said.

"You're right, mother, and I missed them a lot. Americans have drab breakfasts—packaged cereal—dry stuff, monotonous."

While the four family members pulled out chairs to seat themselves, Orhan tried to compose himself. He needed a calm demeanor when he spoke to his mother. He had to make her believe he considered the fact that he was not married of no consequence. He knew it would matter to her a good deal, but he had to try to act as if it should make little difference.

Dede and Abdullah said nothing, stunned by the import of what Orhan had told them. It was as if their curiosity consumed their power of speech. How would Orhan reveal his news to his mother?

"Where is your wife?" Selma said in an accusing tone.

"I think she is probably still sleeping." Orhan took a swallow of tea.

Selma thrust a hot *pida* bread at him. "Here, its been a while since you've had hot bread for breakfast. Was she asleep when you left the bed?"

"I don't know. I didn't sleep with her!" Orhan carefully placed white cheese on the bread, and stuffed the whole in his mouth.

"She's your wife and you didn't sleep with her!?"

Orhan paused to swallow. "She isn't my wife, mother. I want her to be my wife, but she would not marry me before she came to Gaziantep to meet the family she was marrying into."

"Not your wife, and she's sleeping up there in our family apartment as if she were!" Selma put both puffy hands on the table's edge, and pushed herself back. "Orhan, what have you done? What *have* you done to us?"

"Now my daughter, be calm. He meant no harm." Dede said quietly.

"My father, you do not understand. I will be the laughing stock of every educated woman in Gaziantep! You have killed me, Orhan…killed me! I have told my friends you are married. Now I cannot face them!"

Orhan swallowed the final bits of bread in his mouth, jumped up, and moved behind his mother's chair. "I'm sorry mother. I'm sorry. I didn't think. I bumbled. But what's done is done. Anne is here. How can we make her feel welcome? We have to make her happy. I love her. I want to marry her. If she goes back home and doesn't marry me I'll be devastated."

And as Orhan spoke the apartment doorbell rang with a limp sound. Orhan rose, opened the door for Anne, and ushered her to the breakfast table. As if nothing had been said before she arrived, he met her cheerfully, but the three persons waiting at the table sat dark and still, like the stones of the crusader castle that had made Anne so curious.

The rest of the breakfast was sheer pretense. His father and his grandfather began by prattling. They wanted to know what Anne thought of the *pida*, the white cheese, the olives, the runny jam with large pieces of fruit in it? In Turkish she was able to say that she enjoyed it all. Playfully and in English, she turned to Orhan to say that the olives looked to her like miniature shrunken heads. He did not translate her comment.

Abdullah asked about her father, learned of his new wife, learned he was a geneticist very attached to his research—all this through translation. Orhan translated carefully, hoping at each interruption that it would be Nermin who appeared so that Anne might have someone besides himself with whom she might speak at this first breakfast. Selma sat sullen and said not one word.

****

Dear Daddy,   June 20, 1960

I'm here, and I've been storing up images and things to tell you for some ten days now until I could sit down and bang out a letter to you. And now I can only think to tell you "Wow!"

Still, I'm at my typewriter, now and the things I wanted to tell you are coming back. First I want to tell you about the thoughts I had when I left the U.S. and was looking from the window of the plane. There I was, looking down on the forest covered mountains of the country that's been mine from the start of my life, and I had no feeling of loss to be leaving it, no feeling that I was inextricably linked to that culture beneath me. The last decade has been a stormy one in the U.S. and people like Senator McCarthy have made me feel, even as a teenager, that I was counter to my own culture. It felt good to be leaving the rat race that is our culture, and even better to be leaving the psychology of the arms race that we are beginning to become embroiled in. And then, after what seemed like endless hours and plane transfers afterward—

hours when I did sleep fitfully some—I ended up in a window seat in a DC-6 flying out of Istanbul over the Anatolian plain. It was then I recognized that there below us I was not observing my culture either. I was not only at odds with that culture below me, I wasn't even a part of it. I'm used to being a vital part of my culture. You've raised me not only to be observant of where I live, but ready to throw myself into my culture to work to right the wrongs I might see and enjoy the arts I could understand, or at least appreciate. And there below me on the open plain, in the rocky pine forest was a culture to which I am completely alien, disconnected. I can speak only a few phrases of the language, and I know no one as yet who might connect me to this country except Orhan.

An awful feeling! But it was a bit mollified by wanting to reject my own country when I flew above it. Then, I got to thinking maybe I belonged only in the sky. Maybe my source of feeling about my life should only be airy, expansive, sky-born! Was it a kind of illumination? The blue dome of the sky, which I was still in a position to look up to was some kind of Spirit dome. At least that watery blue sky told me that everything was still "up in the air" and I should be content to live that way for a while. It's too early to have anything more to say about this cultural stuff than what I felt as I came, but I'll keep you posted as my sense of it changes. For the moment I'm out of my own culture and in this one, but not of it.

I think it was Keats who used a phrase I've been thinking a lot about lately when he wrote about "negative capability." I think he said something about the most mature people are those who are able to live with, be content with, uncertainty. This capability of living without all the answers, being content with ambiguities is what I'm working on right now. If everything is up in the air for me, I want to just let it be up in the air. The sky in Turkey is brilliant. The sun shines through air that is hot, but clear. I want to take all this color in without passing judgment on it. We'll see. We'll see if I can.

Of course I've met Orhan's family now. His mother scares me. She dotes on Orhan, as we suspected. His father isn't around much, although I like him. It is his grandfather whom I already love though I know only a few words to speak with him. Men have always been my mentors and this grandfather—whose name is long and lovely, Omer Asim Bey—is a complex gentle-man who appears to have taken me on to make me feel welcome. Nermin, Orhan's sister, is terribly young, but I *can* speak with her and teen-agers are always a phenomenon.

Orhan has been eager to spill out the bulging bag of tricks he learned in the U.S. I am wondering if you would think he is the same man. Here in Turkey he is very much a "take charge" kind of guy. As I said, I am trying to take it all in without passing judgments. We'll see, we'll see. The Turks have a great phrase I've learned for "Wait and see." It's *Dur bakalim.* Literally translated, "Stop. Let's look." I'll write again after I have done just that! I love you, I miss you. Anne.

****

Dear Nancy, June 30, 1960

Where to begin? I'm going to use you. Not like we did on the swimming team, to watch and coach each other. But because I just have to write some of this stuff. There is so much to process. I will just have to do it on paper, and would you keep my letters. I'll make them a kind of journal of my time in Turkey. I'll type them because they may get long. Oddly, my first saga is about this typewriter I type them on. I carried it with me on the plane because I knew I was going to want to have it right away. Orhan's things that he shipped back by boat are still not here. But what a fuss this typewriter caused before Turkish customs would let it in. Orhan explained to me later that they were afraid I would sell it at a huge profit once I'm in the country—I guess Turks want typewriters with English script for business, etc. Anyway, this uniformed customs officer was going to snatch it away until Orhan got both assertive and underhanded. He bribed them by paying a great deal more than the duty they wanted to charge and they let it through. That was my introduction to Turkey. But I have my typewriter and I'm grateful Orhan was willing to "arrange" it for me.

Still I've been here three weeks and the time has evaporated into haze and heat. I've had a host of experiences and every thing and every one but Orhan is completely new. Let me tell you about the people first. The bright spot is Dede (pronounced deh-deh which sort of rhymes with bed-bed). I always have liked men and this is the one in Turkey that I'm going to learn most from. He is a Sufi Muslim and in case you don't have a clue what that means—I didn't—Sufis are a mystical group of Muslims who keep a low profile in Turkey, as Islam has, since 1922 when Ataturk founded the Republic. Ataturk insisted that Turkey be a secular state and made it illegal for any faith to proselytize, even Islam. So Omer Asim Bey—Dede, as we call him since it's the affectionate term for grandfather—observes his faith by saying his prayers five times a day. But I think the real heart of his faith is wrapped up in his compassion and his reading. Its not so much the Koran he reads, but a 13th century poet named Yunus Emre whom he adores (and I am determined to learn to read in Turkish). He says this Yunus Emre was a simple peasant who was drunk with the love of God. Orhan says modern Turks are just beginning to appreciate the simplicity and power of Yunus Emre's writing. Anyway, Dede is so far my favorite person in Orhan's family.

Then there's Nermin, his sister, who, at the moment is the only one I can talk to with any ease. She is home now for the summer, having got here only four days before I did from a fancy and expensive boarding school in Istanbul. Like Orhan did, she studies in English in Istanbul, so she knows English well. It is to the credit of Orhan's family that they give their daughter as fine an education as their son, except that I imagine they will marry her off before she goes abroad for any higher education, as Orhan did to graduate school in the U.S. She is giving me Turkish lessons after a fashion. Our sessions degenerate into talking in English about the U.S. and all things Western because she is so enamored of the idea of Western fashions and ways coming to Turkey. You and Nermin would hit it off because you care about things like clothes and the latest music. I'm grateful to have someone besides Orhan to speak with and I'm grateful for the practice she gives me in speaking Turkish, but I'm not learning the kind of vocabulary from Nermin I care about because she doesn't want to talk about Islam and Turkish politics, let alone the subtler similarities and differences in our two cultures. I'm just going to have to learn more Turkish so I can speak with Dede.

Then there's Orhan's father Abdullah Bey. He's very handsome—bushy eyebrows, lots of wavy graying hair—but he knows only a smidgin (sp?) of English words and seems ashamed he can't speak with me. He's terribly involved at the factory and sort of floats above this scene at home in airy serenity.

Then there's Orhan's mother Selma. You heard Orhan describe how she hoped to find a wife for him. I foiled that plan! But it's more than that. Orhan used to be fairly attached to his mother. Now she can't seem to forgive him for bringing me here and me for existing. She can't speak with me anyway, but it's clear she doesn't want to.

Let me tell you about the reception day Selma Hanim has. It seems the women's social scene in Gaziantep is structured by the fact that every woman who is anybody has a reception day—a regular afternoon each month when they are at home to receive guests. Selma Hanim's day is the third Thursday and everyone who is any one has made a note of this somewhere. Every woman's ambition is to have a crowd at her *"kabul"* day because this is the way women here collect their social importance. Selma had told many people that her son was bringing home a bride, so many of her women friends, fittingly curious, were expecting to meet me at her *kabul*. It's a kind of reception like an open house and the guests come and go at any hour. Nermin padded back and forth in her embroidered slippers serving each person from the trays our maid Hatije brought to the reception room door. The protocol is that she serves the guests according to the order in which they arrive, and what she serves is also according to ritual: First chocolate, then Turkish coffee, and finally after waiting just the proper amount of time, tea in small glasses and something sweet and some salty pastry as well. The order and the nature of the refreshments never changes, and if you serve things too fast, your guests are insulted because it means you're trying to rush them through your reception and out again. Ah ah, ah! You mustn't be too eager.

Having been coached by Nermin, I came into the reception primed to behave properly. For instance initially each person sits and goes around the room in a circle asking each woman "How are you," before you say anything else. Each woman answers you in the same ritualistic way. 'I'm fine' or whatever., except I never heard anything but 'I'm fine.' I came in and of course know enough Turkish to do this, and everyone seemed impressed. Alas, though! I wore a sleeveless dress with a jacket. That would have been all right, except I took off the jacket! Seeing that, Selma nearly choked up her coffee which she's not supposed to drink because she's the hostess. Through Nermin, who was circulating to pass coffee, she let me know I was to leave, put on my jacket and return. I did that and returned, ripe for my next mistake. I sat down and crossed my legs. (I didn't know crossed legs were so rude to my elders as Turkish protocol makes them.) Again through Nermin, I was asked to "uncross my legs." But after those two bloopers I couldn't seem to keep my cool and stay there. I slipped out as surreptitiously as I could and Nermin came to tell me that Selma was having still another fit. Nermin begged me to come back. I couldn't. It's odd that Nermin begged because she had told me how much she hates these receptions. For one thing her mother is embarrassingly obese, anyway, but in social situations she seems more demanding and passive at the same time...

Selma's father, Dede, however, even with my few words, saw the way I felt and indicated I needn't go back. He hired a taxi to take the two of us down town to the copper market and that was the end of that reception for me. The copper market is a short, narrow cobblestone street with rows of small open stalls. It's one of my favorite places in all of Gaziantep, and I recovered, pronto. I adore the clutter, the noises made by men banging away to shape pitchers and plates and countless other copper shapes. Dede knew exactly what to do with me, in spite of the fact that he and I can only speak in small dribbles of words. Nermin had told him what happened, and my hero swept me off! Nermin, for instance considers reception days, as I've said, banal and empty, but because she wants to be married goes through all the rituals of helping her mother run hers perfectly. Ah yes, help me! Suggest to me how many and which similarly inane social rituals we have in the U.S. and I shall be placated. All I know now is that they are no easier to endure in Turkey where they are foreign than they are in the U.S. where I've lived with them all my life.

I guess I better explain this "bride" stuff. Did you catch it above where I wrote it? You must not tell this to my father under any circumstances, but I think you don't see him much anyway. Orhan was afraid to tell his family I was coming with him—unchaperoned, no less—unless we were married, so he told them we *were* married. Then, when he got here he saw how complex our being married might make things! When he told me you can guess I was pretty shocked. He only told me at the last moment before we arrived in Gaziantep. Anyway, he got cold feet himself. We never slept together. He slept on the sofa in the living room I think. Naturally, I don't know where he was. What I know is that we spent only one night in the apartment they furnished for their *married* son, before he took the donkey by the tail and flung it back on his parents that we weren't married. Right now they are trying to figure what to do about that, and Orhan is back sleeping in his old room in their apartment. I am up rattling around in the apartment upstairs. As long as no one in the town suspects we're not married, we're doing all right. What we'll do if I decide to stay—maybe we'll get married secretly if that's possible in Turkey—is all up in the air. It will be a whole lot harder for Orhan if I decide I can't marry him and live in Turkey, but I can't do much about that. He's told me he's really sorry. He made his own mix up!

Since they hadn't arranged a hotel for me in the first place, Orhan begged his parents not to send me off to a hotel, and this is the major concession they allowed him. But all this has lent a chaos to my arrival that makes me feel like the snakes that crawl out of an ancient crusader castle here. To this family I'm some kind of spoiler. I'm poison.

But really, another metaphor's struck me these days. I am like an artifact at the bottom of an archeological dig. Pull me out in this culture and I'm a wild curiosity, but they don't know what to do with me. And from my own culture, I'm cut off, displaced. There is no way to hear about, keep current with, or experience any small custom or ritual that I grew up with. It's a terrible feeling so far. I hate to pull this paper tantrum, but it makes me feel less cut off to write it. So…dear Nancy,

I wish we were still sporting it up in the pool together, (no pools at all here) but since we're not, consider yourself used. And consider yourself to have comforted me just by being there where this letter is going. If it only wouldn't take maybe two or three weeks to reach you, and God knows how many weeks to hear from you back. Somehow, more than to hear from you, I needed to write to you.

    More later, good friend. Anne.

CHAPTER EIGHT
ONCE THERE WAS AN OLD MAN, A YOUNG WOMAN, AND GOD
JULY, 1960

Several days after the disastrous *kabul* day, Omer Asim Bey, sitting cross-legged on a floor pillow in the dining room, his water pipe lit and beside him, stayed on after breakfast ruminating. Orhan continued to be preoccupied with the factory, eager to persuade his father his new ideas were workable. His daughter Selma had been as sullen of late as he had ever seen her. If both of them carried on this way much longer, this guest of Orhan's might turn her back on Turkey and never come again. Turkey should not become fixed in her mind as an inhospitable country whether she married his grandson or not. Selma's attitudes belonged to her. Nothing her father could do about them. He was a guest in this house. Ever since his wife Meliha had died and he had come to live with Abdullah and Selma, he had been careful to refrain from any comment to Selma about her behavior. A certain neutrality toward the behavior of those around him was one of the stances he had achieved with the benefit of old age, or was it his Sufi practice? He was not about to give up that aloof stance now. But that didn't mean he didn't want this young woman to like Turkey.

Eyvah! He needed a long draw of tobacco smoke. He leaned forward from the floor pillow, prodded the smoldering shreds of tobacco in his water pipe, and struck a match to invigorate them. Pleasures fade away one by one for a man in his eighth decade. A water pipe had to remain as one of them. The old know what matters. At least he did. Water pipes…God… maybe the poetry of Yunus Emre since it's mostly about God. Any poet who lasts six centuries must matter. No woman could give pleasure for six centuries. And water-pipes? They must have been around some five centuries giving pleasure

This new woman would be pleasant to have around. He would help her with her Turkish; take her to visit the Hittite dig at Karatepe; show her some of the finer parts of Turkish culture; maybe tell her some of the older tales and poetry Orhan hadn't a clue about. Pity he himself hadn't studied more language. He knew Persian, but only for literary use. Whether or not she had a faith of her own, she might want to know a bit about Islam. Why did he sense she would want that? He knew very little of her, but she was probably too well educated to be stimulated by the society of Turkish women. She wouldn't belong, but she couldn't be blamed for that. After a Turkish woman was married, even if she was educated, she was pushed out of the society of her father and brothers, and what Turkish husband told his wife about anything important he was thinking? He hadn't told Meliha much of anything. Orhan's education might make him different; he'd had so much education. But most Turkish men, even if they were educated, didn't speak with their wives about things other than their children and simple household matters. When he met her this girl had called him a 'gentle man.' She appeared to like men. She might not be ready to be dismissed from masculine interests and the world of ideas.

"Dede, you have to help me!" His granddaughter Nermin burst through the french doors of the sitting room and flitted about lifting newspapers, looking behind chairs, picking up any loose object to peer under it. "I'm looking for my Vogue magazine. Have you seen it?"

"What magazine?"

"That American one, Vogue." She raised her voice, irritated. "The one with all the pictures of clothes in it. I have to take it. I have to have a picture to show the dressmaker when I ask her to make my dress."

Looking at the pile of newspapers beside him, he said "Now what would I be doing ogling a magazine with all those toothpick-figured Western women?"

"You *delikanli,* you! You're the only man around who will admit he might ogle them." His granddaughter reached down as she passed him and scruffed the gray hair on his forehead. The Turkish phrase for youth '*delikanli,*' crazy blooded, that she had used for him pleased Omer Asim Bey.

"*Vah, vah,* all those lovely bare arms! I might well ogle them. For an old man like me, a picture's as good as the real thing."

"See what I mean! You're crazy blooded." Nermin continued to rush around the room. "Where *is* that magazine? I have to have it. I'm late."

"Draw her a picture."

"*Aman,* you're no help! My magazine must be somewhere else." She left the room, slamming the door so hard the frosted glass rattled.

That girl was the crazy-blooded one, the old man brooded. She was no ordinary Turkish woman, but she scarcely knew it. Her ideas about life—a woman's life in particular—were dangerous. She might be adolescent and only interested in clothes and froth now, but fundamentally she thought women should be educated and use what they learned. He did too. He had never been so backward as to claim women shouldn't be educated. But she was learning all the wrong things. Nermin was studying languages, literature; she was even interested in archeology. Archeology was an interest of his, yes, but he shuddered at the image of a woman so sure of herself in a man's world as to be able to go out and dig about in huge holes in isolated areas with men ogling her every move. Who would marry a woman so bold, so sullied? Selma and Abdullah should marry her off with dispatch. Surely they could arrange some good marriage for her. Otherwise they'd be sorry when she'd invaded a man's world so far that a respectable, influential man from a good family would never want her.

His thoughts drifted back to the woman Nermin's brother had brought home. She was a smart one, but she was foreign. *Allahallaha,* youth was all crazy-blooded. The idea of making an American girl come here and try to be Turkish! This An-ne also probably had a stash of ideas useless to a woman, at least if she'd studied the history and literature he'd heard she had. What could she have thought she was getting into in Turkey? Even he, a loyal Turk knew it was crazy-blooded to leave all that American gadgetry and set up a household in a place like Gaziantep—at least if you had a choice. Much better if parents choose mates for their children. Parents understand what marriage is all about.

Later Nermin came back to the sitting room, and this time Anne was with her. She spoke in careful Turkish, louder because of her grandfather's difficulty hearing, as if her new guest could understand. "Anne's going with me to the market. Orhan was sorry for going off to the factory with father, and asked me to take her. He just doesn't know how much better it is for me when his friend's here. We're going to do everything together. I'm going to take her to a dig, I'm going to—" her voice trailed off. "Lively—this dead old place can be lively, Dede!" Nermin flung her arms akimbo, and shook her shoulders as if she were dancing to some wild American music. "I can't find mother. Will you tell her for me? I've gone to the dressmaker's. I'm going to show Anne the vegetable market as well, and we'll be back for dinner?"

"Tell the truth." Omer Asim Bey said playfully. "You didn't look for your mother. You know if I tell her when you're gone it will be too late for her to object. *Pek iyi.* I'll tell her. Did you find your bare-armed lovelies?"

"In my room, yes."

"All that fuss for what might better stay hidden under your bed."

"You old rusty-mind! You don't mean that."

"Respect your elders," he grinned. "Your mother hears you speak like that and she'll not let you go back to school."

Nermin turned abruptly. "How do you know how I feel about going back to school?"

"Don't look at me as if you're reading every wrinkle on my forehead! I know! That's all."

Nermin stamped her foot. "I'm bored, Dede, bored! How will I ever come back to Aintab when I finish school? I just hope—" she indicated

Anne with a flick of her eyes—"she can't understand. I don't want to spoil this town for her so soon. How can an educated woman stand it here in Eastern Turkey? How, Dede?"

"I'm not an educated woman."

"*Janim,*" her tone turned affectionate. "No, you're not. Too bad! We have to go. Tell mother."

"If I see her."

They were gone. Tame a girl like Nermin? How? How had she got that way? Her mother hadn't been that way. It was hard to believe that her mother had once been prettier than Nermin. Selma had been demure as a young girl, clever but meek. She had been quick, facile in the domestic arts. Did that make a difference? Praise for Selma had come early, praise for the ninety-nine ways she knew how to cook eggplant, praise for the skill with which she embroidered open cutwork, Gaziantep's signature craft. She had planted good seeds for homemaking, but hers had been a shriveled harvest. Diabetes and too much flesh had taken her physical confidence, and servants had robbed her of her domestic skills. When his wife, Meliha, died and he came to live in this house he had seen things he hadn't wanted to see. His daughter might plan, complain, give adept orders to her household, but she did whatever she did sitting down. No whisper was left in her of that lithe wisp of a girl she'd been. Her mother Meliha had been more alive the day she died than Selma was now. "*Vah, Vah,*" he sighed.

Selma was lucky, at least, in her husband. Abdullah Bey was all factory methods, social graces and no nonsense. No complaints or softness about him. He provided well. Abdullah had built one of the best apartments in this section of town for his family. When Meliha died, they had convinced Omer Asim Bey it was senseless for him to think of keeping a separate household. If his son Ahmed had lived…by this time, he, too, would have had a young family, and their grandfather might have lived with them…No, he was better placed here. The crazy bloods of this household were quite enough.

The door opened again and the doorman Ali came in with his market baskets.

"*Selamunaleykum, Omer Asim Bey.*"

"*Aleykumselam, Ali Efendi.*" The two men exchanged the traditional Islamic greeting. "You're late. I hope you weren't buying our dinner."

"I was. I started early, but there's more to buy with a guest at every meal. Some days there is too much to do."

"And others, there's not enough. You read our poet lately?"

"Lately, our house is never quiet. Our baby is ill, and Hatije fusses over it—she's always fussing."

"Come to me, then. We'll read together."

"Since the master died, I've missed Yunus Emre." Ali spoke over his shoulder, not loudly enough, as he carried his baskets into the kitchen. The master of whom Ali spoke was the master of their Sufi order. Omer Asim Bey glanced at the back of the young man's baggy village pants. To make those pants he'd have to buy double cloth, he was that tall. How did it come about that a barely educated village boy, muscular, strong-handed, should want to read poetry? This was an unusual lad. He had begun coming to the same Sufi group to which Omer Asim Bey belonged, and he had also discovered he liked the poet Yunus. If when seeing a young shoot of wheat you could nearly taste the juice, if you felt the sun in a clod of dirt, if the face of the moon could give you an enormous shove, then you understood Yunus. Life had its inebriates in every age. Mystic spirits sprung up in diverse places. One spiritual inebriate less often found another, but he and Ali had found each other.

A small group of men in the Gaziantep area had come together as a Sufi group. In their gatherings, the audiences with their master, the chanting, the *zekir* ceremonies in which one of their number whirled, Omer Asim Bey had gained a sense of purity, rightness. Their master had died last year, however, and the group met now only on rare occasions. This boy, Ali, had come from the village Omer Asim Bey owned. His village, though it was not a remarkable place, was more special in the old man's mind because it had produced another Sufi, another who loved Yunus Emre. In other ways it was ordinary: the school was never full; the grape crop was often sparse; the wheat was going to be poor this year. After the earthquake, the villagers had built back their destroyed mud-walled houses lethargically, but they could hardly be blamed for a tired response to such a disastrous act of God as that earthquake. A few years back he himself had more energy. He'd pulled official strings, been politically clever, and the government had helped rebuild the houses, and built a school as well. He had helped find a teacher—all soon after public education was inaugurated. It had made too little difference. Only about half the families sent their sons to school, and he knew of no daughters. But still, that village had produced this Ali, a lover of good poetry, a lover of Yunus and *Allah*.

****

In the heart of the Gaziantep shopping area the wide asphalt paved street where cars are able to pass only with care gives way to a cobblestone passage so narrow as to be negotiated only at a horse cart's peril. In that area Nermin and Anne paused in front of an ancient stone arch, the entrance of the *sebse han* or vegetable market. Anne glanced in the arched doorway of the high stone building. "*Abo!* This is the color I came for!" Anne said. An explosion of color lined each side of the market's central aisle: the wine red of stacked small eggplant, the flame red of tomatoes, the muted green of bell peppers. She could not have named the profusion of fruits and vegetables, even in English, but she saw the varied shapes and colors as a bright collage. Further into the huge hall past some five or six vegetable stalls, were two butcher's shops where skinned sheep hung chest-down on hooks. Arranged below them were their severed heads for sale. Even the ghastly took on a certain beauty.

As the two women paused at the huge open arch, a villager jostled them from behind. Suspecting the man's gesture might be intentional, Nermin took Anne's arm and pulled her into the market's central aisle where they meandered moving along among the stalls. As they passed, each seller sprang to life from his seat to urge them to buy. Where the air was redolent with the smell of rotten fruit at one spot, they moved faster. "The very grime of this place gives it charm," Anne said. Then, fearing Nermin might misunderstand, she said, "Our supermarkets are odorless, sterile places where everything's wrapped in plastic."

"This place! Charming? I don't think. But I thought you'd want to see it. We will leave. They all know you're foreign and stare! It's not only because you're blonde." Nermin paused. "Oh, I don't know. If I had courage I would stare back at them...Now, to my dressmaker. She knows about you because I told her daughter. Her daughter is a school friend of mine from primary school. To receive an American will honor my dressmaker."

Chatting aimlessly, out again in the cobblestone street, they moved behind two women in long coats and headscarves until the women moved up on to the narrow side-walk and stopped at a store whose open door was flanked by bolts of fabric. When the women no longer made a path for them, it was impossible to speak. Instead they had to pay attention to winding their way around countless loitering villagers. When they reached the crossroads at the center of the business area there was more room to walk, although care crossing the street meant they stopped for both a shiny Chevrolet sedan, and a horse cart. Neither the few cars, nor Nermin and the other pedestrians, appeared to pay attention to the dust-covered red traffic light at the intersection.

At last, they turned into a narrow dirt street where at a weather-worn wooden door Nermin lifted a heavy iron ring and knocked. The tin ring of metal on metal brought a slim girl to the door. She was barefoot except for wooden clogs below her faded long-sleeved cotton dress. "Welcome, welcome." She kissed Nermin on both cheeks, and when she was introduced to Anne, kissed her hand and put it to her forehead. Then she led them across a packed-mud courtyard, and up a narrow stone stairway which ran along the outer wall of a stone-block house. At a small cemented entrance-well, they stopped, removed their shoes, and donned the slippers which lay arranged for guests. Remembering her bare feet would be both large and gawky, Anne winced as she removed her shoes, but no one appeared to give her feet a glance.

Inside the room seemed friendly. Faded red and brown woven *kilims* covered its floor and the walls had scarred wood paneling. The dressmaker sat sewing on a low settee, her headscarf slightly askew. She rose and motioned her guests to sit on a second low settee, the only other furniture in the room. While Nermin unfolded the cloth she'd brought and opened her magazine to show the seamstress a picture, the young girl disappeared to make tea. Anne listened to the Turkish. The woman's enunciation was careful, and since she knew the subject was a dress, Anne caught many of the words.

The daughter brought tea in tiny glasses. When Nermin had finished hers—the hosts did not take tea themselves—she stood and the dressmaker dropped to her knees, pins in her mouth, to take Nermin's measurements. Her daughter recorded them in a small notebook. "*Bel*"

"*Bel* means waist." Each word the dressmaker spoke through her pins, Nermin translated. Her measurements finished, the dressmaker held the material to Nermin and pinned it to specific places with practiced hands. Then with large scissors, she cut the cloth. The scraps fell to the floor. Finally, she unpinned the cut cloth, folded it, dismissed Nermin as her customer and settled on the settee to engage the two young women in conversation as her guests. Anne was beginning to catch more phrases of the simple Turkish when Nermin asked for permission to leave, and reluctantly, the dressmaker granted it.

"It feels good to release my head to English again," Anne said when they were picking their way through the uneven stone street. Even though she had attempted only a few words in Turkish, the visit had exhausted her. "That's impressive, to be able to look at a picture and cut out a dress on the person instead of from a pattern. We must have lost that art in the U.S."

Nermin caught Anne's arm. "Look! Gaziantep is famous for its *baklava.*" They were passing a shop window behind which a man with a long stick of a rolling pin was rolling out a thin circle of dough on a flour-dusted table.

"Orhan said I should wait to taste Gaziantep *baklava.* Now's the time." Aware that she was watching another unique skill, Anne lingered in the shop. At length, when she noticed Nermin was growing impatient, awkwardly, using Turkish, she bought her first *baklava.*

Once more in the street, Nermin walked rapidly. "You did good. Very good," she said.

"It makes me sad that the first things one learns to talk about in a language are so mundane! I want to be able to talk about more than food and clothes."

Nermin did not seem to want to talk. "I don't understand you," she said, moving on.

"I think I thought I was going to land, sprout wings and fly to the top of some minaret to shout Turkish wisdom." Anne shifted the heavy bag she carried. "Instead, I'm grounded by a string bag. I haven't a clue how to say anything I care about saying in Turkish. When you're helpless in one language, you begin to feel you are dull in any language. I've always loved learning. In college my relationship with books was better than it was with people. Ideas jumped out at me, became experiences. I remember feeling sorry for my mother because, smart as she was, she got buried in domestic affairs and was never free to use her mind." Anne glanced at Nermin, saw she was not listening, and continued anyway. "My mother settled for using her intelligence to help my father use his brain. To me that was a capitulation. The price for a well-run home was the burial of my mother's potential. Then she died." Since Nermin continued to be pre-occupied, Anne ceased talking. Studying Turkish wouldn't seem so dead if she could only get to the vocabulary for ideas. What was the word for idea? What was the word for feeling?

Nermin walked now with head bowed. At the dressmaker's, while Anne was not looking, the dressmaker's daughter had slipped an envelope into her hand. One glance at the neat engineer's print of the address had informed Nermin that the moment had come! His letter was here. How clever she'd been to arrange this secrecy. No one knew she'd received a letter but the dressmaker's daughter, and that girl was not only innocent in the ways of the educated world of Gaziantep, she was sworn to secrecy. Oh, how much Nermin wanted to have Jim see her in that sleeveless dress the woman had cut just now. Her mother wouldn't let her wear it in Gaziantep, but…She couldn't picture Jim's face anymore. She'd heard that the face of someone you loved was more difficult to remember. It had been nearly two months since she'd seen him. But this envelope was real. It meant he still existed. Should she show Anne? She wanted to, but…No. Anyone who knew might try to stop her. She had to be free to do what her heart told her. It wasn't only a romantic dream. Affairs of the heart were fuzzy, and this was matter of fact. Still, no one should know because this relationship had to be worked out without interference. The fact was, she, an educated woman, would be happier married and in the U.S. If she came back to this town she'd be out of place—like riding the underside of a donkey. Still, she didn't want to leave Turkey forever. It was, after all, her country. This made Jim a natural for her purposes. He was a scientist and his archeological laboratory was in this country, so he would need to return again and again to Turkey. He had looked so American the day he came to lecture to her science class, she could not believe he was intelligent, too. Dignified, serious, he had described his research to girls who had made mud pies in the very dust he wanted to sift for artifacts. But he was shy. If she hadn't insisted she help him with his Turkish, if she hadn't been much bolder than she ever dreamed she could be, he never would have known her name. Jim's knowledge intrigued her. Archeology was a richness Turkey possessed that few Turkish nationals appreciated. Foreign reverence for their archeological wealth was beginning to wake Turks to the treasures their own soils held hidden. Nermin wanted to be one of those alert to this richness.

    She put her hand in her pocket to make sure the letter was still there. It would have been too daring to try to tell him what a deception he was involving himself in by using this address. He didn't know it wasn't hers. She had simply told the dressmaker's daughter she might have a letter and would she please keep it until the time seemed natural to give it to her. Even if the dressmaker herself had happened to see it, Nermin could hardly begrudge a widow a bit of gossip to spice up her life. The dressmaker might talk, but Nermin's mother was of another class. Any talk the widowed dressmaker might do would bounce about in another set of reception rooms in quite separate houses from those Nermin's mother frequented. Her secret was safe.

    Jim wasn't the sort who would take to intrigue. For all he knew, her parents had been told all about him and how much he appreciated their daughter's help with language and arrangements. His innocence was part of his charm; he had no inkling of her dreams about him. She would keep them to herself, at least until he recognized he might be dreaming as she was. She could wait. There was school to finish, time to let things happen. Meanwhile, it was both exciting and harmless to be in love with a man who was too shy to touch her. How could anyone think it was improper?

The two women reached the family apartment and climbed the stairs. Nermin left Anne trying to speak with Dede about what she'd seen, and rushed to her bedroom. Flinging herself on her bed, she tore open the letter. It contained five carefully printed sentences:

"How is your summer going? My work is going fairly well. However, I find I need someone to translate who understands better what's involved in archeology. Does your grandfather happen to know of anyone? If he has suggestions, would you write me at the village address below. Best, Jim."

How innocuous, how stodgy! Wild with disappointment, Nermin dropped off her elbows and buried her face in her pillow. How could he have written such a say-nothing letter? Still, at this early stage what had she expected? She had to wait, ignore his stuffiness. Finagle and wait. Manipulate and wait. Meanwhile, nothing, nothing she said or did about Jim or with Jim could ruin her dreams about him: dreams of travel, dreams of the U.S., dreams of helping him do his research. Fantasies, they were. Pink, orange, bright, bubbling dreams. Nermin lay prostrate flung out like a sheep-skin pelt on her bed, until slowly she grew more calm.

CHAPTER NINE
ONCE SHE WAS, NOW SHE'S NOT, LEARNED AUGUST, 1960

The morning sun shining through the window of the sitting room made a bright red rectangle on the rug beside the table where Nermin and Anne sat for an English lesson. Since Nermin was helping Anne with the Turkish vocabulary of archeology, they had chosen an account of the history of the Gaziantep castle. Before she explained the more difficult Turkish words, however, Nermin seemed driven to complain about Gaziantep in English. "Eastern Turkey is backward. We don't even try to attract tourists. If this were Western Turkey, the town would have made a history of the castle in English." With a dramatic gesture she fell back in her chair to pout. Having made a decision that during this session she was going to tell Anne about Jim, the Turkish in this lesson she might teach Anne was of only secondary interest to Nermin. For the two weeks since the letter had come she had been thinking about Jim all on her own, and that was unexciting. She needed someone with whom she could talk about Jim. Besides she needed Anne's advice. Jim was, after all, another American.

To focus the lesson back on the castle, Anne glanced at the picture of it. "Glad I don't have to depend on this picture for an image of the Gaziantep castle."

"Turkish printing is terrible. Better to print no books than to print photographs so fuzzy as this. In school our best books are printed in England." Nermin continued to frown, unable to find a way to turn the talk in the direction she wanted.

"The way a book's printed isn't what's important, anyway. This one has history in it about the castle…no matter what language its in, I want to read it if I'm going to learn anything about Gaziantep's history. What I need are historical facts." Anne stretched a foot into the patch of sun on the floor. It was already late August and the morning was cool enough that the sun felt good on her bare ankle. "I can speak better with Dede, now, but even he doesn't know the kind of specific facts I want."

"If I knew more archeological words in English, I wish—"

"Don't be hard on yourself. You have things you like to talk about— fashion, things like that. You do that well. My interests are just different."

"But I'm interested in archeology, too. I…I have a friend. He knows archeology in Turkey and needs help with the language."

"Who's that? I thought you said Turks weren't interested in archeology."

"He's not a Turk. He's an American."

"Where'd you meet an American?"

"At school. He lectured to our class and I helped him with translation. I had a letter from him. Remember the dressmaker's daughter? He sent it through her."

"What's wrong with a letter coming to you here?"

"My mother would ask too many questions."

"Oh! Then, he isn't writing you now for translation help!"

"It…it was a friendly letter"

"What does that mean?"

"Nothing. A letter from a friend. He still wants translation help." Anne looked alarmed. Nermin decided she was not sounding casual enough.

"You scare me. It's, it's not a good idea. Don't get involved with anyone from the States. Please don't!"

"Why not?"

"Because you don't know what you're getting into. To marry into another culture...oh...you know that's why I'm here in Turkey...and...and I just don't know."

Nermin sat up straight. "To have a friend...to marry him!? That's different. I didn't say I wanted to marry him."

"That's good. Keep it that way. If you marry, you marry a whole culture and it takes more than love.... I think I love your brother...but can I learn this language? Can I live in Eastern Turkey?"

"I just want to work with this man...not marry him."

"But when you work with a man, the marrying part begins to be attractive. You remind me of me. The lure of the different, the chance to get out of this town, the idea of being a bridge between cultures—that all appeals to you...but—"

A knock interrupted Anne, and she was relieved. The doorman Ali, his baby daughter whimpering in his arms, burst in without waiting for an answer. "Forgive me," he said. "I come like summer thunder. This child—she was supposed to stay asleep, but, excuse me, her cloth, she soils it steadily...never stops crying. Is Hatije in the kitchen? She can give it her breast."

"Yes, she's in the kitchen, I think." Nermin rose to go find her. Anne had understood Nermin's Turkish and part of Ali's. The chance to observe a Turkish villager like this bear-like man intrigued her, but she could only guess at what gave him the urgency he was expressing. It had to be the child. A small face and one flailing bony arm was all that she could see of the little thing, wrapped as it was in a grayish piece of cotton wrapper. The face was as gray as the wrapper. Alone with him as she was, Anne longed to be able to say something to this father in sympathy, but to frown was all she found to do.

Hatije swooped in with Nermin behind her and took the child from her father's arms. The village woman's *shalvar* was pushed well up her calves—she'd been mopping a floor. Ali took his leave and the mother dropped to a squat on the floor, knees up, and put the child to her breast.

"She's been ill for some time," she explained. "She has many, excuse me, stools in a day. She nurses only fretfully." The young mother pushed back a thin strand of fine brown hair falling lifeless over the child's face. The head seemed to Anne far too large to go with the fleshless arm protruding from the wrapper.

"Have you taken the child to the doctor?" Anne's Turkish was adequate for that simple question, and when Hatije replied that they had not, she also understood. But when Hatije explained that they had taken the child for a "lead pouring" the previous week, Anne became lost in strange language and asked Nermin for help. Nermin translated as Hatije described a recent day in the village. An old woman hovered over a small fire burning on the rooftop of a village mud house. The flames had long since gone to ash and a bellows was needed to enliven it. Hatije's mother and Hatije were joined by the old woman's daughter who fed the fire small sticks. Hatije described how the other younger woman scattered burning seeds on the fire and the odor of them filled the air as the older "woman with hands" put a pot of lead to the coals. The younger woman continued to puff with the bellows, and the spark in the fire came to life. The metal heated. Hatije's mother, the old woman, and her daughter huddled closer about the fire muttering their chant. When the lead neared the molten stage, the old woman dipped a bowl of water from the bucket and hovered with it in readiness. The chanting grew more fervent as the lead grew hotter, until at last with a practiced flourish the old woman lifted the vessel high and poured the molten lead into the water bowl A puff of steam burst from the bowl. When it cleared all four women hung over the small bowl to peer at the lead's patterns before the older woman's hands shot into the air. Anne heard Hatije's tone of disappointment as she described how the old crone's hands had dropped. As the child in Hatije's arms stared out from deep-set, dull eyes, Anne was shocked to see it looked older than its mother.

Fumbling for a comment, Anne asked Nermin if she would tell Hatije that she, Anne, would be happy to contribute the funds, if Hatije would take the child to the doctor.

Either Nermin did not make the offer clear or Hatije did not want to understand, because the young mother made no acknowledgment before she rose and carried the child downstairs to the family's rooms.

The baby reminded Anne of the pictures she'd seen that were intended to appall Westerners into contributing funds for starving children. But this child belonged to a woman Anne knew, and that seemed achingly different. "She's so resigned. How? It's her child."

"Your word resigned. I don't understand. But you must learn that village mothers don't expect their babies to live until they do. In our country we have a word, *'ejel'*. It means the day you are destined to die. Hatije probably feels her child was not destined to grow up."

Anne moaned. "It's so passive, just to accept fate. Nothing is so sad as the death of a child!"

The sitting room door opened once more and Selma Hanim, her headscarf askew, entered to ask where Hatije was. It was time to start dinner.

"Her daughter is ill. She took it downstairs to their room. It looked terrible."

"Have they been to the doctor?"

"You know they can't afford a doctor!"

"Get my purse from my room," Selma ordered. Take her ten liras and tell her to take the child up the hill to the clinic. Then come back and help me make dinner."

Nermin went obediently to find the purse, and when she headed downstairs to Ali and Hatije's quarters Anne asked to go with her.

In the month Anne had been in Gaziantep she'd seen several chubby-cheeked rosy babies bundled either on village mother's backs, or carried through the streets on the arm of a scarf-wearing, long-coated woman. To find that a child so malnourished lived in their same building shocked Anne. "She must be feeding her wrong!" she speculated.

Nermin expressed surprise. "I don't know. We can ask her?" That Anne cared so much seemed odd. In the room where she and Ali lived, they found Hatije squatting to rock the child's wooden low-sided cradle on the *kilim* covered floor. She turned from the cradle and shyly motioned them to sit on the only piece of furniture in the room, a low, lightly padded *sedir* covered with a muslin slipcover. Anne sensed their presence was distracting Hatije from caring for her child, and found words in Turkish. "We don't want to disturb you."

"My mother sent us," Nermin added. "She thinks you should take the child up the hill to the clinic." Nermin thrust the ten-lira note out. "Here is the money to do that."

Hatije made no move to rise and take the note. "Tell Selma Hanim I am grateful. The child is quiet now. Perhaps when it wakes."

Anne lowered her voice and asked, "What's the baby's name?"

"Dursun," Hatije answered.

"That means, 'let it stay,'" Nermin translated before she said to Hatije, " Our American friend wonders what you feed it."

"Nothing. She eats nothing," Hatije moaned. "She is a year and a half and breast milk is all she takes."

Nermin turned to Anne. "Did you understand that?"

"Breast milk is all this child has had!" Anne was shocked. *Eyvah!* Tell her that when the child is well, we will help her feed it solid food. I'm sure she should have something besides breast milk."

"She doesn't walk yet. She's very weak," Hatije added.

Nermin sensed they should stay no longer. She rose, crossed the small room and peered at the child's hollow-eyed face to avoid looking at Hatije. She had now achieved a position where she could thrust the folded note into Hatije's sleeve. The next time her mother could give her money for herself, Nermin decided. In the face of illness Turks had a ready phrase to say, and leaving, Nermin used it: *"Gechmish olsun* let it pass and stay passed."

Hatije looked at the child and mumbled. "This is my second child. The first was a boy. The boy was born strong and grew weak. This one, she has been weak from the beginning, but...I wanted her to live."

A silence followed. Hatije's face, when she looked down at her child reminded Anne of Mary's resignation in Michelangelo's Pieta. It seemed irreverent to break the silence, but since she wanted to do the Turkish thing, she said, *"Gechmish olsun"* in a tone she hoped spoke of how much she cared.

Hatije looked gratefully at Anne.

Nermin wanted to leave. They did.

Climbing the hall stairs, Anne moved heavily, unable to understand her own strong feeling. Was it that she'd so rarely seen a child ill like that? "That really got to me," she said.

Nermin didn't comment. Hatije was the maid who didn't read, she explained and when Nermin spoke with her the barrier of the village woman's ignorance was forever in the way. "People are different for you," she told Anne. "You treat Hatije like she isn't ignorant, like she understands…like any other woman. You're like Dede. He knows what you're feeling when you talk with him. I can't get away from my own feelings when I talk with someone."

Selma had the orders organized to produce the noon meal when her two emissaries returned. In Hatije's absence there was rice to be picked over for tiny rocks, carrots to be peeled, and lettuce to be washed. The three women settled in to the work.

As she peeled carrots Nermin asked herself if Anne could be right about marrying Americans. But when she nipped her finger with the knife, she had to concentrate on stopping the small stream of blood. Later, she promised herself, she would need to take time, consider why Anne had counseled such caution. In a way she wished she hadn't spoken about Jim.

Abdullah and Orhan came home from the factory for the noon meal, and Selma, stimulated by the pleasure of doing her own work, bragged that her help had been excellent, that if she could only keep it, she might do away with Hatije's cooking help.

At the end of the meal Anne was allowed to bring the melon to the table. She was watching Orhan deftly cut his pale-green crescent into precise bite-size pieces when Ali knocked and entered the sitting room. He held his villager's cap, which he seldom removed, limply in his two hands. "Excuse me…I don't mean to disturb you. I came to ask…" he paused, "might Hatije be excused for the rest of today? God give you life, our daughter died."

****

Dear Nancy,   August 28, 1960

I haven't heard from you yet, but I'm going to use you again. I have to tell somebody this stuff. The thing that strikes me regularly these days is how different Orhan is now that I'm in Turkey. I can't tell if it's because we're not married, or if he would act in these same ways were we married. The other night we dared to walk out together on the streets of Gaziantep. Now this would be no big deal if the Demir family had told everyone for sure we were married, but we're not, and the town doesn't know whether we are or not. So it was running the risk of calling down the disapproval of the town biddies either now or later to walk out with me unchaperoned. The early evening is my favorite time of day here because it's cooler and when there are clouds, the sunsets are wonderful. That evening the sun lit a fiery gold edge around a mushroom shaped gray cloud as we were walking in the more open part of town where we could see the sky. Orhan is as romantic as I am. He really liked walking in that kind of brass-gold light. But then as we moved to the older part of town the sunset faded—or at least the streets were so narrow we couldn't easily see the sky—and two young boys ogled us. Particularly me. Orhan was outraged. I tried not to notice, and anyway their looks didn't look that lewd to me, but Orhan turned and growled at them. He said something like "Have you never seen a human being before?" In Turkish of course. I was just pleased to have understood his Turkish. I couldn't be bothered about the stares. I am understanding more and more Turkish now. My language progress is the only thing that reminds me of my old self. I was always good at languages and now that I'm using another language and hearing it all the time, I'm able to really use my skills.

And I'm going to need a lot more Turkish soon. Nermin will be going back to school in Istanbul and I won't have anyone here in the family besides Orhan whom I can speak with—whom I particularly want to speak with, that is. What I mean is I really want to be able to speak with Dede, and that's coming, but it will have to be Turkish. To get back to Nermin. She reminds me of me when I was an adolescent. She is rebellious. She follows trends ardently and seems most interested in froth. She has a crush on an American archeologist working here and I've been here just long enough to think that's pretty dangerous. She of course is a fuzzy thinker about the implications of any relationship with this man (whom I haven't met—she met him in Istanbul at her school and helped him with translation). Still, I've learned just enough from being here this long to know that intercultural relationships are not near so thrilling when you get to their nitty gritty. Anyway, I like Nermin a lot, particularly for her spunk, and I'm going to miss her when she goes back to school.

    The "position of women" in Turkey worries me most. This country is not so influenced by Islam that it outright cloisters its women. It's more subtle than that. The way women are expected to act has more to do, I think, with Turkish women's expectations for themselves. The women I've met seem to prefer each other's company, socially, rather than mixed company. Most of the women I know anything about have no desire to do anything in life but be mothers and good homemakers. There's nothing wrong with those expectations, of course, but women like you and me have dreams of doing something more like a career along with our families, and there's not much room for that idea here. There's not much room for any idea, and besides that for my athletic side which you know about from the swim team, there's not even a pool to swim in. If I'd been a plump home economics major, I'd be fine here. I could learn to cook the Turkish cuisine, which is outstanding, and I could learn to do the open-cut work embroidery, which is the Gaziantep trademark on linen. But you know me. You know that I really want to spend my life dealing with ideas of some kind, and domesticity is only a second priority for me.

    So when Nermin leaves there will be Orhan, his mother Selma, his father, and Dede left for me to relate to around this house. Orhan is still pretty fascinating in himself, and he clearly cares about keeping me happy, but he feels quite naturally that he must spend most of his days at the factory because after all, the business of cloth manufacturing is what he went off to learn. And he **has** learned a good deal about that, and almost because he brought me home with him and I'm an embarrassment to his family, he wants to show them that on the main thing he went for—learning the business end of the family factory—he has done well. I understand that—now much better than when I first arrived—and can live with that. Still, I have to try to imagine what it would be like staying in this culture, cut off as I would be from my own culture. Orhan's father is an interesting man, but he's preoccupied with things out of the home. His mother plain doesn't like me. I'm just too foreign for her. Not that I'm an infidel—just foreign! If I were pretty it would be obvious what Orhan sees in me so that she could brag to her friends about how Orhan had found me and brought me here from America. I'm not. If I could talk to her and cared to talk about the things she's interested in I might win her over. I can't. If she needed more physical help and I could provide that, she might at least be grateful. She doesn't. She has servants. If she were gracious—seemed to care about making me more comfortable in any way—she might succeed. She isn't.

But then there is Dede. I adore him. More and more I can even talk with him. He is not only a gentle man, but he clearly cares about me. He cares about introducing me to the things I really want to know in Turkish culture—its archeological history, and his mystical branch of Islam, the Sufis. He says when Nermin leaves he'll give me a consolation prize. He'll take me to Karatepe, where there are ancient Hittite ruins. (He knows the Turkish woman in charge of the site.) I know enough Turkish now to enjoy a trip like that with him. And the next time his Sufi group has a time in which they perform their ritual—that includes whirling, he says—he'll get permission and take me to the ceremony. (He calls it *zekir* in Turkish and I don't know exactly how to translate that, but it's a ceremony where they chant and repeat the names of God.) He says we may have to wait a while for that, however, because since their master died without leaving a deputy behind they have not found a new leader.

I have another problem. I think I wasn't at all realistic to think I could figure out if I could live in this culture in only these three summer months. I think I need at least six, but I can't expect the International office there at the U of W to wait for me through the autumn and the busiest time of the year. Don't know what I'm gonna do about that yet.

I've rattled on long enough. I'll stop for now. Take care of yourself. I seem to have a lot of help taking care of myself. (In an odd sort of way.)

Love to you, Anne

****

Dear Daddy,   September 1, 1960

How goes it? I am picturing you getting ready for your fall class schedule. Soon I'm due back to help meet the new International students. But it's odd. I'm not ready to come back yet. I'm just not ready to cut this culture out of my life before I'm more familiar with how it goes for its natives, and might be for me. I don't feel I've given it a fair chance yet. I have little feel for the things about it that could be rewarding for me.

Orhan is trying hard. Last evening he took me to an amazing event, both for me and for this town. He claims the educated folk of this town really enjoy Western classical music, but they can't get enough of it. He brought, as you know, a number of 33-rpm records when he came back. So...he arranged for a room at a place rather like we might find in the basement of the public library in Seattle, for a record concert! He set up his record player there and invited all the educated elite of the town who wanted to join him to come and listen to recorded Western classical music. Some people even brought their records as well, and because there wasn't time to hear everything, and because every one seemed to like it so much, people agreed to schedule another evening like this. A Turkish version of a classical music concert. I loved the evening, and I loved Orhan for making it happen. It gave me still more of a sense that he really is trying, both for himself and for me, to make me want to marry him and live in this town.

What, oddly, and maybe most importantly, I think I'm beginning to feel growing in me is a sort of sense of common humanity. Orhan's family has a doorman who doubles as his father's chauffeur and he's married to a very sweet woman who is the family's maid. They live on the lower floor of this apartment building. Tonight their baby died. I saw the child—a little girl named Dursun about eighteen months old and too weak to have ever begun to walk—this afternoon. What shocked me most, I guess, was that here was a child starving to death with plenty of food in the house. Her mother doesn't seem to understand that at this age she needs something besides breast milk and grapes, which are the only other food her mother claimed she would eat. It was probably the grapes that gave her the diarrhea that took her. Ali, her father, claims she's been weak since the beginning, and of course I don't understand pediatrics enough to put together what might be the right diet for her here in Turkey. Somehow this death hit very close to home. It shouldn't have happened. When you get that close to life and death in a country, it's hard to think you don't belong in that country.

Then there's Dede. No one knows better than you, Daddy how I've always needed a father figure. Well…Dede is almost old enough to be your father, but as I am able to talk with him more and more, I really like him. Old people can be terribly conservative, and in many ways he is immersed in the past. Still, his values are just the ones I appreciate about Turkey. Sufism, being mystical, is probably the kind of Islam that I can feel the most affinity to—its basic tenets seem to be very much in harmony with the more universal elements in Quakerism. Sometimes we're just silent together. Tonight when Ali came to tell us the baby died, Dede could see I felt terrible, and afterward we just sat in silence together while Orhan went somewhere with Ali.

Still, there are so many of the big things I miss here. I'm not talking about how I crave a hamburger—Turkish cuisine will always make up for food lacks. But can I ever mix socially with those same women who were at the concert Orhan organized the other night and talk about anything that has any real interest to me? How can you talk about music? Although the appreciation of it is the best social evening I've had here so far. Will I ever have a woman friend that I can speak with about ideas? values? Not that I had that kind of friend at home, but I felt there was the possibility for it. I don't feel that in Turkey. I'm just hoping this country might surprise me that way. I haven't been here long enough to expect that kind of mutuality yet, though, and it's important to me.

These things are all very subtle, and I'm terribly glad I've come here to try to get a handle on them. I just haven't got a grasp yet!

I know I miss you…bad! And I love you, good!

Anne

CHAPTER TEN
ONCE THERE WAS A CHILD WHO WASN'T
SEPTEMBER, 1960

The road into Sam Koy in September was two dry, hard ruts, and would remain that way until far into the autumn. Orhan aimed to drive in the ruts without swerving. The hardened mud should not scrape the bottom of the family's 1959 Chevrolet. The car slipped out of the ruts only briefly as he drove slowly on the three-kilometer stretch from the main road into the village, but that jolt unseated the small coffin perched on the back seat between Dede and Anne.

Dede had insisted that even though women were not customarily present at burials, Anne should be allowed to go with Ali, Orhan, and himself to the burial. It was in the village where Omer Asim Bey owned most of the land, and his proprietary feeling about it added to his certainty. Anne would surely want to see something of village life. He had asked for and received Ali's permission to take Anne in the back seat along with the coffin. This foreigner—an infidel but a gentle woman—would honor Ali if she was with them, even though the priest might not welcome her at the burial itself.

With the jolt, Ali turned to inquire of Omer Asim Bey if the coffin had shifted and made the two passengers uncomfortable. The comfort of this old man whose station in life was one he could never hope to attain was important to Ali, and Anne's comfort was important to Orhan.

Out of the corner of his eye, Orhan saw Ali take out his *tespih* and with his long fingers begin to fiddle at the beads. These were no mere "worry" beads. At a time like this before the burial of his daughter Ali was repeating the names of God. Orhan hadn't seen him fingering his beads in the city, but he wasn't certain he didn't. In the city Orhan saw less of this young man, since he was his father's chauffeur and Orhan himself seldom wanted someone else to drive him. He wished now that he could think of something reassuring to say about Ali's baby daughter, but he didn't know what that would be, and was relieved when Dede spoke. "A sad errand we're on, Ali Efendi. The next time we'll hope our women will help Hatije eat better during her waiting time. There's no reason why she shouldn't have a stronger, healthier baby."

"I think that way, too, Omer Asim Bey. For me, this baby died six months ago when she was a year old, and I saw she was weak. Village girls need to be strong. It's Hatije who is shaken by this death. Last week when we brought the baby here to the village for the lead pouring Hatije took strength from each view—that row of poplars down by the stream bed, still green in this dry season…the water piped so it is clean as it is now."

"If you have to plant your daughter in the earth, village earth is best," the old man said quietly.

"I had no faith in last week's lead pouring. I went instead to find the *hoja*. But this priest is new in the village and I didn't know him. His turban was askew and his shirt was dirty. When I asked him what amulets to use he only shrugged and said, 'If *ecel* is coming for your daughter, eh, it's coming.' When I told him I had faith in the power of the Koran he seemed annoyed, but he told me to make three amulets. I was to write one to put under the threshold, one to put around the baby's neck, and one to put in her bath water. That last had to weigh the same as seven Korans. I paid him. I had no faith, but I paid him."

"To do it without faith is useless," Omer Asim Bey said quietly, and Orhan listened with interest. Orhan had eschewed what he thought of as the superstitions of his grandfather's Islamic faith, and now his hunch was that his grandfather, also, gave no credence to this business about amulets.

The car hit another bump, and the coffin shifted again. Ali reached behind to steady the crude wooden box perched on the back seat between the old man and Anne. "*Sagh ol,* Orhan Bey," he said. "I appreciate the transportation help. It would have been a long walk to the village with a coffin."

"One day, villagers will have their own cars, like in the U.S.," Orhan said "One day—" The car jolted again into a rut when Orhan removed a hand from the wheel, and he put two hands back to right the car before he continued. "One day we will educate our own engineers and technicians and manufacture our own steel and make Turkish cars!"

Omer Asim Bey threw back his head and clicked his tongue. "Not just me, but your grandson, Orhan, will be in his grave before that happens!"

"If we're going to have progress, Dede, you have to believe in it."

"What's progress? Cars are handy, but the back of a donkey's more reliable. What's the hurry?"

Orhan, having thought Anne could not understand Dede's Turkish, was astounded when he heard her say in Turkish, "I agree." But then he realized he wasn't sure if he was more startled by her Turkish or her agreement. "We shouldn't argue on the way to a burial. Later, sixty years too late, I shall invite you, my grandfather, into the twentieth century."

Ali appeared to be embarrassed by the respect they were showing his daughter. "Go ahead, argue! What is progress?"

"For me," Orhan began, "progress means lots of things. Healthier children, more education, better houses, more cars. Would you like to have your own car, Ali?"

"Where would I go? I'd like more money. Then when I need one, like now, I could hire a car. I look at that hill," Ali motioned to the back of *Duluk Baba,* the high hill between Gaziantep and Sam Koy, "and I want to re-visit the tombs that are up there. Without a reason, I don't go there, and when I did go there as a boy there wasn't a road."

"For you, to visit those tombs," Dede said "is to re-visit your past. For me, it is to dig into history. Still, the journey I want to take is the journey into my heart—to find what it all means."

Orhan chuckled. "Is that why you visit all the archeology digs you do?"

"Maybe not..." Dede shrugged. "Don't ask me to be consistent. This much I know. When we start moving faster in this country we'll leave behind some of our best heritage. Who reads poetry with this much rubber tire between him and the earth? You young fellows go off and fall in love with technology and forget the rich life we've already got. Look at those fields of ripening wheat. The grapes will be coming..."

"Yes, but Omer Asim Bey," Ali was careful to remain respectful, "You often speak of the village as some ideal place. Why do you think I left it? There's no work here if you can't work the land. And what villager who works the land appreciates it? We are ignorant."

"*Estaghfurullah!* Don't talk like that!" Dede interrupted. "You're not ignorant, Ali, and there are others like you. You don't always know why you know something, but you know it."

"But to educate villagers—broaden their sense of their own potential—that can't rob them of their natural wisdom," Orhan persisted.

"I want to educate the villager. You know that," the old man countered. "But it isn't the villager who gets robbed of his dignity in clamoring after the West. It's you young intellectuals. You reject your past and recklessly want another future. You waste your intellect on technology. You make our culture seem adolescent, shallow."

"But our past has much to get rid of: Islam's corruption, our attitudes about women—" Orhan began to hope that Anne was not understanding this talk. Still, he would have been happier to know which parts she was able to understand.

Dede had interrupted. "Yes and there's a heap of good to winnow out of our past and take into the future. You want so much to be Western that you've lost your sense of history. Wisdom is neither non-Turkish, nor all ancient. We have it right here! In our homeland!"

Enlivened by the argument and embarrassed that he should feel so enlivened on the way to a burial, Orhan shook his head. "But in this age with all that Turks must do to catch up, the passive search for wisdom we've already got is a luxury. I say we have to leave that to old men like you, my grandfather." Orhan wanted to turn and grin at Dede, but the road prevented him.

"Nay...progress is different. Every time a child is born, progress has to start all over again. Each child has to start out fresh on the road to becoming what a human being can be. You can't pass on that kind of progress."

Ali sounded confused. "Don't some humans pass on the good that's in them?"

Dede sighed. "Don't know. Some people catch it; some don't."

"I'm confused," Ali admitted. "Orhan Bey's kind of progress is easier to understand. I could learn mechanics, but I like better the way my father spent his time. He was a shepherd. He had time to learn poetry, sing. I have no voice to sing, but when I was with my father, he sang and played the horn, and I wandered the hills." Ali pointed again at *Duluk Baba*. "I often went to those tombs. They say some foreigner dug them out and found they had already been robbed. The tombs themselves with their round stones at the door and the stone coffins inside are still there. When my father had his flock near them, I used to go to them. They were cool inside, and when I shouted they did strange things to my voice. I liked to think about the families that were buried there and what they must have been like. I was crazy over ghosts—old ghosts were even better. I thought I could make myself see them in there."

Orhan stopped the car. They had reached the open space near the fountain in the village. Three village women squatted at pipes protruding from two stone walls built at right angles. From three pipes of the six flowing the women caught the water in their jugs. Though the water flowed fast, the women appeared to be settled for a long wait before they could rise with a full jug. Meanwhile, through the car's open window he heard them prattling with each other in their harsh, high-pitched village tones.

Ali got out of the car and spoke back in the open window. "We just passed the graveyard. I saw no signs that a fresh grave had been dug. Last night I sent word to the *hoja* we'd be coming. Now I'll have to find him, see if he's ready. If we have time I'd like to show you my father's headstone in the burial ground. He deserves a big one with a turban…but" and the villager was off.

"I remember Ali's father." Dede said. "I can still see him, his cheeks puffed out playing the *zurna. Zurna* players have powerful lungs and Ali's father's wind was famous even among *zurna* players. At weddings, at harvests that man was able to play—blow in, blow out without pause—for hours on end. Ali told me that when the day came he could no longer play the *zurna* as he thought it should be played, he made up his mind to die, and he did. *Ejel* had come for him."

"No need for us to sit in the car while we wait. The sun will move and there won't be shade for long under this tree. The water in this village comes direct from the ground. Let's have a drink." As he spoke Orhan fished a water bottle from the back seat. Dede and Anne got out and hesitantly approached the fountain. Orhan followed them and as they approached one of the women, seeing his bottle called to them. "The water's good. Take some," she said proudly, indicating the pipe. Orhan filled the water bottle and took the first swig. It tasted pure, cold. Dede explained that he had recently encouraged the villagers to pipe their water by putting up some of the money himself. Some of the poorer villages, he explained, were not so progressive as to protect their water by piping it from where it left the ground.

Disturbed by the attention the car and its three occupants attracted Orhan was uneasy when the village children began to cluster around them to stare. He had not thought ahead. There was no way he could leave Anne alone while he joined the ceremony at the mosque. It would have a good deal of kneeling and praying anyway, and in this instance when he didn't much know the child who had died, he would feel awkward. He decided to ask to be excused and take Anne on a walk through the village.

When Ali came back, he brought three friends with him and Orhan excused himself observing that Dede would not be the only man to help Ali carry the coffin to the mosque.

As he and Anne started up the packed earth path between the courtyard walls of the village houses, he recognized that anyone who came through any of the wooden doors in the walls and met them on this path would think that he and Anne were married. He liked that idea.

"How do you say it. 'For practical purposes?' Anyway, what I mean is that people here in the village will think we are married. I will not ask you what you think about that. I will tell you it is true, though." He was uncomfortable asking if he could take her arm, so he took it. She seemed to give it willingly.

The sight of donkey droppings, the odor of every kind of animal manure in that dry mud corridor going up the hill, embarrassed him. Nothing about a Turkish village but the air could be called clean, and when odors like these floated into the air, it could not be thought of as clean, either. The path running between the walls—wide enough for perhaps two animals to pass and no more—was dry in this season, but in its center were dry rivulets which would run muddy and smelly in a wetter season. They reached an opening in the path where a woman sat in the center of a pile of dung—probably from cows—carefully fashioning patties with her two hands, which she plastered on the wall beside her to dry. He glanced at Anne. What would she think of a woman forming dung patties with her bare hands?

"They use it for fuel don't they?" she said. He noted she said no more. No comment about the bare hands or the wall plastered with dung patties.

"You heard that talk about progress. It would be progress to bring electricity, or maybe some kind of natural gas to the village. For fuel these women shouldn't have to form dung patties with their hands. Villagers should be able to use animal manure for their crops, anyway. Even when it's prosperous, life's too hard in the village!"

"Still, I can see why Dede waxes romantic about it! Those women at the fountain were spontaneous, welcoming—" Anne stumbled on one of the dried ruts and Orhan caught her by tightening his grip on her arm. They walked on.

"I wish we knew someone. I'd love to go behind one of these doors. I'm sure there's more to be seen than dung patties."

Behind those wooden doors there were stables, and above them the living floors of the village houses, but Orhan hesitated to speak with any of the villagers, masquerading as a young husband as he was. Pretension never felt right. Besides, although villagers were forever friendly, he felt foreign enough that he was never sure what should be said to them. Every stranger in a village was considered a 'guest of God,' he knew, but that presumption was awkward. Dede could do it. He owned so much land in this village. But to pose as a guest of God was too much of a pose for Orhan, and he hesitated. If he were in some way their employer, that would be another matter. They passed a place where a faded *kilim,* its colors further dulled by dust, hung over the wall. Anne paused to look at it. "How are these used?"

"If a family's well off, they cover the floor in their living quarters, even the *sedirs* where they sit, with these *kilims.* When they can't afford so many *kilims,* they cover as much as they can—woven cotton's better than mud to *walk* on. No one wears shoes in the house. Most people have thick-wooden-soled sandals to wear where they need them in their courtyard. Shoes are only for coming out into the world. I wonder if many women even have them. I don't know. When we get back to the fountain, observe. Most of the women will be wearing sandals. They wandered further, and met only one woman going to the fountain who greeted them with a nod of the head and a stare. Since Anne's head was uncovered, the village woman looked at her strangely. Orhan decided to turn and go back.

The woman making dung patties sat beside her work, still, but she took their return past her as a reason to stop. "Welcome to our village," she said. Anne caught her phrase and answered with its traditional reply: "Glad we're here." Hearing Anne beside him speak Turkish made Orhan feel pleasantly proprietary. He decided, however, that it was not acceptable for him to say anything to a village woman he didn't know, and since Anne could speak so little more, he guided her on. For himself, he nodded in a way he hoped the woman would think was cordial. The chances that the woman had heard and noticed Anne's accent were unlikely.

He spoke further only when they had moved on down the path out of hearing distance. "Now you know why these people need progress.

They need electricity, machinery for harvest...many things could make life easier. You've seen one more reason to bring Turkey out of ancient times."

"What I wonder about is their life as a community. Do they help each other...or do they compete and back-bite?"

"I have no idea. Dede knows them better. I commented once to him that villagers looked strong, healthy to me and he said that's because the babies that are not born strong don't live. Darwin taught you Westerners about 'survival of the fittest,' and here in the village, life teaches it to them."

"That woman must surely build up her natural immunities. One couldn't exactly call a pile of dung 'good clean dirt' I admire both her tolerance and her skill."

"Village women have many skills. I wish we could get you inside one of the houses to see women rolling out their huge, thin bread patties. They do it with a long rolling pin."

"How come you've seen it?"

"As a child, I used to come here with Dede. He thought I should know something about village life."

"Your grandfather's a remarkable man."

"He'll show you a lot of Turkish life in the time you're here. The longer you stay the more he can show you. You know, he was the one who insisted that you be invited today. It's not a woman's thing, burial ceremonies. Ali warned us you probably wouldn't be welcome at the actual ceremony today. He knew the village priest—*hoja* they call him—would not want you there. I don't like that about Islam. It isolates women as if they hadn't equal powers of understanding to men."

"It's good of you to see it that way." Anne hesitated. But—"

"I know. You don't know if you can live in a country that treats its women that way. Well modern Turkish men are better. Some of us have tried to break through our culture—reject that part of it. But we're not supermen. We don't always see ourselves well enough to get rid of those old cultural ways. Often, I catch myself thinking in the old way. All I can say is...I will try."

Anne said nothing, nor could he tell what she was thinking and they had arrived back at the village fountain. Waiting there, were Ali, Dede, and a group of younger men, Ali's friends. Since they were waiting for him. Orhan couldn't avoid going to the mosque with Ali and the other men. "I'd guess you'll be most comfortable waiting in the car. We'll go now, but the prayers won't take long. You can go to the car and sit to wait. Don't let the little boys who gather round to stare bother you. They won't be thinking of you as human. You are just some kind of curiosity for them to gawk at—a new happening in their village, as is the car."

"I'll pretend it's the car they're gathered for."

"Good attitude."

When the men had carried the small coffin to the village mosque the ceremony began with Muslim prayers. Orhan had always felt uneasy kneeling, bending touching his head to the floor in public. He reassured himself now with the idea that his fellow Muslims were too busy practicing their own ritual to notice the awkward way he practiced his. That idea didn't help. He didn't like praying in this way. Might be better to do what Anne said she did at her Quaker meeting, sit in silence, if he were to pray at all. No chairs to sit on in a mosque—only *kilim* covered floors, ripe for kneeling. At least the *hoja* made the ceremony short. Only a child, a girl at that. The six men went to the burial ground, lowered the small shrouded body into the tiny grave hastily prepared for it and took their leave. Ali excused himself and left them. He would walk back to the city later.

When they returned to the car they found a stately *shalvar*-clad woman standing beside the open window of the car speaking with Anne, and when they departed Dede insisted that Anne stay in the front seat where she had sat to wait for them.

"I had a great time," Anne said. "That woman you saw beside the car came and shooed the children off. She was forceful. She kept saying '*Ayip, ya!*'"

"That means disgraceful."

"I guessed that, because the little boys slunk off and she stayed on. We couldn't speak much, but she protected me while she rattled on. She told a whole string of stories. I caught only a few words, but I can pretend I get more. While I nodded and smiled I stole looks at her headdress with all the coins dangling from it."

"I'm not sure, but I think that was the *muhtar's* wife."

"Who's the *muhtar*?"

"The village head man. He probably got wind of your being there and sent his wife down to be hospitable. You had a better time than I!"

"We'll have to teach you how to pray better," Dede had strained to hear their conversation and when he could not, he still felt he wanted to quip.

"As long as you don't insist I actually pray!" Orhan spoke loudly to accommodate Dede's hearing. "Dede… Do you think Ali's O.K.? Is it all right to leave him to walk home?"

"He wants to see his friends. Besides, he needs time alone to come back to himself, that fellow. I'd guess he feels relieved and is confused by his own feelings. The worry and uncertainty that child has caused is ended. He'll feed on this evening's long shadows. The heat and dust will make him all the happier. The 13 kilometers back to the city won't be long enough."

"I'm hungry. Mother said she intended to keep Hatije's mind off the fact that we were burying her daughter by keeping her busy cooking. Maybe we'll have *ichli koefte*." Orhan grinned before he caught himself. Anne might think he was callous. Maybe he was. "Could be all sorts of interesting things for dinner," he said, thinking he was ravenous.

CHAPTER ELEVEN
ONCE THERE WAS AN ANCIENT TIME
OCTOBER, 1960

"Dust and bumps. This rotten road is finished and we're here," Dede said, as Ali stopped the car at *Karatepe*. "I think you'll like this place. Otherwise I wouldn't have brought you all this way." The old man climbed carefully from the back seat of the family's Chevrolet, and Anne followed. Aiming to remain in the shade Ali eased the car into a space between a huge boulder and a clump of pine trees for the four or five hours they would be exploring this Hittite archeological site.

Anne adjusted her jeans. The heat of the road had made pants increasingly uncomfortable in the car, but for climbing around this site as she would be, she was glad Orhan had suggested she wear jeans. For the first time in Turkey she was wearing pants. Nermin, who wore jeans around the house, had suggested that they were not to be worn on the street, and taking that cue, while in Turkey Anne had made a skirt and blouse her habitual garb. A skirt was cooler. Her jeans in these three months had become tighter and made her think about what Dede had said to Orhan before he'd brought her here: "I want to fatten her mind. Feeding on the past is what she needs—to eat ideas, feed on a sense of history. We'll stuff her like grape leaves with ancient carvings, poetry. Let her burst!"

Now she had countless questions: How…why did the Hittites settle in this mountainous terrain? The countless huge boulders must have been here in ancient times, but what about the weather-beaten pine trees? If the Hittites dominated Asia Minor from 1800 to 1200 B.C. how many times since then had these scrubby pine trees burned off and come back? A site as high as this would be easier to protect. Who were the Hittites' enemies?

At a promontory where they could look out over the valley below, they paused. "The people of this site were probably later than the period when the Hittites dominated, but these stones were uncovered only recently and archeologists don't know too much yet," Dede said, taking Anne's arm. "Come *Amerika-li kiz.* I want all your first looks to be taken beside me." He guided her toward a tin-roofed, open shed where a collection of huge carved rocks, some slabs, some chunks, lay haphazardly beneath the sheltering roof. Other pieces had been assembled outside as if they were waiting their turn to get in. They wandered aimlessly under the roof which Anne decided was a kind of overstuffed open-air museum.

"Hittite carvings are one thing. Hittite statues another," Dede said, waving at a carving opposite them. "The statues have a rough, blocky, over-sized quality. The carvings depicting scenes have a more refined touch." He pointed to the main figure on one of the carved slabs. "Enormous noses must have been a sign of greatness—intelligence. The important men all have huge noses." The scene on the carved stone was of a feast where the big nosed King sat eating, fanned from both sides with what looked like palm fronds. "They—" Dede stopped. A woman was coming toward them. She wore pants with a brown shirt and a tattered European sun hat over her scarf. "Here's the important person here. She can tell us about the Hittites." He spoke still louder so that the woman approaching would hear him, and afterward muttered to Anne under his breath that he could not remember her name.

"*Hosh geldiniz, Bey Efendim.*" The woman shook Dede's hand first, then Anne's. Her hand felt rough.

Dede asked how the excavation was going and the woman told them her small crew was almost ready to stop working for this autumn. She would be leaving soon. The woman spoke English to Anne when Dede introduced her. "We're piecing it all together only gradually," she said. Then she turned to Omer Asim Bey, and asked in Turkish, "Is it not more impressive, now, Bey Efendim, than when you saw it last?" She suggested they browse in the shed and then go out to see the gate, and the old man took Anne's arm and urged her out of the shed, as if they were going to the gate. When the woman had gone he guided Anne back to the shed.

"I didn't want a stranger around to spoil your spontaneous reactions. You've now met a Turkish-educated woman who's using her education."

"How did **she** happen?" Anne asked.

"Probably raised in Istanbul with highly educated parents. Women like her exist in Turkey, but men are baffled by them—don't seem like women to us. I think, however, she's married. Orhan may have heard about such Turkish women—maybe even known one when he went to school in Istanbul. But there are none he could meet in Gaziantep."

With his usual diffident manner, Ali approached the shed and Dede called to him. "Come. These carvings are important. You must see them."

The villager heard several of Dede's stories before he said. "*Abo*, what a job! You mean men can be paid to dig here?"

Having ambled through the clutter in the shed, the three of them moved out to the gate. It was not a swing gate, but a series of stone slabs arranged to line a wide passageway on a bluff overlooking a bend in the river below. The scenes on the stones told a story. On either side stood lion-like beasts of stone and beside them continued a row of stone slabs some one and two meters high. Each slab had either flat-carved figures or chiseled hieroglyphics carved into its surface. Omer Asim Bey pointed to a stone and said that when he was last here he'd been told this stone with its cuneiform writing had been found to tell the same story in two scripts. Ali squatted beside the stone to study it, and after several minutes touched it with the tips of his fingers in awe. When he rose Anne took her turn kneeling beside the stone. When she ran her fingers over the symbols, they were not only rough to her fingers, but so cold she was startled. "If I had some kind of mystical powers I might decipher these meanings by touching the symbols," she said reverently.

Dede watched, approving. "For sure, you get more connection with the past than if you stood back and looked." He bent beside Anne to touch them himself. "If these stones are removed from this setting, crammed into some junky museum, people will lose the sense of the people who carved them. I like to touch them. Rub them. Get them into me." When Anne rose from the stone, he took her arm again and guided her out to the end of the gateway. "Now let's look at the stone lion! Life was rugged for the men carving these beasts. But the men carving must have sensed that the figures they chipped from stone would outlast their lives. They were making a permanence bigger than anyone's pain. Of course stones by themselves would endure, but carved they would endure with a story and that story would tell the dreams of the men who carved it." Dede shrugged. "Maybe they didn't think that way, but I can't believe they didn't have some sense that their work would be timeless."

That idea, Anne mused, that a stone carving in itself will be timeless goes against our Western idea that the individual is all important. She wished she had the Turkish to speak this idea, but she didn't. These ancient workmen must have wanted their work to last because the carving in itself was important, not because their work had their name on it. It didn't.

Dede spoke as if to himself. "Stones stay around long enough to speak of those who carved them. I look at them and see a man's sweaty face, but he is nameless. There must have been long dull hours in the carving, but there must have been men who sensed the magnitude of what they were doing. The stone was lifeless, but the carver could give it eyes, albeit dull ones. The life was in the eye of the carver." He shook his head. "Now centuries later, these carved eyes, dead as they are, still remind us of the kings and carvers' eyes that glittered once." Then he looked at Ali. "Life's topsy-turvy, eh?"

Ali answered in a voice too low for the old man's deaf ear. "*Hichten geldik, hiche gidiyouriz,*" from nothing we came, to nothing we go."

"Eh, what was that!"

"Nothing. *Bey Efendim.* I was just thinking of Yunus Emre. Yunus wrote poems; these men carved stones. My father played the *zurna*. Men find ways to hit at nothingness."

They had reached the outer point of the reconstructed gate, and Anne suggested tentatively that they eat. She wanted to come back later by herself.

Ali and Anne went to get the food from the car. Omer Asim Bey chose a picnic spot under a tree. They brought the *kilim* and he supervised the spreading of it. The only space he'd found in the shade overlooking the valley below was cramped and rocky, but the view would have to mollify the hard feel of the rocks. As Ali and Anne were spreading the *kilim* and laying out the food, Dede said, "I'm the big-nosed King. I'll watch. You two do the work." Anne made a small pyramid of the *ichli koefte* Hatije had made them. The ten football-shaped patties piled one on another looked like short fat cigars. She was glad they wouldn't taste like tobacco.

When she offered Dede a glass of the lemonade she'd asked Hatije to put in for them, he hesitated. "Lemonade? With a meal? Never eaten a meal on the ground with anything to drink but water! You try my olives, I'll try your lemonade!"

"Turkish olives make me think of shrunken heads. Do I have to?" She held out a piece of *pide* bread on which Dede placed two olives. "Who wants a shrunken head? You Ali?" She tossed her head asking that question, and noticing the gesture Dede frowned, and she was uncertain why.

"I do," Dede said. "But I can't drink sweet lemonade with salty cheese. Crazy!"

"That's the difference between you and me!"

"More difference than our sense of taste," the old man offered a sly grin.

"Long live our differences then! But please I can't swallow this olive!" Anne tried to spit the black thing out with a hand covering her mouth, but discretion was impossible. "What about the lemonade? Ali, would you take it again on a picnic?"

"Only thing better would be water." Anne in noting that Ali's deference had vanished saw Dede was frowning again, and recognized that the old man might think she was being too flirtatious. She was relieved when after the meal Ali got up, excused himself, and wandered off.

Anne settled herself without clearing up, sitting where she could lean against a pine tree. The dry air smelled of pine needles. "How is it that you care about the past, Dede, and Orhan doesn't?"

"*Eyvah!* What a question."

"Maybe there's no answer."

"There most certainly is an answer. You should know it." Dede shouted.

The old man spoke loudly naturally because of his difficulty hearing, but she also wondered if he thought she would understand better if he shouted. "Orhan's generation is the first one growing up after Ataturk changed us overnight. Can you think what it was like to go to bed one night using Arabic script and by law the next morning be required to use the Western script and a new alphabet?"

"*Aman!*" Anne was proud. She had not only understood what he said, but she'd found the right word to exclaim.

"There were many changes like that around 1923 when the Republic was founded. Orhan wasn't born, of course until the mid-thirties, but he was born into a changed world. Ataturk emancipated women—said we ought to rip off the scarves covering their faces, educate them!"

"Poor you! Suddenly you had to look at women's faces!" She dared to joke with this old man and it felt good.

"*Aman.* I didn't mind! But I was too old to admit it. Orhan's generation was the only one that could admit it. They took up Ataturk's cause and clamored to be part of Europe. Everything that had kept Turkey from being part of the West was bad, corrupt: religion, technological backwardness, education based on memorization of the Koran. They wanted everything to change all at once. When you're in a hurry—and that generation is—you make slashing choices. They haven't time for Turkey's past."

"But—"

"Yes, but!" That's what I tell him. He's not ready to hear our 'buts' yet. We have to be patient with him."

"But he's impatient."

"He'll learn. You wait. Turkish intellectuals of his generation are going to learn. I know it."

"If I could be sure of that…" Could she dare to speak with Dede about her sense of the way Turkey isolated her? If she chose her words carefully… "You have to understand something about me. I had a wonderful childhood. My parents, like Orhan's were well enough off and able to give me every educational advantage. As a child I didn't care about other people, I cared about books. There was always a library as a hang-out for me. Librarians were my first mentors. I devoured books by the shelf full. I would pick a subject—rocks, say—and read everything I could find about it. I adored living at my own edge."

"*Aman.* That's your country. Here there are few libraries. Even Turkish boys couldn't do that."

"Then when I was an adolescent and needing my friends, I had another great chance. My parents were," she paused to find a gentle way of describing her mother and father who had each shunned the Catholic and Quaker faith into which they were born, "…not very religious. There was this man who worked specially to help the adolescents understand religion at the church where I went with one of my girl friends. When I began to break away from my family as most adolescents in the U.S. do, I bounced right into the charge of a minister at the church. He became like my father, so that at this adolescent time when I most needed certainty, answers, I had them in a kind of rational religious faith."

"What's a rational religious faith?"

"I don't know what I mean by that. It just came out. I had a liberal belief. I thought I had all the right answers. They made sense. It wasn't so much the faith I clung to, it was the church youth group. I can still hear that minister's soft voice telling us what we could do to keep our teen-age passions clamped beneath our tight clothes."

"*Eyvah*! Tight clothes. No good!"

"We were all supposed to stay chaste! Go no further than kissing.

This man drew whole hoards of high school kids to the church each Sunday evening to think about 'boy-girl relations.' Imagine going to the church to learn about wholesome sex!"

"The old man shook his head. "*Eyvah!* A Turk like me never even uses that word in mixed company. Can't get my mind around that one."

She had said too much. She had come to feel that in Dede mercy was understanding, but she could have overtaxed his mercy. She wouldn't describe all the odd-ball boys she'd given her heart to. He'd never believe that it was a matter of pride with her to remain chaste. "I'll say no more. I don't want to strain your sense of the believable."

"Oh, I believe you. Not because I believe what you tell me is possible, but because I do not want to believe the opposite. There's a Turkish saying. 'Don't say impossible; the impossible is possible.'"

"I got to college and had to conquer a new world. I thought I had all the answers—at least intellectually. I was too cocky for most young men in the U.S. They mature late anyway. So…I'd had friends in high school—I had the church group for my social life—but in college, I was an intellectual and religious. I frightened the men." She paused. "Remember, in the U.S. we choose our own partners, and we want to date when we get to college, but the harder I tried with men, the more I frightened them."

"You would have frightened me!"

"As old as you are? I might have frightened you!?"

"I don't know." Dede still seemed playful. "I'm a Turk. I can't translate my reactions to the U.S. I've never been there."

"You've at least tried to imagine how I feel. But I sense you resist what I'm telling you like water resists my body when I'm swimming. Gently. I've had other resistance since I've been here and its been rock hard." She paused. Had she said too much? She glanced at Dede, but he wasn't looking at her. "I know about water and I love it. I joined a swim team when I was socially so unhappy in college. I practiced swimming and competed in swim meets and filled all my time with study and rugged exercise and forgot about being a misfit."

"How did Orhan find you, then?"

"I'd finished college when I met Orhan. Besides he was foreign. He needed someone to take care of him. I helped him and for me he was exotic. You never saw your grandson as a foreigner. He was very different."

Dede looked at Anne, puzzled. "You really seem to have all the answers."

"Oh Dede, it's all bluff." She shook her head. "I'm used to having the answer so I talk as if I do. But I don't. I really want to make it in this country. But I don't know if I can. All my life, learning has been my biggest pleasure and now I don't see how that could go on here. The only thing that makes me feel I'm learning here is the fact that, though its a struggle—slowly like this—I can say all this in Turkish."

"Eh? You can't see yourself living here? I can. Make yourself a bridge. Be the connector. Connect Turks and your people!"

"Pretty grandiose, that idea! I've only just begun to learn the language."

"I'm talking about just being here. Being here you become a bridge, like it or not. You don't have to say anything. You're important. We have a proverb: 'A man is slave to what he says, sovereign to what he does not.'"

"*Eyvah*! How Turkish it is to have a proverb which speaks only about men! I'm a woman. I don't want to be sovereign, I just want to have more say."

"Clever woman! You take words and twist them into new meanings. Now you better let me have my after dinner sleep. I don't think I've ever been spoken to by a woman so forcefully. I didn't think I'd like it, but I know I like you. I'll go to sleep and think about it." Dede grinned at his own idea.

Anne rose. "Yes, I want to stand up. Shake myself. Wander around." She was exhausted from so much speaking in Turkish. Flies buzzed about the remains of the picnic on the *kilim,* but just to move seemed a relief. She would come back later to clear the picnic, not disturb Dede now. Still, the cheese needed wrapping. The olives needed to be put back in their container. Silently she did what needed to be done with the food, spread a napkin over the basket, then wandered back to the shed to look again at the carvings.

The banquet scenes carved in stone reminded her of the pictures of ancient Egyptian figures she'd seen. All the figures were in profile, none in full face. She reached out to touch the figure who was clearly the King and drew back, sensing it might be irreverent. Instead she touched the bare chest of one of the palm bearers. Where were the women? Wandering through each of the rows she found a figure clearly recognizable as a woman who appeared to be suckling a small figure standing beside her. Otherwise her headdress and skirt looked very much like those the men wore. What did this say about whether women were honored among the Hittites? She would have to read more.

For a long while she lingered, imagining herself into that other world. Then she moved slowly out to the gate, and ambled along that row of stone blocks. Some of the slabs were too high to see over. The carvings of animals—square-limbed, heavy horses and lions—seemed more powerful than the representations of humans. The suggestion of movement in the stones with depictions of horses and chariots excited her.

To glance at the lower side—the side of the stone slabs that might have greeted oncoming travelers in Hittite times—she moved to the end of the wall made by the row of block carvings. As she moved around it, her foot slipped and she fell off a two-foot drop below the outermost block. Her ankle twisted under her, and pain ran up her leg. To break her fall, she had thrust the palm of her hand forward. When she lifted her palm she saw it was bloody. Tiny rocks pressed into the lacerated flesh. Her hand hurt more than her ankle.

Oddly, the sight of the wound sent a rush of what seemed like joy through her and she held the hand out against the blue sky. It became only a shadow, a silhouette against the sky and was transformed. It was not only painless, but weightless. The pine trees behind it became feathery and delicate. The blood on it became invisible, eclipsed by the dome of the late summer sky. As she held up her hand and realized it was painless, she wondered if this hand could be suggesting something about living in a strange land. This land was not her land, nor was it the Turk's land. It was a land where human beings had been planted to act as stewards of whatever they found here. It was a land where she could be as much one with the forces beneath it as the Hittites had been. She had fallen on this earth, rocks might have wounded her, but what was a tiny wound in the grand scale of things? On this mountain, ages back, Hittites had both flourished and fallen on these same rocks? And this fall had given her a deeper kinship with those who had lived here.

Lowering her hand she lay still in the spell of that illumination. If she tried to move, she might learn that she could not move. Her ankle throbbed, but not so much that she needed to know what had happened to it. The world struck her as bathed in some kind of sacred light.

At length—she had no idea how long it was—she called to Dede, and her shout broke the spell. She called his name countless times before he and Ali appeared coming around the end of the stone wall above her. "What's happened?" The alarm in Dede's tone told her she must look worse than she knew. She tried to move and could not pull her leg from under her. "I've hurt my ankle. It might be broken."

"*Aman, aman.* It must hurt."

"Not badly, it's numb. I can't move."

"*AllahAllaha,* I'm sorry. What will Orhan say? I've let you hurt yourself."

"Dede!" she said sharply "How could you have prevented this?"

"*Eyvah!*" Carefully, he lowered himself to sit beside her.

"Don't blame yourself—it's an accident. It may even have been fated!"

"You, a Westerner, talking about fate? That I should live to hear it!"

"Here we sit talking about the meaning of it all," she said casually. I think we better get me to the car. Could Ali carry me?"

"He should bring the car first. I'll go for him. You stay here."

Anne grinned. "I promise I won't move."

It seemed a long while until the old man came back with the young one. Her leg had gone further numb. The spell of the illumination had worn off.

"I'm sorry to make all this fuss," she said glancing at Ali's face. Clearly, he was embarrassed.

His picking her up aggravated the pain and she put her arms around the doorman's neck and when she hid her face against his shoulder, she thought she saw Dede wince. Formalities, taboos? Oughtn't they to disappear in times of extremity. Ali carried her back to the car and Dede trailed behind.

"If you'll put me down and let me lie here on the *kilim*, I'll rest and wait until we're ready to go. Let's not spoil the trip."

"*Aman,* you **are** crazy! We will put you down while we fix the car so you can have your leg high—only that long." Ali was sent to find two straight branches and cut them free of greenery so they were bare sticks.

Because the woman in charge of the excavation might have medicine for pain, Dede left Anne sitting, and went to find her. She might also, he explained, know more than he about what to do initially with injuries.

Anne glanced again at the carved animals. The lion looked fierce. Before lunch she had thought this same lion had appeared inebriated.

Dede returned with the woman in charge. She brought aspirin, and was uncommonly agitated. "This has never happened before. Never. Never," The woman repeated her words. "I'm so sorry, so sorry!" Ali came with water and the woman helped Anne drink from the goatskin. "You'd better have two aspirin. It's a long road back to Gaziantep." She looked at Omer Asim Bey, who was now carefully washing Anne's hand. "Will you take her all the way, or do you want a doctor in Osmaniye?"

"Please. Let's wait until we get home where we know doctors. There isn't much pain," Anne pleaded. The woman wanted to know how it had happened and Anne was relieved to be reminded she spoke English. She told of the incident in English, all except the illumination, for which she could find no words in any language.

Dede arranged the sticks in the back seat, padding them with the *kilim*. Again Ali picked Anne up. This time, in the presence of another strange woman, Anne felt embarrassed to put her arms around his neck.

Traveling, finally, downward on the bumpy road Anne was relieved that she had no need to speak. The car moved slowly down the mountain. They had almost reached the asphalt main road when a new idea came to her. She had thought she might need more time in Turkey, and now the decision was made for her. Whatever was wrong with her leg, she would need to stay and give it time to heal. The bumps in the road shook the car miserably. To distract herself she thought about that strange moment when she was at one with a world that seemed ancient and wonderful after the accident. What was that experience all about?

They reached the paved road and the bumps nearly ceased. It was dusk as they started over the mountains and the view of the grassy hills as the car began to climb seemed familiar. "I like the brass color of the light at this hour. Somewhere off there is a castle Orhan was going to take me to."

"But it's only as old as the crusades. Compared to crusaders the Hittites make a better adventure! You've proved it! But I have to say, I can't understand how you stay so calm."

Anne hesitated. "After the accident…I had an incredible experience. Suddenly the world was beautiful. I was beat up, but… history was beautiful."

"You **are** an odd one!"

"Maybe this country has sharpened my senses. I want to read now—read all I can about Hittites, and come back to Karatepe. I just hope, I hope I haven't ruined your trip."

"Ruined? We got there didn't we. Can't say I'm not worried about what Orhan will say, though."

"*Aman!*" Anne tried to reach a hand forward to touch Dede's shoulder and couldn't. "You mustn't worry that Orhan will blame you. He knows me well enough to know I do what I want no matter what I'm told to do."

"*Eyvah,*" the old man shook his head. "We're learning that about you, yes. You're proud of it. We are baffled."

CHAPTER TWELVE
Medicine Never Was Once like the Western World's

The Kurdish women with their tattooed faces and orange and scarlet clothing were too demonstrative in their suffering, too loud as they sat on the bench across from Anne and Orhan in the waiting room of the American Hospital. They embarrassed Orhan. At one point they burst into shrieks when their male patient uttered a loud sigh, and at another time one of the women even keened her misery. He was grateful for the stoicism of the others waiting to see the doctor. They were probably his fellow Turks.

Hatije had reported that Anne had been restless. As the only woman in the house besides Selma, she had been asked to stay with Anne in the apartment upstairs through the night. As early as they could expect the clinic to be open Orhan and Anne had come up the hill to the hospital. Orhan's patient had not complained about having to wait until morning for medical attention, and was still behaving remarkably. Hatije who was ready in the night to provide anything the injured guest needed, had said Anne appeared to be in pain, but had asked for aspirin only twice. Now, Anne showed no sign of being in pain, but she had said almost nothing to Orhan. He was allowed to go with her when she was taken in a high-backed wood and wicker wheelchair to a windowless room where there was an X-ray machine. As an aid lifted her onto the table, she winced but her over-all quiet manner, her calm, amazed Orhan.

They returned to the huge, high-ceilinged waiting room and sat side by side on plain benches, leaning against the stone block wall. Awkward it was, bringing this foreign woman here and treating her as if she were his wife. Good, however, that Gaziantep had an American Hospital, a mission hospital that had remained in the city long after its Medical School for Armenians had closed its doors. He was also relieved that in this clinic waiting room (frequented only in emergencies by the educated families in his social circle) he had seen no one to recognize and greet him. The reputation of this hospital meant that the first recourse for medical needs the educated in Aintab explored could be right here in this city. Only later, those who could afford the expense and the time went to Istanbul or Ankara for Western-trained medical opinions and treatment. In any case, among the educated in Aintab most medical affairs were dealt with surreptitiously. Since in Anne's case she was not really his wife, he felt still more secretive about bringing her here, but Istanbul was a long way away. This hospital's treatment would have to be good enough. He felt more protective of this woman than he could ever in his life remember feeling about any one or any thing. He had brought her to Turkey, and Turkey's rugged terrain had laid her low.

This was a remarkable woman. Her unwillingness to blame anyone for this accident amazed him. "What good does it do to find someone to point a finger at!" she'd said. "Does it make the pain less acute, the wound heal faster?"

"I am really sorry," was all that came to Orhan to say.

"Odd. Nothing's real. Ever since this happened I've been in Turkey, and not in Turkey. My leg's numb, and I'm in a new country doing things I've never done before even in my own country. I had a strange experience when it happened. I was there, yes really there on *Karatepe*, but I was in a Hittite world. An ancient, beautiful world. That's all I can put into words about it—ineffable. And now I feel I'm moving about inside a coating of clear plastic—a kind of plastic balloon. Nothing's real."

"You should have made me take a psychology course while I was in the U.S. People kept saying things about themselves I didn't understand. Americans seem to be masters at what you call introspection. You use that word as a matter of course, but I have only just learned what it is."

"Odd you should say that. I've missed something here, but I couldn't put my finger on what I missed. Maybe it's introspection. Not here, but nudge me when you're feeling introspective. We can talk."

An aid came back with the wheel-chair: the X-ray showed the ankle was broken. Anne was to be taken to the operating room to have a cast put on. When she asked the American doctor if it was going to be possible to have a walking cast, he had frowned from under his bushy eyebrows, run his hands down the sides of his spotless white coat, and informed her that regretfully, they were not set up to provide her with a walking cast. She would have to get about with crutches. At least, to talk about her medical problem she had not had to use Turkish. Orhan had brought her to the city's only English-speaking doctor whom he had only recently heard about, and was curious to meet. This doctor had come only a year or so ago. Now again Anne had astounded him at the stoic, but intimate way she had spoken with her own countryman. Good thing this American was already married.

As they put her cast on, Anne chatted as if she'd had countless casts applied to her leg. "What will happen to my job? I'll not be able to go back for at least six weeks." Later, she asked, "What am I going to do with myself for these immobile weeks?"

"We'll have record concerts more often," he promised. "Somehow we'll get you English books to read."

Did she mean it when she said softly, "It's a good chance for me to read in Turkish." Then she had another thought "But what about exercise?" and discussed with the doctor her concern about gaining weight.

"You'll exhaust yourself just navigating up and down stairs," the doctor indicated the crutches. "Your underarms are going to feel it." Orhan was surprised that this American doctor would speak so intimately to his patient. By comparison Turkish doctors were taciturn.

Later Anne asked if Orhan or his mother knew a woman who could teach her the open-cut-work embroidery they do in Gaziantep.

"If I did, I am not sure I would let you do it," he said. "Bad for the eyes."

"I already feel protected, Orhan. Be careful not to over-protect me."

"You mustn't feel like a Turkish wife!" He joshed and at the same time railed at the irony. Would that she did begin to consider herself a Turkish wife!

At home again, Anne struggled to the front steps with crutches. (They had had to wait while the hospital's carpenter sawed off one of several sets of crutches in the hospital storeroom.) Then, as she made her way slowly across the marble of the outside entryway, it occurred to Orhan that she would have a worse struggle to climb the three flights of stairs to the family apartment. Crutches took skill and there was no way he could help her with them. He had been able to support her this morning on the way to the hospital when she had half limped, half hopped down the hall stairs. But now she would be on her own with new crutches. Chagrined, Orhan asked Ali to make a chair with him. The two men joined hands and with their four hands together aptly lifted Anne up the first flight. If the press of her body gave Orhan an erotic kick, what was it like for Ali? Maybe he didn't recognize his own feelings.

At the top of the first flight of stairs, they rested momentarily on the landing. They had started up the second flight when Orhan stumbled. Anne would have fallen back down, except that Ali, with quick agility scooped her into his arms, lifted her high, and carried her on up to the landing between the second and third flights. Orhan, when he recovered, looked up at the villager waiting there with Anne in his arms, and tried to hide the shame churning in him. Uncertain he had succeeded, he waved Ali on up the stairs to the door of his family's apartment.

Had his mother waited dinner for them? Would she be civil to Anne? He knew he couldn't expect her to be sympathetic. Someone other than herself was seizing the stage with health problems.

Selma complained that the *pilav* had gone cold waiting, and the vegetables were overcooked and mushy, but her refusal to speak to

Anne was what caused Orhan the real chagrin. Selma had heard Anne speaking Turkish with Dede. Clearly she knew Anne would understand if she did speak. But this injury had somehow made Selma more sullen. She said nothing at all to Anne at the table.

Dede spoke nearly non-stop. He described the way *Karatepe* had changed and developed this time as compared to the last time he had been there. He recounted a tale about how the carvings might have come about. And when he had been speaking an inordinately long while—Orhan suspected he might be making up a tale—the old man told about a Hittite King, whom he claimed with a grin, had a "dangerous lack of inhibitions."

"And why don't you tell us about our princess—her lack of inhibition?" Selma interrupted her father's story. "Tell us!"

"I was working up to that," Dede paused for drama. "Nermin has…written me a letter. She never writes me. I guess she thought I would put a good face on her news, make it softer. But she miscalculated. She thought that what an old man tells you, you will not mind. But I can't make hard truth soft. My age teaches me nothing about how to do that. Does any decent girl of good family announce casually to her grandfather that she herself has found the man she wants to marry? Does she?"

"She wants to leave school!?" Selma added.

"Nermin!" Orhan nearly shouted. Were they speaking of his baby sister? "What does she want to do that for?"

"To be married. She thinks she wants to be married." Abdullah said grimly.

"Oh, no!" Anne spoke in English.

"You knew something about this?" Orhan asked in English.

"No. I did not. But Nermin told me something that helps me guess."

"What we have to do is go to Istanbul." Selma broke in to command. "And Orhan you have to go with us."

"I can't do that! I can't leave Anne in this state."

"Dede will remain with Anne. We will leave our car, hire another, so that Ali can drive those at home wherever they want to go. We have talked about it. Dede is willing."

"But I can't do that! I'm needed here." Orhan rose and walked away from the table.

"You are more needed in Istanbul. We will go to see this man she wants to marry and you will have to be our spokesman." His father remained calm. "You will have to explain to him why he cannot marry our daughter."

"What? Why?"

"He is an American. An archeologist! We cannot speak his language. You can!"

"You think we could persuade Nermin to explain to him?" Selma scoffed.

"We have made the arrangements. We will leave tonight and go as far as Adana. Nermin told Dede this man is leaving the country. He's worked here since last spring. He'll work here again, but he's going to England for his research now. Nermin wants to be married and go with him. If this man is going to leave the country and Nermin is going to go with him, we have to act fast."

"We have to talk to the young man. Tell him he cannot marry her. She's too far away. We must bring her back here."

"You have to go, Orhan. Don't worry about us." Anne spoke again in English, but the Turkish speakers understood from her tone she was releasing him.

Abdullah looked at Anne and in Turkish said, "You are most kind at this time to let us have our son. I think you must understand how much we need him."

Orhan was again astounded at Anne. In Turkish, she managed to say, "I agree. You need Orhan. I look forward to being with Dede. We will have a good time!"

When dinner was finished, Anne asked if Orhan would join her for coffee in the sitting room, even if it were briefly, before he went to pack his things for the trip. He owed her the granting of that request. Besides, after the kind of morning they had had, he wanted to sit, to quietly drink the coffee. Only to be quiet would restore his sense of balance. His mother had gone to begin packing the things she and Abdullah would need. Abdullah went off to the factory to settle things for his absence. Dede went for his usual afternoon rest. They were alone.

"I detect something you may not see about all this," Anne began.

"What do you mean?"

"This guy is an American. I am an American. There's some sense in which your parents are holding me accountable for all this."

"They couldn't. How?"

"Well, I did know about this American!"

"You did!"

Nermin told me about him when she got a letter from him about a month ago."

"A letter!"

"She showed it to me. It was all of five lines, completely innocent. He wanted translation help which is what Nermin had been giving him in Istanbul."

"Why didn't you tell us about this?"

"She trusted me to keep it a secret."

"But didn't you know there would be hell to pay if Nermin has anything to do with him?"

"Of course I knew. That's what I'm saying. I feel right now some of the hell there is to pay. I don't break my word because I'm afraid of paying hell."

Orhan put down his coffee cup, jolted by a sense of the dilemma Anne must have faced.

"I did tell her I thought her dreams were a big mistake. Intercultural marriage was something she should consider carefully before she dreamed about it."

"A mistake is it? A mistake it would be if you married me?"

"That's not what I said just now. That's not what I told Nermin."

Abruptly, Orhan shut his mouth. He had nothing more to say, especially in English.

On his way out to the factory, Abdullah came back into the sitting room. Sensing an awkward silence he paused, then spoke to Anne. "I did not ask you before. Was the medical care satisfactory this morning?"

"It was quite all right, I was pleased to be able to speak in English to my doctor, and I liked him."

"Glad to hear that. He's only been here for a year or two. My wife and I paid his family a welcoming call—that was what is expected of us. We had a son in his country, after all."

"Anne might like to meet his wife," Orhan speculated.

"We met her. She seems pleasant. Yes, when you get back, you must arrange for Anne to meet her." Abdullah said, and left.

"Now I'm certain your parents connect me with this crazy dream of Nermin's!" Anne's voice shook.

Again, Orhan tried for the right words in English. "Maybe it is this way. I think my parents are very angry with me for considering getting married. I was not supposed to do that. They had a young girl of a good family in mind to ask for me—the family in fact is among our dearest friends and I know the girl well. It's not that I don't want her. I want you."

"But because you've disappointed them by bringing me, I think I disappoint them as well. When they blame you for Nermin, I am part of that."

"There is psychology again. What is the word, subtle? It is all too subtle for me."

"Go off. See what you find. I'd be willing to bet that Nermin herself has hatched all this up, that the young man hardly knows a thing about it."

"You cannot mean that."

"Yes I can! I saw his letter. There wasn't anything in it to make Nermin dream as she is. She reminds me of me. She gets an idea and lets her imagination go wild."

"My father dotes on Nermin. He will never believe that it is not this ogre of a man who has got us all into this. Impossible. He can't accept that his daughter could do any wrong."

"There's where psychology's missing. I won't argue. Go and see."

CHAPTER THIRTEEN
ONCE THERE WAS A TIME THAT WASN'T

The dry heat-waves shimmered in the air as Anne and Dede moved slowly back to the cooler marble entryway. Orhan, Abdullah, and Selma had just pulled off in a taxi going to Adana on the first leg of their journey to Istanbul. Anne had asked for help descending the apartment building's stairway so that she could wave the family off, and when Orhan had suggested that was too much to do on crutches, she suggested that it would show his parents that she didn't object to being left on her own. "Besides," she said, "I like having Ali carry me back up the stairs." Orhan gave her a dark look which was only partly playful, then added a promise to telephone her the following evening. By that time he and his parents would have reached Istanbul, seen Nermin, and know better the facts of the situation. The car the family had hired pulled away.

Anne turned to Ali beside her expecting he would carry her again. But Dede raised a hand to indicate he disapproved of Ali's picking this woman up. "Wait 'til you're inside the entryway," he commanded. It made sense in Turkey that no one should see Ali take a woman, particularly this foreign woman who was supposed to be Orhan's wife, in his arms. Once they were inside, Ali carried her as if she were a lifeless stone rather than a female body, and Anne wondered what all the fuss was about. Still, she admitted to herself, she didn't understand all the nuances of the way Turks reacted when they observed men touching women.

Having negotiated two flights of stairs, Ali stopped outside the family's apartment to wait for Omer Asim Bey. From her perch, Anne glanced down the stair well at Dede. He seemed to be climbing with inordinate difficulty, and her concern for the old man crowded out any speculation about this culture's ideas about sexual innuendos between men and women.

Dede caught up with them on the landing, and removed his cap. His sparse hair was moist and matted where the cap's band had skirted his head. *"Eyvah,* its been years since I've had to amuse a young lady," he said, winking at Anne. "Ali, help me! Go down town and collect the names of all the films at the cinema houses. Take a pencil. Write them down, and if there's anything other than half-bare-bosomed girls on the poster telling about the film, write that down, too. You got a pencil at your house?"

"No, give me one. I'll do it, Bey Efendim."

Dede turned to Anne. "Do you think you'd like to try a Turkish movie house?"

"Let me have a snooze. Then I'm up for anything." It had already been a long day, but she would make it longer rather than be rude and ignore Dede's concern to keep her entertained.

As Ali opened the door of her apartment, Anne had another idea. "Bring a chicken from the market, will you Ali? I'll roast it tomorrow. Make Dede an American meal." Ali looked at her blankly as if to be privy to her plans was not part of what this doorman considered part of his job.

Later, she was awakened by Ali's knock and what sounded like the squawk of a chicken. When she had negotiated the distance to the door she found Ali standing on the landing, a live scrawny brown feathered bird, bound at the legs hanging from one huge hand.

"What do I do with that?"

"Kill it, prepare it for roasting." Ali grinned, amused at her surprise at the state in which he delivered the chicken.

"Weren't there chickens to be bought already killed?"

"Villagers bring them live like this. If they don't sell them, they take them back home. I can kill it for you."

"Yes, kill it. Then what?"

"You dip it in hot water and the feathers can be pulled out. You want Hatije to do it?"

"I want Hatije to help me—tomorrow. What's Dede decided about a film?"

"He wants to go to an early show. Hatije's making a soup for your supper."

The wooden floor of the movie house creaked as they entered. The lights were not yet dimmed. Anne maneuvered into an unattached wooden chair, which groaned and shifted as she sat down. The crowd around them was young, a few swarthy *shalvar*-clad village men, countless boys in their early twenties, a very few women with their families, wearing proper coats and scarves. Waiting for the film to start, she and Dede cracked and ate the squash seeds he had bought. Others around them also pulled the dried seeds from the small paper bags they came in and cracked them with their tongue and teeth. Anne tried and decided the skill needed had to be acquired. She couldn't do it.

The lights went down, the film started, and she entered yet another world. The film was an Italian comedy. It was both odd and difficult to follow dubbed-in Turkish coming from the mouths of Mediterranean-type actors, but the film would have been that much more strange if she had heard Turkish emerging from a familiar Hollywood face.

Dede seemed restless. "You feel that draught?" he wanted to know. She did and asked him if it bothered him. He turned his collar up for protection, and claimed it didn't.

The movie was a situational comedy, and Italians, she decided, knew how to be funny. Little language was required to follow the plot. Anne laughed a lot and forgot to notice if her companion was equally amused. When the story of the film got more tangled, Dede laughed as well, and for the rest of ninety minutes it was as if they had both forgotten where they were until the screen was once again plain silver and the lights came up on the people-cluttered, garlic smelling stuffiness of the movie house. With the lights on, most of the crowd sat docile waiting for the next film. Anne and Dede and a few others filed out. Dede flagged a taxi, and on the way home they were silent until Dede asked again if she had felt the draught.

"We should have moved out of it. I enjoyed myself a lot. An hour and a half in which I had not one thought of anything other than what was on the screen." She tried and found it difficult to explain in Turkish that the accusations Orhan's family made at midday dinner had lost their sting. Dede appeared to understand.

"See here! *Amerika-li Hanim.* You forget the things they said. They'll get things straightened out. My daughter is like her daughter—they're two schemers. But the mother will get her way. When Selma wants something, she turns to iron to get it."

"That doesn't mean I won't be blamed for starting it." Anne struggled again in Turkish.

"*Evvah.* They're not seeing straight. One chat with Nermin and they won't blame you. They want to think of her as a sweet, shy Turkish girl, but God love her, she's bold, crazy-blooded—obsessed with being different. She's the spice in our lives, but we should know she's difficult once she gets a taste of independence." Dede reached over to pat Anne's knee. "Don't worry...It's as well you couldn't go to Istanbul. If you're not there, it'll be hard to put the blame on you."

Anne noticed he had patted her, and asked boldly whether affectionate gestures weren't taboo, surprising herself with her own audacity.

"I forgot you're not part of the family. Anyway, never pay attention to taboos. Don't think all Turks are culture bound."

Waiting outside the family apartment for Ali to open the door, Anne noticed Dede huddling and shaking. She saw his discomfort just as she remembered she'd left her scarf in the taxi and gestured wildly with one crutch for the driver to wait. The driver stared at her.

"Are you used to men's stares?" Dede asked. "That driver looked at you as if he's never seen a woman before."

Ali retrieved the scarf for her, and when she was once more gathered into the villager's arms, Anne said, "That taxi driver may never have seen a woman on crutches. It came to me the other day what people in the street must think of me, even without crutches—particularly the children. They must think I'm some sort of mentally retarded person. They don't expect me to understand when they giggle and laugh. I'm too different to notice. In the U.S. I liked being different. I didn't want to be ordinary. But now when it's impossible to be ordinary, I want to fade back into being just like everyone else."

Because she had spoken to Dede partly in hopes Ali would hear, Anne was disappointed to see his stony face show no register of understanding. Her Turkish could have been too awkward. She was disturbed again when she looked behind from Ali's arms and saw Dede struggling to climb the stairs. When she suggested that Ali put her down and help Dede, the old man protested, but while she waited for him on the landing, Dede accepted Ali's helping arm. "Are you all right?"

"Just slowed up," Dede said, breathless. "That draught must have got to me."

Before he went in the door of the family's apartment, Dede slumped back against the wall, his untrimmed beard bristling on his chin. "You won't be afraid upstairs alone tonight?"

"Sir!" Anne mocked dismay. "Did you think that all these months I have not been up there alone? I like it. Tonight I know that on each of the floors below me there's a man who would adore to slay a dragon to protect me!"

"Yes, but I'm going to sleep long into the morning. Get Ali to take you to the copper market for old pieces. Try a shopping spree."

Anne put her hand on his arm. "What is it about you that you know what women want?"

"My secret? You're asking for my secret? I try to think what sounds terrible to me, and that's what a lonely woman might like."

Anne said good night thinking that on the following day there was no way she wanted to go around the copper market on crutches. She was as eager for quiet as Dede. Besides, the chicken needed to be plucked.

She arrived in Selma's kitchen the next day in the late morning pleased with herself for having negotiated the stairs alone on crutches. Ali squatted, knees high on the floor of the tiny kitchen with the parts of the small kerosene cook stove spread out on the floor in front of him. He had found a small hole, he said, plugged it, and now expected the puffer would maintain its pressure and burn well. Hatije explained that she would now be able to boil the water to dunk the chicken in for removing its feathers. "It's when the stove won't work that I know I belong back in the village where a fire either burns or, if you don't have fuel, it doesn't. When you don't have fuel, you don't cook. Village life is better."

"We can learn this life. The baby will not die next time if we learn this life," Ali said gruffly. "This life's better. Next time Hatije will feed herself better and feed her baby better."

"What good? I either have milk or I don't."

"You mustn't talk like that. In the city people are more clever. If they can't manage something they find other ways. You have to be more clever in the city, that's all. You have to grow up."

Uncomfortable, hearing this kind of intimate talk between a man and his wife, Anne wondered if she should leave. But she had asked Hatije to help her pluck the chicken, and it wasn't right to leave her to do it all by herself.

"You can read." Hatije spoke to Ali, but this time she glanced at Anne as well. The two of them could read, and she couldn't. "How can I be clever? The city confuses me."

"You are not stupid," Ali raised his voice and again Anne wished she were not witness to his anger.

"I am not stupid. What I know how to do, I do well. But, I am too old to learn new things."

"Too old! You're only twenty."

"Teach me to read, then. Teach me to tell time."

Anne took Ali's glance at her as a kind of signal. "I could teach you to read, to tell time," she said, being careful to keep her voice low and calm. She glanced at Hatije and saw there were tears in her eyes.

"Don't cry. Don't. We're talking about how you can learn," Ali said, again gruffly.

"You've forgotten the difference it makes when you can read," Hatije said, simply. "I watch. When the city confuses you, you don't let it. I have lost two children, the last one because I was in the city. I don't understand many things."

The water was boiling. Anne could involve Hatije in thinking about something else. "How do I pluck this chicken, Hatije? I don't know. You do."

Silently, Hatije removed the headless chicken from its perch on the floor, fished out a large flat pan to place it in for its water bath, and poured boiling water over it. Ali left the kitchen.

When the chicken was prepared for the oven, Anne peeled potatoes, and asked Hatije to cut the cauliflower. There were only a few vegetables available this season for the Western style dinner she hoped to have, and cauliflower was one of them.

To rouse Dede to come and eat proved difficult. She sent Ali to call Dede when the food was ready. A very long time after she was at the table waiting, he appeared. The scrawny fowl's meat appeared to be difficult for him to chew—he moved his jaw only with great effort. The potatoes she had mashed were by her own standards too soupy, but Dede claimed they delighted him, being soft and easy to swallow.

Once the meal was over, the afternoon loomed long and too quiet, and Anne changed her mind. She would enjoy a trip to the copper market.

Ali stopped the car in an open spot in the shadow of the town castle. "The copper street is too narrow for this car. Can you walk?" he asked, before he remembered his passenger sported a cast.

Without answering Anne worked her way from the back seat of the car and maneuvering her crutches, started down the uneven cobblestone paved passage. Ali followed her thinking he might be needed. An old peasant woman squatting on the dung smeared cobblestones peered with red-rimmed eyes at Anne? Most of the shops were closed, their iron shutters still pulled down across their fronts as they had been for the mid-day dinner hour. Midway down the narrow inclined street she stopped at an open stall where a man was huddled over a tiny pile of hot coals. Piled helter-skelter on shelves behind him were a number of dirty, tarnished old pieces of copper. Inside the stall two boy apprentices and an older man etched designs on bright new copper. A grimy shirted man—was he the owner?—rose when she stopped at the outer edges of the stall to look, and hastily pulled a rickety wooden chair out of a corner. Then peering at the stained chair seat with a frown he spread his handkerchief on it. Anne thanked him and sat down. The chair shifted under her before it stabilized. "What have you in old bowls…perhaps candlesticks."

The man pulled out several bright new copper bowls to show her before Anne made him understand she was interested only in old copper. With this new aim he fished in a dark corner, drew out a bowl so tarnished it was black, and rubbed it with his shirt sleeve. He was able to uncover for display the design beneath the grime. "Feel that weight!" he said, handing her a bowl. "In the old days, they used heavy copper." Anne found it difficult to find the language to convince the man that she cared more for the design than the amount of copper in any one piece, and when he rummaged again he finally found two cone-shaped bowls. When he wiped them off, she saw that they both had attractive designs, and offered him a price she knew was too low for them both.

Since she was "special" he said he could sell them only at a price considerably higher than she had offered. At length, satisfied that she had gone through the formality of bargaining she agreed to the lowest figure he had asked and asked that they be polished and brought to the family's apartment. The tea the tradesman had ordered came and she sat drinking it while he lined up a row of tarnished candlesticks on the floor in front of her. Most of them appeared to have been made more recently from thin brass. Were candles available for sale in Gaziantep? The man admitted that he didn't know. In the end, she chose the candlestick that needed the least polishing and asked him to clean it up while she waited. Finally, having fished in her purse and withdrawn a crumpled set of bills, she let Ali take the packet, picked up her crutches, and worked her way over the uneven cobblestones back to the family's car.

When they reached home, Hatije appeared at the top of the stairs, her head-scarf askew, looking agitated. "Omer Asim Bey is ill," she said, "He looks very ill, but he says he will not have a doctor." She turned to Anne. "You must persuade him, *Hanim.*"

"But who do we call?" Anne turned to Ali. "Do you know?"

"Me, a villager. How should I know?"

"He's burning up. He asked for pills, but they did no good."

One look at Dede when she reached his bedroom, and Anne's hands went cold. His chest appeared to have caved in beneath the blanket. His bristly gray hair had gone limp and clung to his forehead. At first she tried to humor him. "You look as if you lost some battle!"

"I'm still fighting!"

"Don't you want help—the kind a doctor could give you?"

"No. What's that American phrase? Do it yourself."

"But this is something you can't do yourself! I'd like to call a doctor."

"No. I'll be better tomorrow."

"If you'll only tell us which one, we'll bring him here."

"Nonsense. I'm not so ill as to need a doctor."

"I think you're being stubborn. You're clearly very ill."

"It's an old man's privilege to be stubborn. I'm ill. I'll either get better or I won't."

"But..."

"If *ejel* has come it has come. If it hasn't, it hasn't."

Anne turned to Ali who had joined her beside the old man's bed. *"Ejel?"*

"He's right *Hanim Efendi. Ejel* is the day you're destined to die. That's the way we think."

"Death...? If you men don't know enough to be afraid! Dede...I beg you. Tell me the name of a doctor I can contact. Please."

"Later, if I am worse, I will tell you."

"That isn't good enough."

"Later."

"You promise?"

"I promise."

Using her crutches, Anne lowered herself to the edge of Dede's bed and felt his forehead. This old man lay bargaining with her like another rebellious adolescent!

"You're burning up with fever. I want to bring you an aspirin." He allowed her to give him an aspirin, and taking it with water he began to cough. His face went red. The veins in his forehead looked as if they would burst. Anne turned her head, unable to watch. It made her angry that there was nothing she could do, but she cared too much for Dede to be angry with him. Since fright appeared to have paralyzed Ali, she ordered him to the kitchen to ask Hatije to prepare a clear soup, and he left the room.

"Don't want soup. Want you to read me Yunus Emre."

"Read poetry? In Turkish? That should be Ali."

"He has work to do. You read." He indicated a small book on the table beside his bed. "Find one with a refrain. Easier to get the Turkish. Better music."

Anne took the book, opened it, and followed his instructions.

"Dust onume hubb-ul vatan, gidem hey dost deyi deyi
Onda varan kalir heman, kalam hey dost deyi deyi"...

She read on, understanding almost nothing of the difficult language, but catching a certain spirit from the refrain, *"Hey dost deyi deyi"* She guessed this repeated phrase was like an "Alleluia."

"It's about going to my death singing. I know that poem well," Dede said. *"'Hey dost deyi deyi,'* Hear the song in that?" The old man's voice came out as anything but a song.

"I wish I understood it."

"Doesn't matter. Catch the spirit!" Dede grew animated. She continued, reading mere words. *"Ten curuye toprak ola, tozam hey dost deyi deyi."*

"My flesh shall be dust, blowing on wind, while I sing *'hey dost deyi deyi,'"* Dede affirmed.

"That poem's about how to die!" Dede said in a voice that was almost gleeful, and awe overcame Anne. Had he no fear?

"You must believe in life after death," she murmured.

A long pause followed and she began to wish she had said nothing.

"I don't know. Is there life after we die? I don't know. But I know this: the people I see who die as if they were going to a great adventure are the ones I want to be like." He spoke with his eyes shut. She felt no need to comment. Carefully, she pulled her leg off the bed where he had made her put it, adjusted her crutches and rose to go to inquire about the soup. Tears blurred her vision.

In the kitchen Hatije was preparing the soup tray. She finished and Anne began to pick it up before she saw she couldn't carry it with crutches. Instead, she followed Hatije who carried the tray. Two people entering Dede's room created commotion. He didn't stir. When she spoke to say that the soup had come, he still did not rouse. Anne seized his wrist. He had a pulse, but he was unconscious. It had happened. They had to have a doctor and she had no idea whom to contact.

She sent for Ali and asked him to go himself up the hill to the doctor who had put her cast on, tell him what was happening. Ask his advice. If you can, get him to come. If he understands Omer Asim Bey is unconscious, he may be willing."

For what seemed an endless time she sat beside the bed waiting. When she could no longer sit doing nothing she picked up the Yunus Emre book and studied the poem she'd read before. She understood several of the lines, and tried translating them, making them poetic:

"One day from a scrap of cloth, they will make a shroud.

I'd fling off these clothes, wear the shroud, singing Alleluia."

The music of those two lines in English satisfied her. Most of the lines she couldn't grasp, let alone translate and get any musical effect. Dede had said the words were simple in Turkish. They didn't seem simple. But she could hear their music.

Ali came back with a different doctor. This man had an elaborate drooping mustache. What did his carefully styled mustache have to do with his profession? Since he had been willing to come when they needed him, however, and he seemed to know what to do she was grateful. He claimed the only place to treat the old man was the hospital. He was not in grave danger, he said, but he would be if he failed to get treatment. They needed to get fluid into him. The doctor promised to return to the hospital and send an aide with a stretcher to help Ali take him there.

When the doctor had gone, Anne went to the window of Dede's

bedroom and stared out into the back courtyard of the building. A headscarved woman in the yard next door dumped a bucket of water out over the packed earth. The water spread and formed a dark patch in the dust of the courtyard. Watching the water create that black earth, Anne felt herself encased by some kind of glass jar. Nothing seemed real except the late afternoon sun which glared from every surface it hit. Later, she watched Ali and the hospital aide, a man in a crumpled white uniform who was even larger than Ali, carry Dede downstairs on a stretcher and roughly, but with uncanny skill get the unconscious man into the back of the hospital's makeshift ambulance, a jeep. When they appeared to have finished, Dede was a limp hump and Anne felt compelled to get into the seat beside him and hold his head as gently as she could. Would he survive the shaking he would get as the jeep traveled up hill over the cobblestone street? So this was a Turkish medical emergency: a combination of crudity and skill at making do.

At the hospital the procedures appeared to be routine. The hospital personnel seemed to know instinctively that Dede was the sort of patient who required a private room rather than a ward bed, and once their patient was settled in a bed, Anne and Ali waited for nearly an hour on a hard bench in the hospital entrance way for news of him. Anne remembered during the wait that Orhan had said he would call as close to nine o'clock as he could, and grew anxious. She dared not miss a chance to let the family know what had happened. Her watch said ten to eight when the aide returned to tell them Dede was settled and they could see him.

Omer Asim Bey looked like a lifeless shrunken puppy when they were allowed back into his room. There was a crude metal rack at the side of his bed from which hung a bottle with a clear fluid and a tube running into his arm. He seemed restless, not quiet. Anne wondered how anyone could be at peace with all this apparatus surrounding them. She moved to the bed, careful to keep her crutches controlled under her arms, and noticing Dede's hand lay on top of the counterpane, she gingerly touched the back of it. He didn't stir. She had hoped he would show some sign of life before she had to leave to get the telephone call, but he did not.

Stealthily, allowing herself only fifteen minutes to get home before the time Orhan had promised, she left Ali with instructions to stay and bring word to her when it seemed right for him to leave. Maneuvering down the stairs on her crutches from the second floor of the hospital, she remembered that she had easily found Turkish words to leave Ali with instructions, and was proud of herself.

The taxi she hired let her off in front of the house and as she made her way awkwardly across the front courtyard, she remembered she had come away without making provision for getting back into the house. The family had an elaborate locking system, but Hatije, thank God, was at home.

She had just perched herself beside the telephone table when the phone rang. She picked up the receiver, but Orhan's voice came only dimly through the static. Turks never left out formalities, she remembered, as Orhan spoke his formal greetings in English and she heard them only as gibberish. She began to speak in English and realized she had been speaking nothing but Turkish for some 30 hours. English stuck in her throat. She said nothing.

"We have only seen Nermin until now. She is impossible!" The connection improved as he said the word "Impossible" and his voice roared in Anne's ear. "My father... horrified at his princess." Then the connection went bad again. She thought she heard the word stubborn, but could not be sure. She wanted to break in with news of Dede, but Orhan seemed too animated to hear anything beside his own news. "Say's she is not coming home. If they will not give her a proper wedding, she and this young man will go off and be married. Mother is so angry, she does not speak with Nermin. My father is so shocked he can hardly talk to her. I try to give advice and Nermin says 'Practice what you preach.' Proud she knows the English proverb. We meet the young man tomorrow. He may be easier, reasonable, do you say? I wish you were here. This family needs a stranger with us—to make us be polite to each other."

Disturbed about the suggestion she was a stranger, although she knew she was, Anne sensed it was the time to let Orhan know about Dede. But static filled the silence.

...."Can you hear me?"

"Yes...almost."

"Something has happened. I need advice."

"What? What? Talk more slow."

"Dede...is...ill."

"What?"

"In the hospital." she shouted.

"Yok janim! How?"

"He...he just... several hours ago. He wouldn't let us do anything until...well he went unconscious. Now Ali's with him at the hospital. I'm frightened."

"We should never have left you. I will start back...We will change plans...see the man sooner. I will come. Tell Ali to stay with Dede. Bring you news in the morning. I will call in the morning.... You need our number. Have a pencil?"

Anne picked up the stub that lay beside the phone and when he told her wrote: Saray Hotel. 1562 Istanbul. "Send love to Dede," Orhan said and she wrote "love" after the hotel's telephone number. To write that word reassured her.

She put the phone receiver back slowly and pushed herself up with her crutches. What could she read? She wandered into Dede's room to look, and found the Yunus Emre poetry. Opening, it fell to the same number, 89. The last lines jumped out at her.

*"Yunus Emre var yoluna, munkirler girmez haline,
Bahri olup dost golune dalam hey dost deyi deyi."*

Since there was no way she understood this poetry, she found her dictionary and looked up the words she didn't know. The construction was difficult. But reading was something to do. Translation might be a good exercise. She was no poet, but she could play with it, make it as poetic in English as she could. For a long while she wrote with the stubby pencil, trying different words, phrases. Finally she wrote the lines,

"Go Yunus, learn the way, like a diving bird
You shall surface in love's lake, singing Alleluia."

When the words were strung out with the right rhythms, she paused to take in the meaning, and was shocked. The poem spoke of love's lake, and that was death. Yunus had been writing about death and willy-nilly she was reading about it! The idea jolted her: Dede might find himself after death bathed in love and singing.

****

Dear Nancy, September 10, 1960

Thanks for your letter. In reading it I realized how eager I am to keep up with stuff in the States. I feel cut off when I don't want to be, and your letter helped. Keep'em coming, please. I'm going to be here longer than I expected.

Guess what I saw! A mountain-top with Hittite artifacts which probably date back to sometime a bit after 1200 B.C. The site is still in the process of being dug out. Orhan's grandfather, however, knows the woman who is in charge of the dig and he arranged the trip. It's the kind of site I'd never have the chance to see at home, and yet the Turks—all but a very few—more or less ignore it. Then I guess most people in the U.S. wouldn't pay much attention to it either if it were in their back yard unless they were archeology buffs. The wonderful sense of history I got wandering around up there was one of those occasions of a lifetime, only marred by a fall I took that meant I ended up with a broken ankle.

I think I told you about Orhan's teen-age sister Nermin. I really like her. She's spunky and just wild enough to set her own hair on fire! But she's put her foot in it now. She wants to leave school to be married, and that of course make's her parents see flames! Adding to their upset—but its not as if they wouldn't be upset no matter who Nermin chose without their help—is the fact that she wants to marry an American. Orhan has gone off with his parents now to Istanbul to catch their wild one, and cage her. So I'm alone with Dede. He took me to a movie last night to keep me entertained. Movie houses here are draughty barn-like places, but you can forget about where you are in a Turkish movie house every bit as easily as any other place you go to escape. I came out refreshed. For a space I'd laughed in another world.

Forgive this being short. I just realized I have to write my Dad and see if he can work the angles to allow me more time here without losing my job. Read between the lines and interpret that idea any way you're inclined. I don't know myself what it means. Write soon... Love you, Anne

****

Hello again, Daddy, September 10, 1960

It was good to have your news. I missed the Seattle summer, but now autumn is so lovely in Gaziantep—cool, clear and dry—that I can't say I miss Seattle weather any more. Not one bit.

As when I was at home I was not aware enough to recognize what a "new" country I lived in, now I am only beginning to be aware of what ancient ground I'm living on. Of course there were probably civilizations flourishing in North America at the time the Hittites were carving the stones and living the struggles I saw depicted the other day, but I'm guessing they did not leave the traces for us to find in their remains as so many civilizations here in the Middle East have left. At any rate, I have that wonderful sense of discovery; a sense that the world is richer than I ever dreamed it could be. It makes me very glad I met Orhan and came here, but I am no clearer as yet about whether I want to settle here, acculturate, and live here for the rest of my life. *That* seems a huge and lonely undertaking, and I haven't yet the guts to make that leap of faith.

However...I am going to have to live here longer than I'd planned when I left home and I'm wondering if you would help me by seeing if it can be arranged to be away from my job for perhaps another two months. On our trip to *Karatepe* to see where the Hittites lived, I climbed around without being very careful and slipped. I've ended up with a broken ankle. It is set, and has what I think we would call in the U.S. an old fashioned cast—they don't seem to arrange for walking casts here, even if the break is simple, as mine was. Instead I am toughing it out with my underarms growing as hard as leather and my crutches showing the scars of heavy use already. Big deal. Life is so easy in the house of Orhan's family that I scarcely feel my handicap—

except that the family has all, except Dede, gone off to Istanbul to put wrappers on their unruly daughter. With my leg, I was left home with Dede which would have been quite delightful if he hadn't fallen ill with something like pneumonia. This has taken him to the hospital and left me holding the fort. I am managing well, thank you, but suddenly I feel as if I am no foreigner as far as my obligations go, but every bit a foreigner as far as knowing what I am doing. An odd state of affairs, but one I'm intrigued to experience.

So, just imagine me living up to my new status! Let me know what they say in the International Student office. Let them know I very much want to be back there soon! Our English proverb to cover this is, "no use crying over spilt milk" If I can have my cake and eat it too, I would be very happy for the spilt milk. Love to you and, what should I say… honor?… to Bonnie!

Anne

CHAPTER FOURTEEN
ONCE THERE WAS A DAUGHTER WHO WASN'T...

A taxi carrying four silent members of the Demir family moved through the automobile cluttered streets of Istanbul. Here in this large city the streets were full of men and women who appeared to be villagers, but they seemed to know enough about traffic in the city to walk primarily on the sidewalks. Had they been in Gaziantep, the driver would have had to sound his horn steadily to clear a path through the crowds of pedestrians. This driver blew his horn only rarely, and it worried Selma. When the taxi stopped in front of a shabby looking apartment in *Besiktas,* she peered out at the building and sighed. Some Istanbul buildings had elevators. This one was only three stories, but she guessed she was going to have to climb stairs.

Having negotiated a narrow stairway and been admitted to this American man's two small rooms, Selma collapsed into the one comfortable appearing chair in his sitting room, and looked up warily at the room's book-lined walls. This man as a husband? What kind would he be? He collects books!? He performed the opening amenities well enough, but after those he had no manners! He left his guests alone and went to his kitchen to bring refreshments when they had been there no more than fifteen minutes. Had he no feeling for how much the

Demir family was honoring him by making this call upon him? Nermin wants to marry this man who has no idea how to receive guests!?

When he had left the room Selma turned to Nermin. "Haven't you told this young man that it is impolite in Turkey to offer food so early in his guests' visit? We've scarcely been here long enough to be settled in our chairs!

Nermin pouted. "Americans know how to receive guests! Why should Jim need to know about how Turks receive them?"

Selma grunted.

Nermin turned to her father. "What do you think of him?"

Abdullah frowned. "He is dignified."

"See! I knew you'd like him."

"But," Abdullah said abruptly, "he can hardly remain dignified if he carries you off and marries you after we've asked him not to."

"But *babam* he's a good person. I want him. If he leaves this country without me, he may never come back!"

"That is not what you told us. You told us his work was going to steadily bring him back to Turkey." *AllahAllaha*. Was this headstrong young girl Abdullah and Selma's daughter?

"You're the one who may never get back to school," Orhan added. "You can't leave school now and expect to come back!"

Selma sat straighter. "If you leave now, you won't graduate. All the effort, all the money your father and I have put into your school—for nothing?" She hoped her tone was commanding.

The young man came back carrying a tray with large cups. Turks would never use cups so large. What could he be serving in such huge cups? He reached Selma with the tray and it appeared that he had made the American Nescafe she had heard tales about. It looked like black-colored water. Selma concentrated on her disgust over his coffee and attempted to ignore this young man's good looks. Blond with blue eyes. By Turkish standards he was not only good looking, but his looks were rare. Orhan's friend was blond with blue eyes, but she hadn't the features to go with it—her nose was large. This man luckily, was also tall, but he was thin like a shred of *kadaif*. He was also a bit too lanky for Selma's taste. He knew some Turkish—at least enough to use

Turkish as he passed the coffee. But why didn't Nermin take the tray and pass it for him? Passing trays was women's work.

When the coffee was distributed and the formalities of social interchange were finished, Abdullah nodded at Orhan to begin with the questions.

"My father and mother have come to Istanbul because they have heard from Nermin that you and she wish to be married. Is this true?" Orhan began, in English.

Selma understood none of the English, but two things pleased her: Orhan's tone was of authority, and this young man blushed red and looked anxious.

"I think it surprises us both. But yes, we're beginning to think that way."

"As you know, there is a set way in Turkey to arrange marriages, and my father and mother are upset that they should hear of this for the first time by letter from Nermin."

The foreigner looked at Nermin with his question before he answered Orhan. "But… have they…heard already? It's…it's a new idea to Nermin and me. It wasn't supposed to get beyond the two of us. I had thought we'd make a decision when I came back to Turkey." His tone was as if he couldn't believe what Orhan was saying.

Nermin shifted in her chair. Orhan, whose hands had clutched the arms of his chair, let go. "Let me translate what we have said so far to my parents," he said, and turned to Abdullah. "It seems that the idea of getting married is a new one to Mr. Martin. He had thought it would remain an understanding with Nermin only. He hadn't intended anyone to hear of it until he left the country and came back. He seems upset that we have heard."

Selma disguised her relief with indignation. "Doesn't he know that one discusses such things first with the parents of the girl, not with the girl!"

Abdullah looked at Nermin with a puzzled frown. "Nermin, what did you mean by saying you were to be married soon? It appears Mr. Martin hadn't that idea."

"I'm sorry, *babam,*" Nermin spoke softly in Turkish, hoping Jim would not understand. "I thought he did."

Selma could not believe Nermin's change. She'd become a demur Turkish daughter again. "If I knew this young man better, I would be tempted to say the whole thing was your idea," Selma muttered.

Orhan spoke again, hoping to avoid an awkward translation hole. "My parents received a wrong impression. They are happy to see it was wrong. They want to know what your plans are, and when you are leaving Istanbul."

Selma decided whatever Orhan said had reassured this Jim Bey because he answered calmly.

"I'd planned on leaving in two weeks. That's when I expect to be finished collecting my notes for this phase of the project. I have work to do in the British Museum which I figure will take about four months. I'll be back this next spring to do more field work. I'd thought of coming then to Nermin's home. I'd like to visit your family."

Nermin turned red while her friend spoke.

Orhan translated and Selma was appalled. For nothing? Nermin had forced them to make this awkward, hasty trip for nothing?

"When I come to Gaziantep, I hope I'll meet Nermin's grandfather. I understand he knows something about Anatolian archeology."

"I hope you will be lucky enough to meet him. I found when I called this evening he's been taken ill." Orhan had elected to avoid telling his family about Dede so as not to add further anxiety to this pilgrimage. Now they could be told.

"What's the matter with Dede!?" Both Abdullah and Selma sensed some new alarm from Nermin's tone.

"I don't know what's wrong with Dede," Orhan continued in Turkish. "Anne says he's ill and in the hospital. I'll call when we're finished here again. Anne thought she'd have more news this morning."

"Dede, in the hospital? How did he get there?" Abdullah asked.

"Some doctor ordered him there. I have no more news than that. Since this business is nearly finished, I'll ask your permission to fly back home this afternoon. You can come when you can get away, then."

Abdullah assumed command. "You're right. Someone ought to go immediately. Yes. Telephone Anne. If Dede is really ill, of course we will all go. Why didn't you tell us?

I didn't want to upset you before coming here. If things had got worse, she has our hotel and phone number to call us."

"We ought to be there. We've come away and Dede is ill," Selma whined

"Until just a few moments ago, mother, you considered this trip essential."

Selma turned to Nermin. "*Eyvah!* I'm afraid to leave you, Nermin. What more will you dream up to push this young man into? My father may be ill, but you are crazy-blooded."

Abdullah was eager to keep calm in front of their host. "We will see what the news is when we telephone," he said, and turned to Mr. Martin wondering how much of their Turkish he had understood. "How do you like Turkey? his tone carried a false heartiness."

Orhan started to translate once more, but there was no need. The foreigner had understood, but he answered in English for Orhan to translate. "In my field Anatolia's a gold mine."

"You understood me. You have learned Turkish," Abdullah said cordially.

"Some. It's essential in my work. Nermin has helped and I'm grateful. I didn't expect to end up being so fond of my teacher." The young man's ears turned red as he spoke. Selma wondered what he had said. She had heard Nermin's name, but understood no more. Clearly, this young man was inexperienced where women were concerned, and his shy manner made him less forbidding. Selma found herself wishing she could speak with him, almost liking him. But why did he leave the coffee cups just sitting empty? Surely he knew that was not good manners.

Orhan stopped translating as his conversation in English with Mr. Martin became more casual. Abdullah sat without understanding and thought of a Turkish proverb. "There's a man who defeats all evil, there's a man who axes stone; there's a man who peels a raw egg, and there's a man who can't peel an orange." Which one was this Mr. Martin?

Abdullah waited only as long as protocol required before he spoke. "Forgive me for breaking in. Orhan will you tell Mr. Martin that the family wishes him well on his studies in England and that with his permission we will be leaving. Explain to him that we must telephone Gaziantep."

As they departed Selma assured herself that her father was surely made of iron. She was glad to have seen this Mr. Martin's apartment. He kept it in order. If he only didn't have so many crude village *kilims* on the walls above his many books, it might be an acceptable place. What kind of a family did he come from? How could she ever find out? Many things to look into regarding this young man. *Eyvah,* she caught herself. Was she accepting in some way the idea of Nermin's marriage to him. No! Nermin needed a good young Turkish man who would join Abdullah and Orhan in the factory. It was out of the question to consider her marrying an American. Thank God he was not insistent. The family had gained time to make Nermin think sensibly.

****

The DC3 over the Taurus mountains was buffeted by every gust of wind. Orhan sat, eyes closed, head back, feeling his stomach rise and sink at odds with the wind's punches. If he'd brought something to read he might have distracted himself from the ugly scene across the aisle where a small child, traveling with its young mother and father was vomiting into an air-sick bag. Instead, he stared out the small window at the snow covered mountains below: their blue shadows, their barren, treeless crags. Beautiful.

He had not been able to connect with Anne again. His telephone call didn't go through. He flew through the afternoon sky unaware of what he would find in Gaziantep. Surely Anne would have managed to telephone them in Istanbul, or at least she would have left a message if anything serious had happened. What was the English saying: No news is good news? In this case that was what he could hope was true.

It was strange to be flying home to Anne who was, in an odd way, behaving as if she already belonged to the family. But she didn't. She hadn't reminded him of the fact that they were not married for a long time, but she didn't need to. The precarious underpinnings of her presence in his family home made itself felt below every event, every discussion his family had had in these three months she had been in Turkey with them. Not even the best friends of their family knew that she was living in the apartment upstairs. He was certain all their friends thought he was living with her and they were as man and wife within the doors of his parents luxurious apartment building. He didn't even want to think about what the educated families of Gaziantep would think if Anne decided to go back to the U.S. permanently and he was left to find another wife here in this town where all his family's friends knew all the other friends of his family. It did no good to think about it anyway. What he had to do was to make Anne happy, make her so intrigued with Turkey and the possibilities which would open to her should she become his wife, that she couldn't imagine herself taking up life again without Orhan in the U.S.

Lately, he'd not done well at showing her Turkey at its best. He'd let himself get too absorbed at the factory in persuading his father that to introduce nylon threads and materials was the wave of the future. He'd been distracted. Now Anne was laid up, couldn't walk, but he could plan another evening listening to classical music with his friends—something, anything to make her feel less cut off from Western culture. Dede had made real efforts, taken her to an archeological dig; Nermin had taught her Turkish and gone enough places with her that she now felt at home on the streets of Gaziantep, but he was the one who could help her feel she knew more people with whom she had interests in common. So far he'd only made limp efforts at music. If Dede was all right, the first thing he would do once he was home was plan another evening listening to music. Yes, Orhan wanted Western classical music in his life, and Anne in her sense of isolation actually needed music and the people who went with it. He would make it happen.

Another wave of air buffeted the plane. After the jolt Orhan attempted to ignore the nausea he felt, and keep the food he had eaten in his stomach. He settled in to be stoic until the airplane circled around the Adana air-field and dropped to the airstrip. The jolt when the plane hit the ground was only an anti-climax.

On the far side of the small cement block airport, three taxis waited. Orhan peered at the drivers to decide which one had the best cared-for automobile and chose the driver of a polished, older Chevrolet. This man not only had a well-kept car that had been functioning several years already, but he was neatly dressed. Probably few accidents. He hired the taxi and went to pick up his bag from the baggage horse cart. Once on the road, he found himself staring at the neat patch on the shoulder of the driver's suit coat. This man had a wife who took care of him. She was probably a retiring, uneducated woman, accomplished in the domestic arts, but with no ideas in her head. Orhan reminded himself that he was no typical Turk. He wanted a wife who had ideas. He didn't care nearly so much about the domestic arts. He wanted Anne, a companion who might not sew his clothes, but with whom he could talk. She had sophisticated ideas. He had to convince her she would not be entirely cut off from her culture.

Since that first hot June night when he had brought Anne home, he hadn't traveled this road over the mountains. Now, the car had passed the snake castle and he had looked for the other castle, *Anavartza*, before he remembered there had been no chance for news while he was speeding home. Anything could have happened. He hoped Anne would be there with news, and not at the hospital when he arrived home. He didn't know the doctor caring for Dede since he wasn't the family doctor. He hoped this physician knew what he was doing. He also hoped Onol Bey, their family doctor, wouldn't be offended at the slight. Dede had been unconscious, unable to tell them anything about which doctor to call. Blame was irrelevant. Anne had handled the crisis the only way she could have. Orhan smiled. The way Anne set her chin when she was determined made him feel both protective and proud of her.

****

Orhan had the taxi driver wait, and when he discovered Anne was not at home, had the man drive him to the hospital gate. Reaching the hospital he was relieved to find, when he found Dede's room, that the old man was awake and mumbling to Anne who sat on the *sedir* beside his bed. Dede's teeth were out. He flung his free hand out to grab the side railing of his bed, and insisted with garbled enunciation that he was well on the road to recovery. Then, after only a few more exchanges, he asked that Orhan return in the morning with his water pipe, and made it clear he expected his visitors to leave. "The doctor's given you permission to smoke!?"

"No. But what's the good of feeling better if I can't smoke? This place is boring, and I can't find any peace here. I want the sound of the bubbles in my pipe to make it seem peaceful. I need a pipe to tell me to tolerate this place."

"But you don't need smoke in your lungs!"

"The water filters the bad effects of the tobacco—most of them."

Orhan paused and chuckled. "O.K. here's a trade for you. I'll bring your water pipe, and you promise you won't make your Islam too attractive to my friend Anne. Get some sleep!"

As he ushered Anne from the room, she said she'd like to talk. They found Ali and he drove them home. Orhan asked Hatije to bring them hot drinks and remain near. He didn't like having her hang about, but it was wise not to appear to be alone with Anne in the house, and Hatije knew no English.

Anne wanted to apologize for the way Dede had been taken to the hospital and to a doctor whom the family didn't know. It took finesse to convince her his family knew well that she had done the best she could.

"There's something more important I want to tell you about," Anne continued, glancing at Hatije who might detect the change of tone. "You can guess I didn't sleep well last night…It turned out that I'm glad I didn't. I can't tell you what I was dreaming, but I woke to a dead silence. The silence of the nights around here is deep. It never seemed so deep at home where there's always a car or some noise that punctures the quiet. Last night the silence was particularly heavy. I woke and whatever I had been dreaming left me frantic, and I was still really upset. I shut my eyes and somehow the rich blue black color of the silence broke over me. Then a voice—the voice of the Muezzin—began '*Allahu Ekber.*' It crashed out of the silence amplified by a microphone. That Muezzin's voice coming unfettered by the sounds and sights of the day had a wild strength. I heard him calling the faithful to a faith which hadn't been mine. But suddenly it seemed like mine because of what it asked of me and the others who heard it—Muslims: to know that God was great. This world I'd come to was going to be all right. That silence existed so I didn't have to be frantic. For several more phrases that man's voice continued clear, eerie, calling the faithful—I might be one of them—to faith. Then as if this one lone man had reached others, three other muezzin voices blared out into the still night to cross each other. Instead of one haunting voice there was a cacophony of competing calls. I knew that from several neighborhood mosques a separate voice was crying out, tangling with the others. A harsh chorus seemed to be calling the faithful. I knew I was somehow connected to them." Anne stopped and lowered her head.

Orhan looked at this woman sitting utterly still, one leg folded beneath her, the other leg sheathed in a cast which protruded like a sharp white beak from the settee where she sat. This was not the girl he thought he would find at home. This woman was wiser, more self-sufficient. He had come home to rescue her, but she didn't need him as he'd thought she did. She might even be embracing the Islam he rejected. "And...do you think you know what it means?"

"Not now, no!"

"Do you think you're going to know later?"

"I...I'm wondering if it follows from the experience I had when I broke my ankle, that sense I had that I was out of my element—somehow in a Hittite world and this Turkish world simultaneously. But it was all right. The present might be askew, but the whole of time was still level."

"I...I don't know what to tell you."

"You needn't say anything. I don't know what it all means. I'd like to, and I might know later. For now I can just live with it, feel reverent."

"You know, of course that I have always kept Islam at arm's length. Your English idiom for the way I feel—at arm's length—fits. Dede can embrace Islam, I can see it means a lot to him, and clearly he and Ali share this great love for Yunus Emre, whom all of us educated Turks understand to be a great poet. We know, but we don't understand how he is drunk with the love of God. This is OK for them, but for you? You who weren't born Muslim. I...I don't know what to think. I know this, though. If you should begin to accept Islam, it would make some kind of difference to me, but I'd try to *act* as if it didn't."

"What I need to tell you is that my being a Quaker seems relevant to me now. We have no creed we're required to believe. We expect new truth to keep coming to humans and we have to be open to it. We try to help each other discern new truth, put it into our actions, not just our belief."

"And Islam scares me. I've watched Islam trample on women with all its outward practices—the insistence on keeping women covered with all the black shawls, the sense that women shouldn't be educated because that will make them bad housewives—I don't even know what is cultural and what is religious. Dede doesn't, but I know some Muslim men who've used Islam to keep women in a degraded position and that means I want to throw it all off. I like your English saying, and it fits here. I want to throw the baby out with the bath water. But then there's Dede."

"For me, that may fit, but I want to twist it. Out of the silence those calling Muezzins made me want to bathe the baby and keep the bath water." Anne put her tea cup on the settee beside her. "We shouldn't talk too long. Hatije will wonder what's up. Your parents are away. We have to keep you pure, my friend, for all the educated people in Gaziantep!"

"Pure, eh?" Orhan put his tea-glass down beside Anne's, and rose from his chair. When he looked at Anne he wanted to seize her, envelop her, press his body hard on hers. But...what she had just told him and her wounded leg made it more wrong now. He felt compelled yes, but compelled to leave her alone...quite alone. "I'll go behind you if you want to climb the stairs," he said.

"Thank you, I'd like that," she said.

The following morning he went to the hospital again. He had decided to take Dede's water pipe with him and when he entered the room with the pipe tube wound round his arm, the old man's eyes brightened.

"*Eyvah!* You brought it!" he hooted.

"*Eyvah* it is! I didn't bring it because I thought you should have it. I brought it because you wanted it. You're my grandfather! Grandsons are supposed to bow to every whim of their grandfathers."

"I need one more favor. I can't ask the nurse for this: fill it and set it up in the corner. Then I'll relish the idea all morning that this afternoon I can get out of bed and enjoy it."

"When are they going to let you come home?"

"I wish I knew. Why otherwise would I have asked for my pipe?" Dede wiped a sliver of saliva from his mouth. "That friend of yours put me here, but I can't be angry with her. I was unconscious. She was afraid."

"She did exactly what I would have done."

"I know that. She is like you. Your name is iron, *demir*, and her iron runs inside her. She's strong. I hope you win her, but I don't know if I hope that for her. She'll need a ton of iron in her if she marries you and comes here to live. She's got it, but maybe she doesn't want to use it all up on marrying a Turk."

****

"Eyvah!" Nermin's pencil had broken for the second time. She sat at the rickety table in the tiny cubicle of a room she shared with another final year student in the *lise* section of the dormitory. She had been trying to write too fast, to make up too much of the work she had put off. The report for her science teacher in English would not be finished at this sitting. She leaned against the hard, wooden back of her chair and stared at the ominous stack of notebooks in front of her on the table. If her plan had worked she would have been gone by this time. She might have been in London with Jim having tossed Science, English Literature, everything academic in the Bosphorus. She might have been reading English Literature instead of studying it.

Her own mismanagement had left her here, and that bothered her. She had been too hasty in telling her family and too fearful to talk things out with Jim. She had counted on Dede to find a way to help when she wrote him and he hadn't. Now, dear man, he seemed to be recovering, but... If he had died her parents would not have stayed in Istanbul to set controls on her, but... She felt a tinge of guilt for even thinking of any advantage to herself if he had died. Still, she had to admit that her feeling of relief at his recovery was tainted with regret that her parents were still here. There were, however, advantages to her family's being in Istanbul. Who else had the money or the inclination to take her to the Istanbul Hilton hotel?

Nermin threw the broken pencil on her cluttered desk. Defiantly she rose and pulled her only low-cut dress out of the wardrobe. Maddening it was that she was going to the Hilton's *Altin Kubbe*—one of the most expensive, exclusive of the city's restaurants, a place where she had longed to go with Jim—with her father! Still, Abdullah Bey had flair! Her father was sophisticated, he made money easily and spent it liberally. She moved to the mirror to put on her make-up and wondered if her made-up eyes would shock her parents. She didn't care. Let them see her made up for the first time on an occasion like this rather than when she was with Jim. But wouldn't it have been great to shock them with Jim and heavy make-up at the same time! *Vah Vah!* Pity not to have all the fun she could dream up.

She was still drawing the painted black line on her eyelid when a younger boarding student came to tell her that her father was downstairs waiting for her. Like the broken pencil, the line of her eyelid was the victim of her haste. She had drawn it once, rubbed it out, and tried to put it back on straight. When the girl with her floppy ribbon came to her door, she gave up, leaving a shaky line. So much the better, she thought. They'll think I'm a novice at making my face up.

She practiced her walking as she traveled sedately down stairs, entered the lounge where her father sat waiting, and watched him cover his astonishment. A good actor! Without a word, he rose, took her arm, and walked her out through the entryway past a clustered group of younger boarders, uniformed and giggling. On the porch outside he said. "When did you start wearing make up? Those girls gawking as we left wore their ribbons, why don't you?" His grin puzzled her. Was he serious or joshing her?

"Daddy, I'm in the top class of the Lise! We all wear make up. You and Mother just don't have an idea about life in Istanbul!"

"We're learning." They reached the taxi. He opened the door to the back seat for her and she slid in beside her mother. He got in beside the driver in the front seat.

Her mother's reaction was immediate. "Can you still see with all that paste on your eyes? Did you think that because it is nearly dark I wouldn't see? When you get to the Hilton you'll go straight to the rest room and rub it off!"

"Mother," she tried to keep her voice low and firm. "You just don't understand. Everyone my age wears make-up in Istanbul."

"You are from Gaziantep. You do not wear it."

"Daddy?" she pleaded. There was a pause.

"If you had seen her in the light, Selma, you would have to admit it becomes her."

"The lights will be low at the *Altin Kubbe,* mother. You won't have to see it."

"Humpf," Selma scowled, but she said no more.

They entered the restaurant high above the streets, and a deferential, tuxedoed gentleman escorted them to a table gleaming with cutlery beside the dance floor. Once they were seated, Nermin, hoping to distract Selma from her make-up, launched into a tale of school life. There had been a recent uproar when the volley ball team had been penalized for going off-campus in their gym shorts. A white-coated waiter appeared and Nermin interrupted herself. Her father ordered eggplant salad, two kinds of *boerek,* fried kalamari, and several other dishes as *hors d'oeuvre,* and swordfish for the main dish. Seafood was a delicacy which could be had only on coastal visits since it rarely came to Gaziantep.

Nermin returned to her story until the food came. When the numerous dishes from a huge tinned copper tray were placed on their table, Abdullah and Nermin helped themselves. Selma, however, slipped only one *boerek* to her plate beside a dab of the "delicate hands" eggplant dish, and ate only listlessly. As Nermin was about to take a fourth *boerek,* she noticed her mother's scowl. Was she still unhappy about the make-up? Something else? Pity she didn't enjoy the food. Whereas Nermin and her father had come to the Hilton both to eat and to dance, Selma had come only to eat. Nermin looked at her mother with a mixture of revulsion and concern. Selma's bulk dwarfed her chair, made her seem like a fat, scowling sultan. How sad that she appeared to be living her life out now through her children's lives. She had nothing of her own: no skill, no craft to occupy her. Nothing to give her pleasure except food. She, Nermin, would never allow herself to fall into that position!

The fish course was slow in coming. "Daddy, dance with me, will you?"

"I was about to ask you to dance."

There were two other couples on the dance floor, which was slippery and hard under the soles of her high heels. Her shoes pinched, and she found it comforting to snuggle up to this familiar man, to feel his warmth, catch the rhythms of his body as he danced. She had been frightened of what was waiting after graduation, she had been trying to avoid going home, trying to bring Jim to see things her way. None of this had worked. Now dancing with her father, she felt wrapped in the familiar world she had come from. It did not have to be changed or fought. She rejected her mother's role in the Gaziantep world, but her father's was a role she depended on and admired. Resting her cheek on his shoulder, she moved evenly, automatically. Too soon the band stopped playing, and there was nowhere to go but back to the table.

Selma had stopped eating altogether. She sat, a taut chin cupped in the palm of one hand, the thumb of her other hand clutching the edge of the table. Her free fingers patted the tablecloth rhythmically. "Your father and I have decided to leave for home tomorrow. Dede is ill and *Ramazan* is coming upon us soon. There are things to be done at home."

Abdullah looked at his wife with astonishment. Clearly, he had not heard of this decision. He said nothing.

Selma removed her chin from her palm, turned her head, and peered at her daughter. "Is it evident to you that your most important job is to finish your Lise schooling and finish it with a record worthy of your intelligence?"

"It always was, mother."

"Then what was this marriage business all about?"

"I don't know. Really, I don't know. I just couldn't let Jim go without...without forcing the issue."

"And how have you forced the issue?"

"He knows that my family knows."

"But he does not know your family cannot possibly accept him as a husband for you!"

"What do you mean, Mother!?"

"I said what I mean."

"Your mother means that we are not ready to let our daughter marry a foreigner when we know that would mean she would not settle in this country." Her father had joined her mother in the attack!

"But you acted as if you liked Jim!"

"You're right. We did." Abdullah had taken over. He looked as stern as Nermin had ever seen him. "But liking someone and taking them into the family are two very different things. As sophisticated as you seem to have grown of late, you have not grasped the whole picture of marriage, and since we can't expect you to before you're married and settled, we intend to control marriage for you. You have acquired a romantic notion about marriage. We see it a great deal more practically than you do. It is impossible," he paused for emphasis, "quite impossible to allow you to marry this Jim no matter how much we like him. Marriage must be studied and practical in order to succeed. This marriage would not be."

"What are you saying, Daddy?"

"I am saying something hard as rock. I had hoped I would not have to say it. You will not hear me say it again." His stern look frightened her. "I will not change my mind, and you will understand my actions in this light from now on until you are safely married to a Turkish young man whom you like and agree to."

Nermin could not find words for her anger. The fish course had come. She ate it in silence.

"Order dessert, please, Abdullah." Selma smoothed the tablecloth in front of her with a practiced hand. "Then perhaps you should take your daughter and dance with her."

"Nermin heard her father order dessert and watched him rise as if to start to the dance floor, and found a form for her defiance. "I will not dance." The refusal eased her rage.

Her father sat down again calmly and said nothing. The waiter brought *krem karamel.* Her father and mother both ate placidly. Had the consistency been anything other than custard, it would have stuck in Nermin's throat.

"I do like this music. The decor here is too modern, but the music is just Turkish enough and just Western enough to suit me." Selma attempted to return the evening's purpose to entertainment.

Nermin remembered Anne with the reference to Western music. "Why didn't you bring Anne with you?" She had been intending to ask about Anne each time she had been with her parents. The other distractions had prevented it.

"You seem to have forgotten she has a cast." Abdullah's tone was defensive.

"But you said it didn't stop her. You should have brought her. She'd love Istanbul."

"We know that. But this time one American was enough."

"So you do connect Jim and Anne!" Nermin spoke and afterward thought better of it.

It had struck her that her parents saw her relationship with Jim as they saw Orhan's with Anne—some kind of rebellion. "And one spunky child is enough?"

"That is not our reasoning. But of course we can't help seeing how unhappy Anne is. She doesn't like our life. She appears to want to live like a villager and think like a worshipper of the past. We have some difficulty understanding her—"

"I don't. She thinks women's customs are empty, that's all! So do I."

Selma straightened. "See! The two of you play on each other. That's why we didn't bring her. While you've been here at school, she has made progress in adapting to our life. She has learned more language.

She and Dede read and go places together. If you saw her now, she would convince you that you want to live in America."

Nermin cringed. Anne, Jim, herself, they were all misunderstood. "You don't understand. You just don't. Anne tried to talk me out of marrying Jim. She's on your side!"

"So...if you and she knew about it so early, why didn't your father and I?"

"Jim must have made that clear, Mother. He didn't know about it."

Abdullah disliked what he was hearing and rose. "Come. We're wasting the music."

She could not go on refusing to dance when their conversation had turned sour. Once on the dance floor, she allowed herself to let go, enjoy her father's movements. Her mind told her to rebel, resist dancing with this man who would not listen to what she wanted. But her body melted with the pleasure of this motion in tandem. Nermin and Abdullah Bey did not return to their table until the band had finished three long medleys.

CHAPTER FIFTEEN
ONCE THERE WAS, ONCE THERE WASN'T ISLAM
FEBRUARY, 1961

Out of the dark, an insistent bass drum note sounded from the street below. Each *Ramazan* morning, Dede had told Anne, a man came through the streets beating a huge drum to call the faithful to rise, fill their stomachs, say their prayers and prepare for the day's fast ahead. Hearing the resounding beats, Anne roused. In early November the doctors had taken Anne's cast off, and the winter had passed in Gaziantep with Anne continuing to learn more Turkish. Dede had gained strength, and their friendship had grown more solid. Anne, as the Demir's guest had hesitated to leave for several reasons, among them a sense that since the International Student Office had already hired a year-long replacement for her, why should she go home before she was more certain of what her decision would be. What would she do? No job waited for her in Seattle! Being as ambivalent as she knew she was, it seemed right to stay in Turkey, know the culture better. That way, when she either accepted or rejected Orhan as a person and Turkish culture as a place, she would know better what she had done.

Now, she wondered, was this the time to rise? Should she dress before going to the kitchen? Should she go in her nightgown and bathrobe? When she announced that she would like to try the Muslim yearly ritual and fast, Dede had been matter of fact. He had said that she was welcome to join Hatije, Ali, and himself for a large breakfast in the kitchen at this hour before dawn, but he wasn't sure that she'd learn very much about Islam from fasting. "I look forward to the fast each year—sharpens the senses—but it doesn't do anything for my sense of what Islam's all about. It's Islam you want to know about, isn't it?"

"Every faith has its rituals. I want to experience Islam's. Even if I could, I don't think they'd let me whirl like the dervishes, but fasting's a ritual I'd like to try."

Now, Anne decided the drum was instructing her to rise and dress. When she got to the kitchen Hatije was rattling pans and Dede sat huddled in the dim glow of the bare light bulb hanging from the ceiling. Ali squatted poised over a kilim spread with white cheese, olives, bread, and a jam the Turks called *rechel*. The kitchen's work table had been pushed aside to spread a doubled rug to accommodate more people squatting around it to eat.

"My bones feel like tombstones!" Dede grumbled, "but I'm here." The doctor had warned Dede that he was not strong enough to fast, but the idea of a month of *Ramazan* without its full ritual, without both the spirit and the practice had so devastated the old man that he decided to fast anyway. "And *Amerika-li Hanim,* you meant it, you're here."

"I am. I may not pray in Muslim fashion, but—" she spoke loudly since Dede had difficulty in hearing.

"I'll teach you. You can bow and bend for me."

Anne picked up a black olive, cut into its leather texture, and chewed it slowly.

"But you don't like our olives!" Dede hooted.

"I don't. But I have to eat something, don't I? They're almost good with white cheese!"

In answer, with his chin, Dede indicated Hatije and Ali. "In this warm kitchen, I hope you're sensing one of the special auras of *Ramazan.*" Hatije had joined them around the rug and torn off a chunk of bread. Ali was stirring his tea. "The camaraderie. There's a poem by Rumi, the other 13th century poet I like. It goes something like, 'I…you…she…he…We.' That's what happens in *Ramazan.*"

Anne said nothing, hesitant to speak loudly enough to make herself understood to the old man. In this dark morning hour, although neither Hatije nor Ali acted differently, she sensed a new affinity with them. Each of the persons gathered around the *kilim* were among the "faithful."

The old man continued to muse. "When I get up this early, the effort washes my soul clean."

"And fasting all day keeps it clean?"

"As clean as it ever gets," he chuckled.

"Omer Asim Bey," Ali spoke boldly. "Hurry! The cannon will go off before you get anything in your mouth."

At that the old man shoved a large hunk of bread into his mouth and chewed with some difficulty. "Tasteless, I should have put cheese on it." His words were fuzzy since he spoke with his mouth full. After several moments when the cannon had still not gone off he spoke again. "Ali. What say we treat this young woman to something to celebrate this first day of *Ramazan.* Ask Abdullah Bey for the car and let's go up to the foot of *Duluk Baba.* It's been a mild winter. There will be narcissus for sure, and maybe iris."

"O.K, *Efendim.* You can't eat flowers, but energy will come finding them."

"We'll go in late morning. I need more sleep. If I say my prayers now, I'll need another three hours of rest!" Dede rose, took another hunk of bread, indicated Anne should follow and shuffled off to his bedroom where he kept his prayer rug. Without turning on the bedroom light, he pulled the rug out and laid it on the dining room floor. He instructed Anne to use his rug, stuffed the bread in his mouth, and knelt himself to touch his forehead to the larger dining room rug. The cannon sounded. "Get that! *AllahAllaha!* We're hearing the first cannon of the season!"

Then he demonstrated the words and motions of the prayer.

****

At a bend, Ali turned off from the paved road onto a barely discernible dirt road, parked, and suggested they walk. "No you don't. I'm an old man, weak!" Dede mocked himself. "I can't walk. Drive a ways up!" he roared, commanding playfully.

"The road is bad, *Bey Efendim!*" Ali's protest was low key.

"Drive on!"

"He's bossy," Anne teased, wondering if she should be so playful with this doorman. "You have nothing but to obey."

Ali grinned and started the car.

"We're lucky. Ramazan starts this year on the first day winter decides to break," Dede said. "The sun's trying, but the earth is rejecting its caresses. We'll see. Have the flowers managed to get a start? But we'll never find them so near the road."

Going up the hill toward *Duluk Baba* the car bumped mercilessly over the jutting stones and eroded ruts of the road.

"The government has a re-foresting project here," Ali informed them, forgetting that Omer Asim Bey most certainly knew of the project. "This is the road the water truck takes to water the young trees. Not meant for ordinary cars."

"But the flowers have an advantage here. The same watchman who keeps villagers from grazing their goats on the young shoots of pine trees keeps the goats from eating the narcissus and iris." Dede appeared to ignore Ali's difficulties driving.

The car bumped upward for another twenty-five yards until Ali saw what he was looking for. "There. See that clump of narcissus. We can stop." Without waiting for approval he maneuvered the car around so that it faced downward poised for a get-away and stopped. Was he remembering Anne's accident on their expedition some five months ago?

Anne followed Dede as he removed himself slowly from the car, walked over to the clump of flowers, bent down, and put his nose in it. "The first sign of spring," he straightened. "Each year I lose more of my sense of smell, but I just push my nose closer. What a wonderful smell!" He drew in a deep breath.

Anne put her nose in a clump of the short-stemmed tiny white flowers and agreed. "What's hard to believe is that narcissus grow here wild." Anne rose.

"Later, there'll be tulips, too. I remember a Dutch bulb grower came here once. Got all excited, said he was coming back. Never did that I know of." Dede moved slowly back to the automobile, removed a *kilim,* and began to spread it on the ground. Anne and Ali both jumped to help him and in their haste bumped heads. Ali blushed red and moved abruptly away.

Dede saw Ali's chagrin. "Come back, Ali. It's all right. You have to get used to this forward American woman just as she has to get used to us and our backward ways. Go with her now while I sit and before I get too cold. See if you can find iris."

Anne bowed her head as silently she followed Ali moving off up the hill, his eyes fixed on the ground.

Placing his knees high, the old man braced himself against the slope where he was perched. The view of Gaziantep from higher up on *Duluk Baba* was one he'd cherished, and this one from lower down was almost as good. When you have to be satisfied with something less than the best it's like life, he decided. From this distance Gaziantep's castle on its promontory stood out. He counted five minarets in the area near it. The city's buildings looked like mud-colored blocks which meant that from here his imperfect sight and loss of hearing didn't matter. What he needed was the suggestion of what he knew well and his imagination could fill in the rest. A phrase he had read came back to him: "Nothing matters, everything matters," an amazing contradiction. It had taken a long time, but he thought maybe he understood it. The ground's cold began to penetrate through the *kilim* to his tail bone. The late February day was not warm enough to lie down even though it was sunny. He rose and returned to sit in the car.

He was dozing when he heard Anne chattering in a tone far too bright for her to use to speak with Ali. He couldn't hear what she was saying, but he roused and found Anne and Ali standing just outside the car's window peering in at him. Anne carried a delicately striped brown and gray iris. He opened the window, hoping to hear, and Anne thrust the iris at him. "Look. We dug it up—we'll see if it will transplant."

"It should. Narcissus bulbs do fine when you move them," Ali added.

"I know a bit about how things do when they're transplanted. If I can take root in this country, we ought to be able to transplant this iris."

"How nature mismatches her colors!" With a stubby finger, Dede touched the delicate iris. "That brown and grey would be drab if they were put together in something humans made. But nature gets away with it."

"What say we go back to the main road and double back to *Duluk Baba?*" Ali asked. Anne says she hasn't seen the tombs."

"What are they like? I'm not sure I want to see tombs?"

"Yes you do. They're family burial caves that were dug in Greek and Roman times with shelves carved out of the walls for graves. They have huge, round stones for doors, open now, but once these rounds were rolled across a tomb's entrance to shut it. It's like the tomb your Jesus was buried in. Of course, they've been robbed of anything moveable—bones and all—but you must see them."

"As a boy, I played in them," Ali added. "When I was a boy on this hill—our village is just on the other side—my father came here with his goats. I came with him and on hot days, it was cooler inside the tombs. On rainy days it was dry."

"It's prayer time. Ali and I will say our prayers while you, our infidel, will wait in the car. Then we'll go."

"That's progress. You call me an infidel to my face, now," Anne smiled as she climbed into the car. "It's also risky."

"If you're an infidel you're a devout one, yes, but you don't bow and bend when you pray like we do."

"I did this morning in the house," Anne's voice faded as her two companions faced east and knelt. She had felt awkward this morning bowing and bending and now as she watched, the two men's motions seemed awkward, hard to associate with her Quaker idea of quiet prayer. But maybe prayer with motions was more active.

When the two men were finished Ali drove to the main road, and instead of turning to go home, by their agreement Ali turned instead to go further out of town to the road which wound up to the open tombs. But a short ways onto that road Dede leaned forward and touched Ali on the shoulder. "I think you had better turn and go back. I'm too tired to endure 'til *Duluk Baba.* We can go another day."

When they were leaving the car at the family apartment the look Ali gave Anne and the smile she returned upset Omer Asim Bey. He must make it clear to this young woman that she must not be so forward. To her, a smile meant nothing. She was used to being friendly. But Ali? He was bound to misunderstand.

Although she herself was not fasting, Selma had been preparing all day for the *iftar* meal at which the family would gather to join Dede and Anne in breaking their fast. In these short winter days, the dark came early. Those not fasting had to be ready for dinner at an earlier hour than was the family custom. "In the winter I want my evening meal earlier in any case," Orhan said to his father as they came in together from the factory. The two men had left home after the noon meal without their usual rest so that they would be ready to come back earlier for the *iftar* as the cannon sounded.

"What a wonderful spread, *Anne,* my mother," Orhan said as he appeared in the dining room where a table covered with white china serving dishes gleamed under the crystal chandelier. "What's this?" He removed a lid from a soup tureen. Selma smiled, pleased with her son's flattery, and said nothing. Selma and Hatije had rolled countless small balls of rice and meat for *yuvarlama* soup. Beside the soup tureen was a plate piled high with what looked like brown oval shaped balls: *icli kofte.* In addition a host of vegetables in meat sauces were scattered over the table and at each person's place was a huge hunk of bread. In the U.S. Orhan had bragged to Anne that the Gaziantep women were wonderful cooks. His mother was proving him right.

When the family were already seated at the table Dede arrived.

"*Selamunaleykum,*" he said as he settled into a chair. "Has the cannon sounded?"

"*Alleykumselam,*" Abdullah returned the greeting.

"You were almost late," Orhan teased.

"I'm slower these days." Dede grinned. "My bones creak. If you were around when I say my prayers, you'd hear them complain, though I think *Allah* doesn't."

At that moment the cannon's boom sounded from the castle at the center of town and Selma stood to ladle out the soup.

"I like the way you put yogurt and mint together in this country, Selma Hanim. The soup's wonderful. Health to your hand!" Anne said.

Selma muttered the traditional reply to food compliments: "May it be to your health."

Anne countered Selma's tonelessness with enthusiasm. "Turkish is handy. There are so many traditional replies that you never have to wonder what's right to say. Oh, but I was hungry!"

"Are you fasting then, *Amerika-li Hanim?*" Abdullah asked, surprised.

"She's going all out. Wants to feel what it's like," Orhan said proudly.

"She knows, as we all do, that you don't really experience another faith unless you give it a fair chance, practice it a bit, don't just sit around and hear about it," Dede said. "Have **you** ever fasted, Orhan?"

"Maybe once, when I was a school boy."

"And do you remember what it's like?"

"No. I remember nothing of it."

"And now your generation eschews Islam, I know." Dede shook his head at the same time he put his soup spoon to his mouth and several small balls dropped back into his soup bowl.

"I'm highly respectful of your practice, my grandfather, but—"

"But what? Out with it!"

Orhan hesitated. "But...well you already know that the educated of my generation think Ataturk did a great thing for Turkey when he sliced through the power of Islam. Islam kept us from entering the modern world."

"*Allah* be praised. Let's have a good argument!" Dede moved forward in his chair. "I'm ready! What about the modern world was so worth wanting?"

"On the first day of *Ramazon* I don't like to speak so openly, but yes, I feel Islam's methods of education, its ignorant, power-hungry leaders, it's all been stultifying to Turkish society, kept us from catching up to the European world."

Dede put his arm on the table, fist in the air, "Is it stultifying to have a reverent attitude toward life?"

"That's not what I'm talking about."

"You Ataturk worshippers are only partly right. The Islamic system of education, when its merely memorizing the Koran, is not enough. There's more to education than Islam offers, but that's not to say Islam's held us back."

"Surely my grandfather, you don't deny Islam has been a conservative force in our society."

Abdullah who had been quiet suddenly raised a finger. "But my son, not all conservatism is bad. As a cultural entity, Islam has influenced us in some good ways."

"Tell me. Which ones?"

"For example, Islam's strict laws. They may have been too strict. But think of all the times you choose to do the right thing when there is no one to make you do it but yourself. That's because Islam helps set Turkey's moral climate." Abdullah glanced at his father in law who was chewing distractedly. "It makes people question themselves. Anyone who practices unbridled free choice, anyone who heeds no one's good but their own—the moral climate Islam gives us ought to make them question themselves!"

"It also questions the materialism that those who want us to become more European would have us adopt." Dede said, "I'm glad it does."

Selma frowned and rose abruptly. "Who wants more soup?"

"I'd like more mother. It's delicious."

"Eat your soup, then, and stop being disrespectful to your elders," Selma muttered, as she passed Orhan his bowl.

Dede stopped eating. "He's not being disrespectful, Selma. This is an issue we all ought to be clearer on. You see, I agree that if memorizing the Koran is all there is to education, that's too narrow—education should broaden our minds, even give us engineers for technological progress. But in the Western world from what I read science has become a God, and that frightens me."

"I agree with Dede." Here was a substantive topic, one Anne had ideas about. She entered the fray. "In the West we worship scientific truth. Scientists are venerated as if they were priests."

"And look at the benefits science has brought us," Abdullah added.

"Still…" Omer Asim Bey swallowed a mouthful of bread. In our rush to reap the benefits of science we Turks seem to have forgotten the eternal truths—we've forgotten to be good to each other. We don't know what it is to revere anything bigger than ourselves. The creator, who, after all, set science going is bigger than all of us put together, bigger than science and all its truths."

"I can't speak for Turkey, but in the U.S. the turn things have taken, exploiting our resources, exploiting people, seems to have something to do with plain old human greed," Anne added.

"Turkey's not developed far enough to have turned greedy. We work for an easier life for the common man. Simple things like electricity in the villages, running water in all our homes, better fuels to keep us warm."

"My son, don't forget you're at the table. Pass the *koefte,*" Selma grunted. Absorbed in his argument, Orhan had set down the heavy plate of *ichli koefte* Selma had passed him.

Orhan picked up the plate and passed it. Dede received it and absent mindedly plopped one of the oblong balls onto his plate. "Deny? How could I? We need the basics and to get them we need plenty of educated engineers. Islamic education won't give us engineers, but—"

"You need to have an education which is broad." For the first time in this family Anne felt equal enough to speak.

"And Islam's education isn't broad," Abdullah said. "For a good liberal education Orhan had to go to a secular institution that you 'infidels' founded in Turkey back when you were still feeling the weight of duty and obligation to the world." Abdullah nodded at Anne.

What she'd said had been accepted. Anne spoke again. "That's a big difference, if its true about Islamic education. In the Western world our religious institutions have been a major force in instigating liberal education, particularly in higher education."

"Oh, yes, I agree. Broader education **is** what we need from Islam in this country. I'm a Sufi. I feel the influence of Islam in liberating my life. But I know Islamic priests who are fanatical and narrow." Dede picked up his *koefte,* and bit off one end. Walnuts and ground lamb fell out and scattered over his plate and the table cloth. Embarrassed, he took bread and awkwardly began to mop at his dish.

Since the subject was important to her, Anne ignored the accident. "Some of our clergy are ardent workers for social justice, but Christians have fanatical narrow clergy as well. For judging religion I have a handy rule of thumb. "When religion separates people from one another, there's something wrong about it. When it works to connect people, then it's probably on track."

"But you're talking about some kind of personal faith," Orhan cut in. "I'm speaking about the unfortunate effects a strong religious force can have on a whole society. Social justice may be shot through the tenets of Islam as well as Christianity, but when have I heard of an Islamic priest who fights for it?"

"True enough. What you hear is the fight to keep women veiled and sheltered. But for another contrast look at the villages." Dede had become more animated and Anne loved him for it. "Women move about open faced in the villages. They're judged by their work and their strength, just as men are." He paused, shook his head. "And let people leave the land, come to the city, and their lives get mechanized. Something's off in the cities. The *muezzin's* call from the minaret has to come through a microphone. I'm more reverent when a bare unamplified voice calls me to prayer."

"In the U.S. we have a phrase for cities: 'concrete jungles'. It suggests how the city removes people from the earth, paves them off from nature." Anne had completely stopped eating. "How can you gather in cities and not lose some of the best qualities of a life lived working the land? In Turkey you might still be able to keep some of that sense of the earth."

"I'm not a nature lover. For me that doesn't matter," Orhan said.

"You ought to be, young man!" Dede said. "If you don't love *Allah* you ought to at least love His creation."

"And there's something else," Anne added. "I've observed that Turkey's a new democracy—that's what your benevolent dictator set up—but I wish Ataturk could have seen the ugly influence of wealth on my country. The threat of the cold war and nuclear attack has put fear into our democracy. Greed's got us."

"What do you mean? The U.S. has the finest democracy in the world!" Orhan raised his voice.

"Ah yes, we have a venerable constitution and we have practiced democracy long enough to have its wheels greased and running smoothly, but rich clever men without moral conscience—the same moral conscience that Abdullah Bey says Islam gives to Turks—have manipulated our democracy. Rich men in the U.S. have more power than the little guy and they use it to get richer."

Abdullah stopped eating, shocked. Orhan grinned. This woman, his friend, was not only showing how clever she was. She spoke in Turkish.

"Don't all humans," Anne went on, "need some kind of democracy of the Spirit where every person is respected and judged for their ideas, their character, their work, instead of the money they make? Can Islam help bring that to Turkey?"

"Stop! All of you! You mustn't argue at our first *iftar*." Selma accented her objection with a jangle of the bracelets on her plump arm. "Remember this meal breaks a devout fast!" She called Hatije to clean up the mess Dede had made on the tablecloth and the family sat silent while Hatije fussed.

When the *helva* came, Anne, still fired by the good conversation, dared another subject. "Today I discovered the people who speak of a certain sharpening of the senses in fasting are right."

"What do you mean?" Orhan asked.

"I mean I liked the feelings fasting gave me...but I'll not go all ethereal on you. Dede says Islam doesn't ask anyone to be an acetic anyway. He says it's unbecoming to refuse the gifts of God. But now my cast's off and my body's back together. Normality means using my mind again as well."

"I've convinced her that it's only the things of the Spirit that matter," Dede quipped.

"He's convinced me that when I use my mind, I have an ally," Anne said.

"Just so long as he doesn't make a Muslim of you!" Orhan grinned.

"He might! He keeps going on about how all paths lead to the top of the same mountain."

"Don't worry. I can't corrupt her. She's been on her own path too long. This guest of yours has a mind all right, but its very much her own."

"You think I need to be told!" Orhan chuckled, then lowered his chin. "*Eyvah!* Maybe I do!"

Hatije brought a bowl of bananas and oranges. Orhan took an orange in each hand and flashed one at Anne. "In your weakened-from-the-fast condition, my friend, I'd like to peel you an orange."

"In my strengthened-from-the-fast condition, my friend, I should be glad to accept your act of courtesy." Anne watched him peel the orange, cutting through the peel with his knife in orderly ellipses. Was he putting on some show of gallantry for his parents? What did it matter? Even if he were play-acting, she liked him as *debonair* as he seemed.

Slowly, Dede rose at his place. "This woman may be strengthened-from-the-fast, but I'm not. Since I want to make it to the mosque this evening, I'm going to go rest. Have Ali come get me in an hour," he said, and tottered from the room.

"He's not yet recovered," Anne said, when he was gone. "He shouldn't be fasting."

"And do you think we could ever tell him that?" Selma shuddered. "Even if he weren't my father, I would know he listens to other people, but never to their advice."

****

Dear Nancy, February 15, 1961

Congratulations on pulling off an uncomplicated relationship! Your new man sounds handsome, conventional and just what I might hope for you. Actually, I think I'm a little jealous. I'd adore to be in love with someone I didn't have to come all the way to Turkey to try out. I'd love to be interested in a good intellectual from my own culture. So much simpler!

I am discovering that the Turks may be known in our culture as the terrible Turks, but in their own culture they are clever and industrious—terrible only in their ambition to climb together with their country into the modern world.

And my Turk? I still love him immensely, but if you ask me—and you do, don't you—if he is the same Orhan you and I knew in Seattle, in school, I would have to say no. He is very different now he is back in this country, and he's really wound up in the family factory. He's summoning all the finesse he can to persuade his father to procure the new machinery and adopt the new methods to introduce nylon and perhaps other synthetic textiles to the Turkish market. Cotton has been the traditional fabric and will surely continue that way, but one of the ways Turkey might begin to see itself as more modern is to be manufacturing synthetic fibers. Orhan wants his family's factory to be doing just that. His father, like anyone who has been doing anything for a long time, resists change. Orhan is working delicately to convince him that this isn't just a flashy idea his son (who has always been too young to have good ideas) has come up with to make his mark. This means Orhan has to show himself to be familiar with every aspect of the factory, not just the machinery. He's working overtime to demonstrate his knowledge and skills. His time at the factory, then, is time he doesn't have for me. That's O.K. I still have Dede, and he has time for me and I love him. I could say, if it isn't one man it's another. I like men, but I can't quite say that. Dede isn't the marrying kind! He's the mentoring kind, though, and that's great. I love the things that he introduces me to. It's *Ramazan,* the month of fasting now, and I've been fasting with Dede and Ali and Hatije, the doorman and maid in the house, and I've discovered I am hardly losing weight as I'd hoped. We get up before dawn to eat, and after sunset we all literally stuff ourselves. But my senses are sharpened in a lovely way and I am feeling poetic and happier than I was when I was not fasting. More about this when the month is over.

 The lovely thing that Orhan has done for me now that my cast is off and I can return to normal social life is to organize another music listening evening. Almost the same group of young intellectuals gathered in the same cluttered community room with phonograph records, and the music made a lovely evening again. It was daring of Orhan to do it during *Ramazan* because it is such a holy time and Western music is hardly considered holy, but the group of young educated people who gathered to bring their records and listen to them are not among the devout. They are rather the young modern Turks who want to pull Turkey by its boot straps into the European and non-Islamic world. But guess what happened that evening. We listened to an Oratorio by a contemporary Turkish composer named Adnan Saygun. It was the Yunus Emre Oratorio and besides being good music, it presented us with the English words as they were sung to several of Yunus Emre's poems. He is a poet of whom it could be said that he was drunk with the love of God, a 13th century Sufi and mystic, and his poetry really sounded good to me. As we were leaving I made the remark that I would like to read more of Yunus Emre, was it translated? They said no, there was very little of it translated. I said then I'd like to try to read him in Turkish, and a married woman named Nevnihal, a friend of Orhan's, overheard me—she speaks good English from her education in Istanbul. She said she'd like to try reading Yunus Emre with me. So we've started! We have spent several mornings already pouring over the Turkish words and we've discovered that his poetry is certainly musical, but a challenge to understand! Still, it's poetry. It's one of the deeper parts of Turkish culture that I want so much to know about, so I am thrilled. After the holiday at the end of the month of fasting, we'll do more. I have a new woman friend and I can begin reading a poet I very much like whom Dede also very much likes. Things are looking up!

Of course people don't know yet that I'm not married to Orhan. They all think I am, and that gives a peculiar quirk to the bond I feel with his family. The four of them know, but no one else does, that Orhan and I are not married, that I'm just trying Turkey out. What we will do if I decide I do want to be married is still a mystery. Can we somehow get married secretly? What Orhan will do to get another wife if I decide I'm coming home is a still worse mystery. He is going to have an awful time. But he knew that when he brought me. I don't think he thought about it carefully, but still he brought me…so…

Still, I really do care a lot for him now, and if I do come back home, I will miss him and Turkey terribly. I shall be updating you after the holiday. I'm really looking forward to experiencing this holiday—candy holiday it's called—named for all the candy the kids get from the relatives and friends they visit during the three days of holiday. Take care, dear Nancy, I care.

Anne

****

Dear Daddy, February 16, 1961

It's the month of *Ramazan*. I am fasting, learning, and finding that there are a few things about this culture that I find puzzling. Do you remember the dinner table conversation we had one evening with Orhan at our home? He told us that night about Ataturk and what he had done for Turkey in the early days of his power. You questioned whether a dictator could ever be called benevolent and Orhan was adamant that Ataturk had done what Turkey needed. He changed the script to a Western alphabet, outlawed women wearing the black shawls which covered their face and head, and generally gave Turks a freedom from a lot of what he considered the repression of the past. I remember at the time you questioned whether he was really so benevolent as Orhan claimed he was because he did things so ruthlessly and fast. I didn't know enough to decide at the time and I still can't but now I'm here I'm pretty confused about the Turkish government and the way the Turkish army, solidly for Ataturk, watches over things here. I think it was around 1950, however, that Ataturk's followers decided it was time Turkey had a free election. Of course that happened before I got here. I can't remember if that evening at home when we were talking Turkish politics Orhan told us about the turmoil that was going on last year in Turkey. Menderes was in power and he was not only supportive of Islam in a way the army found dangerous for a secular state, but he also suppressed freedom of information in the new democracy. So the ever-watchful army stepped in, created a coup and the country is now run by young officers as provincial governors. We have a new governor in this province who seems very liberal and non-oppressive. Orhan's family really like him. There are few enough educated people in this province, the social circles are small enough among the educated, that powerful families like Orhan's know the governor of the province not only for his political policies, but they know his family socially. That's the protocol—a new governor comes and you pay him a social visit if you're "somebody." Anyway, government in Gaziantep seems good, guided by a governor who seems to believe strongly in Democracy.

But Menderes, the Prime Minister whom the Army removed from office, is another matter. Orhan disapproved of the things he was doing to give Islam more support, and was glad the army removed him from office. But there are many Turks, Orhan claims, who agree with Orhan that Menderes and his two cabinet ministers should not have been taken before a military tribunal, tried, convicted of treason and hanged as they were. Orhan claims that Turkey is such a new democracy that it very much needs the army, which he respects, to watch over it, but you can understand how I, as a person who has inbred doubts about any army wonders about all this. Still, its not my place to question the Turkish government because I don't know enough!

Dede is above all this politics, lost in the ethereal clouds of a mystical Islam. The new woman, Nevnehal, with whom I'm reading Yunus Emre is a member of the more liberal group of Muslims called Alevis, and as I get to know her better I'll be able to question her. But at the moment I'm thoroughly befuddled about Turkish government and politics and there's really no one besides you I can talk to about these things. No one has my background and makes the same assumptions about government that I do. Of course, I remember the early 50's when although I was too young to understand well, there was McCarthyism in the U.S…. So…I just remain befuddled. It's a good thing I don't care about politics the same way I care about religion, but that doesn't mean I'm not interested to observe what's going on.

One thing I find refreshing. As a foreigner I can accept what I like of Turkish culture and see if I can get away with not accepting what I don't like…Of course, with Selma its different. She wants me to be thoroughly Turkish, follow all the accepted practices and rituals slavishly. But the rest of Orhan's family actually seems to want me to be myself because I suggest to them a kind of modernity they want for Turkey. I just don't know if I have the back-bone to maintain my equilibrium in this culture! There are too many things I question.

What I'm going to do about marrying Orhan is also, still up in the air. Oh Daddy, I love him, but can I marry him? I've been here now almost eight months and I still don't know. Thank God, there **are** three people alive I know I love…you, Dede and Orhan—odd they're all men! I am beginning to enjoy this new friend, Nevnehal, but I suppose to have a woman I like around steadily, I shall have to wait until May when Nermin will graduate and come home from school. I'm told spring comes early to Gaziantep and I'm waiting for it. The three day holiday at the end of *Ramazan* will help and it seems very good to be reading this poet who's new to me with this woman named Nevnehal. I'm very glad I decided to stay this full year and make a decision only at the end of a good chunk of time. It's hard on Orhan to be left in limbo so long…but if I'm going to marry him, I really have to know what living with him might be like! I can almost hear you saying "good thinking, little one." That helps me endure all this uncertainty.

Give my best to Bonnie. More later. An-ne

CHAPTER SIXTEEN
ONCE THERE WAS A BOY WHO WAS MAY, 1961

"Now we go on the most scary mountain in all Turkey." The May heat had crumpled Nermin's white blouse beneath her cardigan as she sat beside Jim on the back seat of a 1958 Chevrolet taxi. Jim removed his travel-worn fringed suede jacket. They had come by plane from Istanbul to Adana and were now on their way to Gaziantep by road. Rare May rain clouds glowered above them. "For Turks this *Gavur Dagh* is scary road. It will be more bad for you. Anne, my brother's friend, hates it. We all hate it. We travel by road because after Adana the planes go too seldom to our town."

"You think the U.S. has no dangerous roads?" Jim's voice cracked as he said "you."

"O.K. You wait."

Jim whistled softly. Their taxi had swerved out rapidly around a slow-moving mini-bus. An oncoming truck was moving toward them. "Danger? This driver makes his own. You're right. I don't like this road."

"But it's named for you: *Gavur Dagh*—that means Infidel Mountain. Clever, yes? To name something dangerous 'non-Muslim'? It must have a story to its name, but I don't know. In any case, it's your mountain—yours and Anne's."

"Not right! We can't be the only non-Muslims that come over this road."

"But you're the two I know. You know what I mean, silly!"

"Am I supposed to like being reminded I'm foreign?"

The taxi sped on, taking the turns so fast Nermin was several times thrown against Jim. "We passed *Yilan Kale* back there. You know what that means?"

"Since *yilan* means snake and *kale* means castle, I'd guess it means Snake Castle," Jim said playfully, mocking his own language skills.

"You are fast learner! It reaches way up. Does it make you want to climb up—battle the snakes, conquer it?"

"You **are** a dreamer! I'm an archeologist. To me castles don't mean as much since they're above ground—not as old. I like to dig! I've just been in Britain. We in the U.S. think of England as a country with history. But their history's young compared to yours."

Nermin pouted. "You know the castles already. Why do I tell you?"

"Because you're proud of your country, little one. I can't knock that!"

"When you call me little one, I feel like a child."

"Sorry, I won't if you don't like it. I'm keen to meet your parents again in their own home. Glad to be going home with you."

In the silence that followed Nermin admitted to herself that she was anxious. This trip home with Jim was supposed to be a clever, calculated move. If she arrived home with Jim instead of his visiting Dede later, it would be easier to convince her parents to let her marry him. By the very fact that she arrived with this gentleman, her family's friends in Gaziantep would consider her engagement already arranged. If other people took it that way, her parents would have to. Thank God they hadn't made their objection to the marriage clear to Jim. If he knew how her parents felt, he might not have agreed to come. Jim was too decent to want to make trouble, but so were her parents. Surely, they wouldn't be difficult. They wouldn't be rude when Jim was already right on their doorstep. Why, then was she so anxious?

"Have we been through Osmaniye yet?" Jim broke the silence.

"Why?"

"According to my maps, that's the place where the road takes off for *Karatepe*. Now that's an archeologist's dream site. But someone else is already digging there."

"I think that's the place where Anne broke her ankle. My grandfather knows it well." Nermin could think of nothing more to say in English and wished Anne were there. When she talked with Anne there was always a great deal to say. Why wasn't Jim a better conversationalist? English was his language, after all.

The hairpin turns began. Nermin sat holding herself tight around each curve. "Now you know what I mean about scary?"

"Right on. Hard to match this road."

"We should have come by train, but it takes three days." Nermin thought, but did not say that to take so much time would have been unbearable for Jim. Americans were always in a hurry, which meant that planes were always their chosen way to travel. Maybe just at the last minute she should have warned her parents that Jim had come back from England and would be with her. She could have timed it so that her parents couldn't have stopped their coming, but they might have had time enough to get used to the idea Jim was coming. Had she miscalculated? Were she and Jim speeding along toward some terrible scene?

The evening light was failing as the taxi descended. Far below, other cars' headlights were like glow-worms inching along the mountain. The distance down made her still more frightened. The motion of the taxi as it went around the curves began to nauseate her, and through it all Jim's silence made her still more anxious.

At last, after endless silence and too much tension, the lights of Gaziantep shone through the early evening light and the driver, like a donkey who knows he's heading home increased his speed. He was from Gaziantep and needed no instruction for finding Nermin's family apartment. He had told her he knew of her family when she hired his taxi at the Adana airport.

The car stopped in front of the house. Nermin jumped out, and was unexpectedly surprised to have to ring the bell outside the gate because it was not open. Hatije came to open the gate. Her pregnancy was another surprise.

Hatije stared rudely at Jim. "Your parents are expecting you," she said to Nermin while she looked at Jim as if she'd never seen a foreigner before.

"This is my guest, Mr. Martin, Hatije." It didn't seem necessary to tell Jim who Hatije was since it must be clear she was a servant. Besides she couldn't remember Hatije's last name and Jim seemed to expect to be given any person's full name, even if it was only a servant.

Her father must have heard the commotion of their arrival. He burst through the broad front door to meet his daughter on the porch. "*Hosh geldin.* We weren't sure what time—" Seeing Jim, he stopped. His scowl confirmed Nermin's fears. Where was her father's unfailing courtesy? "We were not aware that Mr. Martin was coming with you. We would have—" His voice broke off and he began to shake with rage, unable to speak.

If her father was inhospitable, Nermin could make up for him. She turned to pick up her luggage, and motioned Jim to pick up his bags because Ali didn't seem to be around. She was about to move into the entryway when her mother appeared, her headscarf askew, her cardigan unbuttoned. Using the railing to maneuver the stairs, she started down toward the group in the doorway. Nermin dropped her bags and rushed up to her mother hoping to make her hug her. But she did not reach her before Selma had seen Jim. "And what is Mr. Martin doing here?"

"He's come with me, Mother." Nermin wanted to add, "You have to receive him because he's here," but she could not find words.

"We are not prepared like Turkish villagers for 'guests of God,'" her mother said, using her coldest voice. "Let Mr. Martin come in. We will telephone a hotel, call a taxi to take him there—the others are away with our car—and afterward…make sure he's comfortable."

"Mother!" Her mother's manner and the look of shock on Jim's face robbed Nermin of any more words.

****

The road winding up *Duluk Baba* had reached a point where the hardened dirt path for each tire was nearly impossible to see. Peering uphill over the rocky soil of the mountain where only dry dead grass grew, Orhan judged they must be near the tombs. He looked for a level place to pull off the road, and stopped the car beside a rocky bank. Dede claimed to have been here only last year, but Orhan remembered being here only once, as a boy. Several months back during *Ramazan* when Dede and Ali had taken her to hunt bulbs, Anne had heard about the tombs and had asked to see them. Having determined that due to Anne's injury on the *Karatepe* trip there should be no more archeological expeditions made without him, Orhan had nonetheless been unable to be away from the factory and arrange the trip until this particular afternoon when it was already May. Both Ali and Dede had accompanied Orhan and Anne on this trip. Ali had come in case there were difficulties with the road or the car, and Dede because in the light of their present marital status, a chaperone was needed. He would have preferred to take Anne alone, but Dede knew more about the tombs, also. The old man had got through the fasting of *Ramazan* with no more health problems, but no one had wanted to risk the added strain to his frailty by taking him on an expedition until a time when his health seemed completely restored. Now that time had come. *Sheker Bayram* had finished and after two months of normal eating Dede had insisted that he was quite fit enough for an expedition. *Duluk Baba* was, after all, only a short distance from town.

The four explorers left the car and followed Dede climbing to where he had promised they would find the tombs. They had gone only a short distance when Dede pointed to a dark hole in the side of the hill which appeared to be the opening of a cave. The others followed him. Coming closer they saw that leading down to the cave's rectangular opening was a short path on the two sides of which loose stones were piled so as to make a crude gateway into the tomb. Outside the opening, standing upright in troughs dug out of the dirt were pushed two five-foot high round stones of about nine-inch thickness.

"They must be like the stones they rolled away from the door of Jesus's tomb." Anne said glancing at them, as one by one the three of them passed cautiously down the rocky pathway and past the huge wheels.

"It's a lot to roll away. I'd bet the families only opened the tombs as infrequently as they had to." Dede said. He paused to put a hand on one of the stones before bending his head down and cautiously stepping over the rectangular opening into the tomb. Orhan, alarmed to see him disappear into such a gaping hole, followed him without waiting for Anne. "I can manage on my own," she said, cheerfully. But when she didn't appear, and while Dede was lighting a candle in the dark, he turned back to the light to look for Anne. She had stopped outside the opening to examine the great stone wheels. "It'd be quite a task to roll these things back and forth every time they put a body in the tomb," she mused.

"Death is forever," Dede said, holding his candle high. "But of course these tombs have all been robbed centuries ago so that now there's no trace of the families who owned them, either their bones or treasures." Clearly the caves had been used for shelter. Orhan examined the charred stones where someone had built a fire in the middle of the bare swept mud floor. The low ceiling left just enough room for him to stand, but Ali needed to bend his head. The floor was uneven and had collected several pools of water. It was a peaceful unhaunted place in spite of his knowledge that it had once housed the dead. In the dim light he could see carved arches dug out of the walls with niches large enough to hold shrouded bodies. He moved closer to the niches, put his hand into one of them, and felt cautiously, but not broadly for any trace of bones. As he had hoped, he touched only a flat dry shelf in the area his hand moved across.

Dede announced that he was going to go out and find one of the other tombs where he remembered a large carved sarcophagus, and Ali seemed eager to follow him. Orhan followed reluctantly. He would have liked to linger in this cool dark place with Anne. But she turned and followed Dede.

The next tomb was only some thirty meters away. Just outside its rectangular doorway was a carved pillar, it's markings worn with the weather of the centuries. Orhan speculated that the inscriptions on it might give the names of those entombed inside, but it was a script he neither could read nor recognize. Inside, the cave itself was irregular in shape. A side niche, which appeared to have been dug out after the original room, contained an only partially broken important looking carved sarcophagus, its stone lid perched on it askew. What member of this family had so distinguished himself as to warrant such a significant stone box for burial? Anne approached the huge box and passed her fingers over a circular emblem carved on the base of it. To see her touch it sent a shiver through Orhan. Not just the chill of the tomb, but Anne's boldness, her curiosity, all excited him.

Ali had seen a new bulb flowering outside and rather than enter this tomb, had gone to the car to get tools to dig it up. Dede claimed he was tired and wanted to go back to the car. Anne said that since they had come this high on the hill they called a mountain in this part of the country, she would like to climb higher and catch the view of the other side from the top. When they reached the open air, and he was alone with Anne, Orhan grew still more excited. To guide her around the stones of the scrubby vegetation and help pull her upward, he touched her arm at the elbow. From there it seemed easy to drop his hand down and take her hand in his. That move was elating. He had not so much as touched this woman—a woman the outside world supposed to be his wife—since he had arrived home with her almost eleven months ago. A wild rush of desire flooded over him, gave his climb added energy. Anne followed, meek, silent. Did she feel the same rush?

When they reached the top they stood looking down at the broad plain with its cultivated fields. In the distance deep blue mountains rose from the patchwork plain. Three villages huddled to make cluttered breaks in the pattern of green fields, red earth-colored fields and small budding orchards. Clumps of trees dotted the whole. The scene lay spread out clean—no machines. Scattered clouds mottled the sky above and cloud shadows made blotches which swept across the plain. Anne moved to sit down on a stone. He followed.

"History steeps this land spread out below me." She spoke so softly he could hardly hear her. "I've had a glimpse of how I can have a feel for that history now reading Yunus Emre with Nevnehal Hanim. It's not easy. I see how limited my vocabulary is still, but I like it. I know I can begin to plot how I can learn more about Yunus, more history…I want to absorb the currents of thought, particularly religious, but also cultural, trace the many cultures and people who have swept across this landscape. It may sound grandiose, but I want to somehow be a bridge—set myself up to span the old and the new, span the differences between Turkey and my own culture. I feel the old pleasure I used to feel at making plans. If it's too difficult to read the books I find in Turkish I think I can persuade my father to send me books in English. I don't know what sources I'm going to find to find out about these things, but I'll find them."

This woman, this infidel of a woman who sat easily on a stone beside him was telling him of her excitement at the idea of learning the history of *his* land! Nothing he had grown up with had prepared him for hearing a woman tell him of her pleasure in learning. His own learning, the idea of looking for the best way and introducing *viscon* fibers at his father's factory had excited him, but... he had never thought that any one else might know about that same excitement. And a woman? Anne's anticipation of the reading she might do about Turkish history, about Turkish literature—for her to have such anticipation, to seem thrilled about the possibility of searching out these things, learning about them—blew his mind!" It enlivened him just to think about what it was to have a mind that could be blown. He liked the English phrase.

Being absorbed, he had observed only casually a dark grey cloud sweeping over the plain, until rain burst upon them, and he rose quickly. Unaware, he grabbed Anne's hand and led her back toward the closest shelter which loomed as one of the tombs. The sudden rush of water soaked through his shoes, and looking down he saw water running down the mountain in small rivulets, taking tiny rocks and soil with it. The sight alarmed him. This was the erosion scientists talked about when land is shorn of its forests. Bare rocks are left exposed, soil runs off the mountain. Turkey had to care about this. But now? He couldn't!

He and Anne were already drenched when they reached the doorway of the closest tomb, hastily climbed over the threshold, and were out of the rain.

The air was cool in the tomb. So cool that Anne began to shiver. He moved to put his suit coat over her shoulders. As he draped it over her small frame he knew he had never felt closer to any other human being. Another wave of desire surged in him. Beside him was this woman who'd come to Turkey with him as his wife who was not his wife. He had distracted himself from this desire. He had kept above it for all these months. That squelching of the way he felt had been possible only because he had not been physically close to her. Now huddling together in this cold tomb he was undone. The desire he had worked to rein in overwhelmed him. He wanted this woman—bodily! He had to have her. "*An-ne*...what will we do?"

"Orhan," her voice saying his name was muffled in his wet shoulder.

"I want you. I want you. But..." he couldn't bring himself to speak his question about whether she might marry him. "Here...we are rained into a tomb of all places...and we try to decide a big 'if' for our lives. No...I don't try to decide. I know what I want...I only wait for you."

Her voice came to him as a low murmur somewhere into his shoulder: "It's not that I don't want you...I do...but I'm...I'm still frightened. I'm not ready...I need more time. I'm sorry, but I need more time."

"*AllahAllaha!* can I wait? You have no idea how difficult this control is. I don't want to have to control it. I want you, I want you."

Her head came away from his shoulder. Her face lifted toward him, and he kissed her. The kiss carried a force he'd never known before. His lips hard, hers hard against her teeth. He stifled an impulse to bite her.

"We should leave this place," he said, drawing away from her. Then he nearly staggered toward the door, expecting her to follow. She did not. From the doorway, he looked back. His body was blocking the only light which came in the doorway, and she was nearly invisible in the dark of the tomb. "Are you coming?" he paused to wait for her answer.

"I'll come soon," she said, and a wave of anguish shook him. If she did marry him, this woman might always be independent of what he desired of her. But to know that did nothing to assuage his need to have her.

The rain had let up as he crossed the remaining distance to the car and got in to the driver's seat. Ali sat in the front seat, Dede rested with his head back in the back seat.

"Where's An-ne," Dede said.

"Coming. We took shelter in a tomb, and she likes communing with the dead!"

"Maybe you better say she has a sense of history," Dede chuckled. "This much we know. She has a mind of her own."

"*AllahAllaha!* She does!"

They arrived home for the evening supper meal late. Abdullah was waiting for them and Selma was lying prostrate, as if she had collapsed onto the *sedir*.

****

Anne settled into one of the six grimy, overstuffed chairs arranged at right angles on a speckled cement floor in a corner of the lobby of the hotel reputed to be the best in Gaziantep. If they put a Turkish carpet on this floor, would this lobby earn even one star by U.S. standards? No doubt Nermin's Jim probably was used to Turkey's hotel standards. She had arrived, sent word up to him, and expected any moment now, he would be coming down the stairway in the corner. She hadn't met him, but surely she would be able to identify him. Foreign cultures put fellow nationals in strange relationships with each other. Orhan's family assumed that they would somehow know each other and get along. Since she'd been raised in the same country, spoke this Jim's language as a mother tongue, she had been appointed as the family's ambassador to speak to him for them. Orhan's parents appeared to have a new realism about Nermin. This attempt to trick them into accepting Jim had back-fired, and they were still more determined to search out and destroy any hopes either of the two young persons had had about marriage. It pleased her to recognize that she had gained enough of the Demir family's trust that they knew she had had nothing to do with this man's arrival. They had sent her to explain their position to him.

She was certain she would know him the moment he appeared since there was something about her fellow ex-patriots that clung to them no matter how long they had been out of the U.S. If she could not shake off her state-side looks even if she tried, and she hadn't, it was to be expected that men didn't lose their American looks either. Would he have a crew cut?

He didn't. His tousled hair was long enough to part and comb, but clearly that bit of grooming had not occurred to him on this odd morning. Walking with an unmistakably American slouch, he crossed the cement floor of the lobby, and thrust his hand out from the sleeve of a leather lounging jacket. Anne rose and held out her hand. He looked uncertain. Who had sent the hotel clerk to ask him to come down to the lobby?

"I'm Anne. You must be Jim. I think we've both heard about each other."

"Yes. We're not strangers. It was you, then who just sent for me? As you can see I'm an American, but I'm not typical. I'm slouch shouldered, unathletic, and...even bookish. And I'm from a small town—Yakima, Washington. Where are you from?"

"That's wild. I'm from Seattle. All you have to do is speak the word Yakima, pronounce it like we do in Washington state, and I'm smothered with a wave of nostalgia. Nermin can't marry you!"

"What's the talk about marriage? Nermin and I haven't got that far!"

"That isn't clear to her family!"

"My God!" He dropped into a chair beside the one she'd been sitting in. "Can I be direct? When I come across someone else from the States I feel I can get straight to the point. Maybe you can tell me what this is all about."

"Maybe first you'd better tell me what you mean when you say 'this'?"

He flipped his lanky arms out at angles to the arms of his chair and shrugged. "This...this...I arrive with Nermin—a girl I guess I've had a few remote thoughts about marrying. But instead of a civil welcome, her parents are really angry and I get pushed off to a hotel."

"Pronto, you've come to the point. It's amazing to me how our countrymen can be so direct and Turks can be so… circuitous? I've been here almost a year and I seem to be picking up their circuitous ways. I'd forgotten. Since you're from the same country, I, too, can be direct—"

"You can. You must be able to guess who I am, but I swear I don't know who this family thinks I am—some kind of imposter?"

"Did you know Nermin hadn't told them you were coming with her?"

"My God!"

"She had it figured that if she presented you to this town as if her engagement were a *fait accompli* her parents would have to accept you."

"But I thought I was coming on some kind of friendly visit. We're not engaged!"

"That may be irrelevant. Before, in Istanbul, they told her what she probably hasn't told you: they will never accept you as a son-in-law. There are a lot of things that have nothing to do with you and who you are, that mean they can't let her marry you. But you must be aware of what a determined little cookie you bit into. I think I've observed most Turkish daughters are docile. This one isn't. She's far from dutiful."

"I'm not naive. I've seen how determined she is. I like her spunk. I'm not socially sophisticated. When she arranges things, I don't have to. But I won't knowingly be her pawn. What's she up to?"

Anne held out her hand. "Touch me. I'm exhibit number one—the first blow to the family. I was acquired in the U.S. and came to Turkey to see if I could marry into their family. I don't know that, yet, but that doesn't make me any less a blow to Nermin's parents. Their son may marry an American! One he chose himself! Then there's Nermin who wants out of this town in the worst way and she's decided you are her way out. She's got an idea about the kind of life we lead in the U.S. and she wants it. But her parents are also determined. They want a good Turkish young man for her who will help with her father's factory. The difference between your foreign marriage and mine is that Nermin is trying to make yours happen here. Orhan couldn't have considered choosing his own mate had he been here under his parents' nose. They are determined, however, not to lose both of their children to foreigners. They were too polite to tell you that you couldn't marry Nermin in Istanbul. Turks hate to tell anybody anything they don't want to hear. Why be impolite if there's no need? Now Nermin has cornered both you and them and they sent you here to this hotel last night to gain time."

"My God!"

Anne grinned. "This morning or last night or sometime they've hit on a plan. They want to make you seem like my friend. That's risky, of course, because if I should end up marrying Orhan, they don't want a daughter-in-law who's a hussy, either. But at the moment it's safer than having Nermin involved with you. They're banking on your decency as soon as you know, told by me, exactly what is so unsuitable about you."

Jim sat a long time slouched in his chair. Then he leaned forward. "That little minx. She's clever. I feel used, but I still care about her."

"I like her a lot, too. She's wonderfully alive."

He sat up straighter. "I've never felt so wanted by a woman in my life! God, it's a great feeling. Should I fight for her?"

"Don't try. It's a fight you're bound to lose. I'm supposed to ask you to cease and desist."

"No!"

"Yes." Anne lowered her eyes.

"What do you want, then?"

"I want you to understand that no matter how dear Nermin may be now to you, I don't think she's worth the fight you would have to get her. I'd guess her parents might be very nasty if they were pushed—polite but nasty. You don't want that." She paused. "I've become matter-of-fact about marriage. There are any number of people either you or I could marry, and we make it more difficult for ourselves when we choose to marry across cultures."

"If I were feeling sarcastic, if I knew you better, I might say, 'don't you sound worldly wise'...but."

"It sounds odd, doesn't it. If I were another man I'd say it must sound avuncular. You don't know me, but I'm asking you to believe me. I'm learning things this year about myself and marriage and 'life'—that big pretentious word—I would have been appalled to know I'd know, but…"

"You sound like you need to talk to somebody!"

"The family sent me to talk about you and Nermin, and for once I want to do what they want me to do."

"I guess maybe I'm not the father-confessor type anyway. Let's talk about what it is to be an American in Turkey. I haven't talked with anyone here whom I can talk with easily since…maybe the Roman era."

"O.K… I don't know what you're finding, but I'm discovering I'm a different person when I speak Turkish."

"I've been here now four times over the course of three years, but I come to dig. I don't talk to the artifacts. I haven't had to use much Turkish."

"I have. But English sentences are shorter. In Turkish I can't be elegant as I might be in English. Turkish sentences are long and can have verbs at both the beginning and end. I didn't grow up thinking the Turkish way, so its taking a long time to switch and use long well crafted sentences."

"What about idioms? Collecting them in any language, fascinates me, but they're hellish to translate."

"Orhan's grandfather is always quoting me proverbs—Turks have a lot of them, but whether Turkish is any more idiomatic than English, I can't say."

Anne began to feel the thrill of easy conversation about subjects she cared about. Their talk went on until Ali appeared in the doorway and stood quietly waiting. Anne judged he was there to remind her of what he had informed her when he brought her to this hotel: he was due to pick up Orhan and Abdullah at the factory. The mid-day meal, would, as usual this day, be on the table as it always was promptly at one o'clock.

"So…" Jim said when he saw Anne preparing to leave. "What's the family proposing I do?"

"Visit no longer than today, pretend you're my friend, and leave. Then you're welcome to come back only after Nermin's safely married—properly…to some acceptable Turk."

"But that's cold-blooded. It takes no account for anyone's feelings."

"If you're concerned about feelings, they have no suggestions. Turks aren't big on considering feelings. If it's hard on you to stay and pretend to be my friend instead of Nermin's maybe you should just leave immediately."

"Why that?"

"*If* it's easiest."

"It may be easiest, but it's cowardly. I won't do it. I kinda like masquerading as your friend, but I'm not willing to go without speaking with Nermin. My God…me! Buried as I've been with archeological artifacts and dug out by a bold girl."

"When artifacts get dug out, don't they disintegrate?"

"Not me."

****

Orhan moved the papers about aimlessly on his scarred desk top while the boy brought in a tray with two glasses and two bottles of *Gazoz*. The two glasses on the tray were still wet from their cursory rinsing. "I hope you will forgive us. In Turkey at this time we have nothing that is both cool and safe to offer you on a hot day but *Gazoz*. My friends in Mersin tell me that soon we'll be bottling American type drinks—Coca Cola, Pepsi, but they are not here yet." He poured from one of the bottles and offered the glass to his guest.

Speaking to this Jim, this fellow-national of Anne's, Orhan felt a resurgence of his apologetic feelings about Turkish backwardness. It was the early 1960's and he wouldn't have known how behind Turkey was had he not spent last year in the U.S. but he had. His need to apologize was exacerbated by the fact that he had taken this Jim on a tour of the family's factory. Since on the factory floor with the noise of all the machines, they could not speak easily, he had now ushered Jim back to his office. The factory's outmoded technology was the real source of his embarrassment.

"I like *Gazoz* after it's had a chance to settle." Jim held up the glass poured for him and watched the sediment in it settle. "The flavor's good."

"How much do you know about the textile industry in the U.S.?"

"Almost nothing. I've run headlong in the other direction from technology in my country. I never appreciated anything about U.S. technology until I got to this country and saw how innovative you are with antiquated machines. I wish I knew more. Neither did I know anything about how esoteric my field is until I came to this country."

"Then you understand. I have said that at this stage in our development archeology is a luxury for Turkey. The U.S. is developed, large. You can afford variety. We're still trying in Turkey to learn the basics. It wasn't the textile industry as such I studied in Seattle. It was business management of the cloth industry. It's to Europe we look for technological changes in our factories. Europe's closer. But we have to learn sound business practice as well. You in the U.S. are masters at business."

"I'm not. But I don't think I'm typical."

"Common sense will show you what technology means for us Turks. That part of the factory we passed first had old 1920 machines. Noisy, yes? They take many people to run and repair them, but we have to use them, we can't afford to make them obsolete. I showed you the oldest machines first on purpose. People from England tell me that section of the factory must be like the first factories in England: dark, damp, noisy. But the last part you saw, there the machines are newer, use less men. Those were bought from Switzerland. Those use only one man to five machines. Those oldest machines we got when an Austrian company went bankrupt years ago. That is many times how things start here, from European left-overs. Still, now we are better off. We buy machines from the West. One day, maybe, we will have more Turks interested in this area's history…archeology. How long that will be, who knows?"

"But if Turkey lets foreigners explore all your archeological richness, you'll have only the left-overs there, too, when we're finished."

Orhan shrugged and Jim put the fingers of his two hands together and looked at the floor. "There's something else I can't understand as a foreigner. Your family has a point of view about Nermin and you seem to feel you can just declare I can't have her and that's that. You've been in the U.S., Orhan Bey. You know we don't think the family has as much to do with who gets married to who as the two people themselves. I may not get Nermin in the end, but I can't just accept your family's decision about her as if I were Turkish. I suppose all this tempest now may be the first sign of why this marriage might be difficult, but all this cultural stuff is…well…what's basic is the way Nermin and I… well, what we do for each other."

"I can't see what Nermin can do for you that you can't find in another woman."

"I don't have the *rapport* with other women that Nermin and I have."

"I'm afraid '*rapport*' is one of those psychological words they use in the U.S. that I don't know."

"Ah, yes. Your friend Anne said something to me about how those of us from the States take our basic psychological knowledge for granted until we run up against a culture that doesn't think so psychologically."

"That's it. I'm unused to your American introspection."

"I guess what I'm trying to say is that Nermin and I are open with each other in a way I find rare."

"How can it be rare? Yesterday by report at the hotel, you were open with Anne."

"I guess I feel caught. Suddenly I'm open with anyone I can speak English to."

"I sent my friend, of course, as a favor to my parents."

"I can assure you her virtue will remain as untouched as the unexcavated temples in Turkey."

"I had no question about you in my friend's case, Mr. Martin."

"And I want you to assure your parents. I wouldn't so much as lay a hand on Nermin unless we were engaged. But I don't understand myself how what began as mere translation help has somehow mushroomed into an attraction that I don't know what to do about…"

"We have heard. But let me use a business example. It is a question of priorities. It is important to my parents that Nermin marry a Turk. You have seen this factory now. You have said you have no interest in technology. But the man Nermin marries **must** be interested in this factory."

"Why?"

"I'm not sure I know except my parents are sure Nermin can be happy only if she marries someone who can fit into the factory. Happy as she might be by marrying you, my parents are looking at the 'long run' as you say in English. You look at the 'short run.'"

"You know why? Because until now your parents have been what we in the U.S. would call 'pussyfooting.' You have been so polite that you have said nothing straight out. You have left things to Anne to say or you have left me to guess the way you feel. Was I invited to tour the factory to express the way I feel? No."

"You were invited to tour the factory because you expressed interest in it. We are only now speaking of Nermin because you spoke of her."

"So now I am expected to fold up my tent and silently steal away like the proverbial Arab."

"We Turks are not overly fond of Arabs, Mr. Martin."

"More veiled language?"

"Yes, Turks are used to veils. You've seen headscarves across women's faces on the streets of this town, have you not?"

"Hell with it! All right I'll leave. Your sister is worth a fight, but the fight may not be worth the fight."

"You seem a happy person. You were probably happy before you met Nermin. You will be happy again." Orhan leaned back in his chair, satisfied with the calm way he had handled this American. "And now Mr. Martin let us go home to dinner."

CHAPTER SEVENTEEN
ONCE THERE WAS A DIG THAT WAS...
AUGUST, 1961

Spring turned into summer with it's dry heat burning the tarmac and courtyards of Gaziantep and the wheat fields and grape vines in the surrounding villages. Anne continued to learn more Turkish and observe more of the way Turks did things. She found herself most intrigued by Turkish village life, so that when there was a murder in Dede's village, she was particularly eager to go there.

A young girl was to be married to a man she did not want to marry in return for a high bride price. The girl had eloped with the young man she loved, and the girl's family had tracked them down, found them, and murdered the young lover. When Omer Asim Bey heard of the murder, he decided to go to the village to speak with the *muhtar,* learn more, and see if there was some action he might take to keep the dispute from becoming a running blood feud between the two families. Since Orhan was the most likely younger member of the family to take on Dede's interest in the village, he asked his grandson to go with him. "I will die easier if I know you make yourself interested in this village," he told Orhan. "You need to meet the head man, begin an acquaintance with the way villagers think, what they care about. Then, if you want your friend to have an expansive heart, take her with you, widen her horizons. 'Wide horizon, you make my heart wide like you are' the proverb goes." Orhan wondered what the old man's proverb had to do with taking Anne, but it would be good to take her, in any case.

When the three of them arrived in the village, Orhan parked the car under the plane trees in the dusty square just at the hour before school began. A flock of school boys, their shaven heads only slightly less dark than their black school smocks, gathered about the car to stare at the three strangers in Western dress who climbed out. Orhan took Anne's arm to guide her through the cluster of boys. "As if they have never seen people before," he muttered.

"They stare at you too!" Anne said, amazed.

Orhan spoke to them. "Will one of you show us where the *Muhtar* lives?" In response, one boy shuffled and nudged another and at length a wisp of a lad of about eight was pushed forward and beckoned to them to follow him. They left the car parked out of the sun under the trees in the town square. Heat radiated from the dusty path between mud walls where the boy led them. After their path turned and they walked a short distance between other mud walls their guide wordlessly indicated a wooden door in one of the walls and left. In reply to Orhan's knock, they heard the sound of clogs approaching the door and a young girl opened it to invite them in. Climbing the slanted ladder to the open air roof where the family lived, Anne caught the stench of animals which had drifted up from the stable below the living quarters.

Reaching the roof they interrupted bread baking. A woman—Anne guessed she was the *muhtar's* wife—dropped the long stick which was her rolling pin and came to greet them. The young girl called the *muhtar* from inside the living quarters before bringing mats and pillows out for them to squat against. The village chief himself emerged from behind the mud wall, and shook hands, still buttoning his shirt with the other hand. Had he been asleep? The *muhtar* and his guests settled and the women returned to bread making.

The man's dialect was like Ali's but coarse and faster. Anne abandoned any attempt to understand and moved to watch the bread making. With her long stick the wife rolled a large circle of dough out thin, like paper. When it was the proper size, she flipped it around on a stick and deposited it on a thin metal plate over a charcoal fire for her daughter to tend. It blistered and darkened in small bubbles immediately and the girl removed the huge circle, carefully laying it on a stack of other bread circles already some six inches high.

Orhan, when he noted that Anne made no attempt to catch the men's conversation, interrupted to politely inquire as to whether *pekmez* was being made anywhere in the village at the moment. If it were, he thought Anne would like to see that process. The *muhtar* called to his daughter, who in turn offered to take Anne to a courtyard where she had heard they were making the grape paste. Going down the ladder, Anne remembered she should make the day's arrangements with Orhan and called back in English. "I brought food," she indicated her shoulder bag. "You'll be busy. I'll stay out of your way."

"But they feed us something here!" After he spoke Orhan remembered with relief that his English would be gibberish to villagers.

"Trust me. If I'm back, I'm back. Otherwise I'm having my own adventure."

Orhan's look indicated it was not a matter of trust. He was worried. Anne decided to ignore his concern.

As they moved along the village path the younger woman asked Anne what language she had been speaking.

"That was English. I'm from the United States."

"But where did you get your *shalvar?*" The girl indicated Anne's full pant legged, cotton print trousers which she had borrowed, to Orhan's chagrin, from Hatije.

"They'll be handy for sitting on mud floors as I'll probably have to in a village house," she had insisted.

"I borrowed these from a Turkish girl. I like the clothes you wear in the village."

The girl, shocked, turned to face Anne in the middle of the path. "And which language is your real language?" Anne didn't know if she should be disappointed or flattered. She had hoped the girl would tell her she approved of her wearing the *shalvar*. At the same time she was pleased that her foreigner's Turkish could be taken for real.

"Turkish is not the language I learned as a child. When you have to ask me, I am pleased."

"I am ignorant. I know nothing."

Anne looked at the young girl. Her white, gauze head scarf trimmed with silver sequins set off her fresh face. "You mustn't say that. I watched you making bread. I can't make bread like that."

The girl made a clicking sound with her tongue, lifted her chin slightly and said nothing more. They arrived at a gate which was standing slightly open and walked in without knocking. Inside the courtyard, next to a pile of manure, a woman with her full pantaloons shoved up above her knees stood ankle deep in a huge tub of grapes. With her bare feet she stomped on them to squeeze out the juice. The *muhtar's* daughter explained to the woman standing in the tub that her guest wanted to see *pekmez* being made.

"She's welcome. Put more grapes in the tub for me." The woman's voice was pleasant enough in spite of a sharp edge which Anne had noticed in the speech of other village women. While she continued to stomp, the woman told them that her daughter had been filling the tub, but she had gone for another tub, and asked again if they would put more grapes in. Anne and the *muhtar's* daughter helped with the grapes until the daughter of the house returned. Then the *muhtar's* daughter explained that she was needed for bread making and left Anne behind. The grapes were abundant, the work that needed to be done, clear. When the daughter of this house set the other tub on the ground, filled it with grapes, washed her feet and climbed into it to press out the juice, Anne saw that someone was needed to put more grapes to be stomped upon in her tub as well. She began for both women to pick up grapes in great bunches and load them into the large cauldron. Wordlessly, the three women worked in a rhythm, each of them doing the task they had accepted. When nearly all the grapes were pressed down into a great glob of skins and stems the *muhtar's* daughter returned. Orhan had sent her to fetch Anne.

Following the girl back along the rutted path to the *muhtar's* home Anne had what she thought might be her first feeling of real connection to the Turkish people. Wordless work with women who were strangers had made her momentarily feel at home! For work, however, she needed *shalvar* and she decided to have a pair made. Neither Orhan nor his mother would be thrilled to help her get them made, but she would go to Nermin's dressmaker. Even on her own, she could do that.

"What did the *muhtar* tell you about the murder," she asked.

"He either truly doesn't know much about it or he isn't saying. We talked about many other things, however. Dede may want to come back."

"But you heard it might have started some kind of blood feud."

"We did hear that, but it isn't worrying the *muhtar,*" Dede shook his head.

"I told you how strange I find villagers," Orhan added. "They eat, they talk, they argue, but not with me."

When Ali stopped in front of the house to let them out, Anne noticed Abdullah standing at the window of their family's apartment upstairs as if he were watching for them. When they entered, Selma sat moaning on the *sedir*, her palms spread wide rubbing her broad thighs. Nermin was missing.

****

Each time the bus jogged on this rutted road through a scrubby pine forest Nermin was once more thrown against the black-shawled woman beside her. The woman was not unfriendly, but repeatedly, she pulled her shawl across her mouth and turned to stare at Nermin as if this uncovered, Western-dressed young woman beside her were from some other country. The road wound narrowly through mountainous terrain in eastern Turkey. Although it was dusty now, its hardened mud ruts were the legacy of a wet spring. In winter this road north from Gaziantep to Malatya was closed. Now without snow it was just barely passable. To forget what she was doing—the thought of which was frightening until she actually reached Jim—Nermin concentrated on the beauty of the multi-colored rocky crags above the bus. The road might be bad, but traveling this back way, she was more assured her family would not be able to trace her. She wasn't sure they knew which village Jim worked in. She herself had had to study detailed maps to find Korocutepe.

Nermin thought ahead to her arrival in that village. Reaching there she would ask in some indirect way where "the foreigner" had pitched his tent. Her plan was to arrive in the evening, just as it was getting dark and approaching his tent with stealth, boldly seize the flap, tear the tent open and surprise Jim. He will be astounded! He will not believe that I have had the courage, even the know-how to run away to him. For very awe he will take me in his spindly, but still wonderful arms and I will be....

If village boys and girls can run away together, those from the city can do it too. Nermin had decided she didn't share her family's ideas about a "good Aintab family" for her. Aintab boys follow the rules, and that makes them dull! Her family never would understand her. She would have to arrange things so they would not have to try. Her mother's face animated with outrage flashed into Nermin's mind. Then she saw her father's face pained with disbelief. Confronted with that dear man's pain, her sense of defiance faded. But she mustn't think about her father. She had to think only of her dream and the awe Jim would feel at the daring this young woman he loved possessed.

When they reached the town of Malatya, a rooster somewhere in the back of the bus crowed in an off-hour announcement of arrival. Once out and in the bus parking lot, she asked one of the ragged hawkers of buses about a bus which would go further. He claimed there was no scheduled bus going any further in the direction she wanted to go. She would have to hire a jeep. It was already late afternoon. A young girl traveling alone did not go off in a jeep with a driver whom she did not know. Besides it was the late afternoon and she hoped to cover a distance of which she was not certain. The only circumspect thing to do was to wait until morning. But why was she concerned about propriety? The whole trip was improper.

She made her way across the open space where several battered but colorful buses were parked to a corner hiring stand to inquire about a jeep. The man they directed her to looked coarse and ugly with hair protruding from his nostrils and ears. Admitting to herself that her concern was not merely for propriety, that she was also frightened, she booked his jeep for the morning. In this late afternoon, she could not force herself to go off in the wilds alone with a sweaty, dirty driver, even if she was in a hurry to reach Jim before her family could find her. She arranged to be picked up in the morning at the hotel the driver recommended. She almost stopped the first well-dressed woman she encountered to get directions to this Anatolia Hotel, but felt suddenly shy when confronted by a cultured, educated looking person—rare on the streets of this town. Instead, she went off rapidly to follow the vague directions she'd been given.

The hotel clerk eyed her curiously and said nothing. There was no one about to help her with her one bag, so without waiting further, she nearly ran up the stairs to find the room for which she'd been given the key. Since the room was on the one upper floor of the building and private she would feel less vulnerable when she was alone behind a closed door. Rather than leave her room, she ate the remaining bread and grapes she had brought with her for her supper. The day's final insult came when she crawled between the sheets of the hotel reputed to be the best in town, and could not be certain they had not already been slept in. An Istanbul hotel would never get away with such slovenliness. She wondered about Gaziantep.

In the morning so as to stay out of sight—her parents could have sent someone after her and in any case she didn't want to attract notice as a girl alone—she ordered breakfast in her room. When the word came that the jeep driver with whom she had negotiated the night before was downstairs, she left her room, paid her bill, and feigned the aplomb of a person who habitually performed this sort of transaction. When she examined the jeep driver in the bright glare of morning, he appeared clean enough, if still not harmless enough. Having no other recourse, she had to trust him.

The road wound interminably into the mountains and she became more aware of the risk she was taking. On the map the road had seemed short. She had not calculated for the switchbacks and curves of a narrow mountain road, nor the distances drawn flat on the map which turned out to be elongated by ups and downs.

The driver's attitude appeared to remain protective during the morning. By midday she was hungry and relieved when he wanted to stop in a village to buy things to eat. After that stop, however, for no reason, he seemed to change. He stopped frequently, got out to linger and ogle his passenger with mournful eyes and at last when it was nearly dark, they came around a curve after which he indicated a village below them in a nook between two hills. She could be relieved. Her destination was reached. The driver drove to a spot some fifty feet from the first mud walls of the village and stopped. She climbed out of the car and dug in her purse for her money. He remained uncomfortably close while waiting for his pay and when she put the money in his hand he caught hers and squeezed it in what seemed an unnecessarily tight handshake. Quickly she turned, her knees watery with fright, and hurried to the nearest of the three wooden doors in the mud wall ahead of her. Why was he still waiting? He had delivered her. She had paid him.

Thank God, a woman answered her call at once. To Nermin's inquiry as to whether a foreigner was working in the vicinity, she said that her son had been hired by the foreigner to dig. His camp was up the gap. There was a road, but it was rough. The woman peered out through the light of dusk at the jeep driver who was still lingering, and offered to send her son with the driver and the girl to show them the way. Then without waiting for an answer, she motioned to the driver as if he were still responsible. Nermin saw she could do nothing to check the woman's arrangements, but since the boy would be with them, she felt safer. Again the jeep jogged a short distance into the hills.

After about a quarter of an hour the jeep's headlights shone on what appeared to be a clearing with two tents to one side of it. She guessed the smaller one must be Jim's tent. The vehicle stopped. It was now dark and there was no sign of life anywhere in the clearing. The young digger with her said there was a night watchman, but that person was nowhere evident. The boy insisted the smaller tent was the American's tent, got out of the jeep with her, and moved toward it. Nermin knew that this was the moment she had dreamed about. But she was encumbered with two escorts! And which tent flap should she fling open!?

Cautiously, she picked her way toward the tent. Midway she nearly stepped into a campfire with dying embers. Dare she walk up, merely fling open the flap? No. What if someone other than Jim were inside? She turned and moved back toward the jeep to ask the young man to describe this American: "Tall…bony, a little stooped."

This was Jim! She decided to ignore the impropriety. She would **have** the moment she had dreamed about.

For a second time, walking rapidly, she approached the tent. But she could not bring herself to daringly rip open the flap. Instead she called: "Je-em" He would know her voice. She waited. No answer… "Je-em." She spoke louder and this time she heard a grunt from inside the tent as if someone were waking, and it was his voice. Her hand lifting the tent flap trembled. "It's me, Nermin!"

"You!"

"Yes, me. I've come."

Before she could drop to his level, he jumped up and out of his sleeping bag. He was wearing his undershorts and a grimy tee shirt hung loose over his sunken chest. "How did you get here?"

She gestured toward the jeep's headlights. "I hired a jeep."

While Jim looked to see the jeep, she took her first full look at him in the dim light of the car's headlights. His legs were thin, his knees boney. Shed not seen him without long pants before. "One of your diggers showed us the way out from town."

"Is he still here? He'll need to help us find a place for you to stay in the village." He started toward the headlights expecting her to follow.

"Je-em!" She felt shy, but the brashness she needed suddenly came to her. "Let me stay here."

"No, Nermin. You know that isn't right. I'll go with you now and come into town to get you in the morning. We'll talk."

When they reached the jeep, Jim spoke to the boy. "Is your family able to accept a guest?" His Turkish, she noticed, had improved.

The boy volunteered his family's home. "We'll all ride back to the village," Jim added, "I'll walk back here when I see my friend's settled."

Nermin climbed slowly back into the jeep hoping Jim would observe how her spirit had sagged. This arrival had not gone as she had hoped. In fact, it was a huge disappointment. Why should Jim be so sensible? She had done a wild wonderful thing to come here to find him. She'd been courageous and Jim was acting as if she'd done nothing at all! She would not be alone with him until morning. Her defiance of Turkish morals was for nothing. *Abo!* He had spoiled it all.

The boy's mother bustled about officiously, proud to be spreading the pillows to prepare a place for Nermin next to her daughter on the floor of their one room house. The boy offered to bring her back to the excavation site in the morning, but Jim suggested firmly that she stay here until he came after her.

Nermin lay rigid on the floor mat until sleep sounds surrounded her. Slowly the tension of the road left her taut body and the hushed sounds of the others sleeping lulled her. She could indulge her anger no longer. She slept.

****

Orhan studied a road-map of Turkey spread before him on the table in his parents' dining room. Selma and Abdullah hovered beside him. "Lucky I asked him where he would be working. If she left sometime this morning, she probably went by bus. Depending on how fast she travels, if I leave this evening and go by jeep, I might overtake her as she arrives." To speak in English only to Anne who sat beside him studying the map, he lowered his voice. "The little she-devil!"

Anne frowned and spoke in English. "Orhan, do me two favors. Don't think of your sister as some kind of tart. She's only an adventurous dreamer who has the spunk to try making her dreams a reality." Then in Turkish she made her second request. "Take me with you. When you get there and begin talking you know very well you'll want me."

"But we're not married!" He must have said that for his parents!

"As far as Gaziantep knows we **are** married. In the territory around Malatya where no one knows us we might as well be married. What matters is to keep the boundaries clear between us." Anne continued in Turkish so that his parents might catch her logic. "Don't you see, one more adventure and I'm more apt to want to marry into Turkey!"

"O.K. One more adventure! My favorite luxury, archeology! It will look that way and let it! We have to go, and go now. We don't want to arrive too late to prevent—God forbid—Nermin's spending a night with this Jim!"

"Surely she has more sense than that!" Abdullah cried. Orhan shook his head.

They agreed. Orhan would make the arrangements for a jeep to go off in the morning and Anne would get a good night's sleep. "I appreciate all the concern for my getting a good night's sleep, but I really don't understand what makes me so delicate," Anne said softly.

"I am concerned for you because I know I don't want to deal with either my sister or her gentleman friend without you!"

Anne went off to bed and Orhan made the telephone calls to arrange for a jeep before returning to the table where Abdullah sat pressing his fingers together in a circle until the tips were white. "You must make it clear to Nermin that she is not coming back to dull times. I should have told her. Her mother and I have begun to make arrangements with a family here. You know the young man as does she. Nermin knows him, but I would imagine she has not thought of him because he's five years older than she and he's been away—Omer Kaya. He's back from Germany. It appears he's asked his father—you know how well we know them—to help arrange his marriage. It is essential we get Nermin back here before that family gets wind of her having gone. Surely she won't do anything foolish, anything irrevocable!"

"We can hope her upbringing is too good for that, my father."

Thinking about the plans his parents had made on the road in the morning, Orhan was still more anxious to move fast and waylay any foolish actions Nermin might make. He thought Anne might appreciate knowing something of his parents plans, and decided to tell her. She settled into the jeep calmly before she spoke. "I'm elated to find there's another road out of Aintab. It may be tougher to go north, but at least there's a road to travel on."

"I'm glad you have sense of adventure. I guess you would not come to Turkey at all, if you didn't. I just wish Nermin was not so much like you. Fits an American woman. It doesn't fit Nermin."

"That's an odd one!"

"My father told me something very interesting last night after you left. He has already started to arrange a marriage for Nermin with Omer Kaya. Nermin's going to like that. He's five years older than she is, but I think she's always looked to him with respect."

"I hope you're right! That may be our only trump card, and I think we'll need one."

"Now you must tell me what you mean by 'trump'!"

"I mean we need some good talking point. Some news that will help convince her she doesn't want Jim as much as she thinks she does."

By noon they had reached Malatya and after a brief stop at an oven to get *pide* and directions they started again on the narrow dirt road to the village where Jim reportedly was digging. The ruts and bumps in the road made the going so rough Orhan was embarrassed that Anne had to experience such a road. At about four o'clock the jeep sputtered and stalled. The passengers all got out, and the driver dove beneath the chassis. Orhan walked Anne to a clump of trees where he spread his coat, suggesting she sit. "This is scenic country. We'll enjoy it more from the shade."

"But I want to talk," Anne began. "This whole trip I've been thinking about Jim. Nermin is headstrong and innocent, both—she'll put him in a crazy position. We know he's no villain, and he does care about her. It's hard. Nermin not only wants what she wants but she has the gumption to go after it."

"I know," Orhan spoke almost inaudibly. He didn't want to think about what Anne had said. He was distracted by the pattern of sun and shade on her hair. He could not remember having felt so tender toward her since coming home to Turkey. Ironic, that his feelings were stronger for her when she was pre-occupied with protective feelings for Nermin.

The driver crawled out from under the car and came toward them looking embarrassed as if he sensed the thoughts he was interrupting. "Excuse me. Has the lady a hair pin?" He explained that the bumps had shaken a pin loose and to replace it he would have to improvise. Anne fished in her handbag and found a bobby pin which he took and crawled under the car again. Orhan made up his mind to try to hire this driver at the factory since he was from Aintab. He had the kind of ingenuity they needed with the factory's machines of varying vintages: inventive, a good mechanic.

When they were moving again each jolt transmitted another kind of anxiety—that the makeshift pin would be loosed. They went only as far as the next village where they stopped to ask if anyone had a jeep. The driver hoped to find a spare of the pin they needed, but it was an unrealistic hope. The young man in villager's cap and black *shalvar* they stopped to ask shrugged. No one, he said, owned any sort of motorized vehicle in the village. Mechanical tenuousness joined the list of other concerns haunting Orhan as they traveled onward.

After dark and late, they saw headlights coming toward them. It was the first car they had passed and they were in luck. It appeared to be another jeep. Their driver indicated stress by flashing his lights and the other vehicle stopped. Its driver had no spare pins. He told them, however, that there was an American in the village ahead who was bound to have extra parts since he was working there. "I know he's there. I just took a woman to his camp."

Orhan heard and his jaw tightened. Could he use this new knowledge to find out what had happened when this jeep driver delivered Nermin? He needed a circuitous question. Anne began to speak and gently he interrupted her to ask, "Is there a *han* in the village where they will accept guests for the night?"

"That village! Too small. They took the lady to a villager's home." The man said more but Orhan wasn't listening. Relieved, he nudged Anne. Had she caught the significance of that remark. He saw she had. "Thanks, driver Efendi. We better get to the village then and find a place to stay before the whole village has gone to bed."

As they moved on, he spoke to Anne in English. "We may be lucky! We know Nermin is in a village home for the night. She is **not** with Jim. We can begin to think about ways to make the trip look like a normal turn of events." He was moved, suddenly to put his arm around Anne's shoulder and squeeze her. "In the morning we might even make it out to the campsite before Nermin does. She'll wait to be sent for, I'd guess. Did you gather—I did—that Jim helped take her to this village house. Sounds decent. Now if we just get Nermin and all of us home safely, secretly..."

Shortly they arrived in the village. It was without electricity, clearly, and they saw only a few dimly lit windows where kerosene lamp-light lit the panes from inside. "Didn't the man say Jim had asked his digger to take her to his house?"

"He may have. I didn't listen. If you understood that your Turkish is much better. Wait here. I will ask these people to take us in. It may not be a comfortable night."

Stories of village hospitality to strangers were legendary, but Orhan had never tested them and it was late. He was wary.

A bare headed man—his gray hair pressed close to his head from steady wearing of his cap—answered Orhan's knock, holding a kerosene lantern up to peer at Orhan's face. Strangers did not come to his door every night.

Orhan invoked village custom to remind the man of God with the traditional greeting: "*Selamunaleykum.* My wife—" it was imperative to lie— "and I and a driver are travelers headed for the campsite near here where they're digging. We had car trouble and have not arrived until this late hour. We feel we should go no further. Have you room for guests?"

The man paused, lifted his lamp higher, and peered at Anne behind Orhan before he returned the greeting. "*Alleykumselaam.* You are guests of God. We are honored." When the host motioned them in, the driver demurred, claimed he would spend the night in his jeep. Their village host led them across a courtyard and up a ladder to the living roof. The woman waiting there perceived the family had guests, lit a kerosene puffer stove and began to prepare tea while another young girl emerged from the inner room pulling a sleeping mat out onto the roof. Orhan speculated the men would be on the roof and the women would take Anne into the shelter of the home's inner quarters.

They were lucky. Unknowingly they had knocked on the door of one of the more prosperous of the village homes. Tea leaves, fresh-looking quilts, the puffer stove itself all spoke of a home that was better off than he might have expected to find in a village. They settled to drink tea and Orhan and the host spoke in hushed tones since there were children sleeping in the shadows at the far end of the roof. Anne huddled close hoping to hear. Their host, Husayn Efendi, claimed this village had no special distinction. Its farmers had traditionally shipped out their fruit crop and harvested its meager wheat. Then this foreign man came to dig and brought the outside world to the village. "This stranger has done many things." Husayn Efendi gestured toward Orhan. "He has brought a guest in Western-style dress to my door!" He grinned to show his pride at having such a guest. "We have an improved road as well. The provincial government decided no foreigner, not even a crazy one who does nothing but dig, should ride over that road the way it was." Then, having forgot the sleeping children their host in a loud, boasting voice and with many hand motions described how the huge grader from the region's cherished American road-maintenance equipment scraped the road as far as to the edge of the village. He claimed that if the youngest village boys had not seen the new smooth road they would have thought when the grader retreated that their village had been saved from a monster attack.

The woman brought tea which came in glasses and with a tiny fluted dish which held irregular shaped lumps of sugar. Even though the sugar appeared to have been around some time, it was another sign of the family's affluence. The tinkle of a spoon in a tea glass—a familiar sound in this unfamiliar village mud terraced home—made Orhan feel proud. His countrymen generously offered their guests hospitality. In what other country might he take a woman off away on a trip, claim she was his wife, and expect to receive the hospitality afforded "guests of God?"

When Orhan told their host that they would get up at dawn and without waiting for breakfast find their way out to the campsite, Husayn Efendi protested. Wouldn't they stay long enough to have breakfast. Orhan held firm. They must get an early start. What he did not tell his host was that he wanted to reach the campsite before Nermin did in the morning. In the end their host agreed, and to be helpful in the morning, he would rouse and take them to the campsite. The morning plans completed, sleeping mats were spread out on various portions of the house's roof-top and Anne was escorted inside to be with the other women. Orhan lay on his back, his head cradled on his bent arms, smelling the odor of the heavy quilt. It had waited, he speculated, for important visitors too tightly folded for too long. Since Anne was inside, he hoped they had a quilt stored under less airless conditions for her. To think about her stirred his feelings of pride once again. What educated Turkish woman would so willingly arrive in this terraced house, and sleep on its mud floor with only a sleeping mat shielding her from its hard surface?

Just as the first light was making it possible to differentiate the house's flat mud roof above him from the sky, Orhan woke. After some fifteen minutes in which the light grew rapidly brighter since dawn was coming fast, he rose and got to his feet. After straightening the clothes he had slept in, he put on his suit coat, combed his hair, and called in hushed tones to Anne. She emerged rapidly, as if she had not slept well and stole down the ladder to the latrine in the courtyard. He hoped that in the morning light when she could see it, she would find it clean. This was no time to shock her. When she returned, he followed her and without causing a stir in the rest of the household, they started on foot with their host toward the campsite. Their driver went with them to inquire about spare parts for his jeep. Mist hung low in the valley and to avoid thinking about why they were here, Orhan concentrated on how this area, this village might be more lovely. Anne walked between Orhan and their host with her head held high. Remembering that she had fallen at *Karatepe*, he wished that she would look more often at the ground. The trail was rocky, and he didn't want her to fall.

The dig and Jim's campsite were not far out of the village and the moment the site came into view, Orhan saw Jim. He was squatting outside a tent with his back to them trying to make his fire burn. As flames burst from the fire pit, Jim rose and saw his visitors coming. As if he had expected them, Jim started toward them. "Welcome. You help solve my problem," he said in English as he shook each of their hands. The minute Jim had shaken their host's hand, Orhan turned to the villager and thanked him for bringing them here. He hoped to dismiss him. Their business in the village should not become a matter of talk. Since he apologized for the fact they would use a strange language the man retreated as if language difficulties were the only reason he was being dismissed. Their host gone, Orhan turned to explain their need for a spare jeep part and suggested that their driver describe his need to Jim. Jim sensed why Orhan seemed to want to divert the conversation from his "problem" and while Orhan and Anne huddled around the fire to watch the coffee water heat, the archeologist took the driver to see if the necessary pin could be found.

When Jim came back alone, Orhan and Anne were drinking the coffee Jim had offered them. The American gestured with his head toward the driver's receding back. "We found a pin that will do for the jeep, and now I can tell you, Orhan Bey what a spunky sister you have." Cradling the coffee Anne gave him in his hands, Jim said, "I want you to know that I see it as taking tremendous courage to do what Nermin did. And of course I'm aware of the disgrace she might bring to her family."

"My parents cannot believe a daughter of theirs could have behaved in this way." Orhan paused hoping that Jim would offer some hint of what had happened when Nermin arrived.

"When did she arrive? How was she?" Anne asked.

"She got here just after I'd gone to bed." Orhan winced. "Nearly scared the pants off me—a woman's voice calling me by name outside the tent, as if she'd done it every day! She had a jeep driver and one of my diggers with her. I put her off by taking her back to town and promising to get her early this morning." Jim shook his head and grinned. "What a woman!"

"But you must see that she's no woman. She's quite a young girl."

"How could I help it? I saw that after the visit to Aintab." Jim looked down at the cup still cradled in his hands.

"And surely you agree that this country needs Nermin's spunk. You can't rob Turkey of this wonderful young woman!" Anne said.

"I want her. I do."

"No...She needs to stay, work with me in Gaziantep. She has the potential when she works with Turkish women on education, on health care, to be as explosive as Ataturk! But if she's going to do that, she's got to be married to a Turk."

"You're not making yourself clear, but you're asking me to get what you're driving at."

Orhan was startled. Just now, in English Anne had spoken about staying in Turkey. Would she mean it in Turkish? But it was her skill in handling her own countryman that put Orhan still more in awe. She seemed to know exactly how to exploit her countryman's hesitation. "She and I are going to make a wild team," Anne said. "Come back and see us in a couple of seasons." Orhan raised his chin. Looked at Anne wide-eyed.

"I'll do that! Don't you think I won't!" Jim said, and this seemed Orhan's cue to thrust his hand over the edge of the campfire and shake the archeologist's hand.

"We knew we could trust you. You are a gentleman, Mr. Martin. I can say no more."

Jim looked down at his coffee cup before he spoke again. "You're on my ground now. I want to show you our work. Still, I understand, that whenever you feel you have to, you can leave."

Orhan began to answer before he noticed Anne staring at him, unbelieving. "Wait a minute. Both of you. Do you think you can ignore how Nermin feels? She must be waiting somewhere in the village!"

"We have to ignore her. We have to act as if she has no say," Orhan said. "I count on you to handle her feelings. You can talk on the way home."

"I certainly will not handle her feelings. That's Jim's job."

Jim looked confused. "I don't know what I'll say, but I'll go. I said I'd come get her. I'll walk in and get her."

"That's best; you go. Meanwhile, show us where your food is and we'll make breakfast while you're gone." Two things startled Orhan: the speed with which Anne assumed this kind of intimacy with Jim and the ease with which she was ready to cook over an open fire. The hike on the Olympic peninsula with Anne and her father explained the second, but nothing explained this familiarity she had assumed with Jim. The American produced a tin with cereal grain, four eggs, a messy paper of the one brand of Turkish margarine, *Sana yagh*, and a can of jam. Jim left promising to bring back hot bread from the village. He had an arrangement, he said, with a woman to bake bread for him each day.

An hour later when Jim and Nermin came into view around a bend, the breakfast was waiting. Nermin, when she saw her brother, quickened her pace, stalked up to him, planted her hands firmly on her hips and spoke in Turkish. "Orhan Demir, don't expect me to take all this without being angry! You have spoiled my dreams, my plans. I am mad! I'm mad at Jim, too, but…" She stopped. Her jaw quivered and for a moment she found no words. Then she caught herself. "I should be touched?" she said sarcastically. "My brother cares about his sister's honor! When I don't care, why do you?" her voice broke.

"You care, Nermin," Orhan said "You care not to lose it. I think you know that without my telling you!"

"Everyone…all of you are plotting to protect my honor!" tears appeared in Nermin's eyes. "I can't do anything to damage it even when I try. Anne, say something! Are you with these men?" Nermin pushed her chin out as she turned toward Anne. "You can't be so stuffy as these men!"

Anne handed Orhan the spoon she'd been stirring the cereal with. "Here. You men start and eat. Nermin and I will walk a while. Save us food. We'll be back," she said and started toward a narrow goat trail which appeared to lead around the face of a rock rising sharp above it. Nermin followed. Once they were around the point of the rock, not far along the trail, but out of sight, Anne chose a flat rock and sat down. "Now, before you say one word to me, think about this village."

"Why?" Nermin snapped.

"That woman…those goats." Anne pointed further along on the path to a woman near a small stream who with a stick was beating at four goats to drive them away from a clump of gorse bushes. Another woman had spread the clothes she'd washed on the same bushes to dry. "Because all this…our educated lives and our loves mean nothing to those women."

"Of course not. I don't see what you say."

"Maybe my point's too subtle, even for me. But somehow—Oh fiddle-faddle. I think if you think about it you don't really want to ruin your own and your family's reputation for being upstanding and—"

Nermin interrupted. "What right have you and Orhan to follow me here?"

"You may not agree, but we think just caring about you gives us the right. When somebody you care about is doing something you're sure is unwise and is going to really hurt them later, you have to do something. You can't just sit by and watch people you care about make what you think is a mistake."

"How do you know its a mistake?"

"I don't know for sure. But Orhan and I think it is. And we can't let you act as if nothing you do affects anyone else. It does!"

"You must have thought about coming to Turkey, marrying Orhan. Did anyone try to stop you?"

"Yes."

"Aman!"

"I'm trying to tell you now what they warned me about then. Marriage is a big deal and we're not merely individuals as we get into it. We're fragments of something bigger, and we do better if we fit."

Nermin looked at Anne, unbelieving. "What's happened to you?"

"I don't really know. I wish it were natural for me to fit better, but I do know it won't be natural for you either. You'd have to give up too much. You don't know now what things you care about in your Turkish background—some of it has to do with your Turkish privileged position that you'd have to give up."

"I...I won't...I'll never stop fighting my family...well my mother! They don't want Je-em. I do."

"But your reasons for wanting him are to fight Aintab. You don't really know Jim. He's just a way to get out for you—you're using him. You can't use people for long. They up and rebel."

"So!?"

"So, if it's Aintab you want to beat, marry an important Turk. Fight that way. Don't run away."

"Oh, you make no sense!"

"I know. I've only begun to think about these things. Together we'd have to figure what's worth it. What's possible."

"But then I'd be using my Turkish husband like you said I was with Je-em."

Anne shrugged. "Don't expect me to be consistent. Just let me be provocative!"

"*Aman!* Stop. You've already said too much. I don't understand." Nermin sat silently nursing her anger while she watched the village women. Then she said, "I'm not using Je-em. You don't know how well I know him. I spent all those hours with him translating. He's using me! I know exactly how he feels about archeology." Then she stopped when it occurred to her that she didn't really know how he felt about her. How could he have turned her off last night if he had known what it meant to her. Resentment rose in her. "*Aman!* I can do nothing now anyway but come back home." She leapt off the rock ledge. "But I'm furious…furious!" She stamped her foot on a bare stone jutting from the path and winced with pain. "I'm furious at Je-em, too! Oh, and I'm hungry. Let's go back. I'm not giving up. But I can't fight in some far off village where I'm so out of place I feel like I'm riding the underside of a donkey."

"I know that feeling," Anne said as she slid off the rock ledge and followed Nermin. "What did Jim say when he brought you from the village just now?"

"Nothing. Just nothing. He said that he couldn't get his work in this village mixed up with his love life. He said after he'd been in Aintab, he felt we need time to think things over. But he has his work. I have nothing." Nermin's voice broke again, but Anne was now in front of her and did not see the tears she forced back.

They arrived back at the campsite to find Orhan squatting like a villager listening to Jim. They had finished breakfast. "We want breakfast," Nermin said. "You men better have saved us some."

Orhan gestured casually toward the remaining food. "Jim tells me the story of his work. It is fascinating. Before we go back I want to see where he is digging."

"I'm up for that. I'm not as hungry as I am curious." Orhan was behaving with the same naive enthusiasm she remembered finding so charming when she'd first met him, a boy-like curiosity. Nermin ate a great deal and slowly. When the others went to see the dig, she refused to go.

An hour later when they had seen what was to be seen of Jim's project—it didn't appear impressive to Anne—a mere large hole in the ground with its sandy sides slipping back in—they were again around the campfire to talk when their jeep driver appeared on foot to announce the car was fixed. Timidly, he suggested they start back since with mechanical difficulties, it might be a longer distance back to Aintab. Jim walked with them back to the village and the jeep. On the way, Orhan continued to press archeological questions on Jim who explained carefully in English. Anne found him somewhat tedious as he recounted theories surrounding the ancient context of the artifacts they were finding. Too much detail.

They neared the village and Jim dropped behind, signaling to Nermin to join him. Observing this, Orhan pulled on Anne's jacket sleeve and they walked faster. Later when Nermin and Jim reached the jeep Nermin looked pale and Jim spoke with a kind of false cheer. As he thanked him, Orhan shook his hand warmly, while Jim told them he'd be leaving this area in a week's time.

"We'll expect to see you when you come back next summer!" Orhan's voice also had a kind of false cheer. "When you're back in Yakima, you'll go to Seattle. Tell Anne's father to bring his wife and come out and see his daughter!"

****

Dear Nancy! August 3, 1961

This is going to be another quickie! Orhan and I have just returned from a trip where we had a chance to explore an archeological dig way north-east of here in Turkey and I got another great chance to explore Turkish village life. Wow, is it colorful. Orhan's sister Nermin was with us and I found myself talking to her about joining her in her ideas to struggle against the fact that in the villages of Turkey these days the men still don't really believe in educating their daughters. I've met all kinds of clever Turkish women and they're wasted, just wasted growing up without even knowing how to read.

Nermin and I have talked about it. We want to fight this! And in getting into an idea of a good fight, I feel more like marrying Orhan and staying here. I can just see you shaking your head and hear you telling me you think I'm nuts. But for you to have doubts is no reason for me not to have doubts or to have them. I'm just in turmoil. Turmoil, Nancy. Turmoil! Turmoil is a big old fashioned word, but that doesn't mean it doesn't describe best the way I feel. Oh, friend, write me and let me know what you think. Quick, quick…before I do something that will last a lifetime and be all wrong!

Love you! Anne

****

Daddy! August 3, 1961

Help, save me! I'm just back from a really amazing adventure into a back woods village out of Malatya in the mountains to the north. I went with Orhan chasing his sister Nermin because she had scared the beJesus out of her parents by running off to find her American archeologist friend whom she was determined to marry. Her parents who have already arranged her marriage to a most respectable family here in Gaziantep were terrified that the family would learn of her running off and that would mean the marriage possibility would be abandoned. We were terribly lucky. We brought her back and no one knows but us six people in the Demir family that she went in the first place. There I go—talking about myself as if I really were married to Orhan like this town thinks I am. Daddy, I'm slipping into it and I don't know if its what I want or not. It's just happening. I found myself talking to Nermin on this trip about joining her in her fight against the aridity of Aintab's culture. And I think when I was saying it I meant it, but do I? I see now much more clearly all the wonderful things about U.S. culture I'd have to give up if I married Orhan and lived here…the music...the intellectual life, the freedom that women have...But somehow I feel like grabbing and running with the freedom I think I might have married into—as a foreigner married into one of the wealthiest and trend-setting families in this town. I'm thinking about using my privilege and social position to set a climate for change. That may just be naive, a pipe dream, but it excites me in a way I have not recognized until I said it and had to truly think about it on the road as I returned from this trip to rescue Nermin.

You see, Orhan's family trusts me now. I think maybe even the others besides Orhan and Dede even like me. I've been a big help to them in helping them control their unruly daughter. They've even set a wedding date for her and she likes the guy they've chosen for her well enough to go along with them. A miracle, to them! Doesn't seem like such a miracle to me because I think Nermin finally woke up to the way she was dreaming! Besides she really likes this Omer she's marrying.

It's me now that I'm wondering about. I think maybe in spite of how awful the phone system in Turkey is, I'm going to ask you to phone me in Aintab here as soon as you get this. It should work better to initiate the call from the U.S. than it would for me to try to make it work from this direction. I'll give you time. Call me on September 1. There's ten hours difference in time. Figure it out and call me at ten p.m. my time. Again I say...Help...help! Golly I'm glad you're there, though!

Love you...Anne!

CHAPTER EIGHTEEN
ONCE THERE WAS A MARRIAGE THAT WAS... SEPTEMBER, 1961

The band was a four piece combo—a set of drums, a violin, an accordion, and a clarinet. Although the wedding was held in the garden of Gaziantep's finest hotel, and it was a warm night, each man of the combo was formally dressed in a Western style suit. Open shirt collars were their one concession to the heat. Anne noticed perspiration on the violin player's upper lip when she and Orhan danced near him. There were over a hundred wedding guests, but only some ten or twelve couples danced. The rest sat at tables surrounding the dance floor watching the dancers and sampling the *sofra* that Omer's family had provided with all it's varied appetizers. Since Selma considered herself too old to dance, Abdullah had only Nermin and Anne from his family to dance with, and he inaugurated the dancing with the bride. But the father of the bride quite naturally turned to dance with the woman whom the other guests considered was his daughter-in-law after releasing Nermin to her husband Omer. Abdullah was a remarkably good dancer for having grown up in a country that considered ballroom dancing improper for persons who were not related. When Anne summoned the courage to ask him where he learned to dance, he told her that Ataturk had encouraged Turks to ballroom dance as a sign they were part of the modern world. He had learned to dance in Switzerland when he went there as a young student. She was eager to ask him more about his life abroad as a young man, but she decided that talking so much when they were dancing was probably not appropriate. Besides, she had never considered herself a good dancer, and it took concentration to be adequate for this accomplished partner. Abdullah Bey's life as a student would have to remain, for the time being, a mystery.

When, later, the band played a tango—the almost mandatory "La Comparsita"—Anne was delighted to be dancing with Orhan. Being a lover of music, he danced well, even for as complex a dance as the tango. She had no idea where he might have learned, and when she asked him, all he said was "Turks have an excellent sense of rhythm." Why should she care where he learned when there was the excitement—the equal motion, the easy rhythm—of moving with Orhan's body? He had only occasionally guided her by the arm, not touched her in any significant way except that one kiss in the cave since they had been together in Gaziantep. This in spite of the fact that Turks other than the Demir family thought of her as married to Orhan. Now she abandoned herself to the pleasure of his holding her—no mere titillation—and let it sweep through her body. When the combo stopped playing she wanted to go on dancing, and was thankful that Orhan had no inclination to return to the family's table either. Waiting for the music to begin again, they lingered in the middle of the dance floor with perhaps five other couples. Although the players were Turkish, the dance rhythms were eclectic: mixed with the singer's popular modern and Turkish songs there was a sprinkling of Latin American music in addition to the tango. She felt free—at a wedding, surely—to show her pleasure at Orhan's holding her. Then she remembered that she most likely would not have been dancing with Orhan at his sister's wedding had the other guests not believed she and Orhan had been married for over a year. The idea startled her. Nothing, however, altered the powerful feeling she savored when her limbs moved with Orhan's.

Nermin had made a striking bride in white satin—an ankle-length dress with a sweetheart neckline. Hardly a month had passed since she and Orhan had accompanied his rebellious sister away from the village where she had fled to find Jim. After spending a night in a primitive hotel where Anne and Nermin had had one room and Orhan another—Nermin being one of the few persons who knew the truth about Orhan and Anne—they had arrived home at midday. Abdullah had confronted his daughter at their front door with the news that her family had arranged for her to marry Omer Kaya if it suited her. He had sent her then to her room to consider her answer, having allowed her to say not one word as she returned to the home she had betrayed. Conversation was to be postponed until she was ready with her answer. Nermin accepted that arrangement without complaint. Perhaps, Anne speculated, she did not herself know how to finesse her arrival home smoothly and Abdullah might have given her an easy way to reenter both in the silence he required of her and the decision he demanded she make.

It took Orhan's young sister only some six hours to decide that Omer Kaya was an acceptable husband, and leave her room for a late supper that same evening. Observing this speed, Anne guessed that Nermin's desire to leave home was more urgent than her fantasies about any particular man. Was it that an escape from home was so vital that any flesh and blood young man might do? This view no sooner occurred to Anne than she decided it was unfair.

Her parents eagerness to have her marriage settled meant that they had encouraged the Kaya family to dispense with the engagement party since Omer and Nermin already knew a great deal about each other and didn't need time to become acquainted before the wedding. Instead the families planned the couple's wedding to follow immediately after the *nikah*, or legal ceremony.

Now watching them together, Anne saw that Omer had probably always been an admired big brother figure for Nermin, and the strength of her respect for him had therefore been easily and rapidly translated into a willingness to marry him—to be connected to him in a way she had hardly considered as a child. Earlier Nermin had probably felt herself to be only Orhan's tag-along little sister with Omer, now she seemed delighted to be his bride.

The legal ceremony, the *nikah,* had caused a minor upset, but only within the Demir family. Traditionally, each party to the marriage selects one witness of the questioning and signing—usually a respected member of the family or a noted political figure—someone they can be proud to have intimately involved with the ceremony. Anne remembered with discomfort the meal at which Nermin had announced to the family that she wanted Anne to be her one witness at the *Nikah.* "That ought to be a good one," Dede said playfully, as if Nermin were joking. Selma closed her lips as she pounded the table with her fist closed tight. There followed a long silence. Abdullah shifted in his chair and sat up straighter. "I don't believe a foreigner would be appropriate as witness at a fully Turkish ceremony."

Another silence occurred until it came to Anne that it might be best to decline. "This is the ceremony where the official will ask you and Omer if you are marrying of your own free will?"

"It is." Nermin spoke in Turkish, as had now become her habit to Anne.

"Turkish isn't my mother tongue. I agree with your father. I'm not really an appropriate witness. Dede would be much better."

At that meal nothing more was said and Nermin did not signal her acceptance of Dede. In fact, Anne did not hear that Dede would be the witness at the *Nikah,* until two days before the wedding when Dede grumbled to her about having had to have his suit altered. He had lost weight and to perform the duty for which she had nominated him he owned only a suit he hadn't worn in several years. Anne's suggestion that Dede be the selected witness seemed entirely right when she heard that Omer's witness would be the mayor of Gaziantep who was a good friend of the Kaya family. Dede's respectability would match the mayor's.

As Anne ruminated now while dancing, she was content to think that if she and Orhan decided to be married they would have to go to some other city where no one of the educated persons of Gaziantep would be available to witness for them. They would be married quite secretly. In Anne's mind any wedding ceremony fell short which was not the simple Quaker ceremony in which the bride and groom stood up in the silence and spoke their vows to each other. Perhaps Istanbul would be the only city large and impersonal enough to accomplish their Turkish wedding. *If* it happened, it would be an occasion which she could leave entirely to the Demir family. Where she would be married meant little. She would concentrate imaginatively on the life they might build together after the wedding. She was, however, still uncertain, still wary, about how she would find that life.

"I cannot believe this woman I hold in my arms is the same woman who went with me to a village, helped rescue my sister." Orhan's low voice sounded gentle in her ear. Spontaneously, she pressed her head closer to his lips, and remembered after the gesture was made that Selma, if she saw it, might frown on this show of affection. She took comfort, however, in knowing that Dede sitting beside Selma there at their family's table, consuming food with gusto from the myriad small dishes spread out before him, would understand her frustrated affections. At least she hoped Dede would. Other than some gesture to acknowledge the closeness she felt, how could she have made clear her thanks for Orhan's compliment?

"And how do you feel about having Omer join you and your father in the family enterprise?" she asked. "It appears you're not threatened."

"Another engineer joins my father and me. With Omer, it will be two of us who push my father to develop *viscon* fibers. That will be better. My father will not think I want new things just because I am his son. I push because the factory needs this new thing, even his son-in-law knows it. Omer and I are good friends. He is three years older, but we rode the train to school, to Istanbul, together when we were 'teen-agers', as you say."

"There's something incestuous, methinks about the educated families in Aintab."

"What do you mean?"

Anne's thought had emerged spontaneously. Now she considered more carefully. "I mean…well…everyone seems to know everyone else—all their business. And instead of competing—from where I look at least—it seems they all want a better Aintab, a more modern Turkey, so they push as a body to get it."

Orhan frowned. "Maybe. There are bad things when we know everything about everybody…but we all want Turkey, especially Gaziantep to be part of the modern world."

"You know, of course, that I'm going to miss Nermin terribly in the apartment building. Your mother? How does she feel? The empty apartment was saved for Nermin and her husband wasn't it? Now the Kaya family must have the same deal in their apartment building, so she won't be at home any more."

"I think my mother is very sad at that. She counts on Nermin, and now she is going." Orhan sounded sympathetic to his mother.

"And I'm not a real-daughter-in-law, the kind she can count on."

"That's right. And I don't want you to worry about that. If we marry, you and me will find ways to make my mother content."

"I haven't a clue what you mean by that, but I trust you."

"I'm pleased that you have started a friend like Nevnehal, and she reads Yunus Emre with you. Friends, you need them!" Orhan's sympathy for her seemed still more genuine.

"Ironic, I think she's reading the poetry with me as much because she wants to practice her English as read Yunus. But I couldn't care less about her motives. I'm just glad for the friendship…What amazes me is she's not that much older than I am, but she already has a child!"

"I tell you a secret. I think my parents before I went to study were thinking of Nevnehal as my bride. Her parents are good friends. But I think they did not want to wait to marry Nevnehal. It happened soon after I left for the U.S."

"Would you have liked that?"

"Sure. I like Nevnehal. I rode the train to Istanbul with her, too…to school. But I had met you when I heard she married. I already knew I wanted you." Orhan gave her a gentle, affectionate shove, and she leaned closer, against him. They danced for several minutes in silence. "I hope you learn from Nevnehal it's good to have babies in Turkey. You have both servants and grandparents to help raise them."

"Oh Orhan." Anne could think of no answer, only her own fright.

Orhan squeezed Anne's hand. "I mean...that's when my mother will truly miss Nermin, when Nermin has her first child and the child is not just under Selma's nose in our family's building."

How could she say it? The idea of having a child in Turkey, raising it the Turkish way, made her wary. First there was the fact that almost all Turkish women had their babies with the help of midwives, not doctors, which frightened her. Then from what she'd observed, every time a baby cried, Turks seemed unable to let them cry. They picked them up and nervously jostled them until they stopped. Wasn't it indulgent to refuse to let children cry? Not that she knew a great deal about how to raise children, but common sense told her she'd need to be more self-protective than to pick up a child every time it cried! Maybe her mother's opinions about child rearing—both strict and strong—had arrived in Anne packaged in her very genes.

The music stopped and Orhan suggested they return to keep his mother and Dede company at the table which was still spread with an array of small salads, olives, feta cheese, eggplant dishes, all kinds of foods for sampling.

But when he had guided Anne by the elbow and they arrived at the table, Selma had her own concerns. "You are not married," she said in a low voice to Orhan "and Anne was shockingly affectionate on the dance floor."

Orhan glanced at Anne to see if she had understood his mother's accusation. She had.

"But all of Aintab thinks we are married, mother!" he said, again in low tones.

"We know you are not! It's a disgrace!" Selma did not keep her tone low.

"Come now, my daughter. These youngsters have been living together in the same house now for a whole year thinking about marriage. Surely you can't find fault with the way they've behaved." Dede spoke softly, but Anne sensed his ire and was grateful. He paused before he continued, "You're going to drive Anne back to the U.S."

Selma pouted and said nothing. Anne sensed her thinking: no outcome of her visit might suit Selma better than Anne's return unmarried to the U.S. This young woman, in spite of the help she had been to the family with Nermin, in spite of the fact that Dede seemed to enjoy having her a great deal, in spite of the fact that Selma's son appeared to be genuinely fond of her, still belonged in America and not in Turkey where she made such chaos of Selma's plans for her family.

Orhan picked up a small bowl filled with yogurt, cucumber, and mint, passed it to Anne knowing she particularly liked it and said in Turkish so his mother could understand. "Here have some *jajuk*. It's cool. It will sooth you on a hot night like this." Enough had been said.

"Is there any *imambayildi?*" Anne asked, as she began the *jajuk*. "I want to faint, like the priest."

Selma missed Anne's humor and frowned. "We'll get more. We've eaten it all," she mumbled. "But I don't know why you want it, you're gaining so much weight."

Dede winked at Anne, a wink which was intended to also be seen by Orhan. Selma had thrown yet another curve. Anne was unperturbed. These men knew the pot was calling the kettle black, even if that idiom didn't exist in Turkish. Besides when she had learned that Turkish men liked their women on the plump side Anne had not bothered to worry about her weight. The remark might be just one more of Selma's necessary snaps at the world which she herself would forget the minute the words were spoken.

Abdullah returned to the family's table after having been sitting with the Kaya family and asked Orhan when the office his son was preparing for Omer at the factory would be ready. "Omer says they're postponing their wedding trip until he can take Nermin to Switzerland in the spring. He'll be ready to join us when they return from Mersin next week."

"What does Nermin say about that?" Dede asked. Her grandfather knew as the other men might not that Nermin would have a hard time settling into a quiet married life.

"I assume she has not been asked," her father remarked quietly after which Orhan rose and invited Anne to dance again.

Orhan had wanted to dance in part so they could speak. "I think I learned in the U.S. something," he said. "I think I know now that all women, not just American women like to be asked what they think. Where Dede learned it, I don't know."

"Dede's proof that a person can learn just from being a sensitive human being."

"Maybe you're right. Maybe I didn't admire my grandfather enough until you came and liked him." Anne liked this pensive Orhan.

"If you consulted me now I would ask if you can find a way we could leave this wedding after the next fifteen minutes of dancing."

"You want to leave?"

"I adore dancing with you. And I realize it's only possible because the Turkish world thinks I'm married to you. But I'm tired. I hate carrying on this deception—that we're married. I'm tired of speaking Turkish chit chat. Can we go?"

"We will leave. I'll take you, we'll walk, soon. But there's something starting now you have to see. It'll be your favorite thing at this wedding. Trust me."

Orhan was peering over Anne's shoulder at a darker corner of the garden where a drummer and a horn player were moving about in the shadows. Suddenly, they both burst onto the dance floor with the gusto the guests expected from them. The drum player wielded his sticks on both sides of his drum, his rhythm syncopated. The horn player played with a continuous piercing sound, his cheeks puffing out and in as he breathed. Like acrobats, they cavorted around the dance floor. They finished one number, and a set of some four couples in native dress and head dress emerged from the shadows into the light to perform a dance. As she watched Anne tried to think of a word to characterize their style. Theirs was a sweeping, pounding rhythm, heavy at the same time it was lively. Both men and women wore the baggy pants she had come to expect Turks to wear, but the women's were more colorful while the men's were plain black. The sleeveless jackets they wore were beaded and ornate. Yes, a wild energy had burst onto the floor.

"And when they are finished, we'll see if there will be a *halay*. You must have seen our line dances in movies."

"Thought they were Greek. Are they Turkish?"

"Let's say many Mediterranean countries have them."

As Orhan spoke the dancers attached themselves at the shoulders and formed a line. Then, they gestured to invite the wedding guests to join them. Orhan led Anne and Abdullah joined them on Anne's other side. The line formed with more guests than had been ball room dancing. Men and women, the young, the old, joined with their arms at the shoulder, their feet moving easily to the side, united in the *halay*. If Anne had been excited by the rhythm of two people moving together earlier, now she was overwhelmed by the movement of this line of dancers, all moving in a dipping, foot shuffling unison around the dance floor. It was as if Orhan's arm on her shoulder and Abdullah's light touch on the other side carried her, all of them swept by the stepping movements of the crowd to the pounding sounds of the drum and horn. The dance finished before Anne was ready to have it be finished.

"*Aman, aman, aman…*" Anne spoke in delight as they left the floor.

"Now, it is time to go," Orhan said as he guided her to the table where Nermin had returned to sit with her new family to say their good nights. "We will not wait to go home in the car with my parents. We will walk." Then Orhan guided the woman, the guests thought was his wife, through the protocol of their goodbyes, and they left.

The city's night life made the streets noisy as they walked out of the hotel. The street where they walked was well lit by the strung light bulbs of the garden cafes lining the sidewalk. Because the night was warm men wearing baggy caps and worn suit coats loitered in clusters of three and four outside the tea-houses. They passed near one group of such men, and Orhan grew uncomfortable. "Even though they think I am married to you, you are a attractive woman and I don't know what they will do."

"At home I used to think I had to walk fast, be certain. Act as if I know what I'm doing and who I am. Don't know what I should do here."

"Try it here. That is a good idea."

Orhan urged her to go faster as they passed one cafe. "No woman of good family would enter here," he told her. "There are few places where families can go, but not so many."

"Where did your family go when you were growing up?"

"Mostly to our friends homes. Not many public places…only one 'garden' with a fountain and tables. We went and sat and ordered drinks like lemonade. There are more now, and I think there will be more garden cafes for families as Turkey modernizes. I hope."

"I admire the way Turkish social life's family oriented. Must be tough for people unable to have children."

"It is. They stay more connected to their parents' families. That would be hard for you. I think."

"You're saying that if we were married the pressure would be on. No matter how cautious I feel, I would need to have children."

"I think that's what I'm saying. What do you think?"

"I don't know what I think. I want children, of course, but I'd like to be married and have the freedom to be a couple without children at least for a while."

"That would be difficult. But if I knew, if I knew you wanted them in time, I could assure my mother. You watch. Nermin will have a child soon!"

They walked now past a building which stood out from the others. Anne noticed that it was several stories high and the stones on it's corners were large and of a darker color. "Why is that building so different?"

"I think the Armenians must have built it. In the early 1900's there were many Armenians in this area. Turks know they were good craftsman. They built solid buildings as well."

"Where are the Armenians now?"

"Marched off to oblivion, many of them."

"What does that mean?"

"It is a part of our history we don't speak much about. Those of us who know it are not proud of it. Many Armenians were killed and many more escaped the country. Some are still here but they do not remind us they are Armenians so they can live a normal life."

"Another reason for the label 'terrible Turk'." Anne looked at Orhan, but caught herself before she ran her hand beneath her chin in the gesture that suggested decapitation. "No…I'm beginning to identify with Turks. When my friends write me about the terrible Turk, I blanche."

Orhan took her elbow to move along the walk once more. "That's what I want to hear. The wedding tonight made me eager. I want to be like Omer. Able to take my bride home and act as if she were my bride. Can you tell me?...I have waited. Can we go somewhere secret and you marry me? Will you marry me?"

"Oh, Orhan You've snuck up on me. I'm not ready. I'm still not ready to promise...still frightened of too many things. You've tried hard. You've made the music evenings, you're helping me find friends, you're speaking to me in a way that shows you're trying to understand...I'm sorry. I'm really sorry. I just don't know yet."

The part of town they walked in now, on Ataturk Bulvari, was quieter and darker. Only an occasional automobile passed them, it's headlights flashing across their path. Other than the traffic, the only sound became their footsteps. Orhan walked without speaking. Anne could not read his reaction and became frightened. Was he angry...hurt...disgusted? He maintained his silence until they had reached the courtyard gate in front of the Demir family's apartment building. He opened the gate, and turned to face her. "I will not say I am not disappointed. I am. But...I will try to act as if I am not disappointed."

As he turned she noticed that the family's car was in the driveway. The family had left and come home earlier than expected. They reached the porch and an agitated Hatije opened the door for them. "It is good you have come Bey Efendim. Selma Hanim came home, but she has fallen ill."

****

Dear Nancy,   September 10, 1962

So...you're planning your wedding! I know it's planned to happen soon, and I don't want the event to actually take place before you've heard from me. A wedding happened here tonight, but it wasn't ours. Nermin, Orhan's sister, whom I told you about chasing to a village in eastern Turkey when she had run away to find her archeologist boyfriend, let us bring her home and switched gears so immediately that she was married tonight. A wedding barely a month after we all but dragged her away from another man she thought she was in love with. Of course the man she married knows nothing about the U.S. born archeologist, or it wouldn't have been O.K. for him to marry her. And that's the *coup* Orhan and I pulled off for his parents which has made me that much more acceptable in her parents eyes. I have helped them keep their daughter respectable enough to marry the very respectable young man she has married. He's a good friend of the family already, a Swiss-trained engineer who will fit very well, thank you, into the family factory.

But I am writing tonight because I cannot sleep. Orhan and I walked home from this wonderful wedding, Nermin's, in which I began to appreciate this culture and all its colorful customs like the pipe and the drum and dancing the line dance called a *halay*. By the time we reached home Orhan's mother had preceded us home and had a stroke! Now, tonight, the doctor has been here and we are waiting it out. Her three men-folk will "watch" with her this night and in the morning we shall take her to the hospital. We do not know yet. We can only hope she will recover. If she does, she may well be paralyzed on her left side, Onol Bey, the doctor says. And you know the drag it would be for me to have an invalid around to help care for. But I am really a bit amazed at myself. This woman, Orhan's mother, has been only grudgingly polite to me, and yet even if I end up her major caretaker, I don't want her to die. I see how important she is to this family and the way they all function: a factory owner and factory manager, a daughter to whom the social position of the family is entrusted, a father to her who is a kind of honored patriarch, a son who is rising in importance both in the eyes of Gaziantep society and the respect he gains from his family, and Selma herself who is indispensable domestically. It is just much too early for Selma to die.

You'll hear from me or from my father as to how this all comes out. But meanwhile, please join me in whatever fashion you can muster to pray…Please God, don't let her die!

Forgive this plea of a letter. I'm really unable to think right tonight, but I did have to write someone after the great wedding I've been to and to process this terrible event that happened when the wedding was over. I still love you and wish all the best for you if you manage to pull your wedding off without mishap and before I manage to write you again.

Thank God you're there to write to. (You don't have to share this God of mine for me to thank God for you!)

Anne

CHAPTER NINETEEN
ONCE TROUBLE STRIKES

Selma lay on the *sedir* in the sitting room, her bulbous body flaccid, unmoving. She wore her head-scarf and wedding clothes still, but her body appeared lifeless. She was unable to speak, and Orhan saw terror in her eyes when she looked at him. Abdullah sat beside her bed stroking her forehead, a lock of his wavy gray hair, usually so smoothly in place, fallen across his brow. Orhan could not remember ever having seen this kind of affection for his mother from his father.

"Ali has gone to find Onol Bey. He should be home by now." The doctor whom Ali had been sent to bring, an internist, was a close friend of the Demir family and had been at the wedding. His father's calm voice soothed Orhan.

Abdullah had lived for nearly ten years with Selma's health problems: her obesity, her diabetes. Her son had been away—at school, and in the U.S.—and was not accustomed to accounting for them. "Is there something I can do, my father?"

"Here, you soothe her. I will decide whether to telephone for Nermin. To tell her is not right on her wedding night." Abdullah rose, stepped backward, shook his head, and stood leaning on the back of a straight back chair at the dining table.

Orhan sat down beside his mother on the *sedir*. Dede who had been leaning against the wall in the shadows spoke. "Could that decision wait until Onol Bey has been here?"

"You're right. No need to decide now." Abdullah pulled a chair out from the table, sat down, and let his head drop to his arms on the table. Suddenly, Selma Hanim howled. She appeared to register that her son was beside her, and a strange animal-like cry emerged from deep in her throat. Never before had he heard such a cry coming from his mother. It jolted him. Dede, Abdullah, Anne, each of them heard and stood shocked. She did not appear to be in pain, but her cries seemed to suggest that she felt a kind of mental anguish, a sense of loss, a foreknowledge that perhaps this was her end.

When her cry had ended, she shut her eyes and it seemed a time for silence. Orhan stroked his mother's forehead as he had seen his father doing. If she was aware, was there anything that could be said? If she wasn't aware, it was a time only for touch. Orhan felt he had joined the others present in a dim light and they had become a kind of silent tableau of the concerned. Each of them longing to do something. Each of them unable to think of anything to do. Helplessness paralyzed them, kept them silent.

Hatije padded in with a tray of glasses filled with water. When she offered the water, Abdullah, Orhan and Anne each took a glass, held the clear liquid, drank of it, and remained silent. Orhan set his glass, half empty, on the floor beside the leg of the *sedir* and took his mother's hand. It was dry, limp, but he felt more comfortable holding her hand than stroking her forehead.

In time Abdullah touched Orhan's shoulder, indicated his desire to take his son's place. Orhan rose noiselessly and moved to one side. As he stood waiting for the doctor's arrival, Anne moved to stand beside him, and took his hand. It did not matter that they were not husband and wife. This woman knew he was caught by this moment, and needed her with him. Wordlessly, she gripped his hand, and he was grateful.

The doctor arrived. Selma howled another piercing cry when she saw her friend, the doctor. After only a short examination, Onol Bey announced she had had a stroke, and that her condition was serious enough that she ought to be in the hospital. It was a question of how to transport her there this late in the evening with few persons and no equipment at hand to negotiate her weight onto a stretcher and into some vehicle. They decided after a consultation to give her what medications they could now and take her in the morning. The sitting room with its frosted glass doors and dining table became a hospital room, with haunting shadows. Onol Bey gave Selma a shot—a medication to thin her blood, keep a further blood clot from forming in her brain—and gave them instructions about what to do until the morning.

Having been at the wedding himself, the doctor anticipated the family's question about whether to inform Nermin. "Nermin could do nothing...but worry. No reason to contact her on her wedding night."

The three men—Anne was not a family member—all of whom felt no less inadequate than they had before the doctor arrived, agreed to divide up the night into watches. Dede would take the first hours, Abdullah, the second watch, and Orhan the last. Orhan sensed that Dede would want to keep his vigil with his daughter alone, and left the room immediately after they had made an acceptable bed for Selma on the *sedir*. The doctor had warned them that they would have to move Selma in the morning because her body could not remain immobile without developing further problems. However, procuring a stretcher, transporting her into an automobile, all those tasks could be seen to in the morning. Anne left to go upstairs and Orhan moved numbly through his bedtime ablutions.

When Orhan rose at four in the morning to take his turn beside Selma after Abdullah, she appeared to be sleeping quietly. Abdullah reported that she had had only one short period of restlessness during his watch. His greatest contribution, he claimed, was to see that she did not fall from the *sedir*. Orhan was relieved his mother's eyes were closed and that she appeared to be asleep. He had seen again the terror in her eyes when she had looked at him the previous night and was haunted by it. Now, since he would be sitting with her, he didn't want to think about his mother's fear of death.

She continued to lie motionless until the morning when her daughter arrived, and she stirred. Nermin being another person important to Selma, the invalid howled once again. The unfamiliar sound after a peaceful night jolted Orhan and threw Nermin into a fit of her own high pitched cries. "Oh, my *An-ne*, what has happened to you? What has happened?"

This sister of his, this young woman who had been so rebellious, so critical of her mother's life style and social life, how could she now carry on with such wild abandon? Her wedding was ruined, she said. She would stay with her mother and take no wedding trip, even a short one. She would not return to the Kaya family's apartment until her mother had recovered. Why had Allah done this to the Demir family? It was unjust.

Orhan listened, wondering about the contrast of his sister's feelings with his. He was fond of his mother, indebted to her and to the way she had hovered over him, had always wanted the best for her son. Still, he did not need to have her alive in the same way that Nermin was expressing. If the day she was destined to die had come, he would feel the loss, yes. It would be a shock, perhaps followed by a numbness, a sense of affection gone, but he didn't have this same need to display his grief that his sister, Selma's daughter, clearly felt.

Almost as if she had waited only to hear her daughter's voice, Selma shut her eyes, heaved a quiet sigh, and died. At this final moment, only Anne was not present. She had felt an awkwardness in her presence that morning, and had slipped into the sitting room to tell Orhan she would wait upstairs. Orhan had assured her he wished she would remain, but she said she would return a bit later which turned out to be too late. He was sad she had missed the actual end.

Dede, Abdullah, Orhan, each in his own stoic way dealt quietly with their grief. Nermin keened, threw herself on her mother's body, and was inconsolable until the doctor Onol Bey arrived. She quieted only to listen to his instructions as to what she and Hatije should do to prepare the body to go to the mosque.

But it was when Nevnehal arrived—Anne having forgotten to telephone her and tell her not to come for a session they had arranged for reading Yunus Emre—that the family acquired a calm, knowledgeable friend. This young woman saw immediately the family's need to have someone help who knew what was to be done on the occasion of death. Selma had always taken charge of the performance of such rituals for the family, but she was dead and her men-folk, in spite of the fact that men performed the rituals outside the home in connection with death, were somehow unable to do what needed to be done inside the home. Although, the strong domestic force of the family now lay dead, Nevnehal, who had recently lost her mother and knew well what needed to be done, had by chance arrived. She took charge, and Orhan found himself grateful.

"It is fitting that one of Yunus Emre's poems we were going to read today has the line 'I shall wear my shroud singing alleluia!'" Nevnehal said, when she had been there only a short time. "I think we'll find Yunus Emre is a solace in death."

Dede nodded.

Although Orhan could not picture his mother joyfully donning a shroud and singing, it seemed a good line to reflect on. The family decided to take Selma's body to the mosque for the *jenaze namazi,* afternoon prayer time. Nevnehal who stayed with them through the morning and telephoned her maid to bring food for the noon meal suggested to Nermin and Anne, that in spite of the fact that women did not ordinarily go to the mosque for such prayers, they should insist on going. "If you have to, you can stand on the sidelines," she said. "You must have the comfort of the prayers."

With a certain numbness, Orhan joined his father moving through the difficult task of getting Selma's body to the mosque where they would be able to procure a shroud and a coffin. This lifeless body was his mother and she was dead. He wondered why he was unable to feel, but since he knew that this dullness was better than being unable to function, he did not question himself. To remember how his mother had howled her last agony, sensed the coming of her own death, and been terrorized by it, now gave him only a kind of hollow feeling. He was also relieved when standing behind her coffin in the mosque to realize that the task he had so dreaded of getting her to the mosque and ready for the priest's prayers was finished. In the dust-colored, walled yard of the mosque now, he heard the prayers through his numbness and even the Arabic language of the prayers, though he did not understand it all, soothed him. He sensed that his mother deserved better than the crude coffin covered with a green cloth which her shrouded body was put into, but he was proud that many of their family friends appeared to help carry that same coffin through the streets. The many strong arms that carried his mother's heavy body to the cemetery made it seem lighter than he ever could have dreamed it would be. The Demir family had good support in this community. For this sense of community, he was grateful.

He moved in a daze, seeing no face in the crowd as individual except several of the male workers at the factory. He would not have expected to see these men at his mother's burial. The wave of the moving crowd reached the cemetery. There were more prayers said beside the freshly dug grave, and in the end he felt himself helping to lift his mother's body, removed from the coffin and shrouded, to be laid in the ground.

As they came out of the cemetery Ali was waiting for Abdullah and Orhan and Dede with the family car, but for a reason he didn't understand, Orhan did not want to remove his feet from the earth and climb into a car. Abdullah must have felt the same way because the father and son urged Dede into the car and for themselves chose to start on foot towards the family apartment building.

Not one word on the long walk home was said between them, yet Orhan felt he had never been so in tune with his father as he was when the two men arrived at home.

****

Dear Daddy,   September 3, 1961

I could never have dreamed how quickly things might change here in Turkey with Orhan and his family. His mother died of a massive stroke this morning. I was going to write you the happy news of his sister Nermin's wedding plans last week, but things were moving so fast around here that I did not get to it, and perhaps that is why I am feeling now that things have so suddenly changed here in Gaziantep. I had not been able to tell you about a happy event before this dreadful one happened.

I think you know that I have had mixed feelings about Selma Hanim. She did not like me. I think it was not so much for myself that she didn't like me, but because I wasn't Turkish and she was a pretty conventional woman. To have Orhan marry me bollixed all her plans for her son's living a proper Turkish life at the top of the social scale here in Aintab.

I think she was beginning to like me, and I know she was grateful that I was useful to the family in helping to bring Nermin back when she ran off. But I was still foreign. She was uneasy. And now all this speculation is moot. She has died, and I find myself genuinely grieving for her.

I have a feeling it is going to take a long time for me to face up to the implications of her death. She ran this household efficiently and well. Now, I am the only woman left because Nermin will go to live with her husband's family. If I should marry Orhan I would be the sole woman in charge of domestic affairs in this household. Believe me, that is a daunting thought! It is strange to think that I came to Turkey to find out if I could live in this culture, and now I think I probably could. But I'm worried that as a human being I don't want to have to accept a role that's not natural to me. No matter what country I end up living in, I want to pull my oar, row my boat. But my future as a human being, a woman in Turkey, has just become heavily weighted. Can I carry that weight? Do I want to accept this role? I know I love Orhan, but whether I marry him has become a much bigger domestic decision than I dreamed it would be. I'm frightened.

I think I have to decide and decide soon now because the masquerade that Orhan and I are married is going to wear pretty thin in the coming days when I am managing things here in the house and Orhan is not actually living with me in the upstairs apartment. Just two nights ago, on the way home from the wedding Orhan asked me again to marry him and I had to tell him I wasn't ready yet. But now I don't have the luxury of not being ready. I must fish or cut bait, which turns out to be only a lame metaphor for the decision I have to make. Oh, Daddy, what do I do? I love Orhan. But can I marry his whole family, which is the way I see it now as having to be?

Maybe you will telephone me. In spite of the difficulties with the Turkish telephone system, I would really like to speak with you. I long for some community of discernment like a Friends Meeting. I have neither that community nor my father. I am alone.

Anne

CHAPTER TWENTY
ONCE THERE WAS A FRIEND

"Feta cheese, *pide* bread—that's what I expect for breakfast now. They're all right," Anne said to Dede on a morning two weeks after Selma's death. They sat at the breakfast table, dawdling. "But I still don't enjoy the shrunken heads of the black olives," she joshed. Dede had only picked at the shriveled olives himself. The old man had been lolling about the house, smoking his *nargile,* behaving morosely, and Anne had grown alarmed.

Nevnehal was expected for a poetry reading session. In an effort to engage Dede, the two women had returned now to the Yunus Emre reading sessions they had had before Selma's death. But before Nevnehal arrived the phone rang. Anne picked up the receiver, and there in the sitting room, she heard her father's voice through less long distance static than she could remember having ever before.

"It's ten hours difference. Have I caught you at breakfast as I'd hoped to?"

"You have. Orhan and Abdullah have gone off to the factory and Dede and I are here at the table indulging ourselves. *He's* finishing off the black olives, me the feta cheese. How did you manage to pull off such a good connection?"

"Don't know. Don't trust it to last. So I'll say what I wanted to say first. Then break into chit chat." His approach reminded Anne of a difference she thought she had observed between Turks and

Americans. A Turk, she was certain, no matter how he or she feared the failure of the connection later, would go through the formal and accepted protocol of greetings expected in a phone call, and only afterward turn to the business at hand. Her father was too practical to do anything but speak first about the plea she had sent him in her letter. He would turn to less urgent matters only if there were time and the connection continued good.

"Good thinking, Daddy," Anne said, aware she was mimicking what her father had said to her countless times as a child.

"Your no nonsense father has made an observation. He's going to point it out to you. I won't tell you what you should do. Mainly because I don't know any better than you do."

"You, in your great wisdom don't know!?" Static punctuated Anne's remark, robbed it of its humor.

"Wonder aside now. This is an observa—" A loud crack like lightning cut off the final part of her father's phrase. Then, aware he'd been interrupted, he continued. "Look, I'm going to say this and say too that if at any point we get cut off I won't try to ring back. It's expensive. We've heard each other and for now that will have to be enough."

"O.K. Much as I like hearing your voice, it's not like another call would be any better."

"Your letter signaled a change. You left home out for an adventure. You left home dreaming. You're no longer dreaming. You've come to what happens to many of us. You've come to a point where the dreams you had don't match the reality you've got. Now you know you can either accept the limitations of the life you've got, or pull out and start over again."

"What a choice! I can't make that one!"

"What...what...I didn't hear anything after 'What a choice.'"

"No matter. I said what you said was no help. Don't you know I want someone to make my choice for me? Then down the road when I'm unhappy I can blame them!"

"Get this! Down the road when you're stewing you can't say your father didn't answer your call and phone you." Her father said nothing more and there was so much static it was acceptable for Anne to say nothing in reply.

Finally, it came to her to say, "I should have known."

Another pause. Her father changed the subject. "There's been a death. How are things?"

Anne felt unfinished with their first subject. "I should have known I can't blame you! You don't think blaming other people ever let anyone off their own hook! You're not going to let me blame anyone but myself!"

Another pause. "I asked how are things going. You're there in a tough place having to buckle down, be domestic. How is it?" More static came before Anne could answer.

"Actually, I've got great help. My new friend Nevnehal is showing me how to run a Turkish household. I'm bumbling, but it's sort of fun."

"If what you wanted was to be important, I detect you—" With that, the phone Anne held to her ear went dead. She turned to Dede.

"Turkish phones are terrible. I had my father on the other end—then suddenly he's cut off."

"Try Allah. More reliable. Apt to do better getting through."

"You're just like my father! Try getting sympathy out of you and it's like getting blood out of a..." Anne paused, searched for the Turkish word, and ended by saying the word "turnip" in English. If turnips had a Turkish name, she didn't know it.

"We don't know 'turnips' in this country. I've missed your metaphor, but I **am** sympathetic."

"I know you are. But sympathy doesn't make decisions for me."

"Right. What you need is what I can't give you. Courage." Punctuating the word courage was the sound of the doorbell. Nevnehal had arrived.

She slipped the jacket from her slim shoulders and shocked Anne. The day was warm and her arms were bare beneath her jacket. She entered the sitting room, took Dede's proffered hand and following the ancient custom solemnly, reverently, kissed it and put it to her forehead. Following that gesture she moved across to Anne and kissed her on both cheeks. These formalities completed according to Turkish custom, she sat down at the table and picked up the poetry book as if she were in her own home. Anne watched her in awe. The simplicity, the reverence of this woman!

A week back, and quietly, Nevnehal had informed Anne that Turkish custom required the bereaved family should not be left alone with their grief for the first forty days after death. Since the Demir family were good friends of Nevnehal's family, she was ready she explained, if it would be of help, to oversee the Demir's domestic affairs—their food buying, their meals, Anne's instructions to Hatije—for the forty days of mourning. Anne had been eager to accept Nevnehal's offer. She was aware, however that Orhan and his father might have trouble accepting such a close arrangement since Nevnehal didn't know that Anne and Orhan weren't married. Nevnehal would be slipping in and out of the Demir's apartment frequently in such an arrangement since the cement block apartment building where she lived, her father-in-law's apartment, was only three buildings along *Ataturk Bulvari* from Abdullah Bey's building. If her friend were often around the house, it would become apparent that Orhan was living in his parents apartment and Anne was living separately in the apartment upstairs.

Nevnehal proposed that she and her maid would cook the main noonday meal in double quantities and Hatije and Ali should make themselves available to help transport the food to the Demir family at meal time. Anne protested. Those plans would be too much trouble. Nevnehal countered that she would be cooking for her own family anyway. She suggested that they should try this arrangement for a short period and see if it went smoothly. In the end Anne had only one difficulty with the plan. It was hard to believe that her new friend could be so efficient and effective as she had become in the Demir household when she was so beautiful.

Nevnehal's willingness to leave her twenty month old child with her mother-in-law and lend her domestic management skills to Anne and the Demir family surprised Anne. Each time she observed Nevnehal with her little boy, Samim, what she saw wreaked havoc with Anne's stereotype of Turkish mothers. Nevnehal was naturally affectionate, but she did not seem like a mother who would pick her child up each time he burst into tears and jostle him until he was quiet. Samim, like his mother, seemed quiet and comfortable being in the world. Was his easiness born of the security of many adults coddling him? Nevnehal, who had told Anne how much she admired the drunken quality of

Yunus Emre's love of God, also had a certain assurance about her. She appeared to enjoy herself and her own life style, and her natural exuberance made her seem, if not drunk, at least entirely content with her own love of life.

By this second week of mourning when Nevnehal arrived to help find ways to "pick up" Dede's mood the mechanics of operating the Demir household were running smoothly. More than a week earlier Orhan had come from the formal reception room where the family had been receiving guests to the noon meal and had put on a record of Fauré's Requiem. At the meal, however, in spite of the calming music, (he sensed that Fauré's music was entirely foreign to Dede and Abdullah) Orhan became restless. "I will return to the factory tomorrow."

Abdullah put his elbows on the arms of his chair, lifted his head, and asked, "Would it be wrong? I shall take ten days, and then I too can not afford to be away longer."

"I've spoken with Omer. He is eager to begin to integrate his efforts with ours at the factory. Nermin's in no mood to go off on a wedding trip." Before the wedding Orhan had ordered a large and beautiful hardwood desk made for Omer. "The looms at the factory are still running full tilt. Isn't it time for Omer to occupy his new office?" Orhan asked.

"Wouldn't it be wise to consult Nevnehal about what the educated community of Gaziantep might think of this speedy return?" Anne asked. Orhan and Dede, however, did not appear to think it was important to consider what others might think. Abdullah appeared to be as eager as his son to return. In the end, Abdullah announced decisively that ten days was the longest he could afford to be away, and Orhan too should return. That was the way it was!

Dede's state of mind continued to worry Anne. He had lamented that first his son and now his daughter, both of whom were so much younger than he, had died, and he, by some quirk of fate, was left still living. Indeed, something in Dede already seemed to have died, and Anne longed to find something that would cheer him. The scheme the two women had planned for this particular morning—to stage a reading of Yunus Emre—included an insistence that Dede and his *nargile* join them at the dining room table to read aloud. Nevnehal came ready with two particular poems for them to look at. She read the first one over in Turkish, and they began to discuss its meanings—Turkish and English—with Dede listening. It worked. Dede became as lively as he had been since Selma's death. He insisted that they call Ali and read the same poems to him, and for the rest of the morning the four of them—Anne was amused at the motley crew they made—remained round the dining room table after Hatije had cleared away the breakfast things.

They had been reading and talking for some time when suddenly Dede became animated. "Here's my state," he said. "Listen to this: *Yok yere gecirdim gunu, ah nideyim omrun seni?*"

Anne translated for herself as rapidly as she was able to. "My days have passed to a place of nothing, ah what can I say to you, my life?" Her heart froze. This old man, so important to her, felt himself to be important for nothing. She rose, told the group at the table she'd be back and left to go upstairs to her papers to find Marianne Moore's poem. She was daunted by the need to translate English metaphors into sensible Turkish, and only knew she would have to try. Returning with the poem in her hands, she took a stab at the Turkish of it. She described the sea in a chasm struggling to be free and unable to be. She tried to describe the outcome of the struggle and managed in Turkish to describe something like a sea or a person struggling to be free and in its surrendering finding its continuing.

Simply, quietly, she told Dede he was for her like the sea rising in that chasm. "If there were now no such sea when I am feeling the limitations Turkey puts on me, there would be no reassurance for me."

Dede looked at her, and from one film glazed eye, a tear ran down his cheek. Each of those gathered, Ali, Nevnehal, Anne saw it. None of them remarked on it. Instead, they sat on unmoving, unspeaking. They had sat several minutes when Anne became aware that this group had become for her like a group gathered to help her decide her future. Clarity slipped in upon her. She sat transfixed by her own certainty.

Then Hatije padded in. "*Hanim*," she said, "I am dizzy, ill, I would like to ask to be excused from serving the noon meal."

Ali frowned and rose. "You must not do that Hatije. I will serve the meal," he said, shame-faced.

"Are you expecting a child?" Nevnehal asked, and when Hatije answered in the affirmative Nevnehal continued. "What if An-ne Hanim should become pregnant as well? Then you and she together could do the healthy things mothers do to help their babies grow strong."

"I'll consider that." Anne said playfully. "Might be good for me, too." Then, recognizing how much she wanted the play-acting at being married to be over, Anne vowed she would ask Orhan for permission to tell Nevnehal their secret. Nevnehal's advice would be helpful. How would they ever pull off a marriage and keep it entirely unnoticed?

That same evening before Anne went upstairs to her own apartment, she asked Orhan if he would play Mozart's Symphony number 40. "I want no more Requiems. They make sad listening. I want my beauty in the open, but controlled. I want music that combines the order of classicism with the gaiety of romanticism and manages the perfect balance."

"I am happy to do exactly what you want, my love."

Neither Orhan nor Anne spoke as they listened to the resonating melody of that symphony, familiar to both of them. When the music finished they sat on at the dining room table, until the pressure Anne felt to speak rose and could not be tamped down. "I'm ready to be married," she said. "Mountains of things are going to bother me about Turkish culture. I'm going to miss mountains about my own culture. But no matter where I live, I'll still have to find balance, be human. I think I can accept my limits here as well as anywhere." Then she reached across the table to take Orhan's hand.

Orhan sat without moving, and said nothing. Then he jumped up, still holding Anne's hand, pulled her up with him, and kissed her hard. When she remembered it was still early in the evening she pulled away. At any minute someone might come into the dining room. "I think we need an ally outside the family. Can we tell Nevnehal and get her advice on how to pull a secret wedding off?" she asked.

When they asked her, Nevnehal shocked Anne. She wasn't surprised by their secret when it was explained to her how it had come about. Nevnehal advised that married or not, they needed to get through the *Mevlut*. Orhan explained to Anne that a *Mevlut* was the ceremony which happened forty days after a death. In it there was traditionally a reading for the family of a poem by the poet, Suleyman Celebi who wrote the work in 1409.

But Orhan claimed, that he could not wait until after the *Mevlut* now that he knew he was to be married. He proposed that he should go off on a business trip to Istanbul. Abdullah, of course would know the real truth and help make his departure seem natural. Perhaps they would leave Nermin at the house to receive any guests, pretend that all is well at home. They would tell Omer so he would pretend all was well at the factory. Perhaps they would decide to say that Orhan is only at home preparing for the *Mevlut,* not off on business.

"That is not a likely one," Orhan said. "I am going to have a hard time being properly solemn at the *Mevlut* when I am so happy."

"You'll have to become an actor," Anne said playfully, knowing she was asking the impossible. "I wish there were time to invite my father to come as my witness, but that's impossible."

"You're going to feel like you're at home again in the Istanbul Hilton," Orhan said, knowing he was suggesting the impossible.

Anne was puzzled. "I'm not at all sure I want to feel that way."